GET
STRANGE

GET STRANGE

J.C. BRUCE

ISBN: 978-1-7347848-1-7 (Hardback)
ISBN: 978-1-7342903-4-9 (Paperback)
ISBN: 978-1-7342903-5-6 (eBook)

Library of Congress Control Number: 2019920362

This is a work of fiction. Names, characters, places, and incidents are a product of the author's imagination. Locales and public names are sometimes used for atmospheric purposes. Any resemblance to actual people, living or dead, or to businesses, companies, events, institutions, or locales is completely coincidental.

Book design by Damonza.com
Website design by Bumpy Flamingo LLC

Printed by Tropic ⊚ Press in the United States of America.

First printing edition 2020

Tropic ⊚ Press LLC
P.O. Box 110758
Naples, Florida 34108

www.Tropic.Press

BOOKS BY J.C. BRUCE

To Sandy, Kacey, and Logan

Giant Crocodile Devours Burglar

By Alexander Strange

Tropic©Press

A twenty-foot crocodile "as fast as a horse" killed a burglar in Belle Meade, Florida, dragging him into a nearby swamp, police reported.

Mary Jo Simmons was alone in her double-wide when she heard glass breaking. The 76-year-old retired school teacher grabbed a Louisville Slugger and whacked the burglar's hand as he reached through the door's shattered window.

Screaming, the man backed away from the house, police said, but was caught in the jaws of the gigantic reptile.

"Probably should give the croc a medal," sheriff's Deputy Clayton Jones told a Belle Meade radio station.

Biologists have other concerns. The creature appears to be a cross-breed of a North American crocodile and an imported Nile croc from Africa.

"Nile crocodiles are far more vicious than our native species," biologist Annabelle Nott told me. "Unfortunately, they're mating."

The population of native crocodiles, once nearly extinct, has rebounded since they found homes in the warm water circulating in the cooling canals of the Turkey Point nuclear power plant in Homestead.

Could radioactive water alter their genetics?

"Uh, we don't like to talk about that," Nott said.

STRANGE FACT: A crocodile cannot stick out its tongue.

Weirdness knows no boundaries. Keep up at *www.TheStrangeFiles.com*. Contact Alexander Strange at Alex@TheStrangeFiles.com.

CHAPTER 1

THE KILLERS BUGGERED-UP the first attempt on my life when they poisoned my fried okra. They mistakenly assumed the vegetable would end up on my dinner plate.

Negatory.

I'd rather eat sushi than okra, and I'll be starving during the Zombie Apocalypse before I eat raw fish. But my dog, Fred, loves okra. Fresh, steamed, deep fried, he doesn't care that it has the texture of snot.

I was in the checkout line at a local deli, my small cardboard box of fried okra in my shopping basket, when a statuesque brunette with flawless legs and short shorts reached down to pick up the credit card she'd dropped.

Yes, keen observer of the human condition that I am, I did not fail to notice her as she bent over. It's a professional obligation, you understand, as a reporter.

I was absorbed in this task of journalistic scrutiny when I felt something nudge my basket, and I reluctantly turned to see a fat middle-aged man in a floral Hawaiian shirt standing behind me.

"Must be day for drops," he said. His accent was unusual, maybe eastern European. He retrieved a set of car keys with a black fob from my basket.

I was annoyed he distracted me from my anthropological study of the species *Pulchra femina*, but I am nothing if not civil.

"No worries," I told him.

I thought no more about it until I returned to the *Miss Demeanor*, the fishing trawler I live aboard in Goodland, a funky little island town off the southwest coast of Florida. When I poured the okra into Fred's bowl, I noticed a sheen on its crispy brown surface, as if it had been coated in butter. Hadn't seen that when I scooped it out of the deli bin.

Fred bounded over—all eight pounds of him—his tail wagging. He stuck his nose into the bowl, shook his head—sending his huge ears flapping—then shuffled backward.

"What's wrong, buddy?"

"Gerruff."

"Since when don't you like okra?" I nudged the bowl towards him, but he backed off several more steps.

"Gerrrruffff!"

Fred's vocabulary may be limited, but I knew he was unhappy. I picked up the bowl and sniffed. I expected it to smell horrible, and it did. It was okra, after all. But this was different. I couldn't place it at first, then it hit me:

Almonds. Sort of. But chemically. Somehow.

I'm a mystery junkie, and I recalled that the smell of "bitter almonds" is the signature of a particularly lethal poison: cyanide. Not sure what bitter is supposed to smell like, but I knew almonds.

Maybe it was my imagination, but I also felt a little lightheaded and nauseous. I remembered cyanide is a gas at higher temperatures. It's Florida. Temperatures are always high. If Fred's okra were poisoned, maybe I'd inhaled a whiff.

I set the bowl on the galley counter and fumbled about my small pantry for a box of Ziploc bags. I sealed the bowl inside, then walked onto the deck with Fred for some fresh air. I left my inanimate shipmates, Mona and Spock, inside. Since they didn't breathe,

I knew they'd be OK. Then I pulled my iPhone from a pocket in my cargo shorts.

911: "Do you have a problem?"

Me: "Yes. I think someone poisoned my okra."

911: "Did you say okra?"

Me: "Yes, okra."

911: "Are you saying you think someone tried to poison your food?"

Me: "Not mine, technically. Fred's."

911: "Who's Fred?"

Me: "My dog."

911: "You have a dog named Fred?"

Me: "Yes."

911: "Strange."

Me: "No, that's me."

911: "You're strange?"

Me: "In the flesh. Can you send a CSI?"

The line died.

"No. That's my name, Alexander Strange." Too late.

I had one more number to dial. I knew this sheriff's detective. We played poker together from time to time at the dog track, but I dreaded calling him.

Still, cyanide.

"Henderson," I said when he answered his cell phone. "You sober?"

"Whaddaya want, Strange?"

"I think somebody poisoned my okra." When he didn't respond, I asked, "You still there?"

"Yeah, I'm here. But I could have sworn I heard you say somebody tried to poison you."

"Yes. My okra."

"Your what?"

"Okra. You know, green, a vegetable, tastes like buggers."

"Are *you* sober?"

"As a judge."

That got a snort. We both knew judges. In fact, a judge—my uncle in Arizona—owned the trawler where I spent my nights, dry-docked, resting on bricks and oil cans in a weed-covered vacant lot.

Living the dream.

"I'm in Everglades City, about to finish up," Henderson said. "I'll meet you there."

"I'll be at Stan's. I feel a cocktail coming on."

The *Miss Demeanor* rested between two of Goodland's best known watering holes: Stan's Idle Hour and the Little Bar. Stan's is a sprawling outdoor eatery and drinkery specializing in burgers, booze, and bikers. The Little Bar is famous for its exotic menu.

I descended the ladder propped against the *Miss Demeanor's* hull and walked over to Stan's outdoor bar and grabbed a seat. The bartender had green hair, a nose ring, and gauged ears. *Tres chic.* I placed my order and she returned shortly with my drink in one hand—a Cuba Libre, my preferred ethanol delivery system—and a plate of food in the other.

"Try some of these," she said. "They're different."

I'm all about free food so I grabbed one. But given my earlier experience, I took a moment to give it the once-over: No skull and crossbones, no telltale scent of bitter almonds, no expire-by date. I took a bite.

"Tastes fishy," I said. "What is it?"

"Grouper balls."

I picked another golf-ball sized piece off the plate and examined it. "Grouper balls, huh? Must have been a very big fish."

She rolled her eyes. "They're from the Little Bar. My aunt gave them to me. She works there."

"Ah," I said. Sage.

"You live over there, right?" she said, gesturing to the weedy lot next door.

"Home sweet home."

"How'd your boat get that hole in its side?"

"Pirates."

She gave me another eye roll then made her way down the bar offering her grouper balls to other customers.

The notification screen on my iPhone flashed with a new email. Didn't recognize the sender, but when you write about news of the weird a lot of your emails are from people you don't know or really don't want to know.

Mr. Strange, we have a mutual friend who is missing. Please call.

I felt a clunk in my chest. A premature ventricular heartbeat. I get them when I'm stressed. They're not fatal, just scare the bejesus out of me. Which of course is stressful.

I tapped my reply on the small screen's keyboard:

Who's that?

But I feared I knew the answer.

It took a couple of minutes to receive his response. Would have been much faster using text messaging, but I rarely give out my cell phone number. Finally, it arrived and we exchanged a flurry of short emails:

I'm in Goodland. Can we meet?

Who are you?

You ask a lot of questions.

Bring some answers. I'm at Stan's.

As if poisoned okra weren't bad enough, now this. Some days it just doesn't pay to get out of your berth. I took a sip of my cocktail. The melting ice was diluting it. I hate it when that happens, but it's one of the hazards of imbibing outdoors in the subtropics.

I took another sip. *Please, God, don't let it be her.*

A cloud of cigarette smoke materialized in front of me and I waved it away. I shot a death-stare at the middle-aged blonde on the barstool next to me, but she didn't disintegrate.

"Second-hand smoke won't hurt you, honey, I promise," she said. She flashed a smile revealing inflamed gums and yellow teeth.

"Whatever."

She turned away, directing her attention to the bandstand where a group of women were lying on their backs, legs gyrating in the air, doing the *Buzzard Lope*, the signature dance of Stan's Idle Hour.

"Come on now, girls, you know what to do with those legs," the emcee urged as the women continued kicking into the air like a flock of drunken vultures.

Green Hair nodded at my watery drink. "Refill?"

"Pacing myself. Supposed to meet some people."

She scanned the dance floor with its collection of wife beaters, cowboy hats, Harley vests, full-body tats, and feathered boas. The usual.

"One's a cop," I said.

"Don't see any polished shoes."

Not much about Stan's is polished. The bar anchors a small inlet the locals call Buzzards Bay South. That has a fine, piratical ring to it, doesn't it? Docks line the edge of the cove, creating a sheltered marina for pleasure craft and fishing boats venturing daily into the Gulf of Mexico. From Goodland, it's a straight shot south to Key West along the Ten Thousand Islands off the southwest coast of Florida. Like Key West, Goodland is where people come to get lost. It's a tiny refuge for the discontent, the beat-up, scoundrels on the lam, and future victims of the aforementioned scoundrels—a perfect symbiosis.

Green Hair poured another ounce of rum into my diluted drink. "On me."

I raised my glass in salute. "Cheers." Never look a gift Bacardi in the mouth, that's my motto.

"Greetings," a middle-aged man approaching the bar said to Green Hair in an overloud voice. He wore a white straw hat with a flat rim and top. I think it's called a boater. Very popular at political conventions. I glanced past the blonde as he mounted the bar stool and noticed the rest of his getup—madras shorts, white belt, knee-high black sox and wingtips: the Full Cleveland. It's Florida. We get some of that. And who knows, maybe thirty years from now I'll be sitting on a barstool in my cargo shorts, flip flops, and ball cap and some punk will look at me disdainfully because my fashion sense is so Millennial.

While Green Hair filled Full Cleveland's drink order, I picked up my iPhone and scrolled through the rest of my email and text messages. It distracted me from Full Cleveland's annoying chatter.

"I have led a most interesting life," he said in an odd, nasal voice, maybe with a hint of Cajun. "I have sold tractors. I have sold nuclear reactors. But my best job ever? Selling urinal screens."

"Urinal screens?" Blondie squeaked.

"Yes, yes. Traveled all over this great land of ours, selling urinal screens in every town from Miami to Moline."

I turned away and noticed a squadron of pelicans above the marina. One of the birds circled, spotted something tasty, and dove, prehistoric wings akimbo, splatting into the murky water as if shot from the sky. It emerged with a fish swelling the pouch under its bill. Near it, a blob of what looked like seaweed drifted toward the docks.

In a fury of flapping and splashing, the pelican took off again, then alighted atop my trawler next door, perching on the *Miss Demeanor's* roofline, which extends over the bow like the bill of a baseball cap. The bird arched its head and wriggled lunch down its throat. Its feathery neck bulged as the fish descended from beak to gullet. The bird rose to its full height and appraised it surroundings. Proud of itself. Mighty hunter. Then it took an enormous dump on the trawler's bench seat, splattering Fred, who had been sunbathing there, which set him to yapping.

"Magnificent creature," the blabby tourist said, pointing at the bird. The blonde sitting between us lit a Salem and nodded.

"Yes, yes, we all evacuate. When we do it, what better opportunity to capture someone's attention with an advertisement?"

He then rattled on—a nonstop diarrheic fire hose of jabber—about his career selling urinal screens, whatever they were. At first I thought they might cover the windows of Porta-Potties to keep the flies out. But then he told the poor woman they are those colorful, perforated plastic mats in the bottom of the pissers in men's rooms. His job: selling advertising on them—a big hit at truck stops.

"We all gotta go, and when you do—bingo!"

I marveled at his lack of taste and why he thought it was so clever the advertising message on the heat-sensitive screens only materialized when peed upon. The blonde turned to me and offered a weak smile, like I would rescue her.

"You're on your own."

She shook her head, reached into her purse, and set a ten-dollar bill on the bar. "You'll excuse me," she said to the chatterbox. "Maybe you should think about selling tractors again." She slid off the barstool and headed toward the ladies' room. No magic urinal screens there.

Full Cleveland slid over to the empty seat between us and poked me in the ribs with his elbow. He pointed toward the target of the pelican's enormous bowel movement. "You think dat's why they call it a poop deck?" His accent said New Orleans and I could smell the Old Spice radiating off what I surmised was his freshly shaved face—he'd cut himself under his left ear and it was still seeping.

I didn't own a urinal and didn't need any magic screens. And I certainly didn't want to hear any more from this guy. I debated for a moment whether to mention the blood on his cheek, then decided against it. It would only invite more blabber. I pulled out my wallet. It's made of translucent blue plastic with a Superman emblem embroidered on the front.

That captured the green-haired bartender's attention. "Cool," she said. "Where'd you get it?"

"Friend of mine."

"His name Kent?" she asked, playful.

I could be playful, too. "Yeah. We worked together at the *Daily Planet*."

"I always had a thing for Superman." She rested her elbows on the bar and leaned toward me. "Wondered what it would be like to be with a Man of Steel."

"Lois says he's faster than a speeding bullet."

She pursed her lips in mock disapproval. "*You* got any super powers?"

"Yeah. I can make rum disappear." I downed the rest of my drink.

"My name's Gabby, by the way," she said. "In case you're wondering."

"Hi, Gabby. I'm Alex."

Full Cleveland jumped in: "Alexander Strange. Weird news reporter extraordinaire."

I turned to confront him. "You? You're the guy who emailed me?"

He shot me with his finger.

"Do I look like I need toilet seats?"

"Urinal screens." He flashed a brief but mirthless smile. "We need to talk."

I could see my reflection in his mirrored sunglasses. Unlike Full Cleveland, I needed a shave. I could also see a crowd gathering behind me at the edge of the dock. That's when the shouting started.

"Oh, God!"

"What the fuck?"

"Dios mio!"

I slipped off the barstool and pressed against the semicircle of gawkers. I peered over their heads—an advantage of being vertically gifted—and could see the source of the commotion: A tangle of dark, salt-encrusted hair floated off the edge of the dinghy dock, splayed outward like a jellyfish, just breaking the waterline. Beneath the murky water, I could make out what appeared to be a naked body and the remains of a human face. I say remains, because it appeared the crabs and other sea critters had been using it for *hors d'oeuvres*.

I shouldered my way through the rubberneckers, clambered down the gangway to the floating dock, and shouted: "Somebody call 911." Instinctive, but pointless: We were well past the point of medical intervention.

The body shuddered, and then, as if possessed, jolted a foot to my right. A dorsal fin pierced the water's surface.

Fuck me!

I dropped into a full squat and almost lost my balance, pulled forward by the weight of my messenger bag, which not only held the poisoned okra but my heavy digital camera. I felt a hand grip the back of my T-shirt steadying me. I looked over my shoulder to see Full Cleveland. I handed him the satchel and bent down again.

Waterlogged bodies are heavy. I pulled it two feet out of the drink when the shark struck again. The impact twisted the corpse in a counter-clockwise turn nearly tearing my grip away. I hung on, stupidly—did I want to fall into the marina with a feeding shark?—and nearly lost my balance for a second time. I heaved upward and the body emerged from the bay, first to midsection and then, finally, all of her.

Yes, it was the corpse of a young woman.

And there were three other things I realized, some immediately, some later:

One: I knew her.

Two: Full Cleveland was not an ordinary urinal screen salesman.

Three: I thought I knew all about weird. I had much to learn.

CHAPTER 2

I FELT A hand on my shoulder. I looked up and it was Full Cleveland. The green-haired bartender stood beside him holding a tablecloth. Showing uncommon poise, she crouched down and gently draped it over the woman's naked corpse.

She stood up, took my hand, and said, "Come with me, Alex."

She led me up the gangway to an empty table a few yards away from the edge of the dock. "Sit here and I'll bring you something."

Full Cleveland walked over and studied me for a moment, as if I were a curious laboratory specimen. Then he removed his straw hat, wiped his bald head with a handkerchief, and replaced the boater. "I'm so sorry," he said. "It appears I was too late. You're going to have your hands full with the police for a while. I'll call you tomorrow."

Like tomorrow I'd be in a better mood to buy magic toilet screens.

The blare of sirens pierced the air. In a few moments, a uniformed sheriff's deputy swept past my table and strode down to the floating dock and the body. I guessed what might happen next and it did: the sound of retching.

I looked toward the dock and saw several people pointing in my direction. In a few minutes, the deputy walked over and pulled up a chair.

"They say you pulled her out," he said. "Couple people said you seemed to know her. That right?"

"Yes. Her name is...was...Maria Martinez."

The deputy wrote that down in his notebook and looked back at me, expectantly. Like it would be the most normal thing in the world for me to continue talking, telling him about her. But the train from Normal had left the station.

"So, how did you know her?" he finally asked.

I took a moment to gather my thoughts. I had assigned Maria to check out a tip I received regarding missing evidence at the Collier County Sheriff's Office. She believed something was rotten in the department. It made me hesitant to share details of the story to one of the sheriff's deputies, so I decided to give him an abridged version of how we met.

"She was a freelancer," I said.

He raised his eyebrows.

"A freelance writer."

The deputy nodded and scribbled it down. "How long did you know her?"

"Not very. We met a few months ago in Fort Myers. At a press conference. She was stringing for *The Nation*. I work for Tropic Press."

"Stringing?"

"Freelance reporting."

Another nod and more note taking.

"And *The Nation*?"

"It's a magazine."

It is, in fact, America's oldest continuously published magazine and self-described "flagship of the left." I knew this because Maria mentioned it. *Ad nauseam.*

"And this press conference. What was that about?"

"The big announcement for the Ark II."

"Oh yeah. About the lottery to see who gets to go, that one?"

"Yeah."

His head bobbed up and down. "My mom and dad bought lottery tickets."

"Good for them. Anyway, that's where Maria and I met."

The deputy's cell phone rang, and while he took the call I recalled my first meeting with Maria. Our butts were numb sitting in uncomfortable folding metal chairs waiting for the Rev. Lee Roy Chitango to arrive. Maria's wavy obsidian hair framed an upturned nose and liquid amber eyes. Her librarian glasses sparkled under the TV floodlights. She wore mismatched socks, pink running shoes, and a short violet-and-white striped dress. Her press cred said *The Nation*, so I broke the ice with a sure-fire conversation-starter with a liberal.

"Here's a bit of trivia for you: Did you know Thomas Edison, when he lived here, skinned manatees to make belt drives for his phonographs?"

Would she laugh? Would she cry? Would she think I was from the Planet Moron?

Slowly, theatrically, she turned to me as she lowered her glasses, and said: "Everybody knows this. And if that's a pickup line, you're the biggest lame-o in Florida." Then she turned away and pretended to busy herself with her notebook.

The biggest lame-o in Florida? Is there an award for that? Could I get a reality TV show?

"You knew that, really?"

This earned a brief, disdainful shake of her head. I liked the way her curly black hair shimmered. I liked her voice, too. Sultry with a hint of a Cuban accent.

"You must be a Pisces."

She turned to me. Her amber eyes drew into a squint and, I swear, they grew darker, coffee-colored. "How do you know this?"

This. Not that. Very Latina.

"I have a gift." I turned away from her and pretended to fiddle with my own notebook.

"No, really," she insisted. She trilled her rrrrs.

I let it ride for a moment, setting the hook, and then returned my gaze to hers.

"Your ring."

She raised her left hand to her face and stared at it for a moment. "You were looking at my ring, why?"

I was checking out her ring, of course, because I was checking *her* out.

"Because I'm a journalist. I saw your birthstone. Isn't it self-evident?"

"Oh."

It wasn't, really. Birthstones are organized by months while signs of the zodiac overlap months. But I knew aquamarine when I saw it—it was my mother's birthstone. While Maria's ring looked Dollar Store plain, mom's birthstone was mounted in a silver band with delicate filigree. She wore it constantly, including the day she drowned in a Texas cave trying to protect an endangered species of spider.

The deputy ended his call and I finished telling him my story. I didn't bother him with my lame attempt to pick up Maria, but I couldn't help but reflect on how sitting next to her at that press conference had altered the course of her life. Had we not met, she would be alive and well somewhere, not sprawled naked on a dock with her face devoured and bite marks from a shark on her thigh. My heart ker-thunked and I felt flush.

The deputy finished scribbling and looked up. "You feeling OK?"

"I've had better days."

"Sure. Look, is there anything else you can tell me about her?" he asked.

"She lived at a condo in Pelican Bay." I pulled out my phone and gave him the address. "It belongs to her aunt who lives in Connecticut. Her mom and another aunt live in Miami. Don't have contact info for them. Oh, she's got a cousin you may have heard of…"

Before I could continue, he got a call on his shoulder radio. The CSI team had arrived. "Stay here while I meet them."

I shook my head.

"See the boat over there?" I pointed to my trawler. "That's where I'll be." I got up and began walking back to the dock to retrieve my satchel where Full Cleveland had left it.

"Hey," the deputy called after me. "Your name is Strange?"

"Some people think so."

"No. That's your actual last name? Strange, like the movie?"

"I was Strange long before that."

Blame my mom. She never knew the guy who knocked her up. A one-night stand at a Grateful Dead concert, she told me when I was still in grade school. Imagine a mother doing that. Mom never cared for her last name, Strano. Went by Alice Sunshine. When she filled out my birth certificate, she accidently wrote her name in where mine should have gone. I should mention she was stoned at the time.

After she drowned, Uncle Leo adopted me and allowed me to legally change my name. I'd been going by Alex Strange by then. Alex because that's what Mom had always called me. And Strange because Strano is Italian for Strange and Mom hated her real last name and that's as close as I could get to it. And, besides, one of my comic book heroes was named Strange—Adam Strange, savior of the planet Rann.

"A detective from General Crimes will be over in a while, Mr., uh, Strange."

I nodded and started to turn away when a great squawking and flapping erupted from the dock. A half-dozen seagulls were squabbling over my baggie of okra they had torn open.

"No, no, no," I shouted.

I raced to the dock and chased the gulls off. Half the okra was missing from the torn baggie. The birds circled overhead and I could see several of them chugging the chunks of okra down their gullets.

They flapped about for a few more seconds, then began plummeting into the bay, one after another, like a feathered meteor shower.

The deputy stared at the sky, his mouth wide open in amazement.

"It's the okra," I said. "Seagulls are allergic."

I picked up my bag, carefully placed the remaining okra inside, and walked back to my boat. A wave of nausea hit me as I climbed aboard. I leaned over the rail to catch my breath, and then I threw up. Seasick on dry ground.

I glanced back toward Stan's and saw a sheriff's van pull up. A female crime scene investigator emerged carrying what looked like a large tackle box. She was a study in black: black shoes, black slacks, black shirt, black hat and a long black ponytail. At the dock, she set her box down, pulled out a camera, and began taking pictures of Maria's body.

Shortly thereafter, a van from the medical examiner's office pulled in. I'd seen enough. I stepped inside the *Miss Demeanor*. Mona stood guard by the entrance, dressed in full pirate regalia, sword held high. Mona is bald, has enormous breasts, and is made of plastic—a mannequin. A former female friend dressed her in the pirate garb after we bought her on a lark. Her crewmate is a cardboard cutout of Mr. Spock, his right hand in a split-finger "live long and prosper" Vulcan salute. There is no truth to the rumor Spock and Mona get it on when I'm not around. At least I don't think so.

"Today has been a total clown fiesta," I said. "I think I may have gotten somebody killed."

No response from Mona, who never took her brown eyes off the entrance, *en garde*.

Spock seemed unmoved by my troubles.

"Did I mention getting somebody killed, Spock?"

No response whatsoever. Vulcans, even cardboard ones, have empathy issues.

I looked at the bottle of rum in the galley. Then I looked back at Spock. He wouldn't approve. And he would be right. I needed to keep my wits about me. The rum would come later. The guilt had already arrived.

CHAPTER 3

I watched Detective Jim Henderson as he ran a hand over his close-cropped gray hair, wiping off the sweat. Deep creases radiated from the corners of his eyes. Thin as a foremast, he had a taut jawline, unlike many guys his age—early sixties, I guessed. Oddly, his wide, furry moustache—think Magnum PI—did not share the gray color of his crew cut. It was charcoal black.

Did he dye it or could it be a mutation? I never inquired. Some things you don't ask a guy carrying a Glock.

He took a sip of coffee out of the Green Lantern mug I offered, cocked his head and asked, "Starbucks?"

"Costco."

Henderson frowned and scrutinized the cup for a moment. Like either the coffee or the superhero were somehow offensive. As if I should be serving him a Caramel Macchiato in Wedgewood china. He took another sip and looked up. "No doughnuts?"

Banter.

"Got some okra you might like." I could do the banter thing, too.

He squinted at me for a second, his cranial hard drive spinning, then he got it. "Oh, yeah. With all this, I almost forgot."

I walked into the galley and retrieved the okra. I had placed the torn bag inside another Ziploc.

Henderson zipped open the bag, looked inside, then sniffed. "Smells like fried okra to me."

"You could confirm that by taking a bite. Or you could send it to the lab."

He nodded.

We were quiet for a moment. Henderson would ease into the questions about Maria, establish rapport first, even though we knew one another. Smart. That's what his idle chit-chat had been about. It's a fundamental interviewing technique. I use it all the time, too. He would get the conversation going then allow it to lapse every so often, hoping I would feel the social necessity to pitch in, to be polite. Maybe saying more than I should. Also standard operating procedure. But were there ever an occasion to watch what I said, this was it.

It had been two hours since I pulled Maria from Buzzards Bay. The guilt had morphed to anger and it was grinding on me. But Jim Henderson was the last cop I wanted to talk to about her.

I'd met Henderson at the dog track poker room shortly after I moved to Florida from Arizona. This eastward migration, from the Sonoran Desert to the Everglades, transpired after my newspaper, the *Phoenix Daily Sun*, folded and my Uncle Leo—Maricopa County Superior Court Judge Leonard D. Strano to you—offered me a change of venue. "Hop on down to Florida and live on my boat," Leo suggested when the paper went belly up, neglecting to mention that, drunk, he had run the *Miss Demeanor* aground, shattering her prop, crushing the hull, and nearly capsizing her. Which is why she rested on cinder blocks and oilcans, dry-docked in Goodland. A metaphor for my own life.

The boat was not only my home but my office. After the Sun set, as it were, a handful of us pooled resources to create Tropic Press. I had already been writing *The Strange Files* in Phoenix, so with the move to the Gunshine State, my boss, Edwina Mahoney, thought it would be clever to title me the Weird News Editor, Florida enjoying the reputation as the Candy Land of Crazy.

Henderson rested his coffee cup on the bench seat, and slipped a pack of coffin nails out of his chest pocket. He gestured it my way, but I ignored him. He lit a Marlboro, took a deep drag, and turned his head toward the water and exhaled. The onshore breeze blew the carcinogenic fog back into his face.

"You know, even a cop should be smart enough to quit," I said.

He took another drag and exhaled toward me. Defiant. The wind blew it back in his face again.

"I'll quit when I retire," he said, squinting.

After a few more puffs, Henderson flicked the smoldering butt over the side, then opened his notebook.

"The deputy you talked to, he said you seemed upset. You OK to talk?"

"I guess so."

He nodded. Considerate. Playing the good cop.

"How long'd you know her?"

I told him the same version I gave the deputy, the story of how we met. When I finished, he asked, "So, why'd she end up here in Goodland? She with you?"

"No."

"Huh." He wrote something in his notebook.

I knew what he meant by "huh." He didn't believe me. A smart guy would have kept his mouth shut.

"I get it," I said. "Most murder victims are killed by people they know. And I knew Maria. And she bobs up here, right by where I live. It looks bad."

"You used the term murder. What makes you think it's a murder?"

"Because I'm not blind. She has severe ligature marks on her throat, and her neck appears to be broken."

"Could be an accident," he said.

"How's that?"

"Let me ask you: She into kinky sex?"

"Kinky?"

Henderson raised his hands to his throat.

"A gasper?" I asked. "That's what you're thinking?"

"You'd know better than me."

"To quote Bill Clinton, I never had sex with that woman."

Autoerotic asphyxiation, a session of risky sex that got out of hand, would be consistent with her strangulation marks, I supposed. But it wouldn't explain why she surfaced in Buzzards Bay, unless, of course, she had been getting it on in Goodland.

That line of reasoning occurred to Henderson, too.

"Any idea why she would be here other than to visit you?"

"No. As far as I know, Maria has never been to Goodland, at least until now. And besides, this is stupid. Maria's a journalist. Kill a journalist in America and you invite a shit storm of media attention. Whoever did this would have been smarter to just make her disappear—wrap her in anchor chain and dump her in the Gulf."

"So why didn't that happen?"

"Like I would know."

"What's your guess?"

"It's either one hell of a coincidence—kinda hard to believe—or the killer picked this location for a reason. And the only reason I can think of is to implicate me. And your line of questioning makes me think it's working."

Henderson backhanded an invisible fly, a gesture of dismissal. "Just doing my job," he said. "But since you raised the question, what's so special about you?"

"We were working on a story together. But you know that already, right?"

"So?"

"So, it has to be about the story. Otherwise dumping her body here makes no sense."

"This story got her killed, that what you think?"

23

"You tell me." Henderson—and an arrest he made—were crucial elements in the story. Which is why I was reluctant to talk to him.

Henderson ignored my comment and fished out another Marlboro. He fired it up and took a deep drag. This time he managed to blow the smoke downwind. I kept my mouth shut, waiting to see if he would answer my question. He took another drag, cocked his head at me, ready to start grilling me again.

That's when Fred, his big ears at full alert, began barking. Henderson and I looked around for the object of Fred's irritation and spotted a Brown Pelican floating overhead.

No telling if it were the same avian who despoiled my boat and splattered Fred earlier. While I'm willing to believe pelicans can tell one another apart, they all look the same to me. I hope that isn't politically incorrect.

Fred is a Papillion, an eight-pound fur ball with ears jutting out of his head like butterfly wings. Maybe he knew the difference between one pelican and another. Some sort of doggie sixth sense. Maybe that close encounter soured him on the entire species. Bad dog. Shouldn't stereotype.

"Isn't she kinda tiny to be a bird dog?" Henderson asked.

"He, and I think Fred carries a grudge. A pelican attacked him a little while ago."

"Want I should shoot it?"

"You'll have PETA up your ass."

Henderson took another drag on his coffin nail and peered through the open cockpit door into the trawler's lounge. He spotted Mona.

"Who's she?"

"Shipmate. Her name's Mona."

"She inflatable?"

"You're sick."

"You mind if I wander in there and pay Mona a visit?" Henderson asked.

Red alert!

"You wanna search my boat? Without a warrant? Really?"

Before he could reply, his cell phone jingled—*Mission Impossible* theme—and he stood up and turned his back.

"Henderson." He said nothing for a few moments, listening. "Where? Jesus. Nobody's closer?" More silence on his end, then. "Look, I just got here. We have a possible homicide." Another pause. "Alright. Alright. I'll head on over."

He bent down and gave Fred a brief scratch on the head. "Thanks for the coffee," he said, raising the cup in a brief salute. "Gotta run. We'll talk some more." As he turned, I noticed he had a swatch of white on his butt—pelican poop. Should I tell him or not?

Fuck him.

Henderson swung a leg over the gunwale and stepped onto a rung of the boarding ladder. He started to swing his other leg over then stopped and took another sip of coffee and smiled. "Kinda grows on you. I'll return the cup next time I see you."

"What's the rush?" Not that I would shed any tears when he left.

"Standoff outside the Walmart on Collier Boulevard. Asshole in a pickup truck playing Garth Brooks. Loud. Windows open. Another asshole blaring Kanye West. They're both carrying."

"And *you* have to respond?" I asked.

"It's the weekend. I'm the senior duty officer today for this part of the county."

"Oh, so that's why you were so willing to come out to get my okra."

"Oh, yeah, the okra."

I reached down and handed him the baggie. "Forget something?"

He looked and grunted. "Why would anybody want to kill you?"

"Why would anybody want to kill Maria?"

Henderson gave me the standard-issue cop scare, the one they teach cadets at the police academy to intimidate people. I decided to change the subject.

"You gonna shoot the Kanye West guy or the Garth Brooks guy?"

"Brooks is a liberal, right?"

"They both are, I think."

"Huh." As if it made the decision harder. Henderson descended a couple of rungs—a neat trick while holding a cup of coffee and a baggie filled with cyanide-laced okra—then paused.

"I gotta ask you," he said. "You ID'd her right away. I could barely tell she was human. How could that be? Her face …"

He didn't have to say any more. It wasn't her face. It wasn't even that magnificent mop of obsidian hair.

"I recognized her ring."

CHAPTER 4

AFTER HENDERSON LEFT, I walked to the Little Bar and ordered a cheeseburger to go. Back aboard the *Miss Demeanor*, I gave Fred some Alpo, poured a Bacardi and Diet Coke, which, without a lime, technically is not a Cuba Libre. I drank it too fast. Then I poured another. And drank it. Fast. The cheeseburger stared up at me, impatient. Was I going to eat it or not? A cow had given her life for me. But I'd lost my appetite. I pulled off a chunk and dropped it into Fred's bowl. Fred had no qualms. Nice to be a dog.

I poured another shot of courage, then fetched the phone from my cargo shorts and dialed my boss, Edwina Mahoney. She didn't answer—a relief in a way. So I left a message:

"Hi, Ed. Alex here. I had a free moment, so I thought I'd call and let you know I got one of our reporters killed."

I swirled the ice in my drink for a bit, wondering how long it would take Ed to call me back. When she didn't, I logged onto the Tropic Press website. Our *This Month in History* report caught my attention. It was May 5, the anniversary of Alan Shepard's launch into outer space—the first American to do so. It was also on this date Christopher Columbus landed in Jamaica and claimed it for Spain. And in 1965, a rock band named the Warlocks played their first gig.

I downed my drink and reached for the bottle.

Spock glared at me.

"What?" He can be such a prig. "You never drink, do you, Spock?"

Then, I reflected on how his planet had been destroyed. And how stalwart he'd been.

"Sorry, Spock, it's the rum talking. But at least it's not Romulan Ale. Trust me on this, never drink anything blue."

If he had an opinion on the matter, he kept it to himself.

I glanced at Mona. She stared unblinking at the trawler's entrance, sword at the ready. As usual, she had nothing to add to the conversation, so I turned back to the *This Month in History* article on my phone.

The Warlocks. You may not have heard of them. But after their first few gigs, the boys in the band—some guys named Jerry Garcia, Bob Weir, Phil Lesh, and Ron "Pigpen" McKernan—decided to change their name. You know them now as The Grateful Dead.

I know them as the band my mother, the Deadhead, followed around the country. It was at one of their concerts she got knocked up. Hence me. So, all you Warlocks, thanks. Wish my mom hadn't become a stoner, but, hey, if not, I might not be here.

And Maria Martinez might not be dead.

The Bacardi beckoned. Before I poured, I took a final look at the website: Also in May—in the year of our Lord 1780 on the 19th of the month—the skies turned black at high noon over New England. To this day, nobody knows why. It wasn't the Apocalypse (obviously), an eclipse (verifiably), nor an alien invasion (as far as we know). If that happened today, I imagine the president's spiritual advisor, the Rev. Lee Roy Chitango, would declare it God's wrath on all the evil, homosexual, God-denying, unpatriotic, hedonists. And he'd use it to sell more lottery tickets to the Ark II.

The sky wasn't black in Goodland, but the end of the day neared. I spent the rest of an unsettled evening brooding over Maria's murder and worrying why her body floated up near my boat. I tried, but failed, to purge the image of her devastated face. And was someone trying to poison me? Could it be a coincidence that both of these things occurred on the same day?

And Henderson. I'd known him since we ended up at the final table of a Texas Hold 'Em tournament at the dog track. While we weren't pals, we weren't strangers, either. But you wouldn't know it from his line of questions. Did he believe I would be so stupid as to dump Maria's body next to my boat? Of course, Florida's overcrowded prison system is not unduly burdened by Rhodes Scholars. But, still.

If Maria could speak from the afterlife, she would warn me not to trust anybody at the Sheriff's Office.

"Spock, I'm freaked out, furious, and frightened. Any words of wisdom?"

Nothing.

"You're no fun, Spock." I poured another, intent on adding seriously fucked up to the alliterative stream. But I might have been there already.

THE STRANGE FILES

Electronic cigarette explodes

By Alexander Strange

Tropic ⊚ Press

Electronic cigarettes are marketed as a safer alternative to inhaling cancer sticks.

Don't tell that to Aaron McKenzy of Miramar Beach, Florida. The 38-year-old graphic artist was trying to quit smoking by switching to vaping. But when a faulty battery in his electronic cigarette exploded, it knocked out his front teeth and burned off the tip of his tongue.

"Imagine a bottle rocket going off in your mouth," said fire department spokesman Bob Jendusa.

When the battery blew up, it flew out the tube into McKenzy's closet, catching it on fire, which may have been a lucky break because it set off the smoke alarms in his apartment. That led fire fighters to find his unconscious body in his bedroom.

A spokeswoman for Sacred Heart Hospital reported McKenzy is in good condition, but due to the nature of his injuries, he could not speak to the media.

STRANGE FACT: Urea, a major chemical component of urine, is used to add flavor to cigarettes.

Weirdness knows no boundaries. Keep up at *www.TheStrangeFiles.com*. Contact Alexander Strange at Alex@TheStrangeFiles.com.

CHAPTER 5

"MR. STRANGE," THE man on the phone said, "we met yesterday. My name is Lester Rivers and I am with The Third Eye."

I checked my watch: Mickey's hands were on seven and six. I felt a dull ache behind my eyes. Rum and Coke will do that when consumed to excess. Fred pawed my leg, demanding to be carried down from the trawler to the litter-strewn boatyard so he could do his morning business.

"Thought you were a toilet seat salesman," I said.

"Urinal screens."

"Listen, whoever you are, this isn't funny."

"It's whomever."

"Whatever."

Fred's scratching on my leg intensified. I put my finger on the iPhone's red button, but stopped when he said, "Don't hang up, I need to talk to you about Maria Martinez."

How did he know?

"I'll call you back in five."

I carried Fred down the ladder propped against the boat's hull. Fred began his regular circuit. He romped over to the side of an oilcan and raised a leg. Then he meandered to a little grassy patch, circled a couple of time, and squatted down to finish his morning ablution. We climbed back aboard and I gave Fred a treat before returning the call.

"So, what's your story? You a toilet guy or a detective?"

"The matter we need to discuss is on behalf of my employer, The Third Eye. It's about Maria Martinez."

"That's why you wanted to meet yesterday?"

"Yes. We need to talk. Can you meet me downtown?"

"I guess, but what's this about?"

"In person. Not over the phone."

"You're killing me."

"No. But there's a killer out there, which is why we need to talk."

The Third Eye is a well-known detective agency based in Boise, Idaho. They are headquartered there, of all places, because Idaho is one of the few states that allows private investigators to be unlicensed. That loophole has allowed the agency to hire not just former cops but also ex-special forces operators, hackers, journalists, and even a few self-avowed psychics.

The Third Eye is actually a fanciful appellation, a capitalized nickname. The agency started out as Investigative Inquiries of Idaho. The news media and pundits began calling the outfit Triple I and it evolved into its current handle. They formally changed their name to Third Eye Investigators a couple of years ago. I admired the name. It evoked a sense of the mystical—perfect for an outfit employing psychics.

Maybe that was Rivers—a psychic. I'd find out soon enough. I agreed to meet him for lunch at Citrus on Fifth Avenue in Naples, the trendy downtown shopping and dining district.

"But if you're with The Third Eye," I said before we rang off, "what's with the baloney about toilet seats?"

"Urinal screens, and jibber-jabbering about toilets does tend to clear out eavesdroppers."

"Huh."

"The woman sitting between us? You may recall she left the bar shortly after I began my little spiel."

"So I noticed."

"Good. Dat's what journalists are supposed to do, notice things."

Dat, not that. The Cajun coming through again.

"So, then, a little test," he continued. "What did you notice about me yesterday?"

"I pass the test, you buy lunch?"

"Sure."

"Well, you have terrible taste in clothes."

"And my face?"

"I didn't see much of your face—you wore a hat and sunglasses."

"So did you. But I can describe you in intimate detail, from your overly long hair—you really should get to a barbershop, young man— to that oddly shaped scar on your forehead. Looks like a horseshoe. You rather remind me of that Star Wars actor, only you're younger, of course. And you're bigger. Actually, you favor your uncle, Superior Court Judge Leonard D. Strano. It's his boat you live on now, right?"

"My uncle? What does my uncle have to do with this?"

"I contacted Judge Strano in Phoenix while tracking you down. You list him as family on your Facebook page. He helped. I mean, I knew you were in South Florida somewhere—that's obvious from your blog—but you've fallen off the grid, haven't you? No physical mailing address. No utility bills. Vehicle still registered in Arizona—that's illegal, by the way. Your colleagues at the news service refused to talk to me. Probably thought I might be a process server. So, rather than waste more time, I just called your uncle."

"How'd you get my cell?" I asked. I block my Caller ID on outgoing calls and only a few people have my number.

"On the responding deputy's report. Pulled it up this morning."

"Usually phone numbers are redacted."

"Only the copies given to the press and public."

"Oh, this is Third Eye stuff."

"The Third Eye knows all."

"How do you do it?" I asked.

"The Third Eye knows all, but does not tell all."

Full Cleveland, Man of Mystery.

"And the whole toilet seat rap?" I asked. "You're a detective *and* a toilet seat salesman?"

"Urinal screens. And before you sneer at advertising in unlikely places, you may wish to recall that the county where you live was founded by a man, Barron Collier, who got rich selling ads on street cars in New York."

"He ever sell ads on outhouses?"

"Don't know, but if he could have made a buck, I'm sure he would have."

"Whatever."

"Only teenagers say *whatever*. But to answer your question, I work for The Third Eye as a skip tracer. Missing persons. Usually, I'm assigned to track down people who want to disappear. It's harder than you might think to just up and vanish. I enjoy traveling. The work keeps me busy between gigs."

"Gigs? That what you shamuses call your assignments? Gigs?"

"Oh, no, that's what we musicians call our engagements."

"You in a band, too?"

"Yes. The Black Ops?"

"Black Ops? Like Delta Force or Navy SEALS?"

"Indeed. We're all veterans."

"You Guitar? Drums? Vocals?"

"Trombone."

Drifting Planets in our Future?

By Alexander Strange

Tropic©Press

Beachgoers on Florida's Atlantic coast were alarmed recently when a bright flaming ball appeared on the horizon streaking in their direction.

"It lit up the night, I thought somebody touched off a nuclear weapon," Steve Bennish, 24, of New Smyrna Beach told police. "And then it just disappeared."

Emergency operators up and down the coast received hundreds of calls from worried residents reporting UFOs.

The sightings drew the attention of the Near-Earth Object Program at the Jet Propulsion Laboratory in Pasadena, Calif. Astronomer Terry Eisenberg told me the light show could most likely be attributed to a small asteroid knocked out of its orbit that entered our atmosphere at a shallow angle making it appear to grow before it vaporized.

"We missed that one," he said. "Too small. It may have put up a heck of a light show, but I doubt it was bigger than a basketball."

What would cause it to be jarred from its orbit? I asked.

"Lots of things. Let's hope it wasn't a drifting planet," Eisenberg said.

Drifting planet?

Eisenberg said scientists have discovered the galaxy may be filled with "millions and millions" of Jupiter-sized planets wandering aimlessly through space.

And what would happen if one of these gas giants wandered into our solar system?

"If we saw it coming, my advice would be: Don't buy any green bananas."

STRANGE FACT: Despite its size, the planet Saturn's mass is so light that if you were to place it in a big enough bucket of water it would float.

Weirdness knows no boundaries. Keep up at *www.TheStrangeFiles.com*. Contact Alexander Strange at Alex@TheStrangeFiles.com.

CHAPTER 6

I HAD TIME before driving to Naples, so I called Edwina Mahoney again. And, as before, there was no answer. I finished a column about UFOs that I had already started and posted it. Tried Edwina again with the same result. Finally, I stepped down to my berth and threw on a pair of running shorts. I grabbed my shoes and Fred's leash and walked back up into the lounge.

Fred saw the leash and launched into his happy dance, jumping up and down and whining. As I tried to sidestep him, I bumped into Mona and she toppled. I dropped my shoes and caught her before she hit the deck. Mona rested on a weighted stand with a dowel rod inserted into her left heel, but the peg wobbled. I made a mental note—again—to repair it.

I tied my shoelaces, leashed Fred, and walked him over to Mrs. Overstreet's single-wide at the Drop Anchor Mobile Home Park.

Mrs. Overstreet loves Fred and is happy to dog-sit on the days when she's not waiting tables at the Little Bar. I gave Fred a scratch, then a treat, and handed him over to her welcoming arms.

"Did the one-legged man ever find you?" she asked.

"One-legged man?"

"Yes, he came by the Little Bar yesterday looking for you. I told him you were probably at Stan's."

My quizzical look seemed to trouble her. "I hope I didn't do anything wrong."

"No, of course not, Mrs. Overstreet. I just don't recall talking to a guy with one leg. Can you describe him?"

"Let's see," she said. She pulled Fred up to her face and nuzzled him. Fred loves attention. "He wore a flat straw hat, shorts, was a little heavy, and of course he tried to hide his, pro...pro..."

"Prosthesis?"

"Yes, that. He tried to hide it by pulling his socks up high. But I could tell by the way he walked. With a limp."

"Huh."

As I started to leave, the door to Mrs. Overstreet's trailer opened and a girl stepped out. I recognized her green hair.

"You," I said.

"Hey, Alex."

"Gabby, right?"

"Right."

I looked back and forth between her and Mrs. Overstreet.

"You two have met, I see," Mrs. Overstreet said, smiling. "Gabriel's my niece. She's staying here for a few days."

"Until I can find a place of my own," she said.

"Gabriel?"

"Call me Gabby. Everybody but my aunt does." She turned to Mrs. Overstreet and gave her a kind smile.

"Small world," I said. "Welcome to the hood."

Gabby stepped over to her aunt and gently patted Fred on his head.

"Thanks for your help yesterday," I said. "I lost it."

"No problem." She paused for a moment then said, "You knew her, didn't you?"

"Yeah."

"I'm so sorry."

She scratched Fred behind his ears for a few seconds then returned her attention to me.

"Looks like you're going for a run."

"Yeah."

"I'd join you, but I've got to practice."

"Gabriel's a singer," Mrs. Overstreet said. "She's moved here to play with this new band, the Swamp Vixens, and they're opening in Naples tonight."

"A singer and a bartender," I said. "You're busy."

"Got to pay the rent." She glanced at her aunt. "Soon as I find a place. But I probably won't be at Stan's much longer. I'm in training at a restaurant downtown that pays better. And it will be closer to where the band plays."

"Your band need a trombone player?" I asked.

"Uh, no." She laughed. "Why? You play?"

"No, but I know a guy."

I have a four-mile route I run most mornings. Goodland is shaped like a catcher's mitt, and the half dozen inlets, canals and small bays that poke their way inland form the fingers on the mitt. My normal route took me past the two story, wood-framed Marco Lodge and the Crabby Lady Restaurant along Bayshore Way. Then I retraced my steps back toward Stan's, past the Little Bar and the shoebox-sized post office, then jogged out to Goodland Drive for the long run to San Marco Road and back.

Panting by the time I returned to the *Miss Demeanor*, I had sweated out the alcohol from the night before. When I first arrived in Goodland, someone had abandoned a rusting boat trailer on a ten-by-twenty-foot concrete pad adjacent to where my trawler now rested. I'd rolled it to the far corner of the yard and used the pad as a small exercise area. I dropped and did a hundred pushups, a hundred squats, and finished with a hundred sit-ups. As I stood up, I felt something funny sticking to my back. I brushed it off. A cigarette butt. Fucking Henderson.

I climbed aboard and checked my cell phone. Edwina Mahoney hadn't returned my call. She'd been getting harder to reach lately, so much of her time eaten up in efforts to find investors in the news service. I couldn't begrudge her that. If she succeeded, it would be a financial windfall. Until then, I called the *Miss Demeanor* home. The trawler wouldn't be seaworthy until her prop and belly were repaired, and while not as shiny as some newer watercraft, she was spacious—a characteristic of trawlers, which make them wonderful live-aboards. Leo had arranged to have power and water run to the boat, and a service came by weekly to empty the head's waste tanks. A bit Spartan, but better than living in a box under the freeway.

Leo and I agreed that if I kept an eye on the boat, I could stay until he arranged to have the repairs completed. I kept tabs on what I would eventually owe him for utilities. I had a few thousand left in the bank from my severance package from the newspaper, which, with my modest salary from the Tropic Press, kept Fred and me afloat, as it were. But if Edwina were successful in finding some investors in the service, it would certainly make life easier.

I showered, then pulled on a pair of khaki cargo shorts, a red Weezer T-shirt, my black Cincinnati Reds ball cap, and slipped into my black Nike running shoes, the ones with the red shoe laces. I am nothing if not color coordinated. Then I grabbed my messenger bag and climbed over the gunwale.

I kept my car in a vacant lot across from Stan's. I was driving a maroon Chrysler Sebring convertible with nearly 250,000 miles on it, a vehicle sold to me by my uncle when one of the previous Mrs. Stranos (the current Mrs. Strano was *Numero Cinco*) grew tired of it. The matching maroon cloth interior was indelibly stained with splotches of yellow when *Numero Cuatro* left it parked, top down, under an exfoliating olive tree in Uncle Leo's front yard back in Arizona.

I dropped the top and turned onto Goodland Drive, which connects the village to the rest of Marco Island. Connects it except when it floods. Locals say it happens more frequently these days. At San Marco Road, I turned left and made my way off the island to the Tamiami Trail, which leads directly into downtown Naples, the last major coastal city on the southwest coast of Florida.

Naples is the political, cultural and financial hub of Collier County. In Naples it's Bentleys, Lamborghinis, and Mercedes. It's multi-million-dollar mansions along the Billionaire Coast and happy hours in which the champagne and chardonnay begin pouring before noon. In Goodland, where I lived, it's Harleys and pickup trucks and modest one-story brick and clapboard houses painted in a riot of colors. And it's always happy hour if a cold Bud makes you happy. Not so ritzy, but a lot funkier.

I dig funky and it's within my means. But downtown Naples is quaint with its swaying palms, ritzy shops, and sidewalk cafes. I was pleased to meet The Third Eye guy there if he was springing for lunch. And I needed to discover why he had an interest in Maria.

I tuned the radio to the local news station. The Sheriff's Office had not released the ID of what they were calling a "drowning victim" found in Goodland. Nothing about the standoff in the Walmart parking lot Henderson responded to—guess he hadn't shot anyone. And meteorologists were concerned a tropical depression might be spinning up in the Gulf.

I found a parking spot on Fifth Avenue, a block from the restaurant. Lester Rivers sat under a yellow umbrella at a table on the broad sidewalk still wearing his Full Cleveland getup. He lifted his straw hat and ran a handkerchief over his bald pate. Forecast said the high would be in the upper 80s.

"Nice look," I said.

He set down his glass—looked like an Arnold Palmer. "You're so observant."

"In truth, a neighbor of mine is more so than me. She said you have an artificial leg. That's what the knee-high socks are all about? Not just a fashion statement?"

He nodded.

"Car accident?"

"In a manner of speaking. A bus and it encountered a roadside bomb outside Kabul."

I winced. "I'm sorry. Your leg. Blown off?"

"Not exactly. I crawled out a window but the gas tank exploded, rolling the bus over and pinning me. The bus caught fire. I couldn't pull free. By the time help arrived, my left leg below my knee was charred bone."

I felt my face getting hot and perspiration beading on my forehead. "I'm so sorry. Really."

He offered a mirthless smile. "You asked."

A waiter arrived. Lester ordered another Arnold Palmer and an artichoke and arugula bruschetta. "I'll just have a Diet Coke for now," I said.

"Lost your appetite?"

"Again…"

He waved me off. "I get around all right."

"Well enough to keep me from tumbling into the bay yesterday," I said. "Thank you for that."

"I need you alive and well, Mr. Strange, he said. "We have work to do."

"Meaning what?"

"Meaning we need to find Maria's killer."

I felt my stomach tighten. I took a sip of my Diet Coke, hoping to calm it down.

"Cops seem to think it could be me," I said. "Why don't you?"

"Brett Barfield says you're, and I quote, 'a gigantic hemorrhoid,' but he says you're trustworthy."

Barfield's a former cop I know. After he quit the Scottsdale PD, he signed up with The Third Eye. We'd worked together to track down a polygamist holding a 16-year-old girl, a niece of Uncle Leo's wife, captive. Barfield shot his balls off. Literally. Which sounds horrible, I know, but you had to have been there, had to have witnessed her tied to the motel room bed, had to have seen this douche bag coming after us with a butcher knife. I remember asking Barfield about his aim: "Whatever happened to shooting at the center of body mass?"

His response: "Oops."

Rivers removed his sunglasses and looked at me. His eyes were cobalt and penetrating, revealing an intelligence obscured by his goofy getup. "There's something else. I saw how you reacted when you recognized Maria, how you held her hand, how you kept repeating her name. I saw the thousand-yard stare in your eyes. I've seen the look before. Too many times. It's the look of a man who's lost a friend in combat."

I didn't recall holding Maria's hand or saying her name. In fact, most of those first few minutes after I pulled her to the dock were a blur.

"That's how you knew her identity?"

"Yes. And your statement to the responding deputy, which, like I said on the phone, I read this morning."

That aroused my curiosity. "The police have released her name?"

"No. Her name is in the notes, not in the report released to the public."

"And you can get access to those notes."

He shrugged.

I told Rivers about Henderson's visit aboard my boat. About how his line of questioning gave me the creeps, as if he suspected me in Maria's death. But how it felt too pat. Maybe I was paranoid, but it smelled like a set-up to pin the murder on me.

I also told him my fear someone tried to poison me in the deli checkout line. He had listened to my story without interruption, but this animated him.

"Date and time," he said.

"Huh?"

"This okra incident, it happened yesterday, right?"

"Yes."

"At precisely what time?"

I told him.

"The delicatessen will have video. We'll see if we can get the ID of the people who were in the checkout line with you."

"Won't the police do that?" I asked.

"They won't take this seriously until they have a lab report back on your okra. If they even do a test. Based on what you've told me, I'm not comfortable with this Detective Henderson. But even if he does follow through, by the time the tests are completed, it could be too late."

"And you can get this video?" I asked, surprised by his aggressiveness.

"We'll get it." He didn't say how and I didn't ask.

"There's one more thing," he said. "You shouldn't have invited Henderson on board."

"About the okra?" I asked, stupidly.

"About Maria."

"Why not?"

"Fruit of the poisonous tree."

"Huh?"

"It's a legal term. You allowed him on your boat without a warrant. If he came aboard without your invitation, any evidence found there could be ruled tainted—a consequence of an improper search, a.k.a, the fruit of the poisonous tree—and could not be used in trial."

"Trial? What trial? I have nothing to hide."

"Isn't dat special."

"It's that, not dat."

He nodded. "I gotta do something about … *that*. Keep reminding me. "

He was about to take a bite of his bruschetta, then paused, leaned back in his chair and shook his head. "Damn!"

"What?"

"I've made a mistake. I should have thought of this before inviting you here. They're going to get a warrant to search your boat. Probably today. You better get back there and make sure there's nothing incriminating lying around."

"Why would there be?" I asked.

"You said it yourself. Her body surfacing near your boat, it's not just odd, it's suspicious. It may be a remote possibility, but I agree with you, this could be an effort to frame you."

He rested his fork on his plate and wiped his brow. "Maybe I'm being paranoid, too, but if someone went to the trouble of dumping her body there to incriminate you, why not also seed the crime scene with other bits of evidence that could point in your direction? Maybe, just maybe, they expected you to be found dead at the same time. Bastard killed the girl then offed himself. Wouldn't … *that* … have been tidy?"

"Death by cyanide is tidy?"

"Well, maybe not for you."

CHAPTER 7

"Brothers and Sisters, let us pray."

The Rev. Lee Roy Chitango was holding forth on the *OhGodOhGod* Radio Network, broadcasting live from the Museum of Holy Creation, a sprawling religious theme park on 400 acres in eastern Collier County—Florida's fastest-growing tourist attraction.

Ten enormous marble tablets formed a Stonehenge-like circle at the museum's entrance surrounding a towering "eternal flame" symbolizing the burning bush that spoke to Moses on Mount Horeb.

Each of the marble tablets was inscribed with one of the Ten Commandments, all in different languages—English, French, German, Spanish, Italian, Japanese, Portuguese, Mandarin, Russian, and Korean.

Curiously, there wasn't one in Hebrew.

I asked Chitango about that, having interviewed him several times for *The Strange Files*. All the conversations were phoners. He did no interviews face-to-face.

"This is a Christian theme park. A park for Christians," he said.

Notwithstanding that most of the park focused on the story of Genesis, the world's creation, all drawn from the Old Testament.

"Well, if it's a theme park for Christians, what's the with Dozen Dancing Virgins?" I asked.

The Virgins were a Rockettes-styled troupe that high-stepped its way across the altar at the end of each of Chitango's televised services to the tune of *Spirit in the Sky*, a 1969 song recorded by an Orthodox Jew named Norman Greenbaum. Not all the dancers were blondes, but most were, which led some smart-ass journalist to dub them the Boogie Barbies.

"Jesus wants us to multiply," he responded to my question. "What better way to get that started than with dancing virgins?"

Chitango's rant played on the radio as I sped back to Goodland, keeping the speedometer a steady ten miles an hour over the limit, hoping not to get pulled over. Lester Rivers was afraid I had no time to spare.

Chitango's sermon for the day condemned atheists.

"Dear God, we pray for the souls of these misbegotten *heatherns*," Chitango intoned. He always mispronounced heathens, a carryover from his childhood in rural Oklahoma, where he recalled in his autobiography being mesmerized by the late Oral Roberts on the radio.

I'd asked him about Oral Roberts' claim to have seen a 900-foot-tall Jesus who threatened to "call him home" if he didn't raise eight million dollars from his followers.

"God did tell Oral he would call him home, and, of course, he eventually did once Oral completed his ministry," Chitango said. "He sits with Jesus now. But the vision of the towering Jesus came earlier, when God told him to build his City of Faith Medical and Research Center."

"This inspired you to build the Museum of Holy Creation?"

"No, God spoke to me directly about that."

The Almighty had apparently spoken to Chitango about non-believers, who the Sermonator declared should registered with the police.

"Just like sex offenders. And homosexuals. And those transpeople. We have a right to know the evil ones among us. And, my friends, I can promise you this, come the Reckoning, there will be no berths aboard the Ark II for the faithless. And there will be no transgender bathrooms."

The Ark II was an enormous seagoing bunker under construction on a secret island in the Caribbean to house the "Selects"—the survivors of the End of Days. You, too, could board the Ark II if your lottery number came up—a kind of natural selection process Darwin would be proud of. Except Chitango didn't believe in evolution, the Earth being too young, now only approaching its 6,666th birthday.

Chitango did believe in joyful procreation—an activity reserved, by definition, for heterosexual congress. More babies, more tithers—an outstanding business plan. The Boogie Barbies served as a sort of mascot for that. They would soon be joining an elite group of "primary tithers" who would be given a tour of the secret construction site of the Ark II. Reporters from both the *Tampa Bay Times* and the *Miami Herald* had pestered Chitango about the identities of these tithers, but he wouldn't give them up.

It would be easy to dismiss Chitango's lunatic ravings, but some politicians, no doubt cognizant of the ratings of his syndicated radio and television programs, were stepping carefully lest they offend his swelling sea of followers among the Christian evangelical right. Five years ago, if you had mentioned Chitango's name, you would have gotten puzzled looks. His rise to superstar status was nothing short of, well, a miracle.

At a recent press conference, a U.S. Senate candidate from Miami, Ricky Perez, responded to a question about the Ark II and the Rev. Chitango's pricy lottery tickets to raise funds for the ship's construction. Only two thousand of his followers would win the lottery, but, hey, salvation isn't free.

"So, Representative Perez," the reporter from *Miami New Times*, asked. "Isn't Chitango's lottery a scam?"

The reporter pronounced the reverend's name Shit-an-Go as

opposed to She-Tango, as His Holiness preferred. Many of his detractors did.

Perez didn't miss a beat. "The Rev. Chitango is a man of God, a man of vision. Unless we change our ways—which is why I am running for the Senate, to help change America—we will need a new Ark to weather the storm ahead."

In the past few months, the good reverend had invited Perez on his show multiple times and picked him in the crowded Republican primary race for the Senate nomination.

"Ricky Perez, his words are music to my eyes," Chitango said in a broadcast the week before. "When Ricky Perez is in the Senate, we will enact laws at long last to register the users of morning after pills, we will stand up to the sodomites, we will return prayer to the classroom, and we will have stronger libel laws to stop the vicious lies the fake news media says about us."

I turned off the radio as I crossed the bridge to Marco Island. A few minutes later, I pulled into Goodland. A sheriff's cruiser, an older unmarked Crown Vic, and a crime scene van were parked in the Little Bar's parking lot. A uniformed deputy guarded the entrance to the boatyard, just inside a ribbon of yellow tape. Inside the fence, two CSIs in moon suits scoured the weeds near the stern of the *Miss Demeanor*.

"Check this out," one of them said, her voice muffled by the hazmat suit's headpiece. She pointed to something near the waterline. The other CSI walked over and took several photographs, at one point stooping near the object and placing a ruler next to it so the photos would show the scale of their discovery.

The first CSI stooped down and picked up a length of braided yellow rope, maybe ten feet long, and held it aloft in her gloved hand. The other moon suit walked over with a large paper bag. The first CSI coiled the rope and carefully placed it in the bag. Lots of rope like that around marinas. But this one was different: It had a noose on one end.

"What's going on?" I asked.

The uniformed deputy stuck out a hand to block me.

"Stand clear," he ordered.

"You guys got a warrant for this?"

"We do," said a familiar voice behind me.

I turned to face Henderson who was holding an envelope I presumed contained the warrant.

"What the hell?" I said.

Before he could respond, the technician holding the bag with the rope walked up.

"You'll want to see this," she said to the detective. "We found this rope near the water." She opened the top of the bag. "Look but don't touch and don't breathe on it. You can see that here"—she pointed to the noose—"looks like blood." The moon suit then walked the bag over to the crime scene van, set it inside, and clicked the lock on the vehicle.

She pulled off her headpiece as she returned and I recognized her ponytail. "You were at the dock yesterday," I said.

She nodded her head. "Correct."

"What's with the space suit?" I asked.

"Standard operating procedure at homicide scenes to make sure we don't contaminate any evidence."

"I turned to Henderson. "Homicide scene?"

The other CSI had climbed the ladder up to the deck of the trawler. She, too, removed her headpiece and yelled down to Henderson. "Door's locked."

The uniformed deputy asked Henderson, "Do we break it or do we have a key?"

Henderson turned to me. "Your choice."

I dug into my cargo shorts and retrieved my key ring. "It's the big brass one," I said.

The deputy walked over to the boat and ascended the ladder. Once up top, he drew his sidearm, unlocked the door, and stepped inside.

Seemed overly dramatic to me. Probably wanted to impress the CSIs. Daring cop enters dangerous vessel.

Then a frightened shout and the deafening blast of a gunshot boomed inside the boat.

The CSI on the boat froze. Seagulls squawked and burst into the air along the shoreline. Ponytail raced to the trawler followed closely by Henderson, who pulled his Glock. "Garcia, you all right up there?" he yelled. "Garcia!"

A moment later, the deputy reappeared on deck. His smoking pistol dangled by his side.

"Sorry about the noise, detective" he said. "She startled me."

"She?" Henderson asked.

With nobody blocking the gate, I followed the parade into the boatyard. There could be only one *she* aboard the boat. "Mona," I said.

"Mona?"

"My mannequin."

Henderson and the ponytailed CSI began climbing the ladder and I followed.

"You can't be here," ponytail said. I ignored her and stepped inside the lounge. Mona was lying on her side, a bullet hole punched through her left breast. A hole in the lounge window, too.

Great, another repair.

Henderson turned to the deputy, his face purple with rage.

"I'm sorry, detective," the deputy said. "Really. I saw the sword in her ... its ... hand and then, I swear, she lunged at me. I just reacted."

Outside on the deck, the CSIs were giggling. Henderson whirled toward them and they choked it off.

"Jesus fucking Christ," Henderson snarled. "You," he said to the deputy, "off the boat and take him with you." He jerked his head toward me.

"Mona, baby," I said, "the paramedics are on the way."

The CSIs lost it again.

"And you," I said to Spock. "You just stood there, did nothing?" Fucking Vulcans.

"Off the boat!" Henderson bellowed. The deputy gestured me toward the door. I decided to go along. Better than getting shot.

"Henderson," I said, "in all fairness to the deputy, Mona can be a little tipsy."

"OFF THE BOAT!"

The deputy and I descended the ladder. When we reached the bottom, I turned to him but he avoided eye contact.

"Seriously, man, the stand she's propped on, it's broken. Could have happened to anybody."

A few minutes later, Henderson climbed down and the search continued.

The techs dusted for prints, sprayed for blood spatters, and collected fiber and hair samples. Using what looked like some sort of plaster, they made impressions of footprints in the boat yard. And they photographed everything.

While they worked, Henderson suggested we talk. With no place to sit in the yard, we walked over to his aging unmarked sedan.

"You need a new ride," I said.

He ignored that.

"Before we begin," he said, "I am going to read this warrant."

"Seriously, man, a Crown Vic? Think about your image."

He started reading, droning on for about five minutes. I couldn't tell you what all he said, being preoccupied with recurring thoughts about Maria. Had she been hanged. By that rope?

When Henderson finished, he pulled a little card out of his shirt pocket, hidden behind his Marlboros, and read me my rights.

"Am I under arrest?" I asked.

"No. You are what we like to call a person of interest." He finished reading the script then asked me if I wanted a lawyer.

"Just get on with it."

He pushed the start button on an audio recorder. "Tell me some more about your relationship with Ms. Martinez," he said.

"I got a better idea," I said, "tell me why you're asking me that question *after* you decide to search my place? Aren't you jumping the gun here?"

He shook his head. "You live in the heart of the crime scene, where the body surfaced. You knew the victim. You said so, yourself. You also were able to identify her despite her face being unrecognizable."

"Yes, I told you, I recognized her ring."

"Weren't you more than just friends?"

"Meaning what?"

"She worked for your outfit, the news service, right?"

"You know that already."

"She was asking questions about the Edgard Dominique case, right?"

"Ah," I said and waited.

"You put her onto the story, didn't you?"

"Yes. How you guys fucked up the case."

His face empurpled. "I didn't fuck up anything."

"This is personal, isn't it?" I could ask questions, too.

"Were you having a sexual relationship with her?" he asked, his voice growing louder. I'd gotten to him. Thought I should do it some more.

"Fuck you."

"We're searching her apartment next. We going to find your prints and DNA there?"

"Let me save you the trouble," I said, my voice a few decibels louder, too. "I've been there. I've already told you we knew one another. That doesn't make me a murderer."

Henderson paused, hoping I'd blurt out something incriminating, my anger or anxiety getting the better of me. But I've done a few confrontational interviews myself.

"Let me ask *you* something," I said, regaining my composure. "Maria Martinez's story would have disclosed a major screw-up in your department, all directly related to an arrest you made. If anyone sitting in this car would have a motive to kill her, why wouldn't it be you?"

Henderson didn't blink. Instead he channeled Sgt. Joe Friday. "Where were you the night of the murder?"

I took a deep breath. "You know, this is the second time you've tried to trick me. It's insulting. Like I would know when she was killed. Really?"

He sat, stone-faced.

"But the first time was when you invited yourself aboard my boat. Sneaky way to snoop around."

He remained silent, waiting for me to get to the point.

"Satisfy my curiosity, you see something on the boat to use as a trumped-up excuse for a warrant?"

"I already read you the warrant."

"Come on."

He paused for a moment then said, "You're not a very good housekeeper."

"What?"

"The coffee cup you gave me. It had lipstick on the rim. We've bagged it and will test it for her DNA.

"It won't have her DNA," I said. "Maria never set foot on my boat."

I started running through the very short list of women who spent the night on the *Miss Demeanor*. It's not that I'm a monk. It's just, well, you meet a girl, you finally get to "Your place or mine?" and you live on a beached trawler in downtown Nowhereville. Guess what? It's usually her place.

We were quiet for a moment. It looked like the CSIs were wrapping up. Henderson clicked off his recorder.

"And besides," I said, "you already ruined the chain of custody by carting off my cup the way you did."

"But I got my warrant." Smug.

"So, when are you going to release Maria's name to the media?" I asked. The morning news reports and the brief story in the newspaper merely called her an "unidentified female" and a possible drowning victim. Even in Florida drownings are news, but not exactly rare. The accounts made no mention of the ligature marks on her neck.

"Probably tomorrow," Henderson said. "Mrs. Martinez is in South America with her sister and we have been unable to locate her. Her cousin—you know who he is, right?"

I nodded.

"He's coming, but we've also contacted her aunt in Connecticut and she's flying down first thing tomorrow. She'll formally ID the body."

"Oh, Jesus," I said. "Don't let her see Maria like that. It will haunt her for the rest of her life. I'm already having nightmares."

"Has to be done," he said. "Not sure if the ME can get good prints off the corpse, and DNA tests take time. It's not like TV. We don't have our own lab for that, and we have to send it off to the state."

"What about my IDing her?"

"Think about it," Henderson said. "The ring is all you identified."

"Aw, jeez."

"Well, you know, you could save us all some time and confess."

In the end, he didn't arrest me or warn me to stay in town. He didn't apologize for killing Mona, either. But once the corpse was positively identified as Maria, I was sure he would be back. Maybe next time with handcuffs.

THE STRANGE FILES

Dog Shoots Woman in Foot

By Alexander Strange

Tropic©Press

A Labrador retriever-bulldog mix named Trigger shot a 46-year-old Clewiston woman in the foot during a hunting trip this week, police said.

The woman left her shotgun on the ground, fully loaded with the safety off, when Trigger stepped on it. She is expected to make a full recovery, but her name—Henrietta "Minnie Pearl" Thaxton—will be added to the list of humans who have been accidently shot by their dogs in the past few years.

Other examples include a dog who jumped on his "seriously intoxicated" owner's bed knocking his .380 pistol on the floor and discharging it, and a Nebraska hunter who got a buttocks-full of buckshot when his dog jumped on a shotgun he left on his boat.

In a happier twist of fate, a three-month-old German shepherd shot a Vero Beach man in the wrist two weeks ago with a revolver when the man tried to kill the dog because, he told police, "I couldn't find a home for him."

The dog now has a home. As does the man: county jail.

STRANGE FACT: While there have been six reported incidents of dogs shooting people in the past year, there has not been a report of a cat shooting a human in more than a decade. Perhaps they are more cunning and don't leave any evidence.

Weirdness knows no boundaries. Keep up at *www.TheStrangeFiles.com*. Contact Alexander Strange at Alex@TheStrangeFiles.com.

CHAPTER 8

I TOOK FRED for a walk after relieving Mrs. Overstreet of her dog-sitting duties. He took a little-dog dump in front of the Little Bar and I scooped it up in a blue plastic bag and responsibly dropped it in a trashcan.

Fred accompanied me on my migration from Arizona to Florida. Technically, he belongs to Uncle Leo's fifth and current wife, Sarah. When I headed east, Sarah asked me to take Fred along for the ride.

I let Fred loose to play for a few minutes among the weeds and debris in the boat yard, then I scooped him up and we climbed the ladder to the trawler.

"Fred, I have to warn you, Mona's been shot."

Fred responded by licking my face. That Fred, he's a dog who can handle adversity.

As I stepped over the gunwale, my cell phone chirped. Caller ID said Full Cleveland, which is how I'd entered Lester Rivers' name in my contacts list.

"You're answering, so you're not in jail," he said.

"No flies on you."

"So, what happened?"

As I walked into the lounge, I told him about the rope with the noose and blood stains, the fiber and hair samples, and the coffee cup and how Henderson used it as an excuse for a warrant. I also told him a deputy drilled Mona and blown a hole in my window.

"You were right, Lester. I should never have invited him aboard."

Rivers paused, then said, "Assuming the rope didn't belong to you…"

"It's doesn't…"

"…then I think our earlier conclusion holds: The killers either want you in jail or the morgue."

"Either way, I'm out of play."

"Right. If you're being framed, the motivation has to be to distract the police from finding Maria's real killer. You in jail, the cops stop looking. Case closed. And now they've got some evidence to use against you."

"Yeah," I said, "but the evidence can't hold up because I didn't do it."

"Charming," he said. "But let's concede the evidence is circumstantial. You've still been named a person of interest. Maybe one morning we find you hanging from the transom by another length of yellow rope. Poor soul. Couldn't handle the guilt. Offed himself. Or some such. Once again, case closed."

"And what about the okra?"

"You tell me. Why'd you try to poison your dog?"

"That's all very clever, but would your normal everyday thug be that smart?"

"You noticed anything normal about any of this?"

"Point taken."

I glanced over at Mona and saw Fred sitting at her feet.

"I'll be damned," I said.

"What?"

"Fred. He's trying to console Mona."

Rivers ignored that. "Tell me about the hair samples," he said.

"What about them?"

"You said they took hair samples from your stateroom, right?"

"So?"

"So, Mr. Strange, are they likely find samples of Maria's hair there?"

"What's with the mister?"

"It's how I roll."

"Call me Alex."

"How about Alexander?"

"Whatever."

"The hair samples. Will they find Maria's there?"

"Of course not," I said. Then thought for a moment, "Well, I don't think so."

"Meaning what?"

"Lester, Maria's never been here, but I've been to her place. What if a stray hair of hers hitched a ride with me back to the boat?"

"Seems farfetched."

"Maybe, but if I'm being framed, how hard would it be for the killer to plant some throw-down hair from Maria aboard the *Miss Demeanor*? And if her hair were found on the boat, the police would conclude I had lied when I denied she'd ever been aboard. And a lie like that would probably be sufficient cause to issue a warrant for my arrest."

"It would be an excellent way to frame you, I agree," he said. "You have a devious mind. You would make an excellent criminal."

"Thank you so much."

"Or a detective."

Lester paused for a couple of beats then said, "Listen, Alexander, if we're going to work on this together you need to fill me in on your relationship with Maria, what you know about her, and the story you assigned to her. It's what I hoped to talk to you about when I met you at Stan's."

"You thought that might help you find her?"

"Yes, and now maybe it will help us find her killer."

"Will this stay between us?" I asked.

"No. I need to tell my boss at the agency. But I can promise you it will go no further. The Third Eye has considerable resources. You can trust us, Alexander. We deal with confidential information all the time. It's what we do."

What I do is raise shields when people ask me to trust them. But I knew I was in over my head.

"Tell me everything you can recall, Alexander. No detail is too small. You never know when something seemingly insignificant at first takes on larger meaning later."

"Gotcha. In that case, you better pour yourself a drink and relax," I said. "This will take a while to tell."

CHAPTER 9

I'D BEEN MAKING the rounds at the courthouse when a tall, lean, African-American woman named Naomi Jackson motioned me to follow her into the law library. Her earrings glittered, exposed by her short-cropped ebony hair. They matched the gold badge on her bailiff's uniform.

"Hey, Stranger Danger," she said, "I got something for you."

A tip? That's music to a reporter's ears. But I kept my chill.

"In exchange," I said, matching her hushed, conspiratorial tone, "I will do you the honor of fathering your next child."

This earned me a punch to the shoulder. Naomi knew that I knew she played on the all-girls' squad.

"My strange, melanin-deprived friend, if I ever decide I need a sperm donor, I will definitely reach out to you. In a manner of speaking. But your jizzum will be delivered in a jar, not a johnson."

"So, besides breaking my heart, wuzzup?" I asked.

"You remember the prostitution bust out in Immokalee last week?"

I recalled a *Naples Daily News* story about the arrest of an Immokalee pimp, the result of a months-long investigation by a task force from the Collier County Sheriff's Office, the Florida Department of Law Enforcement, the FBI, and Customs. Maybe the Justice League of America and The Avengers, too. It was one of those gangbangs where credit had to be shared so noses didn't get bent out of joint, but a single cop did the bulk of the work—Jim Henderson.

"There's more than's been in the news," she said. "The perp's a Haitian named Edgard Dominique."

"Nobody says perp anymore," I said. "Keep up."

Naomi hooked her index finger over the top of my T-shirt and drew me down to her, eye-to-eye, beak-to-beak. She'd been chewing mints and her breath smelled of wintergreen. I hate wintergreen. "I heard 'em use it on a CSI rerun the other night. If it's good enough for that hottie Finn Finlay, it's good enough for me."

She let me go, and I reflexively took a step back. "You should see your face," she said, chuckling. "Wasamatter, lesbian talk embarrass you?"

"No, just the opposite. I had this vision of you and Finn Finlay and, well, I may need a moment to compose myself."

"Oh Lord!" She shook her head.

"So, anyway, you were talking about this Haitian guy, Edgar?"

"Edgard. With a 'd' on the end. He's twenty-nine…" She paused for a moment and looked at me reflectively. "Close to your age, right?"

"It's the miles, not the years."

"Edgard, he got the miles—a sheet miles long. Mostly minor stuff. But enough to hold him. The task force dropped a warrant on Edgard's crib. Figured they'd find evidence he might be tied into one of them human trafficking operations."

"Thought they'd bag Edgard, turn him, then work their way upstream to bigger fish?" I asked.

"Exactly. But here's where it gets twisted. When they searched Edgard's crib they found a laptop with sex videos and an encrypted list—probably clients. Most of the videos were poor quality and were of heterosexual couples and a few two-on-one fast breaks. Looked like some kind of sex club. The guys were mostly white. The women a mix. But on one of the videos there was a dude having sex while …"

She averted her eyes and her skin darkened. "I can't believe I'm talking to you about this. You ever heard of feather flicks?"

"No."

"They're like snuff flicks, only not."

"That clears it up."

"People with a feather fetish get off, have the Big O, with feathers. On the laptop, this dude…" She shook her head and her face was strained. "…popped his cork while strangling a chicken."

I patted her on the cheek. "Very funny." As I turned to leave she grabbed my arm. Her eyes were wide.

"No, I swear, I'm not messin' with you. He did it with a chicken."

I don't like being punked, but I went along with her for the moment. "Is that illegal?"

"Depends on the animal. Could be cruelty. Not sure about chickens."

"You recognize the guy?"

"I didn't see it. Just heard about it. Was told it was a dark room and he faced away from the camera, but they could hear the chicken and its white feathers stood out."

"Chickens. OK, that's sick," I said. "But something tells me there's more."

She nodded. "The list."

"What about it?"

"It's gone. The hard drive on Edgard's computer, wiped clean. The list, the videos, all bye-bye. Somebody got inside the evidence room and completely trashed the drive."

"No way."

"Way."

She glanced over her shoulder, looking for eavesdroppers, but we had the library to ourselves. I'd never seen anyone in there. I assumed lawyers mostly used it as a backdrop for their phonebook ads, looking all serious and scholarly with hundreds of law books in the background. I'd never seen any of the books actually pulled from the shelves.

"Evidence storage is closely monitored," Naomi was saying. "Internal Affairs is all over it. And they've shipped the laptop off to the FBI for analysis. It's very hush-hush."

"If so, how do you know about it?" If this were leaking all over the courthouse, which is what happens with juicy news, the story would be out in no time.

"Judge Henry. He got word from the prosecutor about the hard drive being erased."

"Including the stuff about the chickens?"

"No. That's new." She giggled. "I just heard about it."

Henry Goodfellow was the Chief Judge of the Circuit Court and a longtime friend of Uncle Leo, himself a Superior Court judge in Arizona. They met in Las Vegas years ago and struck up a friendship based on their mutual interests in drinking, carousing, and, of all things, chess. At Judge Goodfellow's urging, Leo bought the *Miss Demeanor*. Indeed, Goodfellow, probably just as hammered as my uncle, was aboard when Leo drove it aground.

"Now you know you didn't hear this from me, right?" Naomi said.

"I don't even know you."

"Well, then, here's one more angle. Edgard may get off."

"That's random. How come?"

"Because his public defender wants a deal for him: Immunity, witness protection, relocation, the whole enchilada, in exchange for his testimony."

"Who's the PD?"

"Her name is Gwenn Giroux."

"Ja-who?"

Her last name is spelled G-I-R-O-U-X, but the X is silent. Ja-ROO. Like kangaroo only not. It's French. Her family's from Montreal."

I pulled out my notebook to write her name down. First name Gwen?"

"Yeah, like the singer Gwen Stefani, but she spells it with two Ns. G-W-E-N-N."

As soon as she mentioned Gwen Stefani, the lyrics to *The Sweet Escape* started rattling around in my head and I knew I'd have an earworm for hours. It's some kind of mental disorder, I'm sure. Worse, I find myself rewriting the lyrics, usually to ill-effect. On the other hand, I have an impressive collection of obscure rock band T-shirts, most of whose music I've never heard.

"So, Gwenn Giroux is going to get this pimp, Edgar, off?" I asked, trying to push Stefani's baby doll voice out of my head.

"Edgard. That will be up to the trial judge. Judge Henry got pulled into this because the state attorney wants a special grand jury empaneled to investigate how evidence at the Sheriff's Office could be tampered."

"That happening?"

"Don't know. No secret the judge and the sheriff don't get along."

"Any gossip about the names on the list?"

"No, but who could pull this off?" She answered her own question: "Somebody with juice. Somebody with something to lose."

Naples isn't a big city. But it's a rich city, with lots of moneyed celebrities. What if one of them were on that list?

"Naomi, surely the SO made copies of the list, right?"

"They were going to clone the drive, preserving the chain of evidence and all, then work on decrypting the list. But they never got the chance."

"Why not?"

She shrugged.

Then she did something I never imagined a cop would do. She raised up on her toes and gave me a peck on my cheek.

"Be safe, Stranger Danger." Then she turned and walked out of the law library.

I sat down and gave myself a few moments to process that. What did she mean "be safe?" That didn't compute.

En route to my car, I called Edwina Mahoney, my old managing editor at the now-defunct *Phoenix Daily Sun* and the brains behind our online news venture. I told her I wanted to drop everything and chase this story.

"Absolutely not," she said. "Your column is too important to the news service. We've got some traction and, while it's hard to believe, your weird news report is one of the prime marketing points. What that says about the human condition, I shudder to think."

"But this is weird."

I wanted this story. It would give me something to sink my teeth into. Weird news is fun, but it's like a diet of candy. Sometimes you need some meat.

But Edwina seemed unmoved.

"What if the Vice President or the Speaker of the House is on the list?" I argued. Both owned second homes in the Naples area.

"Yeah, and maybe the Pope is on the list, too," she said. "Or Vladimir Putin."

"Exactly. This story could be sensational."

"We're not the *National Enquirer*."

I replied: "Of course not."

I thought: *They're making money.*

Then I said: "But if we could find out how the computer got hacked, or if we could get the list, it could be important news."

There were a few seconds of dead air and then the sound of her exhaling whooshed into the phone. Edwina has a vile temper.

"I just can't spare you now. I'm sorry. There's … there's something in the works."

"Works? What works?"

"Really, I can't discuss it."

"Oh, shit," I said. "You've got an investor, don't you? Who is it?"

"I'm not talking about this."

"Just tell me it's not that fucker Murdoch."

"I CAN'T TALK ABOUT IT, ALL RIGHT?"

"Gotcha, Ed. Take a Midol. Can't blame me for asking."

"You are such a pain in the ass."

"Yes, but I'm your pain in the ass, so what about the story."

"Story?" She'd lost track.

"Sex ring. Missing evidence. Chickens videoed without their permission."

She took a breath then she said, "What about this kid you were telling me about?"

"Did I say anything about children?"

"No, you dolt. The young woman you met up in Fort Myers."

"Maria?"

"The one working for that liberal rag. She still around?"

"Yeah…"

"You said she's hungry?"

"Yeah…"

"All right, here's the deal. Assign it to her. Freelance. She gets paid nothing unless she turns up something we can use."

"She's too inexperienced for this, Ed."

"So were Woodward and Bernstein. Neither of them could find the men's room at the *Post* before the Watergate break-in."

"Ed, you want *me* to assign this? I'm not an editor. I've never supervised anyone."

"Time to grow up."

And that's how Maria Martinez began her short-lived stint as a freelancer for Tropic Press. When I pitched it to her, she didn't hesitate.

"I want this," she said.

While not being allowed to chase the story annoyed me, there was a minor consolation prize: Maria called me "the bomb" for giving her the assignment.

"Uh, Maria. Nobody says 'the bomb' anymore."

"Really?" She trilled her *rrrrs* again.

"Yeah. You could say I'm totally dope."

"OK. You're totally a dope."

I hadn't heard from Maria in a few days and I worried the story might have gone cold on her. Then she surprised me by calling.

"Alex, I have a proposition for you. I'll buy you dinner if you let me pick your brains."

"You bet. I'm all about brain picking with pretty women."

We agreed to meet at the South Street City Oven & Grill, not far from where she lived at her Aunt Geneva's condo in Pelican Bay.

"She thinks it's cute I'm a"—Maria raised her hands and made air quotes— "struggling writer. But I know she doesn't take me seriously." She waved her fork at me. A piece of romaine flew off. "She will when this story breaks." Maria dove back into her Caesar salad and her Sonoma-Cutrer Chardonnay. My meatloaf sliders were delicious and paired perfectly with my V-Twin lager.

"Alright," she said, taking a break from chewing and guzzling. "I've filed public records requests for all documents, including an inventory of evidence. But the cops say because most documents and files are part of a quote-unquote ongoing investigation they're exempt from the Open Records Law."

"You got nothing?"

"Just the arrest records."

"So, what else have you tried?"

"Spent a day in Immokalee. Figured speaking *Espanol* might help. Got nothing useful other than a few people who knew Edgard and figured he was a pimp. Got some color. No hard news. I may need to go back there."

I nodded.

"I've called the sheriff, the prosecutor's office, and Edgar's public defender, but nobody's talking. It's very mysterious."

"So how can I help?"

"I need names of people at the courthouse I can talk to. Sources."

I took a deep breath. Naïve. Before someone will talk to a reporter about confidential matters there must be a relationship, trust. It's not like there's a website you can punch up: Have-Secrets-Will-Tell.com.

"I can't reveal the name of my source," I said. "But I will call my source (being careful not to identify my source by gender) and see if there's anything new."

That got a big smile out of her. "*Muy bien!*"

"Let me ask you something: You talk to the arresting officer yet? Henderson?"

"Not yet."

"Why not?"

"I don't want to tip him off that I'm on the story."

Naïve, again.

"Probably too late for that, Maria," I said. "Public records requests are discoverable public records themselves. And you've been trying to score interviews."

"So, Henderson may already know I'm pursuing this?"

"The courthouse is a beehive of gossip. He may not know exactly what you want, but I wouldn't be surprised if he's heard something."

She thought about that for a moment, then said, "Well then, why don't I go to *the* primary source and set up a jailhouse interview with Edgard Dominique?"

The odds of Edgard's attorney allowing an interview seemed remote, but I admired her moxie.

"What have you got to lose?"

"I might be able to establish some sort of rapport with Edgard," she said. "I spent two years in Haiti in the Peace Corps after college. *Mwen pale Kreyòl.*"

"Meaning?"

"I speak Creole',"

This I did not know. "Tell me something else in Creole'.

"*Kote twalèt la?*"

"Nice. And what does that mean?"

"Where's the bathroom."

"Where's the restroom?"

Her eyes got big. "Yes, Alex, I gotta pee."

"Oh." I pointed her in the right direction

Evidently, she found more than the potty. She must have passed the bar en route because our server arrived shortly thereafter with another round of drinks.

"Cheers," she said.

We tinked glasses. "You're full of surprises, Maria. Tell me about the Peace Corps."

The question seemed to sober her a bit.

"I got my masters at Columbia, but I couldn't find a job. And that didn't make my mother happy. Four years at Miami, two at Columbia, and no idea what I wanted to do with my life."

I understood. I'd been on the six-year plan at the University of Texas, double-majoring in beer pong and video games until I met a girl who worked at *The Daily Texan*.

"So, a friend of mine signed up for the Peace Corps," she said. "She wanted to go to Haiti, help the earthquake victims. I signed up, too."

I've known several people who were Peace Corps volunteers and, uniformly, they described the experience as transformative. "How was that?" I asked.

She took a big drink, set down her glass, and looked at me, her eyes moist.

"Great. Until the gang rape."

I sucked in my breath. "Gang rape?"

"We were in Léogâne. It's a small town west of Port-au-Prince, the epicenter of the quake. Killed more than a hundred thousand people. There were four of us, walking along a dirt road back to camp when we were attacked by five men. Karen and me and two other guys. I got away. But not the guys. They were beaten. And not Karen. She was raped."

She took a deep drink from her glass. "I ran and ran. Finally, got back to our camp and rounded up a bunch of men and we returned. The boys were in terrible shape but they were trying to console Karen. She was in shock. So horrible."

"They ever catch the men who did this?" I asked.

"No." She drained her glass. I hadn't touched my beer. "I don't think they even tried. And as bad as the local police were, the Peace Corps, *Dios mio.* They sent us home. Told us to keep our mouths shut. For the good of the program."

"Jesus."

"I ran away, Alex. I was terrified. And I know if I'd stayed, I would have been raped, too. They had machetes."

I nodded.

"I'm never running away again." She wiped a tear from her eye. "Sorry about that."

"Don't be."

The waiter showed up at our table, and she ordered another glass of wine. I declined. Maria's drink arrived along with the check. She swallowed half the glass immediately.

"I kinda drifted after that," she said. Tried to find a newspaper job. I sent out resumes all over the country. No luck. I spent three days walking around Manhattan applying everywhere. When I walked into the offices of *The Nation*, the senior editor took pity on me and said I could freelance for them. Not a lot of money, but at least a start. Which is why this assignment is so important to me." She reached across the table and gripped my hand. Hard. "I need this."

After a moment she let go and leaned back in her chair. "I'm being morose. Let's order another round."

"How about we get some coffee, instead," I suggested.

"Yuck. Can't stand the stuff."

"Well, then, why don't you let me drive you home?"

Maria was sloshy and I thought she might put up a fuss. But she surprised me.

"Good call," she said. "I got a bottle of Patron chilling in the fridge."

Maria's condo was on the second floor of a three-story pink stucco building, flanked by royal palms and edged with flowering red and white oleander bushes. We took the elevator, Maria being in no shape to walk up a flight of stairs. Her compact living room appeared tidy. A sliding glass door opened to a small balcony overlooking a lighted courtyard pool. A loveseat and coffee table nearly filled the living room and faced a wall-mounted flat-screen television. The dining area held a small round table that Maria used as a desk. A PowerBook, lid closed, rested atop the table.

She snatched the bottle of Petron from her refrigerator and motioned me to the loveseat.

"More than just a pretty bottle," I said after taking a sip, although tequila is not high on my list of tasty alcohol delivery systems. She threw back a shot and poured herself another.

"Your Aunt Geneva has excellent taste in art," I said, nodding to a Kassandra Clarke lithograph above the TV. "And this is a very nice place. You're lucky to have it."

"Yes, Geneva and I are very close, like I told you." She spilled a dollop of tequila on her skirt, but didn't notice. "And she and Uncle Larry are ridiculously rich."

Maria then launched into a family history. Geneva Marcano, one of her mother's two sisters, couldn't have children of her own and considered Maria "the daughter she never had." She and her attorney husband lived in Connecticut. Her other aunt, Sophia, she didn't like very much.

"These three sisters, you think they would be close. But you know how it is sometimes when three women are together. Eventually, it's two against one. Mama and Sophie live next door to each other in Hialeah. And they got much closer when Sophie's husband left her."

"And your father?" I asked. "You haven't mentioned him. Is he still alive?"

"No. He recently passed away. And I never talk about him. You have to understand, Mama got pregnant in Cuba. She came over to the States during the Mariel boatlift. I was born here two weeks later."

"You just made it," I said.

She took a sip of the tequila. Didn't down it all at once this time.

"Mama was the last of the girls to get out. She's the youngest. She was only sixteen when she arrived in the States, and she never married. Sophie's the oldest and has always been like a mother to her. But she's so possessive. It's like she wants Mama all to herself. I hate her. And her moron son, too." She finished her shot of Patron and picked up the bottle. She looked at my nearly full glass, shrugged, and poured herself another.

"So you have a cousin?" I asked, trying to keep the conversation alive. "Is he in Hialeah, too?

She looked at me curiously. "It's his residence of record, but he lives in Washington."

"Residence of record?"

"You don't know?" She laughed. "*Estupida!* I mean me, not you. How would you know? He is your next United States senator from Florida. Ricky, the weasel, Perez."

"You've got to be shitting me."

" It's embarrassing, but yes."

"Wow. You're full of surprises."

Maria wagged her shot glass at me. "You have no idea." I wondered what she meant. But before I could ask, she raised her palm to me and shook her head.

"Alexander, you must tell me," she said, then paused as if reflecting on how to frame the question. As she got drunk her speech pattern became more formal as she struggled for coherency.

"You're not just helping me because you want to get into my panties?"

Not just.

"Don't be ridiculous, Maria," I managed. "I think of you as the little Latina sister I never had."

"Gawkkah!"

Or at least that's what it sounded like as she involuntarily spat out her drink. Her eyes were watering and tequila streamed out her nose.

Plastered.

"Liar, liar," she giggled. "You want me so bad you can't stand it."

With that, she stood up, bumped into the coffee table, wobbled, and began staggering toward the bedroom, stripping off her clothes with each step. First came her T-shirt. She paused theatrically and unclasped her bra, exposing her small but firm breasts. Next, she slipped off her skirt, nearly falling over in the process. Then she turned, wiggled her ass at me, and lurched through the door.

Captain, the warp core is overheating.

What should a gentleman do? I couldn't very well ignore her invitation. That would be rude. And disingenuous. Especially since her little striptease left me furiously tumescent. Then, again, she was shit-faced. And she had spent some of the evening talking about rape. I had a flash of a morning-after conversation in which she accused me of taking advantage of her. I hate it when I imagine things like that.

Captain, it's a miracle, the nacelles, they're cooling off.

With some misgiving, I made my way into her bedroom where she lay on the queen bed face down. I sat beside her and placed my hand on her bare back. No response. I ran my hand gently up her spine to the nape of her neck. Still no reaction. Her locks were cascading onto either side onto her pillow.

"Hello, anybody home?"

That's when she began snoring. At first, it sounded alarmingly like gagging. Then it calmed to a steady purr.

I bent over and kissed a spot between her bare shoulder blades, sighed, then rolled off the mattress. Should I feel disappointed? Or relieved? Or a little of both?

Back in her living room, the bottle of Patron beckoned. Half full or half empty? One last shot would certainly make it half empty. I poured one.

So Maria came from a politically connected family. Prosperous enough to send her through Miami and Columbia. She survived the Peace Corps, which toughened her. Interesting resume.

One shot of Patron became two, and it dawned on me through a mild haze that driving back to the island at that moment might not be my best plan. Not until I dried out a bit. I was too tall for the loveseat, so I walked back into Maria's bedroom and plopped down beside her. She'd invited me, after all.

My eyes blinked open at 4 a.m. Wide awake. I had metabolized the beer and tequila. Good job, liver! Surprisingly, I didn't have a headache. This is not always a tequila aftermath. Maria was still snoring, dead to the world, so I saw no point in trying to wake her. While her striptease had been arousing, my instincts warned she would not be so lascivious if her much-needed sleep were disturbed. Probably wouldn't feel much better later, either. I predicted a monster hangover in her future. So, I slid out of the bed, retrieved my shoes, turned off the light in the living room, and slipped out the door, making sure it locked behind me.

An act of gallantry, I told myself.

She disabused me of that notion few hours later during an agitated text message exchange:

Maria: Where r you

Me: Back home. How r u?

Maria: Why did u leave me?

> Me: Woke up. Had to let my dog out.
>
> Maria: Prick

I immediately called her, but it rolled over to voicemail. I called again. And again. Finally, she picked up on the fourth call.

"Maria, why are you pissed off?"

"Why? Why? You don't know?"

"Uh. No."

"I invite you to my bed and you just walk out? Do you know how that makes me feel? I thought you liked me."

"Maria, honey…"

"Don't call me honey. I'm not your honey. Obviously."

"Hey, you fell asleep."

"Oh. You just have your fun and split. Wham, bam, thank you, ma'am."

"What fun?" my voice rising. "You passed out. I didn't lay a hand on you."

Technically, I did touch her, but not inappropriately.

"So you got, what? Impatient? Had some place better place to go?"

I also didn't leave a note. I didn't deadbolt her door (which, without a key, would have been impossible, in my defense). I failed to understand that she'd offered herself to me and now felt rejected. (Never mind that she was unconscious.) And I left her without a car, hers still parked at the restaurant. (Oops.)

I asked what I could do to make it up to her. Bring some coffee? Maybe with some aspirin? That earned me a, "Fuck you."

When being solicitous didn't work, I pointed out we were still colleagues and I wanted to help her with the story, and that this "misunderstanding" shouldn't get in the way of our working together.

"Yeah, you like that, don't you? Help the cute little rookie. Make sure everyone knows you were the brains behind her success. Well, I'll show you."

"Maria, I agreed to make some calls for you. I still will."

76

"Don't bother. I'll get my own resources."

"It's sources, not resources."

She hung up.

This is not the last conversation you want to have with a pretty woman with whom you fancied having carnal knowledge.

But you don't always get what you want.

THE STRANGE FILES
Cat Burglar Meets his Match

By Alexander Strange

Tropic ⊚ Press

Tampa police have been on the lookout for cat burglar. Literally, a burglar who steals kitties.

"I came home from work and my front door was unlocked," Stacey Miller told police. "I knew something was wrong right away when my Honeybunch didn't come to greet me."

Honeybunch was among more than a dozen cats who vanished after homes in north Tampa were been broken into.

"We weren't sure who we we're dealing with," Detective Sam Agliata told me. "But our staff psychologist thought maybe this was some kind of sexual fetish."

If so, the burglar failed to practice safe sex during his most recent—and final—burglary.

Harmon Villamonte of Temple Terrace returned home from church last Sunday to find blood on the floor of his entryway.

"'Lil Demon had blood on her fur, too," he told police.

'Lil Demon is a 35-pound bobcat. Villamonte has several exotic animals in his home, all rescued when they were young. "'Lil Demon got caught in a rabbit trap and still walks with a limp," he told police. "I can't release her back into the wild, she wouldn't stand a chance."

Tell that to the cat burglar. Police found him in Villamonte's back yard, passed out and bleeding. As soon as he is released from Tampa General Hospital, police will question him in regard to all the other missing cats—and what, exactly, he was doing with them.

STRANGE FACT: A group of kittens is called a kindle.

Weirdness knows no boundaries. Keep up at *www.TheStrangeFiles.com*. Contact Alexander Strange at Alex@TheStrangeFiles.com.

CHAPTER 10

I FINISHED TELLING Lester Rivers my story of how I knew Maria Martinez. Then I checked my watch and declared it happy hour. Ordinarily, that would mean a Cuba Libre. But I had invented a new drink for a change of pace. A martini made with half Grey Goose vodka, which comes from France, and half Boodles gin, Travis McGee's fave. I called it a French Boodle.

It didn't taste all that great but the pun was terrific, so how could I resist? I had my laptop with me on the newly renamed poop deck, sipping my drink and finishing my column about 'Lil Demon.

That resulted from a tip I'd gotten from a group of fans calling themselves the Army of the Strange. Some of the soldiers, though, seemed to be enjoying recreational chemicals a bit before hitting the send button: "Flog not the dolphin," "Jeff Probst is an alien," and, "Beware the cannibal" were also recent contributions.

With the events of the past two days, I hadn't time nor inclination to do any real reporting, but I kept a reserve of material for emergencies, the story of 'Lil Demon among them. Previous contingencies included hangovers, attacks of slothfulness, and sleepovers. Fishing a dead colleague out of Buzzard's Bay and being nearly poisoned qualified, too, I reckoned

I'd just taken a second tug on my French Boodle when my iPhone chirped.

Caller ID said Edwina Mahoney.

"Well, Ed, I've got some disturbing news," I said.

"Who'd you kill?"

"Maria Martinez."

She paused. I gave her a moment to process what I just told her. It had to be a shock. She finally came back on the line.

"Uh, Alex, no offense, but who is Maria Martinez?"

"Jeeez, Ed. She worked for us. The freelancer checking out the feather-flick, sex club story? You told me to assign it to her?"

"Wait a minute. I've been a little distracted. You say murdered? Dear God."

Then, after a beat: "Did it have anything to do with this story?"

"I can't imagine otherwise, but I don't know for sure."

"Well, tell me what you *do* know for sure."

I ran it down, starting with how Maria planned to interview Edgard Dominique, how I pulled her mutilated body out of the bay, the evidence found around my boatyard, and Henderson's questions. I also told her about The Third Eye's involvement.

"Oh, yeah," I said. "And I think somebody tried to poison me."

"Jesus Christ," she said, "this is a nightmare."

She mumbled "damn, damn, damn" for a few seconds, and I felt compelled to interrupt. "Look, Ed, I know you're stressed right now, and I hate to add to that, but I'm chasing this."

"Yeah, yeah. Nobody puts Baby in the corner. We stick up for our own. Yadda, yadda, yadda."

That Edwina. Hard on the outside, cynical in the middle.

"I've got a backlog of material I've accumulated for the column," I said. "Enough to keep it going for a few weeks, anyway."

"Fine."

Another pause.

"Alex, do you think you might be in danger?"

"Hard to say. I've thought about it." Every waking moment, but I didn't tell her that.

More dead air.

"Want I should file a few extra columns just in case?" I asked.

She ignored me.

"First things first," she said. "You gotta lawyer up; you gotta stop talking to the police. And I need to know you're all right. How are you holding up?"

"What, our worker's comp overdrawn?"

She waited for me to get on with it.

"I'm a wreck, actually," I finally said. "Goddammit, Ed, she asked if she should arrange a jailhouse interview with Edgard Dominique and I told her 'why not?' Well, maybe the *why not* is that it got her killed. Those two words may have set all this in motion. What if I'd said something else? None of this might have happened."

"All right, I'm flying out," she said. "I'll catch the first plane out of Phoenix tomorrow."

"No, you're not," I said. "You've got a dozen people counting on you. Their future's in your hands. If this deal you're working on goes through, if you find an investor for the news service, it could be life changing for everyone. Including me, for that matter."

There were a handful of us, all jobless after the *Phoenix Daily Sun* folded, who borrowed from relatives (in my case, Leo), cashed in 401Ks, and refinanced homes to start the Tropic Press. Edwina had been a genius in securing grants from nonprofits that helped us launch, but we always knew we'd need additional investors.

We weren't the *Texas Tribune* nor *Pro Publica*, not yet anyway, but we were edgy and we'd gotten some attention. Attracting a major investor or two would allow us to repay our startup loans and maybe even a little more—perhaps a lot more. Even if the sale of the news service brought only a modest amount by the standards of modern online acquisitions, it could represent a financial windfall. Me, not such a big deal in terms of my personal survival. If this gig fell apart, I could always deliver pizzas. But there were people with families, kids to send to college.

"Want I should send someone else?" she asked.

"If I need help, I'll call. But remember, we've got The Third Eye on our side."

"All right. But stay in touch. I want to hear from you every day."

"Will do."

"One more thing."

I waited.

"Your weird news report, it *is* important to the news service. But we both know you're capable of more. If you're going to do this, give it all you got."

"Thanks, coach."

She rang off.

I thought about that for a few minutes. I spent my time since leaving Phoenix with one goal in mind: To have no goals. To live in the moment. Enjoy myself writing zany stories about Florida Man and Florida Woman. To be ambition-free.

Ambition means living for tomorrow instead of today. Ambition is stupid. Or so I told myself. Maybe kidded myself. And, lately, the sense I might be adrift felt just slightly more tangible. Not that I wanted to draw up a ten-point plan for the future, but would it be such a bad idea to have a more meaningful reason to get up in the morning?

I owed it to Maria to find her killer. And, I knew, I owed it to myself, too.

Of course, none of this would have happened if Edwina had let me pursue the story in the first place. I was a little pissed at her for that, but more upset with myself for not being more adamant about keeping the story for myself. And there was another inescapable but cowardly thought I didn't want to dwell on: It could have been me, instead of Maria, floating in Buzzards Bay. Or lying face down in a bowl of okra.

I opened an audio recording app on my phone. It took about an hour to chronicle everything, starting with meeting Maria to Lester Rivers' warning. I saved the file, then emailed a copy to Edwina. Just in case.

My phone rang again.

"The game's afoot," Rivers said.

"So, The Third Eye is on the case?"

"Roger."

"Good. At lunch, you said you'd been hired to track Maria down. Give me the details, would you?"

"Sure. Maria's aunt, one Geneva Marcano, she and Maria talked daily, but a few days ago the calls abruptly stopped. She called Naples PD, but they brushed her off, said her condo is outside city limits. So she called the Sheriff's Office and got the usual runaround when people report missing adults. Geneva's husband, Lawrence, is a lawyer and his firm used us previously, so he dropped a dime. I landed the assignment."

Like the cops, Rivers knew that most adults who go missing either turn up or have a good reason to get out of Dodge. When he knocked on the door at Maria's condo, a logical first stop, nobody answered. Neighbors said they hadn't seen Maria in a few days. Geneva was named on Maria's checking account, making it easy for The Third Eye to run her banking activities and credit card purchases. She had made a five-hundred-dollar cash withdrawal from an ATM machine, but there had been no activity since. The cash withdrawal suggested money for a trip, but the lack of subsequent credit card activity didn't jibe with that. Lawrence Marcano asked Rivers to track me down because Maria had told Geneva about a reporter working with her.

"My boss is not happy," Rivers said. "We were hired to find Maria and she was killed on our watch. It's bad for business. I've been assured if we need help it will be forthcoming."

"Forthcoming?"

"Yes. The Third Eye … well, Alexander, you need to know the three men who started the firm. They are former Special Forces. All served in Afghanistan and Iraq. They are, um, a fairly humorless bunch and are not shy about taking extraordinary measures."

"Extraordinary?"

"The agency will do whatever it takes to bring the people behind this to justice."

"Isn't that a a little corny?"

"I'm paraphrasing. My superior expressed himself more colorfully. I was told to locate the, uh, individuals responsible for this and then turn that information over to our Special Operations Department."

"What do they do?" I asked.

"They make problems go away."

CHAPTER 11

AFTER TALKING WITH Rivers, I poured myself a second martini. With everything whooshing through my brain, I knew I would have a hard time sleeping. Maybe a second French Boodle would help.

Sometime during the night the skies lit up, sending flashes through the portholes. A clap of thunder shook the boat and Fred whimpered. Normally, he sleeps at the foot of my bed, but I leaned over, picked him up, and scooted him under the sheets with me. Fred, like most dogs, is terrified of loud noises. He cried a bit more then settled down, but thunder interrupted our sleep throughout the night as the storm swept through.

When I awoke, I noticed the digital alarm clock flashed 4:23, 4:23, 4:23. I never get up that early. I reached for my iPhone and it said 6:15. A power outage. For how long? This posed an interesting arithmetic problem, made all the more challenging by a mild headache. They say there are three things you should never ask a journalist to do—add and subtract. So I cheated, tapped the calculator app and subtracted 423—whoops, now 424—from 615. The result: 191, which made no sense. I guess they're right about journalists and math.

Fred stirred. He stood up in the berth and shook his head, sending his big ears flapping and his dog tags jangling. Then he whined, letting me know he had to go to the bathroom. I slipped on a pair of cargo shorts and my flip-flops and carried Fred down the ladder.

I set him free to roam the boatyard for a few minutes while I climbed back aboard, fired up the Keurig, and dug through the medicine cabinet for some Advil. The martinis helped me sleep, but now I paid the price. I wondered if I was drinking too much. Which presented another interesting math puzzle: I might knock back two or three Cuba Libres in the course of an evening, made with two ounces of rum. That represented, say, six ounces of rum diluted by Coke. Last night, I drank two martinis, each probably around three ounces of gin and vodka, also totaling six ounces of booze. Same thing. So why did I feel like hammered kudzu, to channel my friend Naomi? Another mystery unsolved. I took a gulp of coffee to wash down the Advil and scalded the inside of my mouth.

Fred was harassing lizards on the concrete pad when I climbed back down to the boatyard with his leash in hand. We walked to Mrs. Overstreet's mobile home and she greeted us in her driveway, arms out, happy to see her favorite puppy.

"Come here, Freddie," she cooed.

I handed Mrs. Overstreet the leash and told her I would be out most of day, leaving for Naples.

"No exercise this morning, young man?" she asked in a mock scolding tone.

"I devoted my morning to mathematical calisthenics."

"Oh, what's that?"

"It's a new kind of anaerobic workout."

My plan for the morning was to track down Edgar Dominique's public defender, Gwenn Giroux. I wanted to find out if Maria ever arranged that jailhouse interview, and if, in fact, she'd spoken to Edgard. The Public Defender's Office is on the fifth floor of the Collier County courthouse annex. I dropped the top on the Sebring, slipped on my Oakleys, and headed toward Naples.

The local news-talk station, which carried the Rev. Lee Roy Chitango's *OhGodOhGod* radio network, and Rush, and Glenn, and the other right-wing chatterers, took a break from its stable of gas bags for a spot of news:

A man plunged 180 feet over Niagara Falls in an apparent suicide attempt, but loser that he was, survived, making him only the fourth person in history to go over the Falls without a safety device and live. A woman running for Parliament in Italy, Giolla Rivoli, posed topless for a campaign advertisement saying she needed to "energize" her campaign. And the Richard Nixon Foundation was up in arms over an auction house's plan to sell a vial of his blood.

Up in Orlando, a vigilante calling himself Mister Manners struck again. Upset car owners called police complaining that their turn signal lights had been shattered. In each instance, the vandal left a note declaring: "If you're not going to use your turn signal, then you don't need them." It was signed M.M.

In local news, a transformer at a Florida Power & Light substation blew up overnight, causing a massive power blackout. Marco Island and portions of Collier County east of the Tamiami Trail were without electricity for nearly two hours. A spokesman for the utility said the company didn't know the cause of the explosion, but they had tentatively ruled out a lighting strike. There were no follow-ups on the Goodland drowning victim.

After twenty minutes, I pulled into the county parking garage. On the first floor of the structure, a row of cars had been cleared out for the weekly farmer's market. Softball-sized tomatoes, fresh flowers, sweet-smelling baked goods. A skinny gray-haired man in a fedora sat at the exit of the garage playing a lovely tune on an electric violin, hoping for tips. I dropped a dollar into his jar, grateful he wasn't singing or I would have gotten an earworm.

A dozen protesters were milling in front of the main entrance holding signs aloft and chanting something about fracking. "No more drilling," several shouted in unison. The Collier County Commission had recently granted approval for a Texas oil company to drill exploratory wells east of Naples. You won't see it in the tourist brochures, but oil has been pumped from the Everglades for decades. The quality's crude, to coin a pun, but drillers were becoming more ambitious. As I weaved my way through the crowd, one of the protestors thrust a brochure at me. I thanked her and slipped it into my messenger bag.

Like most government buildings, getting into the courthouse involved passing through a security screening. Unlike the airport, the guards allowed me to keep my shoes on after I emptied my pockets and placed my bag on the X-ray scanner. I didn't take my belt off since I wasn't wearing one. I'd traded in my shorts and flip-flops for khakis, Top-Siders and a polo shirt, un-tucked. The deputy manning the scanner extracted my company-owned iPad and camera, from the satchel.

"Nice," he said, placing the camera back in the bag. "Bet you can take great pictures with this." People say that a lot. Like owning an expensive gun would make you a great shot, too. But I kept my mouth shut. I had enough problems with the cops.

I entered the elevator and pushed the button for the fifth floor. I'm not good with confined spaces, but I've learned if I just breathe deeply and think of something pleasant—like owning a vial of Richard Nixon's blood—I can handle the claustrophobia. After what seemed an eternity, the door opened and I prepared to step out when I realized we were only on the second floor. Two guys in suits stepped in, pushed the button for three, and the car began moving again. Then stopped. Then more people stepped aboard. And the walls continued to close in. And I continued breathing deeply. Then, after a lifetime, the door opened on five.

I turned right down the meandering hallway toward the courthouse annex. I strode past the law library, where Naomi and I had met, and entered the public defender's suite of offices through double glass doors. Twenty-four chairs, upholstered in maroon cloth, were arranged in four neat rows filling most of the space. All empty. To the left, a receptionist sat behind a sliding glass window. It looked like a dentist's reception area, but without the threat of medieval torture behind the closed doors.

I walked over to the window, and as the receptionist looked up I turned on a smile—mid-wattage, no need to paralyze the girl—and asked if it would be possible to see Gwenn Giroux.

"You a reporter?" she asked.

"Why, yes, I am. You must have psychic powers."

She gave me a curious look, tilting her head ever so slightly and wrinkling her nose. "The press briefing will be at 10 o'clock," she said. "You're early."

Instinctively, I looked at my watch: 9:15. Then my brain re-engaged and I asked, "What press briefing?"

The receptionist was in her mid-twenties, plain featured, with straight dishwater blond hair, peach lipstick, applied heavily, but it matched her nails, so points for coordination.

"Edgard Dominique." She practically spat it out, like what else would it be?

"Huh?" Had Gwenn Giroux managed that plea deal, got him off the hook? Naomi told me they were holding him on other charges, too, including probation violation. How could he get out so soon?

I changed tactics.

"Say, you're new here, right?"

She flashed concern, like maybe she should know who I was, that she might be in trouble or something.

"Three weeks."

"I thought so," I said. Then waited.

"That's random. Why'd you ask me that?"

"It's just, you know, you're so nice. Not like most county employees, so grouchy." Two millennials, bonding.

She beamed. "No problem!"

I'm not sure when "no problem" took the place of "you're welcome," but correcting her would be counter-productive. So, instead, I smiled back, upping the wattage. "I just need a moment of Ms. Giroux' time, I really do. I'm not here for the press briefing, but, since you brought it up, can you clue me in on what it's about?"

I'll never know if that tack would have worked because at that moment a tall redheaded woman in black slacks and a white blouse walked into the waiting room from the inner offices. She wore a pair of red-gold wire-rimmed glasses framing her emerald eyes. A small scattering of freckles dotted the sides of her face, giving her a girl-next-door look.

"Oh, hello, Ms. Giroux," the receptionist said.

The redhead turned in our direction and smiled.

"This gentleman is looking for you."

I walked over to her, extended my hand, and she took it. Her fingers were slender and cool. Her nails were pink and her grip was firm. She was ringless and appeared to be in her late twenties or early thirties. But she could have been younger or older. She had the physique of someone who spent serious time at the gym. Zumba classes. Or yoga.

"Alexander Strange," I said.

"Gwenn Giroux," she replied. Her voice was breathy and a pitch lower than I expected, not exactly sultry, not come-hither, but maybe smoky. I was filled with a powerful sense of *déjà vu* and it took me a beat to recover.

"I believe we had a mutual acquaintance." I finally said. "Maria Martinez, a reporter I worked with."

Her brow wrinkled. "Worked? Not anymore?"

"You don't know?"

Her body tensed, her grip tightened, and she shook her head. "What?"

"Ms. Giroux, we need to talk. Can we go someplace private?"

She looked undecided for a moment, then nodded to the door she just walked through. "My office."

While I followed her down the short corridor, I pulled one of my business cards from my messenger bag and handed it to her as we entered her compact workspace. Like every lawyer's office I've been in, there were piles of paperwork stacked here and there, the clutter of someone who is busy. And there were several Bankers Boxes stacked by her desk, the lid open on the topmost container exposing several framed documents and other office bric-a-brac. There were no personal effects on her credenza. She was packing up.

She glanced at my card. "I remember your name. Maria said you hired her."

"Yes."

"So what's happened?" She walked around her desk and sat in her chair. I remained standing.

"Her body was fished out of Buzzards Bay. Actually, I'm the one who pulled her out."

Gwenn's hands flew to her mouth and her eyes flew wide open. "Oh my God," she whispered, the sound muffled by her fingers. And after a moment, "I read about a drowning victim."

I sat down across from her and shook my head. "She didn't drown. At least it doesn't appear that way. The ME hasn't issued a ruling yet. But all indications are she was either strangled. Or hanged."

"HANGED!"

"CSIs found a rope with a noose near where her body surfaced." I put off telling her it was discovered under my boat.

"A rope...." She seemed to withdraw into herself for a moment. She gripped the arms of her chair, then she looked around her cluttered desk as if she were seeing it for the first time, as if everything on it had turned unfamiliar, then picked up a white piece of paper.

"Like this?"

She flipped it over to reveal a photograph of a man in an orange jumpsuit hanging from a yellow rope. Despite his distorted face, I still recognized him from his picture in the newspaper when he was arrested.

Edgard Dominique.

CHAPTER 12

Lester Rivers and I were sitting in the *Miss Demeanor's* small lounge sipping coffee. "No doughnuts?" he asked.

"Cops, dicks, toilet salesmen, you're all alike."

He rolled his eyes, then asked: "So what happened at the press conference?"

There was a bright flash of light, then two seconds later a thunderclap. But no rain, not yet. I'd fastened a strip of duct tape to cover the bullet hole in the window to keep the rain out. The hole in Mona's black-and-white stripped pirate dress added a buccaneerish *je ne sais quoi* to her get-up. Maybe I'd add an eye patch, too.

"The sheriff let his PIO do the talking. Said jail suicides are rare, this the first in eight years. That, statistically, Collier County's suicide rate is lower than the national average. But they would be conducting a death investigation to quote-unquote make sure all policies and procedures were followed. Blah, blah, blah. They handed out a press release."

I handed Rivers my copy of the release. It noted Dominique had been held on charges of pimping, pandering, probation violation, and several other counts. None of the reporters in the room had a clue about the connection between Edgard and the hacked computer hard drive. Nobody brought it up. I certainly didn't.

"Did the public defender, Gwenn what's-her-name, say anything memorable?" Rivers asked.

"She wanted to. Her new boss told her to do what her conscience dictated. But nobody asked."

I'd been right. It had been Gwenn's last day on the job. In two weeks she would begin her new career at Judd and Holkamp, one of the largest personal-injury law firms in the South.

"None of the reporters asked her a question?" Rivers asked.

"The newspaper sent an intern who looked lost. The TV pukes did what they always do: they got their video, picked up the press release, and scurried on to their next sound bite."

"Soooo…"

"So, we have a lot of unanswered questions." I said. "We don't know who killed Maria. We don't know why for sure, but it's a fair guess it relates to the Edgard Dominique story. We don't know why they dumped her body here, but framing me looks like a strong possibility. And the only way they would have known about me would have been through Maria."

Rivers frowned. "If so, I hate to think how they got her to talk."

My throat tightened and I felt a thump in my chest. I took a couple seconds to breathe. Lester noticed, but gave me some space.

"Yeah."

"It's not your fault," he said. That was kind, but we both knew better.

"Here's the other thing," I said. "Edgard's hanging. It can't be a coincidence. But yellow rope. Again. Really? What's that about?"

Rivers looked up from his coffee cup and shrugged. "I spend most of my time not knowing stuff. Until I do."

"Yeah," I said, "and there's one more little mystery. I've saved the best for last. Sorry to bury the lede. Gwenn confirmed that Maria tried to arrange a jailhouse interview with Edgard. Sort of."

"Sort of?"

"Maria showed up at the jail and asked to see him. Like they would just put her in a room with Edgard so he could spill his guts to a reporter."

"Happens all the time on TV."

"Yeah, well in the real world, if an interview with a reporter is authorized at the Collier County Jail, it's all done through closed-circuit television, the inmate in one room, the reporter in another, and the whole thing is videoed by the cops. But it didn't matter. They told Maria to get lost. She made a fuss about it. Started spouting off about the First Amendment and the public's right to know. Very amateurish."

"Which would have made the rounds," Rivers said.

I nodded.

"So Maria stormed over to the courthouse, insisted on talking to Edgard's lawyer. Eventually, she bullied her way in to Gwenn."

"She had chutzpa."

"Maria said she was investigating the hacked hard drive and the missing list. That her sources told her the Public Defender's office was working on a deal. My source, actually, but what the heck. Gwenn said she stonewalled Maria, but didn't leave her empty handed. She told Maria that if she liked, she would forward a note to Edgard. As his lawyer, she got to see him face to face."

"What did the note say?"

"That embarrassed Gwenn. She couldn't tell. Maria wrote it in Haitian Creole."

"And she delivered the note?"

"She did. That afternoon. Edgard was very agitated. Not very surprising, I suppose. County lockup isn't exactly Club Med. She said he pressed her hard about a plea deal. Said he had to get out of jail. When Gwenn handed him Maria's note, he got angry and wadded it up. Then he thought about, straightened it out, read it, again and borrowed Gwenn's pen to scribble a reply, also in Haitian. When Gwenn got back to her office, she called Maria and left her a voicemail, reading what Edgard wrote, although it didn't make any sense to her and she didn't know how to pronounce the words so she spelled them out. Gwenn had to be in court, and was busy getting ready to change jobs, and she might have left the note lying on her desk."

"Don't tell me."

"She didn't think much about it until Edgard's hanging. Then she started looking around for the note, but couldn't find it."

"What happened to it?"

"Her guess, all crumpled up, maybe a janitor threw it out."

"Oh, for crying out loud."

"Funny, those were my exact words."

"And…"

"And so I pressed her on what the note said. Maria's question to Edgard was only one sentence long and, again, the Haitian Creole eluded Gwenn. Edgard's answer in Creole started with the word *kaka*."

"Kaka?"

"Yeah. She can't remember the rest of it. I looked it up online. A kaka is a kind of New Zealand bird."

Rivers shook his head, leaned back, and started cracking his knuckles.

"Please don't," I said.

"What?"

"That thing with your knuckles. It's like fingernails on a chalkboard to me."

"You've got a thing with sounds, don't you?"

"Yeah, I avoid music lyrics, too. They give me earworms."

"It's a disease, you know. A kind of brain disorder."

"Bite me."

"No, seriously. It's called Misophonia. Incurable. Look it up."

"Whatever."

Then he cracked a knuckle one more time just to annoy me.

"When, exactly, did this Gwenn person meet with Maria?" he asked.

"I'm not telling if you don't stop."

He rolled his eyes. "Fine." He shoved his bands into the pockets of his Bermuda shorts.

"Their meeting took place the day after Maria and I had dinner together."

"Like ten days ago, right?"

"Thereabouts. I never spoke to her after that."

We both thought about it for a minute.

"We've got a time gap here, don't we?" I said.

Rivers nodded. He raised one eyebrow, my cue to keep working it out, going Yoda on me.

We're conditioned from television to think that drowning victims float right away. Not so. As water fills their lungs, the bodies submerge. It's only after decomposition begins that gasses accumulate and corpses begin to rise. In salt water, bodies tend to bob up a little sooner. So Maria would have been murdered at least a couple days ago, perhaps longer, depending upon where her body had been dumped and how far it had drifted.

"So, her body floats up in Goodland," I said, thinking out loud. "Ordinarily, it takes drowning victims a few days to the surface. So where was she in the meantime?"

"And with whom?"

Whom.

"Well, eventually she ended up with *who*ever killed her," I said.

Rivers walked to the galley and loaded another pod into the Keurig.

"Any chance she might have left town, or gone undercover, chasing some lead, maybe searching for lost New Zealand birds?" He gave me smirk.

"Anything's possible, I suppose. She could have decided not to tell me what she was up to, maybe to show how tough and smart she was, that she didn't need anybody's help. Especially mine."

Rivers nodded. "Maybe. But in the end, she managed to get herself killed."

We were both quiet for a moment.

"So what next?" he finally asked.

I thought about that for a minute while the Keurig gurgled and his cup filled, then said, "Look, you're the professional detective here. What would you do?"

He sipped his cup of coffee and smiled.

"What I always do. Stir things up. Annoy as many people as possible. Keep being a pest until something vaguely resembling a clue makes a magical appearance."

"Where do we start?" I asked.

"Lawrence Marcano said his wife, Geneva, is coming to identify the remains," he said.

"Yeah, Henderson said she should be here today."

"I should meet with her. Her husband, technically, is our client. Maybe you can join me. We can find out as much about Maria as possible."

"Like…"

"Such as who her friends were, what she might have told her aunt about her investigation, maybe things she didn't tell you. Did she have any enemies, jilted lovers, who else in her family was she close to? Find some threads and keep pulling on them."

I nodded. "Won't the cops be doing the same thing?"

"Absolutely, but there's this note."

"Yeah?"

"I wonder if Maria ever got the voice-mail message. Even if she was upset with you, if she ran across an important lead, don't you think she would have called?"

"She should have. But did I mention how pissed off she was?"

"Yeah, but this girl had ambition. If she discovered something important, she should have contacted you."

"So where you going with this?" I asked.

"Not sure. But if she *did* get the message, wouldn't she have written it down somewhere?"

"Lester, if she did and she left it at her place, the police would have found it by now."

"A note scribbled in Creole? Might not have meant anything to them."

"You thinking maybe I should go over to Maria's condo and look around?" I asked. "I've been there before. Maybe something will stand out."

"Good call. We can get a key from Geneva."

"What else?" I asked.

"This hanging business bothers me. It's too dramatic. I'll ask some people in the agency if they can help, see if there have been any other hanging victims elsewhere, see if there is any kind of pattern here. We recently opened a branch office in Miami. They may know something about this."

Rivers set down his coffee cup and grinned.

"Interesting, all these hangings in an election year, don't you think? Florida really is a swing state."

CHAPTER 13

THE QUESTION OF what to do next solved itself.

The radar on my Weather Central app showed the storm would be arriving soon, so Rivers decided to bail before it hit. I tried to give him a hand while he climbed over the gunwale, but he brushed me off.

"I got this." Grouchy.

I called Mrs. Overstreet to check on Fred. "Let him stay here for a while," she said. "He wore himself out today chasing lizards."

I agreed and said I would walk over to the Little Bar and get something to eat.

"Oh, try the grouper balls or the Buffalo frog legs," she said. "They're delicious."

Mrs. Overstreet is very proud of the Little Bar's fancy menu. But I'd already tried her grouper balls. I had a cheeseburger in mind.

I washed the coffee cups—the Flash and Batman—that bastard Henderson still had my Green Lantern—and set them on the rack to dry. My iPhone chirped as I descended the boat's ladder. Caller ID said Henderson.

"I want my coffee cup back." I said.

"I hope I caught you at a bad time."

"Sorry to disappoint. I was just heading out to my next murder.

You like how I snuck into Edgard's cell? Nice touch using that yellow rope, don't you think?"

"How the fuck do you know the color of the rope?" he asked, his voice rising. "We deliberately kept that out of the release."

"Mental telepathy."

"Jesus Christ, this place leaks like … like…"

"My boat?"

"Worse."

"Well, detective, how else can I annoy you?"

"You lawyered up yet?"

I was. When I met Gwenn Giroux, I eventually told her about the search of the trawler and my status as a so-called person of interest. It didn't faze her.

"Makes sense," she'd said. "Path of least resistance. It would be so nice and tidy if you did it."

I told her I might need a lawyer.

"Call me. You can be my first client." She wrote her cell phone number on the back of a business card and handed it to me. Was that all business or was there more? I was hoping for more.

Henderson continued yammering about lawyers.

"What the fuck are you talking about?"

"Here's the thing," he said. "We need a DNA swab, your prints, and we need a little something else. You're innocent, right? This will be the quickest way to prove it."

"You can't make me do that," I said, although I really didn't know what my rights were.

"Which is why you need a lawyer," Henderson said, his tone now patient, paternal, as if he were talking to a five-year-old. "Here's how it works: You volunteer, you have a lawyer present to ensure everything's on the up and up. If you refuse, I'll get a biological search warrant, then we'll absolutely have the right to take your DNA and anything else we want. Might even do a cavity search. You don't want that, do you?"

"Like you're doing me a favor."

"We protect *and* we serve."

"You suck donkey dick."

"Make it easy on yourself. Meet me at the morgue in two hours."

CHAPTER 14

"Where's the boss?" I asked the receptionist at the medical examiner's office. A short, skinny guy dressed in a black suit, white shirt, and conservative red and blue rep tie looked up from a magazine he was reading. He offered a solicitous smile from behind the counter. Probably make a great assistant embalmer someday.

"He's in the middle of someone right now."

I turned to Gwenn and, on cue, she turned to me. "They make jokes at the morgue?"

I looked back at the comedian. "You should do stand-up."

He nodded. "Yeah, this is kind of a dead-end job."

The door behind the counter opened and a young Asian woman in a lab coat stepped out. She patted the comic on the shoulder. "Thanks for watching the desk for me, Danny."

He rose, gave her a nod, and walked out from behind the receptionist's counter.

"You don't really work here, do you?" I said.

He shot me with his thumb and forefinger. "Nope, making a pick up."

"Undertaker?"

"Assistant," he said. "But we can dream."

He walked out the front door just as the skies opened and a torrent of rain descended. The downpour drenched Mr. Stand Up before he made it to the hearse. I smiled. Thank you, God.

I turned to face the woman behind the counter. She was smiling, too.

"Is this the morgue?" I asked. "Or did we stumble into Comedy Central?"

She stifled a giggle. "We're not all stiffs around here."

"OK. I surrender. Let me ask again, is the boss around, and please don't tell me he's in the middle of somebody."

"Well, actually, he is. Do you have an appointment?"

"Yes. We're here to meet with Detective Henderson of the Sheriff's Office. This is my attorney, Gwenn Giroux. I'm Alexander Strange."

"Strange?"

"I've been accused of that, yes."

She snorted, then stuck out her hand. "Name's Sam."

Gwenn and I shook hands with her. Her grip was surprisingly strong for such a petite woman. Lugging around corpses must be terrific exercise.

"Short for Samantha, I assume?"

"Nope, just Sam. Like Sam Aotaki."

I had no idea, and the blank look on my face gave me away.

"You know, the actress."

Gwenn chimed in. "The actress, Alex, jeez."

"Sure. Well, Sam, nice to meet you. Are you one of the medical examiners here?"

"Intern. Hence the counter duty."

"Seen a plainclothes cop? Thin, gray haired, with a black caterpillar growing on his upper lip?"

She nodded. "Yup. They're waiting for you."

Sam escorted us, taking a shortcut through the main autopsy suite. It held three stainless steel examining tables. Fluorescent overhead lights and a strip of windows high on one wall made the room bright, if not cheery. At the head of the far table, a pathologist in a lab coat, wrote on a white board below the windows making autopsy notes. An elderly woman lay on the steel operating table, her internal organs exposed. I looked away. We entered a smaller, private, autopsy room. Henderson, the ponytailed CSI I'd met before, and another man were waiting for us.

Henderson wore gray slacks, a blue dress shirt, and a Glock. The CSI wore black from head to boot. I noticed her nametag said "Martin." The other guy sported a white lab jacket, jeans, and Buddy Holly glasses. He introduced himself as Dr. Revere.

"As in Paul?" I asked.

"Why, yes. A distant relative. Guess dentistry runs in the family."

"Wait, Paul Revere was a dentist? And *you're* a dentist?"

"Everybody knows Paul Revere was a dentist," Gwenn said.

I turned to Henderson. "And why am I seeing a dentist? I already had my teeth cleaned."

"I'll let the doctor explain."

A flash of annoyance crossed Dr. Revere's face.

"Very well," he said to me, testy. "We will be doing several brief procedures. First, Ms. Martin will take your fingerprints, a DNA swab from your mouth, and collect some hair samples. It's all very routine. I believe you have already consented to this, *correct?*" He gave Henderson the hairy eyeball.

"I'm advising my client against this," Gwenn chimed in. "Unless and until you have sufficient evidence to get a warrant, you have no right to order these tests."

Henderson sighed. "I've already explained this to him. We arrest him, we test him. And there's nothing you can do about it then. All you can do now is delay the inevitable."

I interrupted. "Let's get it over with."

"This is coercive, and you need to know, detective, that I will move to have this evidence disqualified," Gwenn said.

"Fine. You do that."

"All settled?" the doctor asked. He turned to the CSI. "Ms. Martin?"

"Why don't you go first?" she suggested.

"Very well. Mr. Strange, if you would turn toward me, I want to examine your teeth and then we will make an impression of them."

"Teeth?" Gwenn and I blurted simultaneously.

The doctor glared at Henderson. "I'm sorry you weren't informed."

The detective shook his head. "Here's the deal. The autopsy shows Maria Martinez suffered multiple, brutal bite wounds."

"Her face?" I asked. "You saying a human did that to her?"

"Yes," Dr. Revere said. "The victim's face wasn't merely bitten, it was eaten."

I felt a thud in my chest and bile rising in my throat. Gwenn moaned and wobbled. Henderson reached over to steady her. He walked her to an armchair in the corner of the autopsy suite where she lowered her head and covered her face with her hands.

Beware the cannibal. That's what one of the anonymous contributors from the Army of the Strange had warned me. A coincidence? If not, what? I knew nothing whatsoever about the Army. They all used weird names, such as Amun, Eleazar, Sulpica, and Zafrina. Obviously not real. I needed to figure out who they were.

"Dr. Revere is a forensic odontologist," Henderson said, forcing me back into the moment. "Our goal is to find the person who mutilated Ms. Martinez by identifying the teeth marks."

"There are also several bites on her breasts from which we have been able to make very good measurements," Revere said.

It took me a moment to refocus. "So, what? You want to match my teeth with those marks?" I stared at Henderson. "You really believe I would be capable of something like this? Really?"

He said nothing, stone-faced.

"Turn to me, please," Dr. Revere said. "He held a small flashlight in his gloved hands. "Open up."

Too numb to think, I did as he asked.

"Hmm," he murmured.

"Wa?"

"Remarkable," he said, softly, opening my mouth wider and sticking the flashlight deeper inside.

Out of the corner of my eye I could see Gwenn's eyes bulging.

I said, "Wa ish it?"

After a few more seconds, Dr. Revere turned off the penlight, released my mouth, and sat down on a swivel chair by the autopsy table.

"What's going on?" Henderson demanded. Revere ignored him.

"I've been doing this a long time, Mr. Strange," he said. "And I must say in all those years, yours is one of the very few perfect set of teeth I have ever encountered. No fillings, all your wisdom teeth intact, alignment flawless. Very rare. You are a fortunate young man."

"Brush and floss every day," I said.

He turned to the detective. "I won't be taking any impressions of his teeth."

Henderson's face reddened. "Why the hell not?"

Dr. Revere removed his gloves, tossed them in the waste basket, and rubbed his nose. "Our biter does not have perfect teeth. In layman's terms, he is significantly gap-toothed, and his lateral incisor is chipped. These are not his teeth."

I turned to Henderson. "So sorry to disappoint. Maybe you should track down Mike Tyson and arrest him instead." Then, after a moment's hesitation, I added, "motherfucker."

He hunched his shoulders as if preparing to bull-rush me. My inner reptile wanted him to. Henderson topped six feet but I still had him by a several inches and several decades and at least thirty pounds.

But before things got more thrilling, the door opened and the intern, Sam, stuck her head in. "Uh, detective, sorry to interrupt, but you are needed in the receiving area. It's urgent."

Henderson pointed his finger at me, opened his mouth to say something, then swallowed it.

"Same to ya," I said.

He whirled around and stormed out. I turned to Gwenn. She'd regained her composure and seemed to have been enjoying the little exchange between Henderson and me. She struggled to suppress a smile, then gave up. "Cool."

I gave her a set of raised eyebrows and cocked my head, the universal sign for "let's follow him."

"Wait a minute, I haven't got your prints or DNA," the ponytailed CSI said.

"Later."

Gwenn and I walked out of the small autopsy room and trailed Sam and Henderson down the hallway.

"Do you believe this?" I asked Gwenn *soto voce*. "Hannibal Lecter on the loose?"

She shook her head, sending her long, auburn hair dancing. "This is the sickest thing I've ever been involved with. I can't wait to start doing something civilized like suing insurance companies."

We took a few more steps. The entrance to the receiving area loomed.

"Remind me to tell you about the email I got warning me about cannibals," I whispered.

She stopped in her tracks and grabbed my bicep. Her fingernails sunk into my arm. A lesser man might have winced.

"Cannibals?"

"Yeah. I'll tell you all about it. In the meantime, level with me," I said, speaking softly into her ear so Henderson couldn't hear. Her perfume smelled floral and spicy at the same time, and being this close to her, I felt a little tingly. "Do you really know who Sam Aotaki is? And did you really know Paul Revere was a dentist?"

She snorted and elbowed me gently in the ribs. Pals.

Sam opened the door to the receiving room and Henderson strode inside, never looking back at us. Probably too preoccupied with having his murder case blown.

Actually, the explosion was just beginning.

CHAPTER 15

THE RECEIVING AREA of the Collier County morgue is, as the name implies, where the dead bodies arrive for autopsy. Adjacent to it is refrigerated storage for cadavers. A corpse covered by a white sheet rested on a stainless-steel gurney in the center of the room. A middle-aged woman with dark hair and olive complexion was gesticulating and yelling in a heavy Cuban accent at a short white haired man in a white lab coat. Maria's aunt, Geneva Marcano, I assumed, although I didn't spot any physical resemblance. She repeated herself and I finally understood her:

"I am telling you, this is not my Maria's body."

"Whaddya mean?" Henderson interrupted, stepping over to the gurney. He reached over and lowered the sheet revealing the dead woman's ravaged face. "Ma'am, I realize this must be hard for you. But have you thoroughly looked at the body?"

Geneva went nuclear. She raged for at least a full minute—great theater, all in *Espanol*—then she grabbed the sheet covering the corpse's body, ripped it off, and flung it across the small room. "You see this," she said, stabbing the dead woman's pubic area with her index finger. "You see this hair?"

Henderson said, "Uh…"

"Does this poor dead girl look like she shaved?"

"Shaved?" Henderson managed, his voice catching.

I intervened. "You're Maria's aunt—Geneva—right?" I stepped forward, placing myself in front of Henderson. He didn't object.

"Who are you?"

"Maria and I were colleagues. Name's Alexander Strange."

"Strange?" She said it softly, accessing her mental hard drive, trying to pull up some data. Then it clicked.

"You cockroach," she screamed. "You monster. I should kill you with my bare hands."

The guy in the lab coat grabbed her shoulders. Henderson, who had been looking confused, now relaxed and a grin spread across his face.

I took a step back. "What?"

"What?" She shrieked loud enough to shatter glass. "You should have protected her. You should never let her do this by herself. It was too dangerous. You were her mentor. And why did you hurt her like you did?"

I glanced at Henderson. His moustache twitched and a shit-eating grin spread across his weathered face.

"What do you mean, hurt her?" I asked.

Geneva began crying. "She trusted you. She hadn't been with a man since Haiti. She said you could be the one. You had dinner together, *si*? You took her home? But then you left her. Do you have any idea how you hurt her?"

"But I didn't do anything."

"*Pendejo!*"

I glanced at Gwenn out of the corner of my eye. She was chewing a knuckle, her eyes open wide.

"Now my Maria is missing. And they show me this. This body."

Geneva turned on Henderson, who seemed to be enjoying this exchange way too much. She pointed to the cadaver's crotch. "She shaved herself for him," she said. "She wanted it to be special. She told me so earlier in the day. That's why I know this woman is not my Maria. My Maria did not have a bush like this."

CHAPTER 16

"So LET ME see if I've got this," Edwina Mahoney said. "Maria may not be dead."

Lester and I were back aboard the *Miss Demeanor* sitting in the trawler's small lounge. Edwina was on the speakerphone. Fred was napping. Rivers nursed a black coffee. I could have sworn I saw Spock grab Mona's ass, but I might have been hallucinating. I was downing a *Cuba Libre*. Not my first.

"It's a possibility," I said, regaining my focus. "That's assuming Geneva knows what she's talking about."

"The pubic hair's the only reason she believes it isn't Maria?" Edwina asked. "No other dissimilarities?"

"You'd have to see the cadaver, Ed. It's bloated and, well, it's just awful."

"Yes, but if she *is* right and it's not Maria's body, then Maria must be alive somewhere, right?"

"If she's right, maybe. But I have to say, I have a hard time imagining a conversation where Maria talks about shaving her public hair with her aunt."

"But if she's right..."

Lester interrupted. "Here's the way I see it. Maria zeroes in on whomever erased the hard drive. Somebody feels threatened. She's abducted and questioned. Which is how her kidnappers discover her relationship with Alexander. So they try to poison him and implicate him. You with me so far?"

"Keep going," Edwina said.

"If it's her body in the morgue, well, obviously, they killed her. But if she's not dead, there must be a reason somebody wants her alive. The big question is why. If we can figure it out, we'll be well on our way to finding the kidnapper."

"And the killer of that poor defaced woman," Edwina said.

"Right."

"And we have no idea who the murder victim is?" she asked.

"You mean, if it's not Maria," I said.

"Yes."

"If it isn't, then, no, and that's partly my fault," I said. "When I saw Maria's ring on the dead woman's hand I knew it had to be her. Set the entire course of the investigation in the wrong direction."

Edwina said, "but that would be the point, right? Why else kill a young woman with nearly the same physical characteristics as Maria and put her ring on her?"

"Right." I took another sip of my drink.

"They can do a DNA test on the body, can't they, and tell if it really is Maria or not?" Edwina asked.

"They can and they will," I said. "But it could be weeks before they get results back."

"Weeks?"

"Yeah. Collier County isn't big enough to afford its own DNA lab. They're very expensive. They ship all this kind of stuff off to the Florida Department of Law Enforcement up in Tallahassee. There's a huge backlog and it takes a lot of time."

"Even fingerprints?"

"No. Fingerprints they can do immediately. It's their go-to evidence. But that corpse. I'm not sure they can get good prints off it.

Of course, if they could, they could match them to prints found in Maria's condo."

"So where does it leave us?" Edwina asked.

"Young Alexander here is off the hook," Rivers said. "Regardless of the identity of the victim, the bite marks don't match his teeth."

"And how dumb is that?" I said. "Leaving bite marks. And what's with using the same kind of rope to hang Edgard Dominique? Any case against me would never hold up."

"It may be that simple," Edwina said. "They might not be very bright."

"Yes. At best, this strategy would only work for a short time," Rivers said. "Which is suggestive, right?"

"Suggestive of what?" Edwina asked.

"It suggests they only needed to distract the police for a little while. Which tells us the clock is running down on us."

"All this assumes that Maria is still alive," I said.

"You keep saying that, Alex," Edwina said. "Why are you so pessimistic?"

"Just trying to manage expectations." My drink was becoming diluted. I set it on the counter. Might have to switch to something not requiring ice.

"All right. So what happens now?" Edwina asked.

"Now they'll have to take DNA samples from immediate family members," Lester said. "Probably get Maria's dental records, too, if they don't already have them."

"Let's hope for the best," Edwina said. "Isn't that the better path forward, to assume Maria is alive?"

Lester and I looked at one another and we both nodded.

"You're right, Ed. It's the best plan of attack."

"So any thoughts on who this face-eating sicko is?" Edwina asked.

"Maybe a sicko," Rivers, said, "or maybe since they wanted us to think Maria checked out, they had to make sure her face couldn't be recognized. Maybe they just want us to think the perp is a sicko."

Maybe *perp* was making a comeback.

"Why not decapitate her?" I asked. "Or shoot her in the face with a shotgun? This whole face-eating, channeling Anthony-Hopkins thing is so weird."

"As you've said many times, Mr. Strange, weird is your business."

"You're lapsing. We agreed on Alexander."

"I do tend toward formality."

"Kind of stuffy for a toilet seat salesman."

"Urinal screen."

"WHAT THE FUCK ARE YOU GUYS TALKING ABOUT?" Edwina shouted. Edwina is famously impatient about sidebar conversations.

"There's something else," I said. "It's about the army."

"What army?" Lester and Edwina said simultaneously.

"The Army of the Strange."

"The what?" Edwina asked. Lester just stared at me, head cocked, curious if I'd finally cracked up.

"That's what they call themselves. It's a group of anonymous contributors to *The Strange Files*. They use unusual pseudonyms. Every now and then I get good tips from them."

"So, what?" Edwina asked.

"The so what is that after the faceless body floated up at the dock, I got this message. It said, 'Beware of the cannibal.' It's like they know something."

Neither Lester nor Edwina said anything for a couple of beats, then Lester asked, "Have they contacted you since then?"

"No," I said. "But that's not unusual."

"You said their names were weird?" Edwina asked.

"Yeah. Well, they sound weird to me, anyway."

"Such as?" Lester asked.

I pulled out my iPhone. I had a separate folder for all the messages I'd received from the army. "Let's see, there's Jasper and Siobham and Renesmee and Aro and…"

"Vampires," Lester said.

I looked up from my phone expecting to see a grin on Lester's face. He was dead serious.

"Those are *Twilight* names," he said.

"Twilight, as in those books?"

Lester nodded.

"So the army uses characters from *Twilight* as code names," I said.

"Or they're vampires."

I shrugged. "It could be worse, having vampires on your side."

"Vampires never do anything without expecting something in return."

"Reality, gentlemen, reality," Edwina said. At least she stopped yelling at us. "We can work on the question of who this mysterious army is another time."

"Alright, let's recap," I said. "Maria may not be dead; she may be kidnapped. We'll operate on that assumption. If we're right, somebody hanged and chewed up the face of some poor girl to use her as a ringer, no pun intended; somebody planted evidence on and around the boat to frame me, yet another misdirection ploy; and somebody hanged Edgard, the chicken porn freak, with a rope just like the one found under my boat. The bad guys penetrated the county jail both to kill Edgard and to wipe his hard drive of a list of clients. The timing suggests Maria's kidnapping occurred shortly after she tried to interview Edgard at the jail. How they managed to get into the evidence locker to wipe the hard drive is a mystery. Likewise, how they got into Edgard's cell to hang him. There may be a cannibal on the loose. And somebody tried to kill my dog."

"Hmmm," Rivers said.

"What?"

"Well, this all started with the laptop computer being hacked, right?"

"Yeah."

"And your source said the tampering took place while in the sheriff's evidence room."

"That's right."

"Are we sure about that?"

"Where you going with this?"

"We have an awful lot of unanswered questions, and false assumptions can lead us down rabbit trails. For instance, hacking the hard drive in the evidence room is hard to believe."

"What's hard to believe?"

"That someone could break into the evidence room. Unless Collier County is sloppier than any other police department I know, it would be impossible."

"My source said the hard drive was so thoroughly overwritten that none of the data survived, not the list of clients and none of the incriminating photographs," I said.

"Sure," Rivers said, "but how do we know where and when that took place?"

"I'm not following you,"

"Chain of custody. The computer is seized at Edgard's apartment in Immokalee. Then it's transported from Immokalee to the Sheriff's Office. How much time elapses during transit? And who has possession of the computer before it's locked up in the evidence room?"

Edwina: "So it never arrived in Naples intact?"

Me: "Somebody erased it en route?"

Rivers: "Just saying…"

"OK, I see where you are going with this," I said. "We need to be cautious about assuming too much."

"It's a risk in any complicated investigation. You develop a theory, then despite your best intentions you discover evidence supporting your theory and ignore evidence that doesn't. Happens all the time. We just have to be careful."

"Confirmation bias," I said.

"Exactly."

There were a series of beeps, the universal signal of an incoming call. I checked my phone and it wasn't me.

"Gotta go," Edwina said.

"So, now what?" I asked Lester.

"The names on the list are the key to solving this. They point to the people who have the most to lose if the list becomes public. Those are our primary suspects."

"Yeah, but the list is gone."

"Is it?"

"Not following you."

"We don't know how Edgard Dominique got the names on that list, but it is a safe bet a small-time pimp like him was no mastermind. His list can't be the only copy."

"Maybe so. And, if so, whoever iced Edgard—or had it done—has the master list. But it's circular. We need the list to find Edgard's killer and Edgard's killer has the list."

"We just need an opening to the circle," Rivers said.

"And how do we do that?"

"Maria. She's the key."

"This conversation is frustrating, Lester. Sure, Maria's the key. Maria's the whole point of why we're doing this."

Rivers smiled one of his wide mirthless smiles. "Ah, grasshopper, the question is: who could be on the list who also would want to keep Maria alive?"

"Sage. But useless."

"Who cares most about Maria?" he asked. "She got a boyfriend? Apparently not. So it has to be family or someone else very close to her. Or someone who has more to lose if she is dead. We need to talk to Geneva. She may have some insight into this."

"Good luck," I said. "Don't let on that we're friends and it'll go better for you."

"I don't even know you."

I thought some more about what Lester had said. Who would, in fact, want Maria alive? And why?

"Maybe they're afraid to kill Maria." I said.

Lester studied me for a moment. "Keep going."

"I'm just imagining: she's captured, they're going to kill her, she's desperate, so she tells them if anything happens to her somebody—most likely me—will turn what she knows over to the cops."

"Then why try to make us think she's dead?" he asked.

"Oh, yeah. That does kind of shoot a hole in that idea doesn't it."

"Keep thinking." He set his empty coffee cup in the galley's little sink.

"Let me ask you something," I said. "I got a weird vibe from you when we were talking about the Army of the Strange. I know this is a stupid question, but you don't really believe in vampires, do you?"

He leaned against the galley and exhaled. "Let me tell you a story. When I was blown up, pinned under the bus, certain I was going to die..."

He paused, making sure he had my attention. "When you lost your leg," I said.

He nodded. "The pain was unbearable. I knew enough about battlefield injuries to realize I might die from shock before help would arrive."

I didn't say anything, just nodded.

"That's when the angel appeared."

"An angel?"

"That's right"

"I didn't know you were religious."

"I'm not."

"Well, alright, you were in severe pain and falling into shock…"

"That's not it. She was real."

"She?"

"An energy being.. Flaming red hair. She stayed with me."

"To help you?"

"All I know is that at the moment the angel appeared, the panic and the pain disappeared. The angel stayed beside me until I heard choppers approaching. Then she vanished."

"And you're sure you weren't hallucinating?"

Lester paused before answering, and for a moment I was afraid I'd crossed a line, insulted him. Then he smiled and said, "Asked the man who talks to cardboard space aliens."

I held up my hands in surrender. "Touché."

"Let me give you some unsolicited advice: Never dismiss anything out of hand. Weird is your business. Funny business for the most part. I get it. But there's genuine weirdness out there, things we don't understand, the stuff of nightmares. You asked me if I believe in vampires. No, I do not. Because I've never seen one. But I do believe our senses are limited and there's more to the world around us than we can comprehend."

"Like your guardian angel."

"If you want to call her that, yes. I'm just saying, Padawan, keep your eyes open. Your job could turn out to be stranger than you know."

He looked at me, awaiting my reaction, but, for the moment, I was lost in my own head.

"Any of that make sense to you?" he finally asked, breaking me out of my reverie.

"More than you know, Lester."

I told him about my friend Jazzy, a psychic I'd met in New Orleans who a few months earlier had saved my life. How she had been haunted by divinations of her death and how she understood that the trajectory of our intertwined fate was unbendable. And how, because of her courage in stopping a killer, I was alive today.

I also mentioned the apparition I saw when I was trapped with Fred in a forest fire in Arizona. How a tall, red-haired woman—yes, another red-headed woman—guided me to safety. And that I never saw her again.

"I can't explain either of these things," I told him. "The woman in the fire, I've often wondered if I just imagined her in my panic. But Jazzy, I don't know if her premonitions were real, but she believed they were, and she acted on them, and I'm alive today because of that."

Lester looked at me thoughtfully, then nodded his head. "We seem to have something in common. We both owe our lives to mysterious women."

CHAPTER 17

A FEW MINUTES after Lester departed, my cell phone vibrated. Caller ID said it was Naomi Jackson. I'd left her a voicemail message asking if any other reporters were poking around the Edgard Dominique story.

"Naomi, how's it hanging?"

"Mr. Strange, young ladies such as myself don't have parts that hang, you misogynist pig."

"I love you, too. And I'm so glad you called back. Got a question."

"Shoot."

"Are any other reporters sniffing around the Edgard Dominique story?"

"You mean his suicide or all the other stuff, which for public consumption we have never discussed."

"Yes."

"Well, it's been a busy news day. A ball python swallowed a cat over in Lely Estates, the legislature made it illegal for anyone but a state-licensed manicurist to trim toenails, and the candidates were in Orlando with Shamu. That's all I heard about and no reporters have asked me any questions, not that they would."

I decided to take Naomi into my confidence. I told her about the mutilated body and how it might have been misidentified as Maria, and how we were worried someone might be holding her captive.

"Wait, this Maria person, she was doing the story about Edgard's computer? I thought you were."

"No, I assigned it to her."

"Oh."

I detected an edge in her response. "I completely protected you as a source, Naomi. Maria didn't know where the tip came from."

She was quiet, so I pushed ahead and told her about Lester Rivers and how The Third Eye was hired to find Maria. And I shared my concerns Henderson seemed awfully eager to pin it on me.

"Henderson? Nah. He's a straight shooter. But he *is* getting ready to retire. Already put his papers in. Don't take it personal. My guess, his head's out the door. Short-timer syndrome."

"Maybe. But let me ask you. Lester Rivers, the guy from The Third Eye, we've been talking about what to do. Seems like there are two priorities,"

"Talk to me."

"First, assuming Maria's still alive, we've got to make sure her kidnappers think they've gotten away with this deception, that we still believe the body I pulled out of Buzzards Bay is her. As long as they think that, they may want to keep Maria alive. Make sense to you?"

"Maybe. What's the other thing?"

"We need to talk to her aunt. The woman who told the ME that the body at the morgue isn't Maria. Her name's Geneva. She's probably still in town, but I'm afraid she won't see us. She blames me for all of this."

"Geneva, you say?"

"Yes. Geneva Marcano."

"And she's this missing Maria's aunt?"

"Yes, Maria was crashing at her condo in Pelican Bay."

"Pelican Bay. I see"

Naomi's tone seemed strained, but I pushed on. "I hoped you'd have some ideas on how we could keep a lid on this and if there were any way to hook up with Geneva. I assumed you would be up to speed through Judge Goodfellow. But I guess not. Probably shouldn't have pestered you."

"Let me call you back." She hung up abruptly.

I leashed-up Fred, climbed down from the trawler, and took him for a walk around the waterfront. Cumulus clouds on the horizon were turning pastel shades of pink and purple as the sun set. Somewhere out there Maria Martinez might still be alive.

"If she's breathing, we're going to find her, Fred."

"Gerruff."

Good to have loyal shipmates.

Naomi's tone during our phone conversation concerned me. She had gotten chilly when I told her about Maria. I hoped she didn't think my handing the story over to Maria violated our trust. In hindsight, I should have mentioned that to her earlier. Also, she seemed short after I mentioned Maria had been staying at her aunt's condo in Pelican Bay. That was odd.

The sky gradually morphed from purple to gray, and it was time to head back to the trawler.

"Fred, you believe in vampires?"

Fred raised a leg and took a whiz on the base of an oleander bush.

"I'll take that as a no."

Half an hour later, Naomi called back.

"Nine o'clock tomorrow. Judge Henry's chambers. Bring that public defender friend of yours and this Third Eye gumshoe." Her tone was all-business.

"We're meeting with the judge?"

"Yes. You three and the prosecutor and the sheriff and the medical examiner and Henderson and Geneva. She'll be bringing her nephew, the congressman, too."

"How in the world did you set all this up so quickly?" I asked.

"I didn't. The judge did."

"That wise?" I asked.

"What?"

"I mean, Naomi, you want the Chief Judge of the Twentieth Circuit, your boss, to know you've talked to a reporter?"

She paused for a few moments, then sighed. "He knows."

"Huh?"

She sighed again. "You've met the judge, but you don't know him very well. Other than he's your uncle's fishing buddy. But I know this man. I owe my career to him. And I know he cares about doing the right thing."

"Uh, that sounds hokey."

She paused for a moment, then said: "You know what Judge Henry and your uncle do, besides get drunk, when they go out into the Gulf?"

"Fish?"

"Oh, they drown some worms, but you know what they do for fun, the two of them, when they're alone on the boat?"

My heart ker-thunked. "This isn't going to be upsetting, is it?" An image of two wrinkled naked guys Brokebacking around the boat flashed through my mind.

"They play chess. They sit out on the water, let them worms drown, knock back martinis and, as Judge Henry likes to say, 'play for world domination.' Been playing for years. For money."

"Oh, right. Yeah."

"Now do you understand?"

"You lost me at world domination."

"Judge Henry thinks of everything in terms of chess strategy. He's always plotting out his moves several steps ahead. Calculating. When all this kudzu started coming down, he asked me to put a bug in your ear."

So much for my schmoozing abilities. I thought I'd won Naomi over as a source with my charm and panache'.

"And he would do that, why?"

"Because he's smart and he's a politician. And he and the sheriff have had words."

"Words?"

I figured if I kept coaxing her she'd finally get to the point.

"It's an election year. Sheriff's campaign is gearing up. Four years ago he ran on a promise to stop *those damned liberal judges*. He meant Judge Henry, which is hilarious, because he's a Republican, but not Republican enough for some people, I guess."

The tumblers began falling into place. Well before my arrival in Florida, I recalled stories about roundups of illegal immigrants that the American Civil Liberties Union challenged. Something called "Operation Return to Sender." Goodfellow ruled in the ACLU's favor opposing the raids.

"Rumor has it the sheriff is going to run against the courts, again, prove he's tough."

"Sure."

"The judge, he figured this monumental screw-up with the Edgard Dominique case, it could give him some leverage, maybe force the sheriff to tone down his attacks. Judge is up for retention, and he doesn't need any of that soft-on-criminals stuff."

"So if somebody, maybe a naïve columnist like me, rushed into print with a breathless story about tampered evidence, that would be a good thing? Which is why you told me about it?"

"Yes."

"And so, I put Maria on this story…"

Naomi paused and I could hear her catching her breath. When she came back on the line she said, "I'm sorry."

"I get it. The judge wanted leverage. He tried to use public opinion—through the media—to get back at the sheriff. You were helping him. It's politics."

Still nothing back from her.

"Naomi, every source has an ax to grind. I'm not offended. People try to use the news media all the time. Our job's to sort that out." Actually, I *was* offended and my feelings were a little hurt, but I wouldn't admit it to her.

"Anyway, you're right," she said. "Judge figured a story like that would force the sheriff to back down, change tactics."

"So I'm a pawn."

Another pause.

"The judge is trying to do the right thing and it ain't so easy here in Collier County."

"And I should believe that why?"

"Because Judge Henry is the most honorable man I know. I'd do anything for him."

"Anything?"

"Anything."

"You'd sleep with him?"

"No, but I'd take a bullet for him."

Yes, We Do Have Cooties

By Alexander Strange

Tropic©Press

Scientists have discovered that men—and women—do, indeed, have cooties.

The average "intimate kiss" transmits 80 million bacteria, researchers reported. An "intimate kiss" was defined as a "full-tongue kiss with saliva exchange lasting at least ten seconds."

But there is some good news of a sort: Saliva ordinarily protects you against invading bacteria.

Unless that bacteria is MRSA, a dangerous staph infection that's difficult to kill. Cold sores also can be spread by smooching, doctors caution.

Which, naturally, raises the question: Who has more cooties? Men or women?

The French-kissing study did not answer that directly. However, a separate study of the bacteria in men's beards is suggestive.

Beards are trendy. But, scientists say they are foul. In fact, one study in the United Kingdom found that beard samples show men carry more germs in their beards than dogs have in their fur.

Researchers compared samples of beard hair and dog fur and discovered men carry around far more dangerous microbes than their canine friends.

"On the basis of these findings, dogs can be considered ... clean compared with bearded men," Dr. Andreas Gutzeit of Switzerland told the British newspaper the *Daily Mail*.

STRANGE FACT: Two-thirds of people tip their heads toward the right when they kiss. And if they do it for a minute, in addition to exchanging bacteria, they will burn 26 calories.

Weirdness knows no boundaries. Keep up at *www.TheStrangeFiles.com*. Contact Alexander Strange at Alex@TheStrangeFiles.com.

CHAPTER 18

THE REV. LEE ROY Chitango had switched gears, from warning his followers about the Great Atheist Threat, to deliver a sermon condemning gay marriage.

"Brothers and Sisters, Jesus does not want you to lie down with members of your own sex. It says so right in the Bible, Leviticus 20:13: 'If a man lies with a man as a man lies with a woman, both of them have done what is detestable. They must be put to death; their blood will be on their own hands.'

"For a man to marry another man, or a woman to marry another woman, makes a mockery of God's holy plan for us. God has told us that marriage is a covenant between a man and a woman and God."

A threesome?

"The gay-rights *heatherns* are out to destroy our civilization, which is based on the word of God. Hear me, if you are among those poor, lost souls who have lust for members of your own gender, there is help. You can be saved. You can be converted.

"And for the rest of you, my brothers and sisters, I plead with you to help this ministry and to support candidates for office who will defend our Christian values. I spoke to Senate candidate Ricky Perez yesterday, and I have to tell you he is a man of great statue..."

I turned off the radio as I pulled into the parking lot of the Dunkin'

Donuts on Tamiami Trail, near the courthouse. We were rendezvous-ing with Gwenn and then car-pooling over to meet with Judge Henry.

"Why do you listen to that lunacy?" Rivers asked.

"Professional duty. Some days the Sermonator practically writes my column for me."

He shook his head. "Apart from his obvious pandering, his grammar is atrocious."

"You've really got a thing about that, don't you?" I said. "Who and whom?"

"My mother was an English teacher."

"Yeah? Well, *my* mother was a drug addict. So there."

Gwenn waited for us inside, sipping a coffee and gnawing on a Danish. Today, she wore a gray suit, navy blouse and a multicolored scarf around her neck. I resisted the temptation to lean across the table and inhale, see if she wore the same floral and spicy perfume she wore the other day.

Gwenn, darling, you smell of flowers.

Strange, you cad, did you just sniff me like a collie?

I restrained myself and, instead, introduced Rivers. Then I walked to the counter and returned to the table with two coffees and two sacks with a dozen doughnuts in each.

"Hungry, are we?" Gwenn asked.

Rivers grinned. "Bringing doughnuts to a knife fight. It could work."

I asked Rivers, "You get hold of Geneva last night?"

"I did. But only briefly and it did not go well."

"How so?"

"Her nephew, Ricky Perez, he's talked her into using another agency. We've been fired."

"You're shitting me."

"Afraid not."

"What does that mean, anyway?"

"I don't know, but it certainly doesn't make our job easier. I talked to the office. Technically, Geneva's husband, Lawrence Marcano, is the client. My boss will call him today, try to get to the bottom of this. He doesn't like the smell of it, either."

"So, in the meantime?"

"In the meantime, officially, I'm on my own."

"And you're sticking with it?"

Lester gave me one of his mirthless smiles, glanced at Gwenn, perhaps calibrating his language, then said: "Alexander, my young friend, we are going to find these bastards and we are going to rip their livers out."

I turned to Gwenn. "That's detective-speak for ..."

She waved me off. "I'm a lawyer. I'm all about liver-ripping."

We carpooled to the courthouse and I parked the Sebring in the covered garage, leaving the top down.

"I really don't understand this," Rivers said to Gwenn as we walked toward the courthouse entrance. "This isn't a normal role for a judge, is it?"

"It's a little out of the ordinary, but not out of bounds," she said. "Goodfellow reports directly to the Chief Justice of the Florida Supreme Court. All Chief Judges do. He also convenes the grand jury and has broad authority over the entire criminal justice system here."

"Such as?"

"Here are two passages from the Florida Rules of Judicial Administration. I brought this with me in case anyone asked that question."

Gwenn's black three-inch heels clacked on the concrete sidewalk as we marched to the courthouse entrance. The heels matched her leather briefcase, slung across her shoulder. She opened the case while we were walking, glanced inside, and removed a sheet of paper. She did all this without breaking stride. If I were wearing heels I would have fallen on my face. She handed me the sheet of paper and I read it aloud:

"Rule 6: 'The chief judge may require the attendance of prosecutors, public defenders, clerks, bailiffs, and other officers of the courts, and may require from the clerks of the courts, sheriffs, or other officers of the courts periodic reports that the chief judge deems necessary.'

"Rule 8: 'The chief judge or the chief judge's designee shall regularly examine the status of every inmate of the county jail.'"

Rivers' head bobbed. We walked at a crisp pace, but he easily kept up, although limping slightly. "Guy's got juice," he said. "So we got a dead inmate. It's clearly in his jurisdiction. He has the authority to call everyone together, except the three of us, of course."

"I may no longer be a public defender," Gwenn said, "but I still have to work in this town."

"And we *want* to be there," I said.

Gwenn stopped and turned to us. Rivers and I pulled up to face her. "And I want to know who killed my client," she said, her voice steely.

"So your friend, the bailiff, set this meeting up," she continued. "Impressive. But what will everyone else think about you being here?"

"They may find it odd," I said, "but Naomi told me the judge dropped the hammer last night. He called the sheriff and the state attorney, told them he may ask the state Supreme Court to empanel a special grand jury with an independent prosecutor. Neither of them want that. The local prosecutor, what's his name, Harkness?"

"Yeah, Brian Harkness," Gwenn said.

"He's all in favor of a grand jury investigation, but he wants to run it, not some outsider. And the sheriff, that idea gives him the hives."

"And our role is what?" Rivers asked.

"On the surface, we're here because the judge says he wants everyone who could be helpful to be present. *Our* agenda is twofold: get everyone to agree to keep a lid on Maria still being alive—or so we hope—and to connect with Geneva."

"Keeping quiet is SOP in a kidnapping," Rivers said.

I nodded. "It's just there are too many people who know what

Geneva said, that the body in the morgue isn't Maria's. Naomi said the judge would swear everyone to secrecy, and by having this meeting, it would give us some extra insurance."

"Clever," Gwenn said. "Unorthodox, but clever."

"Also, I hope we can push a little bit, see what else we can learn that could help us. And if we're all under the judge's secrecy umbrella, maybe people will open up."

"Might have to horse trade a bit," Rivers said.

"What do we know that would be useful to anyone?" Gwenn asked.

"We know Maria's assignment," I said. "We know she corresponded with Edgard Dominique."

"But we don't know what he told her," Gwenn said. "I'm sick about that. What an idiot."

"Did I ever tell you about dat ... er, *that* ... one time I made a mistake?" Lester asked, giving her a quick smile.

She frowned at him. "That supposed to cheer me up?"

"Guess not."

"You're getting better," I said to Rivers.

He gave me a curious look.

"First time I've heard you say *dat* in a while.

He shot me with his finger.

We entered a conference room adjacent to Goodfellow's chambers. The judge chaired the head of a rectangular oak table chatting quietly with the state attorney, Harkness, to his right. Sheriff Deloit Rankin, in full uniform with a shiny gold star on each of his epaulets, sat to the judge's left. Rankin bore a striking resemblance to Barney Fife. I wondered if he was allowed only one bullet, too.

Geneva , seated on Harkness's side of the table, shot me a stony glare as we entered the room. The heavyset pathologist whom I'd seen disemboweling the old lady at the morgue sat across from Geneva, his hands clasped together as if in prayer. Next to him sat Henderson, who gave us a brief scan then returned his attention to the conversation between the judge and the prosecutor.

Goodfellow looked up, a warm smile opened on his face, and he said, "Welcome."

"I hope we're not late, your honor," Gwenn said apologetically.

"Not at all," Goodfellow replied. "You're right on time."

I rolled up a chair across the table from Henderson, leaving an empty space between Geneva and myself. Rivers lowered himself into a seat by Henderson, and Gwenn seated herself and the end of the table opposite the judge.

I slipped the messenger bag off my shoulder and set it on the carpeted floor and straightened my sport coat. One does not present oneself to a Chief Judge without being properly attired. I wore my blue blazer, neatly pressed khaki slacks, and a white button-down dress shirt, collar open. Spiffy.

Just then, the door to the conference room opened and a slender man with black hair in an expensive gray pinstriped suit strode in. The final member of our gathering, U.S. Rep. Ricky Perez.

"Welcome, congressman," Goodfellow replied. "Take a seat."

Perez scanned the conference room then pulled up a chair between Geneva and me.

"I brought provisions," I said, sliding a bag of doughnuts in the judge's direction. I pushed the other over to Henderson. "Peace?" I asked. He ignored me. "Ah come on, Henderson, they're doughnuts and you're a cop."

"Glazed, I hope," the judge said, reaching for the bag at his end of the table.

"Nothing but," I said. "I heard they're your faves."

Henderson eyed the bag without expression. Then he reached in and grabbed one.

I turned to Perez. "Care for a doughnut?"

"Can't," he said. "I'm on a strict diet during the campaign." Then he winked at me, like we shared a secret or something. My internal Creep-O-Meter pegged.

I didn't bother to ask Geneva. She stared straight ahead, looking past the medical examiner. I followed her gaze out the conference room window. A small passenger jet was making its approach to Naples Airport. Lear? Gulfstream? They all look expensive to me.

Down table, Harkness, the prosecutor, reached in the bag and pulled out two glazed, stuck together. A bonus. The judge slid the bag over to the sheriff, who remained motionless. He couldn't have been more still if someone had shot him with a freeze ray.

"Thank you for bringing refreshments," the judge said, then took a bite. "Ah, glazed, my favorite."

Didn't I just say that?

"We needed an energy boost after our vigorous conversation," the judge continued.

"I'm sorry, your honor," I said. "Did we miss anything important?"

"Actually, we settled on the boundaries of this conversation. The sheriff doesn't want to jeopardize his investigation."

"I'm here at your invitation, sir," I said.

"Indeed."

Goodfellow turned to Lester. "And you must be the investigator from The Third Eye."

"Yes, your honor," Lester replied. "My name is Major Lester Rivers."

I looked at Lester from across the table. "Major?" I mouthed to him silently.

He just shrugged.

"I understand your organization is employed to find Ms. Martinez," the judge said.

"Apparently Mrs. Marcano has now made other arrangements," Rivers said, looking over at Geneva and Perez. Geneva averted her eyes. Ricky Perez stared at Rivers, his expression cold.

"So, why is he here, then?" Perez asked Goodfellow.

"He and Mr. Strange and Ms. Giroux are here at my invitation. Is that sufficient?" The judge had his snarky on.

Perez eyed the judge for a several seconds, then said, "Certainly, your honor."

Harkness broke in. "It would be simpler, judge, to just drag them before a grand jury."

"To which grand jury are you referring, Brian?" Goodfellow said. "Shall I ask the Supreme Court to empanel a grand jury with a special prosecutor to take charge of this case?"

"We don't need to do that," the sheriff said. The freeze ray must have worn off.

"No, you wouldn't like that would you, Deloit?" Goodfellow said. Rankin kept his mouth shut.

Goodfellow turned to me. "Tell me, Mr. Strange, what would you do in response to a summons from Mr. Harkness to appear before a grand jury?"

"Why, your honor, I would invoke Florida's Shield Law."

Like most states, Florida has statutes that protect journalists from revealing their sources. It is not an absolute right, but it serves to discourage overzealous prosecutors from sticking their noses into reporters' notebooks. The federal government, on the other hand, has no such law. But the feds weren't involved, at least not yet.

"Indeed," the judge said. "Which would not be helpful."

The bag of doughnuts called to me. The scent of baked sugar, lard, and dough perfumed the air. But if Perez could abstain, so could I. A test of wills.

"So, to the ground rules," the judge continued. "Everything said in this chamber shall be treated as confidential. You will not speak to anyone about this conversation without my explicit permission. I am convening this meeting as an official court inquiry under my authority as Chief Judge and any violation of this agreement will be viewed as contempt of court. Is that understood?" Heads nodded.

"Your honor," I said, "just to be clear, I am not here today in pursuit of a story. But should I eventually report on this case, I will not use information discussed here today, I give you my word. That said, if I come across the same information elsewhere, it would not be covered by this agreement. I hope that's satisfactory."

Goodfellow didn't hesitate. "It is."

Henderson reached into the bag and extracted another glazed. I remained steadfast.

"To begin," Goodfellow said, "let's see if we all understand the situation. We have a woman in the morgue that Mr. Strange has asserted is Maria Martinez, but her aunt"—he nodded toward Geneva—"believes may be misidentified."

"It is not my Maria," Geneva said in a flat voice never taking her eyes off the window.

"And we hope that is true," the judge said. "And, if it is, then some poor innocent woman has been murdered and mutilated to deceive us."

Ricky Perez straightened in his chair. "What mutilation?" he asked.

I glanced at Geneva, who stared out the window, as if she were in a world apart. She hadn't told him?

"Someone devoured Maria's face," I said. "I identified her by her ring. Your aunt feels otherwise."

"Eaten off?"

"Yes. I'm surprised you don't know. The two of you should talk more."

Perez flashed a brief smile. The smile of a predator contemplating his next meal. Was it my imagination, or did his canine teeth seem unusually large?

"About the victim's identification, any new information on that?" Goodfellow asked the medical examiner.

"Yes, your honor. We don't have DNA results, but we were able to extract partial prints from the victim. They do not match any fingerprints found in the condominium where Maria Martinez lived."

The atmospheric pressure in the room suddenly dropped as everyone sucked in air.

"So Maria *is* alive!" I blurted.

The ME wagged his finger at me. "I didn't say that. Lack of evidence is not evidence. We'll know more when we match the victim's DNA with the samples gathered in her condo. And even if that doesn't match, all we'll know for sure is that the victim is not Ms. Martinez. It does not address her current condition."

"How long with that take?" Goodfellow asked.

"We've asked FDLE to rush it, but it will still take a couple of weeks at the earliest."

"Your honor," I said. "If Maria Martinez is being held by someone who wants us to think she is dead, I hope we can leave here today agreeing to let them keep thinking that. It could buy time to find her."

"Sheriff Rankin?" Goodfellow asked.

Rankin shrugged. I looked over at Henderson and caught him staring at the sheriff. He sat stone faced, rigid, his hands flat on the table. Tense.

"Wait a minute," Ricky Perez interrupted. "I realize I just arrived and have some catching up to do, but aren't we getting ahead of ourselves?"

Goodfellow cocked his head. "Tell us your thoughts, congressman."

"My cousin is missing. But why are we jumping to the conclusion she is being held captive? Because of a body discovered in Goodland who, it appears, is not Maria. You've lost me."

"I identified her as Maria from her physical dimensions and the ring on her finger," I said. "If Mrs. Marcano is right, and it isn't your cousin, then we still have every reason to be concerned about Maria. She would not just up and disappear."

"You know her so well, do you?" Perez said.

"I know she was reporting a very important story and she would not just vanish like this. And there is reason to believe the body of the woman found by my boat was hanged by a rope identical to the one used to kill Edgard Dominique. And we know Edgard Dominique communicated with Maria before his death. So, yeah, I think there is ample reason to be worried about Maria. I'm surprised you aren't."

Perez stood and stared down at me. "I didn't say I'm not concerned, I merely question the assumption she's been kidnapped." He placed his hands on the table and leaned toward the judge. "Has there been a ransom note or any other communication that would support the kidnapping theory?" he asked.

Henderson intervened. "Not yet."

"So, there." Perez sat down and reached out to pat Geneva's hand. She had been slumped over, but straightened as if hit by a bolt of electricity when he did that. She pulled her hands into her lap.

"My Maria would not disappear," she said. "She would not go this long without calling me." She looked past Perez and pointed a finger at me. "I don't like you," she said. That got a quick grin from the congressman. "But I agree with you. Someone is holding my Maria. The only other explanation would be that she's dead. But she is *not* dead. I can feel it."

Perez shook his head but held his tongue.

I wouldn't admit it out loud, but Perez had a point. We had no evidence Maria was being held captive. But while I had doubts about Geneva's "bush" theory, I agreed with her that Maria would not have remained out of contact for so long.

I turned to Judge Goodfellow. "Your honor, do we know how Edgard Dominique's hard drive got hacked and how someone got into his cell to murder him?"

Rankin bolted upright in his chair. "Your honor!"

The judged waived him back then turned to me.

"I think I will direct this conversation, Mr. Strange," he said. "But since you seem so eager to participate, perhaps you and Major Rivers—and you, Ms. Giroux—would care to fill us in on what you have learned."

Devious. No grand jury summons, just a friendly conversation. But sometimes you have to give a little to get a little. So, I spent the next fifteen minutes recapping my meeting with Maria, how I'd been tipped about the missing hard drive (without revealing my source), and how I assigned the story to her.

"Who gave you the tip?" Harkness demanded.

I shook my head.

"There's still the grand jury," he said, giving Goodfellow a sideways glance.

"And what would you do if brought before the grand jury, Mr. Strange?" Goodfellow asked.

"Uh, your honor, I think we already covered that."

Goodfellow frowned, then waved a hand in front of his face. "Indeed. Carry on."

I explained that Maria tried to arrange a jailhouse interview and failed. Gwenn jumped in and shared her story about the note she'd passed to Edgard Dominique at Maria's request and while her copy of his reply was missing, she'd phoned the response to Maria.

Harkness and Henderson were looking back and forth to one another, animated by the idea there could be a clue out there. It seemed to go over Rankin's head. Goodfellow seemed not to notice, either. He joined Geneva in staring out the window, following the path of another jet making its approach.

"We were hoping to check her condo, your honor, to see if she might have written down the phone message," Gwenn said.

Goodfellow snapped out of it. "What's that?"

"Maria's note, your honor."

"Never mind that," Henderson said. "We've already searched her condo."

"What about her laptop?" I asked. "Anything useful on it?"

Henderson paused for a moment.

"What laptop?"

Perez jumped in: "Are you kidding? She's a reporter. You didn't look for her computer?"

A fair question, of course, but what a prick.

"So, in summary," Harkness said, "shortly after Maria Martinez starts asking questions about Edgard Dominique's erased hard drive she disappears. She may be dead. She may be kidnapped. In any event, one theory is that somebody went to lengths to offer a culprit—you, Mr. Strange—to misdirect us."

"Your honor, the only person who has misdirected us is him," Perez said, pointing at me. "Whether Maria is dead or alive, this is the guy who would be Number One on my suspect list."

"So how would you explain Edgard Dominique's death, then, congressman?" Gwenn asked. "You think Alexander broke into the county jail and hanged Edgard Dominique with the same kind of rope and noose used on that poor girl?"

Henderson broke in, turning to the ME. "That her blood on the noose?"

"Same blood type. We don't have DNA results yet, as I mentioned."

"Who would do such a thing?" Geneva asked.

Nobody said a word. Sheriff Rankin looked catatonic. Goodfellow stared at his notes as if memorizing them. I glanced at Henderson. He'd been scanning the room, too. Our eyes locked. Ordinarily, he's got a great poker face, but his moustache twitched and he gave me the slightest cock of his head and a squint. He was telling me something but my universal translator didn't speak cop.

I decided to wing it:

"Mrs. Marcano, Maria believed something is corrupt in the sheriff's department."

Rankin slammed his hands on the table and jumped to his feet. "That's unfair," he shouted, his voice oddly high-pitched, like a kid protesting his hands really weren't in the cookie jar. He glared at

Henderson, then said, "We don't know how the hard drive was erased. Henderson had it in his custody the entire time."

Henderson was glaring at his boss. Guess he didn't like being thrown under the bus.

I pressed him. "You know who got into Edgar Dominique's cell and murdered him?"

"That's none of your business."

Now everybody stared at Rankin.

"Do you know the answer to that question, Deloit?" Harkness asked.

Rankin sat down. "We're working on it. We are pulling out all the stops. I've created a special task force."

I turned to Henderson. He glared at Rankin, his body rigid. "You heading up the task force, Jim?"

Jim. Friends.

"No," Rankin said. "I want fresh eyes on this."

Henderson turned to me and our eyes locked again. His eyes did not look fresh. They looked murderous.

Perhaps an opportunity.

CHAPTER 19

Thirty minutes later, we piled out of the conference room. I cornered Geneva and asked if I could have a moment. She radiated hostility, but after a tense few seconds, she relented.

"I want you to know I'll do everything I can to find Maria," I said, trying to warm up to her.

"Not everything, obviously," she said.

That was a reference to a suggestion offered by her nephew, Ricky Perez, that I write a phony story saying the drowning victim had been identified as Maria.

"Keeping quiet about it is one thing," I'd told Perez. "Lying about it is another."

"You got her into this," he'd said. "It's the least you can do after all the trouble you've caused." He'd said it calmly while smiling. I suppose he thought that would intimidate me.

"Tell you what," I'd replied. "If you feel so strongly about this idea, why don't you hold a press conference and you lie *your* ass off to the news media."

I might also have said something to the effect he should have lots of practice at it. Which got the judge pounding on the table to tell us to settle down. But I noticed what could have been the hint of a smile from Geneva.

In the end, we agreed the best course would be to simply say nothing to the media for the time being. It's not every day I find myself on the side of secrecy. I should have felt uncomfortable about this arrangement, I suppose, but I did not. The public has a right to know about the workings of the justice system, but it didn't have to know that very day.

"If you would allow it," I said to Geneva, "I'd like to go back to your condo and look around."

"*¿Por que?*"

"Henderson seemed surprised about Maria's laptop," I said. "Of course, since he hadn't seen her place—your place—before, I suppose that might be understandable. Maybe if I look around, I might see something else out of place or missing that might be useful."

She thought about it, then nodded in agreement.

"I'm staying downtown. I've been nervous about going back there. Maybe I give you the keys and you go by yourself."

I didn't want that. I wanted some time with her to talk about Maria. See if she might have something useful to offer. Like a clue.

"You have a right to be there," I said. "It's your place. I might not be able to get in without you."

Actually, I guessed the condo had been released as a crime scene, but she consented. Geneva agreed I could pick her up at two o'clock and we would check the place out together.

As I turned to leave, I noticed Judge Goodfellow standing behind me, frowning. But he didn't voice an objection to my suggestion, which I viewed as a sign of approval.

"Your honor," I said, and walked away.

I met Lester and Gwenn in the courthouse lobby.

"She go for it?" Lester asked.

"Yeah."

I drove Lester and Gwenn back to the Dunkin' Donuts to pick up her car. She'd offered to take the back seat to make it easier on Rivers, but he declined. The temperature was approaching ninety and Gwenn removed her scarf. The top two buttons of her blouse were undone revealing a scattering of small freckles and the hint of cleavage.

Gwenn agreed to take Lester back to his hotel. He planned to pack up and relocate to the Pink House Motel in Goodland so we could be closer. Room rates were cheaper than downtown Naples, too.

"See you back on the island, *Major*."

I sat in the parking lot for a couple of minutes after Gwenn and Lester pulled out, checked my email, then texted Henderson:

Can u talk?

Might have been a long-shot, but I had nothing to lose. I wandered inside the Dunkin' Donuts for another cup of coffee. But before I could order, my iPhone buzzed. I slipped it out of my jacket pocket. A reply from Henderson:

Plaza 5 mins

I returned to the courthouse complex, parked the Sebring in the garage again, and strolled over to the little outdoor snack bar on the lawn. I bought a cup of coffee and sat across from Henderson, at one of the tables.

"The doughnuts worked, didn't they?" I said. "Knew I could soften you up."

"Don't push it, Strange."

Cranky.

"I heard not even the NSA would be able to get anything off the hard drive," I said, getting right to it. Either he would open up or he wouldn't. "How could somebody get into the evidence room and do that?"

Henderson sipped his coffee and took nearly a minute to respond, calculating what to say. I waited.

"They couldn't."

"So it had to be before it arrived here," I said. "The sheriff seemed eager to point out that you had it in your possession until then."

He gave me the dead-eyed cop stare again. "I did."

I gave him a cocked eyebrow, an invitation to continue.

"Don't shit yourself, hotshot. I didn't do it."

"Of course not," I said, all sympathetic. "But how did it happen?"

"No idea. That's why we sent the laptop to the FBI." He took another sip of coffee, swallowed, then let out his breath.

"All right, Strange, you're in the clear on this. Not what I thought at first and I'm not going to apologize for doing my job."

"OK," I said. "And I should apologize. I'm sorry I called you a motherfucker." I paused for a beat. "I meant to call you a dickhead, but it came out wrong."

The black caterpillar over his lip twitched. I couldn't tell if it signaled the beginning of a smile or a snarl.

"Feds have any ideas?" I asked.

"Could be one several of things, but it boils down to a program installed on the computer with some sort of kill code that might have been triggered remotely. We didn't turn the laptop off, so it could have been vulnerable, we're told."

"Really?"

"Yeah. I didn't know that either. Turns out there's a bunch of software out there that will do that sort of thing. Anybody can download it. It could've been programmed to wipe the drive if the lid on the laptop were closed before entering a code."

"So how'd a punk like Edgard come into possession of something that sophisticated?"

"His story? He stole it. No clue about the contents."

"Where'd he snatch it?"

"Said he broke into a car. It was in the back seat in plain view. Outside a bar in Immokalee."

"Any security video corroborating his story?"

He shook his head. "No surveillance video outside the bar, no cameras or ATMs nearby, nobody working at the bar knows anything about anything. No reports of a vehicle broken into at that location."

"You believed him, Edgard?"

"No way. We wanted to sweat him. That's why we held him on all those other piss-ant charges. We even put him in an empty cell block, closest thing we got to solitary confinement. I mean, I believed him that it wasn't his laptop. Didn't buy that he didn't know who owned it.

"Then his PD got wind," Henderson continued, "and he completely clammed up, figuring she could get him some kind of deal."

"Why not?" I took my first sip of coffee, and winced. I'd accidently poured in French vanilla cream instead of regular half-and-half. Too sweet.

"Sure, if he would give somebody up. And we were going to do just that. Then he got iced."

"How could that happen?"

Henderson said nothing, just looked out across the grassy plaza.

"Jim?" I said.

Jim. Like we were friends now.

"What's with the sheriff? He trying to lay this off on you?"

Henderson ignored the question.

"What's going on here?"

Another pause. Then he said: "Cellmate."

"Cellmate?"

"Don't have many private rooms."

"I thought you had him in an empty cell block."

"We did. Then he got company."

"So you charge this guy?"

"Nope."

"And the reason why would be..."

"He broke out during the power failure, right before nightly lock down. Lights failed. When they came back on he was gone."

"No shit?" I blurted. I looked around, but we had the plaza to ourselves. "Don't you guys have backup generators?"

"They didn't come on right away."

"Oh, come on. How could that happen?"

"That happens when one of the guards, who also has keys, is bribed."

"You guys still use keys?"

"He shook his head. "It's all electronic. But all the doors can be opened with keys in case of an emergency."

"Like a total power failure."

He shot me with his finger.

"You arrest this guard?"

"Nope."

"And the reason why would be…"

"He's flown the coop."

"Wait a minute." I started putting some of the pieces together. "Hell of a coincidence the power went out at just the right time. FP&L says a transformer exploded. You guys find that suspicious?"

"You're not as dumb as you look."

It took me a moment to process everything Henderson had told me. "What a cluster fuck. No wonder the sheriff looked like somebody stuck a phone pole up his ass. This could turn out to be the biggest law enforcement scandal in local history."

He nodded.

"So why are you telling me this?" I asked.

Henderson looked up. His eyes were bloodshot. He looked like he might have a stroke.

"You saw Deloit. He's spineless. And he's covering this up. I have zero confidence in him anymore."

"And me?" I instantly regretted the question.

His moustache did its twitchy thing again. He seemed to relax a little. His shoulders dropped a few millimeters, relieving some tension. "You can't possibly fuck things up more than they already are," he said. "And besides, somebody needs to know the full picture. Somebody outside."

I nodded.

"And maybe I owe you one. I should have known it was too pat, the body by your boat. It was just too easy. Not even a journalist is that stupid."

"Is that an apology, after all?"

He sighed and drained his cup. "Just what I need a month before retirement. Forty years a cop. Twenty with the city, twenty at the SO, and this is what I'll be remembered for. I should never have put in the papers. Jinxed myself. Should have stuck it out until somebody plugged me. Would have been less painful."

He stood up, walked over to a trash bin, tossed in his cup—a perfect two-pointer—then turned toward the courthouse.

"Hey, Jim," I called after him. "Next time, my place. Beer pong. Shooters. And don't forget to bring me a new window."

"I'll bring you a lot more than that if any of this leaks out before we find the girl," he said without looking back.

"And what about my okra?"

He turned and cocked his head. "Funny thing about that. Still haven't got the lab results yet, but the guy I gave it to, he's intrigued. Said poison is making a comeback. Started with the Russians, when they iced that diplomat in London, you remember that?"

I nodded.

"You pissed off any Russians lately?"

"Pissing people off is practically my job description."

He thought about that for a couple of moments. "Watch your back."

He resumed walking. He looked tired. Older. He moved with his eyes downcast, no longer the tough cop, straight as a foremast. More like a sagging palm bending in a hurricane. Twenty-four hours earlier, he wanted to throw me in jail and I called him a mofo. Now I felt sorry for him.

CHAPTER 20

It's a short drive from the courthouse to downtown Naples. I turned right at the exit onto Tamiami Trail, passed the jumble of Tin City's seafood restaurants and touristy waterfront shops, and soon cruised along palm-lined Fifth Avenue with its trendy clothing stores, fancy art galleries, restaurants, and real estate offices. Signs on the upper floors of the two and three story brick and stucco buildings advertised estate planners, financial advisors, and stock brokers—all there to get their claws into the wealthy snowbirds who flocked to the city.

A snowy-haired guy piloted a powder blue Bentley convertible in front of me, top down, inching along, barely doing the speed limit. I'm neurotic about timeliness, but I had an hour and a half before I would meet Geneva. The Bentley driver kept glancing side to side, hoping someone would notice how cool he looked in the fancy-schmancy car. Nobody turned to stare. It's Naples. Bentleys are a dime a dozen. So are snowy-haired guys showing off.

On the other hand, nobody turned to stare at me, either—me in my classic maroon Sebring, a genuine collector's item. Did they not realize this could be a once-in-a-lifetime experience, seeing a Chrysler with a quarter-million miles on it that still rolled under its own power? None so blind…

There were no parking spaces along Fifth Avenue, so I turned left and found a slot by the Naples Art Association. A sign out front advertised a special exhibition of paintings and sculptures depicting the lives of the Calusa. They were the indigenous people who once called this corner of Florida home, long before the Spanish *conquistadores* splashed ashore. Fierce warriors, they took unkindly to the presence of those uninvited Europeans. The explorer Juan Ponce de Leon, fresh from his failure to find the apocryphal Fountain of Youth, died on the receiving end of a Calusa arrow when he underestimated their cunning. (Some accounts say he took it in the ass.) But the tribe, which inhabited south Florida for more than a thousand years, eventually succumbed to the invaders—not their swords, but their diseases.

They left behind hundreds of sizeable manmade hills, constructed of shell and sand, which gave their civilization high ground against predators and storm-driven tidal surges. Hundreds of years later, rapacious real estate developers would adopt their engineering strategy to create similar mounds upon which to construct hundreds of thousands of homes that, from the air, look like a sea of tile-roofed barnacles on an over-loved coastline. Every new housing development advertised its "lake views"—excavation pits where builders dredge acres of sand and haul it to building sites. It adds a few feet to foundations, maybe—just maybe—enough to keep the living rooms out of the flood plain.

Where I lived, in Goodland, flooding is a foregone eventuality come the next big hurricane—not to mention sea level rise brought on by climate change. The average elevation is a mere seven feet, but sizeable swaths of the little community are barely above sea level. Good thing I lived on a boat. Be nice if it floated.

The *Miss Demeanor* was a custom-made trawler, and replacement parts were a challenge. I made a mental note to call Uncle Leo again for an update on the repair schedule. And to add a shot-out window to the list. I had, on several occasions, offered to buy the boat from him and take care of all of that myself, but he declined. Too many fond memories, he said. Like running aground in Goodland would be a happy recollection. Maybe he looked forward to drowning more worms and playing chess with Judge Goodfellow someday. Maybe if Edwina found some deep-pocketed investors for the Tropic Press, I could buy my own boat and dock it wherever I pleased, maybe head over to Fort Lauderdale, hang out at Bahia Mar with Travis McGee. Or, back to reality, maybe I could get some lunch, fortify myself before my afternoon with Geneva.

I strolled down Seventh Avenue South to the Chapel Grill. It had once been the First Baptist Church, but had been resurrected into a restaurant and bar. A receptionist at the door smiled as I approached.

"Do you have any reservations?"

"Many," I said, "especially about the future of our country given the current occupant of the White House."

She didn't miss a beat. "Besides that?"

We both laughed and she walked me to a table on the patio. My server pitched the day's specials: Parmesan Crusted Red Rock Cod Florentine or Porcini Dusted Florida Snapper. I ordered a blue-cheese-burger, well-done, with extra mustard. Broccoli instead of fries. Some Chardonnay or perhaps a nice Malbec with that? I ordered a Diet Coke.

While I waited for my order to arrive, I slipped out my iPhone and checked for text messages and email. Edwina asked me to update her on the courthouse meeting. I texted her back and told her I would call later. Gwenn texted and asked about my chat with Henderson. I replied I would be pleased to recount the conversation over cocktails if she were free. Nothing from Lester. Probably busy packing. He and I had our work cut out for us based on what I learned from Henderson.

I scanned the restaurant for my server, hoping to see him approaching with my burger in hand. So much for hope.

I turned back to my phone and clicked on a trivia game I played with a cartoonist friend of mine. I didn't have a chance. Think Bambi versus Godzilla, Tiny Tim versus the Hulk, McCain versus Obama. I got stumped trying to identify Beyoncé's husband, Jay-Z.

Two bleached-blond women in their seventies were shown to their seats at the table next to me by—*ta-da!*—my server. He looked over at me, smiled, raised his index finger, the universal sign he had things under control, and scurried away. When he left, the women began complaining about older men in Naples. "All these guys want is a nurse or a purse," the shorter of the two said.

"Or both," her friend replied.

A few minutes passed as I idly eavesdropped on their crabbing. Must be a bitch being old and desperate for companionship. Then, again, being young and alone isn't always a walk on the beach, either. I scanned the restaurant again for my server, but he seemed to have donned his cloak of invisibility.

Tick tock. Tick tock.

I checked the news on my phone: Climate scientists were predicting the rate of sea-level rise would accelerate with the melting of the polar ice caps.

Must get boat repaired.

Biologists at Florida Atlantic University were concerned that crocodiles breeding at the Turkey Point nuclear power plant's cooling ponds south of Miami could be mutating because of exposure to low levels of radiation.

I knew it!

A housewife in Everglades City reported to police that the Skunk Ape—Florida's Bigfoot—made off with her cat.

Yum, yum.

A consumer group had filed a lawsuit against the Rev. Lee Roy Chitango's Ark II lottery, alleging it was a gigantic fraud. No response from the Sermonator.

Tick tock. Tick tock.

I should have snagged one of those doughnuts earlier. If the burger didn't arrive soon I'd run out and find my own cat to eat. The restaurant's sound system began playing Billy Joe Royal's *Down in the*

Boondocks and I involuntarily found myself rewriting the lyrics in my head.

Up in my treehouse
Up in my treehouse
People put me down 'cause
That's the kinda tree I was born in...

I said I have a compulsion to rewrite lyrics. I never said they were any good.

I scanned the restaurant in desperation for my server and—*eureka!*—spotted him leaving the kitchen, my plate held high, as he weaved his way through the busy tables.

Steady now. Don't drop it.

A diner who looked like he'd swallowed a medicine ball suddenly backed his chair into my waiter's path, but he nimbly sidestepped the behemoth and ceremoniously placed the burger and broccoli in front of me.

"Long time, no see," I said.

Maybe they were searching for a cow to slaughter. Or perhaps the crumbled blue cheese needed a few extra minutes to age.

"Kitchen's a mess," he said. "We're getting hammered today." He returned in a few minutes with a fresh Diet Coke without my asking. Nice touch. All forgiven. I dug out my credit card and told him I was pinched for time. He paused to check out my blue plastic Superman wallet.

"Cool."

The burger dripped with juicy goodness and the steamed broccoli glowed a bright green with just a hint of butter and garlic. My theory is if you eat enough broccoli you'll live forever. If you die someday, don't blame me. You were warned.

When the check finally arrived, I added a twenty percent tip. I may not be rolling in dough, but I am not a cheapskate. Bet the geezer prowling Naples in his Bentley didn't tip twenty percent. Hoarding his cash while he hunted for a nurse.

I returned to the Sebring and lowered the lid. Sure, it's warm with the top down, but if you can't stand the heat, get out of the tropics. The sky was cloudless this close to the shore, but glancing toward the eastern horizon, out over Immokalee, storms were building.

I drove south on Park Street, took the first left, then circled back to Fifth Avenue. I got lucky and found a spot on the street near the entrance to the Inn on Fifth. As I pulled in, Geneva walked out of the hotel entrance. I checked my wristwatch. Mickey's hands were on twelve and two. Right on time.

But Geneva wasn't alone. Ricky Perez accompanied her. Geneva seemed tense, walking stiffly. I couldn't make out what she and Ricky were saying to one another, but she shook her head twice in disagreement.

I opened the door of the Sebring and walked over to them. "Hello again," I said. Mr. Cheerful.

Perez turned to me. "Change of plans," he said. "My aunt is accompanying me back to Miami."

My aunt. Claiming possession, taking control.

"But we have an appointment."

"Not anymore."

"I'm sorry," Geneva said, faintly.

A red cap rolled a luggage cart to the curb just as a valet pulled up driving a black Escalade. The driver pushed a button and the back hatch of the SUV opened and the red cap struggled to lift Geneva's two enormous suitcases into the rear of the vehicle. Perez walked over to the driver's side and handed the valet a tip. Couldn't make out how much. The doorman held the passenger door open for Geneva.

"Why are you doing this?" I asked her.

"I just can't bear going there, seeing Maria's things. I'm just in the way here. That's what Ricky says."

"Come on, Geneva," Perez said, his voice gruff. "I want to beat rush hour."

She looked over her shoulder at him, nodded, then turned back to me, her body shielding her hands from Perez. Without saying a word, she slipped something into my palm while we pretended to shake. I held the door for her as she stepped into the Escalade and then Perez sped off.

CHAPTER 21

I SAT STUNNED in my convertible trying to make sense of the awkward scene that had played out between Geneva and Ricky Perez. Why did she have to leave so abruptly? Perez made it clear earlier he blamed me for Maria's disappearance. So maybe he didn't want me anywhere near the investigation, didn't want me snooping around Geneva's condo. Maybe he thought I'd done enough damage.

But that didn't seem to be Geneva's playbook. She might still be pissed off, but, unlike Ricky, she understood the value in taking a second look at her place. Maybe she just cared more about Maria than Ricky did. Or there could be all kinds of nasty family dynamics about which I would be clueless. Too much drama.

I looked at the keys she slipped to me: a silver Schlage door key and a smaller brass key, probably for a mailbox. Time to try them out.

I cranked the Sebring and pulled out onto Fifth Avenue heading west. The seatbelt warning light on the dashboard blinked like a spasmodic Cylon. I like seatbelts about as much as elevators, but I put it on. There was a time when I would have been stubborn about that. Maybe I was growing up.

At Gulf Shore Drive, I turned right. The two-lane street hugs the coastline through Naples and is the main drag through some of the ritziest real estate in the city. Just past the Naples Beach Hotel, the road temporarily dead-ends at Doctor's Pass. I turned right on Mooring Line Drive, then left on Crayton Road. I continued to meander north through high-end residential neighborhoods, passing the city's tony philharmonic center, Artis Naples, and entering Pelican Bay.

I turned on the radio for a spot of news. Animal rights activists were furious about the opening of a fourth monkey breeding facility in South Florida. The poor primates would be used for medical experiments. In Orlando, police arrested a twenty-three-year-old man for decapitating his mother with an ax. And a government report said Florida led the nation in identity theft.

Ordinarily, I would be all over those stories. Monkeys, ax murderers, fraudsters—my bread and butter. But I had other priorities.

I switched off the radio and parked in the nearly empty lot outside Maria's condominium. Many of the units would remain unoccupied until the winter months when the snowbirds flocked south for their annual migration, doubling the population of the city. I had only been to Maria's once before and didn't know where she would have parked her car, a yellow Volkswagen Beetle. I looked around but didn't see it.

I raised the top on the Sebring, got out, and walked over to an alcove at the building's entrance. An aluminum pedestal holding two dozen mailboxes stood like a metallic sentry by the entryway. I found the number to Maria's unit and slipped in the little brass key. An electric bill, a life insurance solicitation from AAA, a letter from Chase bank, and a postcard from a local audiologist offering a special on hearing aids. I hadn't expected to find anything useful, and didn't, but I had to look.

I left the mail in the box and climbed the stairs to the second story entrance to Maria's unit. It looked perfectly normal: no crime scene tape, no nasty fingerprint powder on the doorknob, no sign pasted to the door warning nosey reporters to keep out.

As I slipped the key into the lock, I heard footsteps shuffling behind me. I turned to see an elderly woman, gray haired, slightly stooped, and no more than five feet tall—no bigger'n a minute, as we used to say in Texas. Her face looked like a walnut, wrinkles creasing a deep brown tan. Her eyes were gigantic through her Coke-bottle glasses. She smiled, revealing yellow, nicotine-stained choppers.

"Oh, hello there," I said.

"Hello back atcha," she said, her voice raspy. As she approached I could smell the cigarette smoke on her clothes. She wore a floor-length pale blue housedress and a pink sweater, even in the Florida heat.

"You a copper?" she asked.

"Reporter," I said.

"Reporter? They don't let reporters into crime scenes."

"You must watch a lot of television," I said.

"What's that?" She cupped her ear.

I spoke up: "You must watch a lot of TV."

"So what?"

"I held out the key. "You know Geneva, the woman who owns this unit?" I asked.

"Geneva, sure," she said.

"Well, Geneva said it would be fine if I looked around. That alright with you?"

"Oh, I don't care, honey. You do what you want. I'm just nosey. And bored. When you're done here, come over to my place and have a sit." She pointed to a unit two doors down. "I love company."

"If I have time, I surely will," I said. "If not now, maybe you'll give me a rain check?"

"Drain check?"

"Rain check."

"Gotcha. Just don't wait too long. I've got one foot in the grave and the other on a banana peel."

She turned and shuffled back to her place. I waited until she reached her door. She turned back to me and I gave her a brief wave. She waved back but just stood there, staring.

"Say," I said, "what's your name?"

"Everyone calls me Miss Ellie."

"Ellie, that's a nice name."

"Yeah, just like Ellie May Clampett. And I'll tell you something, when I was her age I turned some heads, too." With that, she raised the hem of her dress and stuck out her skinny, pale leg and twisted her foot back and forth. She wore pink house slippers, a perfect *accouterment* to her sweater. I flashed on an image of her doing the cancan.

"I'll bet you were a terrific dancer, too," I said.

"You betcha."

"What's your name, bud?" she asked.

"Alex."

"Alice? What kind of name is that?" She turned on her heel and slammed her door.

"Alex. Not Alice." But she didn't hear me.

I slipped the key into the lock and stepped inside.

The interior appeared normal, undisturbed, at first. Drawers weren't flung open, belongings weren't strewn on the floor, cushions weren't sliced open. But there were small differences since my last visit. Most noticeably, Maria's laptop no longer rested on the dining room table. And the table was no longer perfectly centered under the small dining area's hanging lamp. The photograph of Maria and the woman I now knew to be Geneva rested on the kitchen counter instead of the living room end table. The Kassandra Clarke lithograph over the TV appeared slightly crooked.

Where to start?

What I knew about tossing a joint I'd either seen on TV or read in detective novels. What would Dirk Pitt do? He'd slip on a wetsuit and dive into the pool. I walked over to the sliding glass door overlooking a courtyard. I could detect no laptops resting on the bottom of the small swimming pool below. How about Virgil Flowers? He'd discover a flash drive duct-taped inside a tire swing. I looked around. No tire swing. Spenser would check out the kitchen then proceed to throw together a gourmet meal using a can of tuna and leftover sprouts. Stephanie Plum would explore all the condo's dark corners, use a cigarette lighter because she forgot her flashlight, and set the place on fire.

Having no cooking ability, no cigarette lighter, no wetsuit, and not seeing evidence of duct tape, I decided to be patient, look around, and just see if anything caught my attention. I really didn't expect to find anything. After all, the cops had been all over the place. But you never know.

Maria's bed had been stripped to the mattress—sheets, blankets, pillowcases, even the mattress pad all gone. Guess they were sent to the lab. I resisted the temptation to raise the mattress or look under the bed. It would be a waste of time to duplicate what the police had certainly done.

The closet doors were mirrored. I slid the left door open. Two pairs of slacks, three dresses, and several blouses hung from pink plastic hangers. Three pairs of shoes rested on the carpeted floor. Two were open-toed sandals, the other a pair of pale blue Nike running shoes, well used.

I slid the other door open but it only held a large Delsey suitcase, the kind with four wheels to make it easier to roll through airports. I'm no expert on women's wardrobes, but the closet had a Spartan feel about it. I looked around the bedroom and noticed a six-drawer dresser by the door. Maybe that's where she kept most of her things. I tugged each drawer open and took inventory. One held a bra. The other, four pairs of panties. A belt and a pair of running shorts and a pink T-shirt in the third drawer. The initials MJM were embroidered on the right sleeve of the T-shirt. I momentarily wondered what the "J" stood for then pressed on. The fourth drawer yielded nothing. A pair of pajamas lay in the bottom of the fifth drawer. I hesitated for a moment before sliding open the last drawer. Would the laptop be in there? Or would a flash drive be duct-taped inside? Empty.

I thought about the times Maria and I were together and what she wore. I recalled the pink running shoes with the mismatched socks she had on the first time we met, and the short violet-and-white striped dress that showed off her nicely tanned legs. Where did she put her dirty clothes? I stepped into the bathroom and saw a wicker hamper. Empty.

Maybe her socks and the dress had been in the hamper and the cops took them for DNA samples. But where the heck were the rest of her socks? And a girl doesn't get by with four pair of underwear, does she? And where were those pink running shoes? Maybe she wore them when she disappeared. Maybe she had on that little dress, too.

Still, it didn't feel right. I walked back over to the closet and pulled out the suitcase, flung it atop the mattress and opened it. I took the dresses and blouses and slacks off the hangers and folded them neatly and placed them inside. I scooped up all the contents of the chest of drawers and laid them in the suitcase, as well. And I topped off the entire pile with the shoes I found on the floor of the closet. With all that, it was still less than half full.

Curious.

I returned to the bathroom and opened the medicine cabinet. There were several jars of creams, some hand lotion, two unwrapped Caress Beauty Bars, nail clippers, a plastic bottle of Advil, and two glass bottles of cologne. No toothbrush, no toothpaste. A used Caress Beauty Bar filled the soap tray in the shower and there were plastic bottles of shampoo and conditioner. No razor.

Perhaps the police had confiscated those items, but if so, why take some and leave others? It felt off. There should be more stuff. No package of unused razor blades or toothpaste or toothbrushes. Or condoms, for that matter. Both the bedroom and the bathroom had the feel of a place that had been swept through quickly, to hastily gather supplies for a trip. But if so, why leave the suitcase?

Unless there had been another one.

I walked back to the closet and inspected the carpet where the suitcase had been resting. There were four indentions in the carpet where the wheels pressed into the fabric. Next to them were four similar impressions, though not as deep.

Aha! There had been another suitcase.

I made a mental note to call Henderson and ask him what the crime scene technicians removed from the condo. Did they pile stuff in the other suitcase? But I would do that after I explored a bit more. I would bet my bippy he would not be pleased with my snooping around, and I didn't want my time cut short.

Not much to see in the living room, and I once again resisted the temptation to duplicate efforts the cops certainly made: No pulling up cushions, no inspecting the backs of pictures on the walls. I was curious, though, about the dining room table being off-center. The leaves of the table were dropped, just as I remembered them. I grabbed one of the leaves and pulled it up and bent down to look under the table. No clues fell on my head.

I poked around inside the kitchen cabinets. Found the nearly empty bottle of Patron tequila we shared. Guess she decided it no longer required refrigeration. There were dirty dishes in the dish-washer, which had not been turned on. I wondered why the cops hadn't confiscated them, but what did I know about forensics? The trashcan under the sink yawned at me, empty.

I opened the refrigerator door and saw a carton of skim milk, a bottle of cranberry juice, and several sealed Kraft cheese bars. Assorted condi-ments lined the door's interior shelves. I opened the milk carton and it smelled it. Sour. Thought about pouring it down the sink, then thought better of it. The freezer compartment held ice cubes and nothing else.

Behind a set of narrow bi-fold doors, were a stacked washer and drier. Both were empty. A second set of doors opened to a small pantry. Inside were boxes of Fruit Loops and Raisin Bran, some crackers, Jiffy crunchy peanut butter, a red plastic can of Folgers coffee, a box of Lipton tea bags, and a six pack of Coke Zero.

I closed the bi-fold doors and walked around the condo for a final look. This had turned into an exercise in frustration. In a moment, I would call Henderson and ask about the clothes and toiletries. If the cops had them, that settled it. But something else nagged at me, and I couldn't quite pull it into focus. I scanned the bedroom once again, recalling the evening Maria passed out and how I blew it—in her mind, anyway—by leaving her. I straightened the Kassandra Clarke lithograph in the living room. Can't stand crooked paintings. Looked around some more, but no synapses sparked. I had missed something, I knew it. I closed my eyes and shut out my thoughts, hoping that would help my subconscious do its job. Again, nothing. I glanced at my watch. Mickey's hands were on four and six. I had a date with Gwenn at The Capital Grille in half an hour. I could definitely use a drink.

Drink?

Now why did that stimulate a neuron? I stopped, breathed deeply for a few moments, and tried to clear my mind. What did Maria drink? Tequila, that's for sure. She also drank Chardonnay. Didn't see any, but at the pace she guzzled the stuff it wouldn't last long. My exploration of her kitchen had revealed milk and Coke Zero. And cranberry juice. Good for urinary tract infections. I wondered, incongruously, if she were prone to them. Then again, maybe she just liked cranberry juice. Maybe it goes well with tequila. What else? Oh, coffee, of course. Couldn't start the day without the kick of caffeine.

Whoa! More synapses fired. What did she say when I suggested we grab a cup of coffee the night she got so hammered?

Yuck?

Then why…

I walked back to the pantry, grabbed the can of Folgers, and pried off the black plastic lid. The aluminum seal had been removed, and it appeared several scoops were missing. The handle of a clear plastic spoon protruded from the grounds.

Maybe she hid her dope down the bottom of the can. Weren't

coffee grounds supposed to confuse drug-sniffing dogs? Although Maria never mentioned using marijuana or any other form of recreational chemistry. I carried the can over to the kitchen counter and slowly, carefully, began scooping out the grounds into a bowl from one of the cabinets.

More than half of the grounds were gone when the edge of a clear plastic bag became visible. I reached in with two fingers and pulled it out. Inside was a small, black Moleskine notebook. I pulled the notebook out of the baggie and began paging through it. A series of what appeared to be passwords were written in pencil in the first two pages. Following each password, in parenthesis, were abbreviations, which I presumed were used to identify the sites the passwords were intended for. The first password read MJM8675309 followed by (FB), which I assumed meant Facebook.

There were the initials MJM again. The numbers 8675309 were from an old song. Written by a guy with a funny name. I tried to recall it but my mental hard drive failed to locate that particular memory. I did remember the name of the song, though: *Jenny.* Could that be Maria's middle name? Maybe. She never mentioned it and since we never put her on the payroll—no story no paycheck—we had no paperwork on her.

I turned the page, and there were two lines written in some foreign language.

Excelsior!

Maria had written down the phone message in this little black book and hidden it.

I shoved the notebook into my sport coat pocket and poured the grounds back into the can. Then I returned the coffee can to the pantry.

I could feel my heart pounding in my chest. I took a couple of breaths to calm myself, then pulled out my iPhone and called Henderson's cell. He answered immediately.

"I need some help with something," I said.

"Good thing I have all this free time," he growled.

"I'm over at Maria's condo…"

"WHAT?"

"Maria's condo."

"Who authorized you to go there?"

"Her aunt. Geneva. Which, by the way, I have to tell you, something's odd with that…"

"Never mind. I need you to get out of there right now and don't touch anything. We're reopening it as a crime scene."

"Uh…"

"What?"

"Well, it's a little late for that now. But before you yell at me again, just answer a quick question for me."

"Get out of there," he demanded, huffing and puffing.

"You sound out of breath."

"I'm walking to my car."

"Sure, but answer this one teensy question. Please."

I thought I could hear footsteps on tile floor. Then the background noise changed. Henderson had left the building.

"Henderson, you there."

"Second thought," he said. "Don't go. Stay right there. I'm coming over."

"I'm leaving unless you answer my question."

"What, for chrissake?"

"When you guys tossed her condo, did you remove a suitcase?"

"Suitcase?"

"Yeah, you know, rectangular in shape, zipper, wheels, holds clothes. One of those things."

"Smart ass."

"Well, did you?"

"Did we what?" He'd lost track.

"Did you take a suitcase from Maria's closet."

"No."

"Did you notice two suitcases in the closet?"

"There was only one."

"That helps. Thanks."

I could hear him wrestling with a car door and huffing as he lowered himself in. In a moment, I heard the car's siren begin to blare.

"Well, Henderson, nice chatting with you. Don't forget about my replacement window."

"You stay put," he yelled into the phone.

"Bye now."

I pushed the red off button and pocketed the phone.

The suitcase missing seemed consistent with her ATM withdrawal. She had been heading somewhere. But where? She had mentioned she might snoop around Immokalee some more, but she hardly needed to spend the night to do that.

I let myself out of the condominium and walked down the flight of stairs. My cell phone began buzzing. Had to be Henderson, so I ignored it.

I walked back to the Sebring, climbed in, and lowered the top. I scanned the parking lot one last time for Maria's VeeDub to no avail. However, I spotted another car that had arrived since I'd entered the building, a black Buick Regal backed into a slot at the far end of the lot. Uncle Leo drives an identical car. This one had a small green and black sticker on the corner of the windshield. At first I thought it might be a Collier County beach pass, then I recognized the lettering: NCR, whatever that stood for.

I drove north through Pelican Bay and exited on Vanderbilt Beach Road, turning east toward Tamiami Trail. The Capital Grille anchored a corner of the tony Mercato shopping center and I wheeled into an adjacent parking lot ignoring the valets in snappy white uniforms who were all too happy to park the Sebring for me. It was still early and there were plenty of empty spaces. During the winter months—known locally as "the season"—a line of snowbirds would snake out the door.

The skies were clear. The clouds over the Everglades that were building earlier had dissipated. So, for a change, I left the top down and walked into the dark, cool, comfortable confines of the restaurant. Gwenn sat at the bar. She turned to me and smiled and the room seemed to grow brighter.

CHAPTER 22

GWENN TOOK A sip from her glass of Jordan Cabernet Sauvignon and purred. She swirled the glass, stuck her nose into it and sniffed it for the second time. Then she took another drink, a full-sized pull this time. "I do believe this is the best Cab I've ever tasted."

The happy hour special featured Wagyu burgers and Jordan for half price. Gwenn hadn't eaten since morning doughnuts. I wasn't hungry, so I passed on the special and sipped a draft beer.

"I know we have things to talk about, Gwenn," I said. "But I have a question first: What *is* that perfume you're wearing?"

She smiled. "You noticed."

I returned the smile. I held back the wattage, no need to cause another power blackout. "Gwenn, I have to say, there isn't anything about you I've seen so far that I haven't noticed."

She frowned.

"Let me rephrase that." I took a breath. "You're very noticeable."

She grinned.

"It's Gucci Guilty."

"Ah ha," I said, like I'd guessed that all along. "G.G. Just like your initials."

Gwenn set down her wine glass and put her hand over mine. "You're funny."

"Funny ha ha or funny weird?" I asked and immediately regretted it. Men are not supposed to show insecurity. We are strong. We are confident. We are tumescent.

"Funny honest," she said. "You're this big guy. And you come across as unafraid of anybody. Sarcastic. Smart ass. But, really, you're still a little boy inside, aren't you?"

"What gave me away?"

Her hand still rested on mine and she pushed up the sleeve of my sport coat. "A Mickey Mouse watch?" she giggled. "And isn't that a Marvin the Martian pen in your pocket?"

"You're on to me," I said.

She grinned and gave me a big wink.

Captain, we have to eject the warp core, the nacelles are about to explode.

"You know," she said, "you remind me a little bit of that actor, when he was younger, who played in the *Star Wars* movie."

"Chewbacca?"

Before she could respond, the bartender showed up with her Wagyu burger and fries.

"Oh, that's fantastic." She grabbed the burger in both hands and took an enormous bite out of it.

She held the burger up and motioned it toward me, signaling I could have a nibble if I wanted.

"Not every day a beautiful woman wags a Wagyu at you," I said.

She raised her eyebrows, offering again.

Looks delish," I said. "But I'm good."

She nodded, swallowed, and took another big bite. I don't think she even breathed in between. After chomping on it for a few more moments, she set the burger down, wiped her hands on her napkin, and took another sip of Jordan.

"What a great idea, coming here," she said.

"I'll say." I smiled at her. She smiled back. A little fleck of meat was lodged in her teeth. I pointed to the corresponding spot on my own teeth and she figured it out instantly. She snagged her napkin off her lap and rubbed her mouth.

"Did I get it?" she asked, smiling at me again.

"Yes."

I could watch her eat all day. I could watch her do anything all day.

"You're staring," she said.

"I'm admiring."

She blushed at that.

"Can I ask you a really stupid question?" I said.

"Shoot."

"OK, and I swear this isn't a pickup line because I know it will sound lame, but is there any chance we've met or I might have seen you somewhere before?"

She frowned. "Am I that forgettable?"

I laughed. "Let me tell you why I ask. Not too long ago, in Arizona, during a forest fire up on the Mogollon Rim, a woman appeared in the smoke while I was trying to find my way out of the woods, and she directed me to safety."

"And I look like her?"

"She had red hair and she was tall like you, but I couldn't make out her features."

She grinned. "No, I don't do forest fires."

"Hmm. It's just that when I saw you, when we met at your office, and I heard your voice, I had this powerful sense of *déjà vu*."

She paused for a moment and looked into my eyes. I wasn't sure what she would say next, then it came out: "It's a brain disorder, you know."

I nodded. "I'm prone to them."

She had been sipping her Cab and nearly spit it out, laughing.

I gave her a moment to regain her composure and said: "I could sit with you all evening, but we have to discuss something I discovered a few minutes ago."

She nodded, but looked back at the burger out of the corner of her eye. She was struggling between giving me her undivided attention and grabbing another bite. She compromised and took a sip of wine.

I told Gwenn about on my talk with Henderson, the details of Edgard Dominique's murder, and how the jailer escaped.

"That sonofabitch," she snarled, her face empurpling. "He should have told me."

"Maybe he figured with Edgard iced, the PD's office was out of the picture."

"Bullshit. They're keeping a lid on it because they've got a corrupted jailer and an escaped murderer, and that will make the sheriff look bad in an election year."

"Then why share it with me?" I knew the answer, but wanted her take.

"I watched you. And I know you caught the looks Rankin and Henderson were giving each other. Something's off between them."

"Rankin's a coward," I said. "He's looking to shift blame and Henderson knows it."

Gwenn smirked. "Goodfellow has the sheriff by the balls; he's blackmailing him."

"Couldn't have done it if the Sheriff's Office came clean right away," I said.

She rubbed her chin, then looked up at me. "And he's using you for leverage."

"Sure. If I spill the beans and write about this, Rankin's screwed."

"But you could face contempt."

"Red Badge of Courage. Politician goes to jail, it's the end of his career. A journalist goes to jail, he's a hero. Besides, I got a great lawyer."

She drifted off somewhere for a few seconds, thinking. Then she refocused. "So, you're Rankin, you want one of two things," she said. "Find the girl and all is well, even if they don't catch the jailer and the killer right away, although that would be a nice bonus. His story would be he kept a lid on it, not because he was embarrassed but out of concern for Maria's safety."

I nodded.

"Or, this drags on past election day, Maria doesn't show up, and the judge loses his leverage."

I said, "That's not really an option. This will leak out, and when it does the story will be about a cover-up. The sheriff can't have that. He needs to find Maria, and soon, which is good. But there's a small window here, not just because it will leak, but if Maria is still alive and being held captive, that won't last forever."

"You care about her, don't you?" she said.

"Of course."

She thought about that for a moment then threw me a curve:

"This forest fire woman. Were you attracted to her?"

"I only caught a glimpse of her, and I don't know why I had that attack of *déjà vu*. But no, I wasn't attracted to her, not like with you."

That earned me a quick grin.

"I only saw her for a moment," I continued. "Then she vanished. Never saw her again. But she saved my life."

Gwenn reached down and patted my knee. "I'm glad you shared that story with me. I thought you had a strange look on your face when we met. Then you told me about Maria and I chalked it up to that. Whoever she was, well, I'm glad she saved you."

She took another bite of her burger, chomped for a bit, then took another sip of wine.

"There's one more thing," I said.

She cocked her head.

"Probably should put down that glass."

She wrinkled her brow, but turned and set the wineglass on the bar. Her eyes lingered on the burger for a second then she returned her attention to me.

I reached into my sport coat and pulled out a small black notebook.

She looked at it for a moment, grasping it in both hands, not quite understanding what I'd handed her. Then she gasped.

"Oh!"

She turned the notebook in her hands and pressed it between her fingertips.

I took it from her and opened it to the page with the lines written in what must have been Haitian Creole.

"This is definitely it," she said. "Where'd you find it?"

"Hidden at the bottom of a coffee can in Maria's pantry."

She frowned. "Didn't Henderson say they searched her place?"

"Yes, he did."

"You found something the cops overlooked?" Giving me incredulous. Like how could they be so dumb or how could I be so brilliant. I preferred to think the later.

I raised my palms. "What can I say?"

"Amazing." She glanced down at the notebook again, gripping it protectively as if it were a map to buried treasure.

"You have no idea how happy I am," she said. "Thank you." Then she leaned over and kissed me on the cheek.

"My pleasure."

She shook her head sending her auburn curls dancing. "This is the single dumbest thing I've ever done, allowing that note to get out of my possession. Oh my God, I am so relieved."

"I'll be relieved, too, if we can figure out what it means," I said.

She read the lines in Creole again and shook her head. "I still can't make any sense of it."

I leaned closer to her to take another look.

"Kaka?"

CHAPTER 23

THE SUN STILL hovered above the horizon when I left the restaurant. It wouldn't set until after 8 p.m. I was eager to get back to Goodland, to call Edwina Mahoney, and to lay out all I had discovered with Rivers. We had a lot to talk about.

My phoned buzzed and I answered. "Hi, Mrs. Overstreet. Everything all right?"

"Yes, but I just got a call and they need me over at the Little Bar to fill in. My niece Gabriel is on her way out, heading up to Naples. Would it be all right if she dropped Freddie off at your place?"

"Sure," I said. "And tell her thanks. You know where the spare key's hidden, right?"

"Yes, I'll tell her."

I rang off, pocketed the phone, and walked over to the Sebring. As I slipped into the driver's seat something caught my eye on the far side of the lot. A black Buick Regal. I did a double-take. It had a green and black NCR sticker on the windshield. I sat still for a moment, hands on the steering wheel, ten and two, wondering what to do next. I glanced at the Buick again and spotted two men in the front seat. They seemed to be staring in my direction.

I took a deep breath then dug into my pocket and pulled out my iPhone. I punched up my recent calls and found the one from

Henderson I had ignored. I pressed it. Henderson answered on the first ring.

"Where the fuck are you?" he demanded. "I told you to stay here."

"Shut up and listen. You got anybody tailing me?"

"What?"

"When I was at Maria's, there was this car in the parking lot. Buick Regal. Black. Don't have the tag but it has a green and black sticker on the windshield with the letters NCR."

"Rental car. NCR is Naples Car Rental. Big outfit here. So what?"

"That car is now parked across the lot from me at the Capital Grill. Two while males in the front seat, looking my way. I think they followed me here."

"Stay put," he said. "I'm on my way."

"Not sure that'll work," I said.

"Just stay there."

"Henderson?"

"Yeah."

"They're getting out of the car."

"Shit." I could hear his siren over the phone. Soon it would be audible in the parking lot.

The two men in the Buick stood outside the car with the doors open. I cancelled the call with Henderson and looked up my recent calls and found Gwenn. I punched her number.

"Hey," she said. "Almost done with my burger."

"Gwenn, listen to me," I said. "I'm in the parking lot and I am being tailed by two men. Henderson is on his way. Stay inside the restaurant. Don't leave."

I didn't hear her reply as the men began walking toward my car. The guy on the Buick's passenger side was my height only wider. He wore cargo shorts, a Hawaiian shirt, and a ball cap turned backwards. Bastard was stealing my fashion moves. The driver, slight and bald, held a pistol against his leg as he walked.

I tossed the phone on the passenger seat and shifted the Sebring into reverse.

Stay calm.

I am proud to say I didn't burn rubber, but I didn't lollygag, either. I K-turned out of the parking slot and drove around to the back of the restaurant. Before I rounded the corner, I glanced behind me and the men were rushing back to the Buick. I could hear a siren faintly in the distance now.

Step on it, Henderson.

I drove in the direction of the Blue Martini, then took a left, leading into the Mercato shops. Another left and I motored toward the exit on Strada Way. If I drove out, I would miss Henderson. So I took another left, which led me around toward the Capital Grill again.

Moments later, the Buick made the same turn and continued after me.

I kept driving. They sped up. So did I. Burned rubber this time clearing the far corner of the restaurant and raced around on the same route I had just taken. Ring around the rosey.

I saw Henderson pulling into the parking lot, siren screaming, so I turned left, once again, and hit the brakes.

The men in the Buick hit their brakes, too, stopping twenty yards behind me. What came down next seemed to play out in slow motion. I know it's a cliché, but that's how it happened:

Henderson steps out of his Crown Vic, his body shielded by his open door. The passenger door of the Buick flings open. The big guy with the ball cap steps out, raises a pistol over the roof of his car, and fires, shattering the window in Henderson's door. Henderson staggers backwards then crumples onto the blacktop.

I watch this play out, mesmerized, as if it were a scene in a movie. Then the shooter turns toward me.

Instantly, I was back in real time. I mashed the Sebring's gas pedal. The most natural of instincts kicked in: Flight or fight. I was definitely in flight mode. I looked in the rear-view mirror and saw the gunman jump back in the Buick, ready to give chase. Then something snapped. I don't know why I did it. I really don't. But in that instant, I thought my head would explode. My vision narrowed. I've never felt such murderous rage in all my life. I screamed and stomped the brakes, screeching to a halt. Then I threw the Sebring into reverse and grabbed the steering wheel with all my might. I could feel my heart throbbing in my chest and I was breathing like a sprinter. I got a bead on the Buick in my rear-view mirror and crushed the pedal to the metal.

The Buick had just started moving when the back of the Sebring collided with its front grill. I could see the driver throw his hands over his face as the rental's air bags exploded. My head smacked the head-rest and my insides liquefied. I looked down at the shifter and threw it into drive. I ran the car forward two dozen yards, then shifted into reverse again. Who knew a Sebring could burn rubber going backwards? The next collision jolted me even more than the first, and the back end of the Sebring climbed over the smoking hood of the Buick.

I didn't bother with the door. I clambered over the windshield of the convertible and ducked down, certain a hail of bullets would follow.

A white and green sheriff's cruiser screeched into the lot, lights flashing, sirens wailing. A young cop, Hispanic, jumped out of his car, gun in hand, and drew down on the Buick.

"Watch out," I yelled. "They just shot Jim Henderson."

The deputy never took his eyes off the car.

The Buick's passenger door swung open, and the big guy rolled out of the car and started running away. He turned quickly and snapped a quick shot in the deputy's direction, but the bullet smacked into the windshield of the Buick. Using a two-handed grip, the deputy aimed and fired three times. The big guy collapsed. Inside the Buick, the driver 's head drooped on the steering wheel. I could smell gasoline.

"I'm the good guy," I yelled to the deputy. "Don't shoot. I'm going to check on Henderson."

He didn't respond, just kept his gun trained on the Buick.

There were more sirens now. I sprinted across the parking lot, head low, to Henderson's inert form on the asphalt. He had fallen on his back and a bloom of red seeped from his abdomen. "Henderson, Henderson, talk to me," I shouted. No response. I shucked my sport coat and tore off my white dress shirt. I wadded the shirt into a compress and held it tightly against his wound. He didn't react. Holding the compress with my left hand, I leaned over and pressed two fingers of my right hand under his chin and detected a faint pulse.

A great whooshing sound erupted, and I glanced back to see the Buick erupt in flames. The deputy yelled at the driver of the car, his head still motionless on the steering wheel. A fire truck pulled into the parking lot followed by an ambulance.

The firefighters tried to rush the burning cars, but the deputy waved them back. "Gun," he yelled. The flames spread engulfing the driver. The deputy retrained his aim on the downed gunman he'd shot and walked toward him. The firefighters scrambled to the burning cars and attacked the blaze.

The medics rushed to Henderson and took over. Gurney. IV drip. One of the medics called for a chopper on his radio. I knew they would fly Henderson to the regional trauma unit at Lee Memorial Hospital in Fort Myers.

A second ambulance rolled up, followed immediately by two more sheriff's cars and a Florida Highway Patrol trooper. Within minutes, cruisers, fire trucks with their flashing lights jammed the parking lot.

Firefighters extinguished the inferno then lifted the driver out of the charred remains of the Buick. The side of his head was missing. He'd been killed by the stray shot from his partner, not the flames.

Cops hovered over the downed gunman's body. He had flung his pistol when he fell and one deputy stood over it. The shooter lay face up and a plume of red stained the front of his Hawaiian shirt where the bullets had penetrated his torso. The medics checked him out and shook their heads. He was long gone, but not unfamiliar. I recognized him as the guy in the checkout line at the deli, the guy who poisoned my okra, who nearly killed Fred.

"Motherfucker."

One of the deputies looked up and nodded. No doubt he thought I was pissed about Henderson. That, too.

Deputies spread out and cordoned off the body, waiting for the Crime Scene Bureau to show up. I walked over to the deputy who shot him. I introduced myself, and extended my hand.

"I want to thank you," I said. "You saved my life."

He looked a couple of years younger than me, and I imagined he would be shell-shocked from the experience.

He looked down and took my hand and shook it.

"Just doing my job," he said. Humble.

Something about him looked familiar, but I couldn't place it. I read the name badge on his uniform: Garcia.

"Have we met before?" I asked.

His eyes dropped.

"Yeah. I killed your mannequin."

The CSIs arrived, three of them, all in black, and began photographing the entire area. Photos first, evidence gathering second. While I talked to Garcia, one of the investigators approached him and asked for his weapon. He unloaded it and turned it over to her. It was Ponytail.

"We can't go on meeting like this," I said.

She gave me a dirty look. "I still need your prints and a hair sample," she said.

The medical evacuation helicopter touched down about a hundred feet away near the Mercato entrance. The EMS crew hefted Henderson and his gurney on board. The chopper revved up, climbed vertically for a few seconds, then banked north, heading for Fort Myers.

More cruisers pulled up and cops began stringing crime scene tape to hold back the gawkers. One of the CSIs photographed the downed gunman. A deputy pointed out the dead guy's handgun to her. She photographed it, too, then carefully unloaded it and placed it in a paper bag.

A news helicopter fluttered overhead and three TV news trucks, their antenna masts erect, flanked the scene. Guys with heavy cameras were videoing and reporters with microphones in hand were reporting live from the scene. I spotted a photographer I knew at the *Naples Daily News*, but shied away.

Gwenn appeared at my side, her eyes wide. "That was insane. I saw what happened. All of us did inside the restaurant. Are you all right?"

"I'm fine." I was uninjured, but a little jittery as the adrenaline wore off. My heart skipped a beat and I felt light-headed for a moment.

Gwenn looked at my naked chest and stomach. "But you're covered in blood."

"Not mine," I said. "Henderson's."

Her eyes never left my torso.

"Jeez, you're ripped."

CHAPTER 24

A HOMICIDE INVESTIGATOR named Wiggins was taking my statement when Sheriff Deloit Rankin approached. "Mind if I have a word?" he asked the detective. Wiggins looked up from his notepad.

"Yes sir," he said. "We'll finish up later."

The sheriff nodded at his car. I walked over to the passenger side of the black Ford Expedition and stepped in. He slid behind the wheel. We left the doors open. The sun had dropped low on the horizon and it would be dark soon. The medics had swabbed the blood off me and given me a gray T-shirt emblazoned with the emblem of the North Collier Fire Control and Rescue District. I wore my sport coat over it despite the warmth.

"I heard you tried to save Henderson's life," Rankin said.

Tried?

"How's he doing?" I asked nervously.

"He's in surgery. Lost a lot of blood." Rankin removed his glasses and rubbed his eyes. "Heck of a day, huh?" he said. Like we were pals, commiserating.

I nodded. "Identify Beavis and Butthead yet?"

"We know the big guy."

I waited a moment for him to finish, but I guess he needed me to ask.

"His ID?"

The sheriff didn't say anything for a moment, just looked out the windshield.

"Off the record?" I coaxed.

He shook his head. "No need. I'm going to ID him to the press." He looked over at the gaggle of TV reporters on the other side of the tape. "I hoped to keep this tight, get it cleared, but after this…"

His voice trailed off. I waited.

"Dombrowsky," Rankin finally said. "Arseny Dombrowsky. We booked him into county jail three days ago on breaking and entering. He threw a brick through the front window of a stop and rob in East Naples, walked in, and just stood there waiting for deputies to arrive. Like he wanted to be busted."

Rankin replaced his glasses and put his hands on the steering wheel, tightening then loosening his grip, working out the stress.

"I found out about that yesterday when it turned out he got transferred to Edgard Dominique's cell block and then vanished during the power blackout."

"Wait a minute," I said. "That guy? Who just shot Henderson? He also killed Edgard Dominique?"

"Yes."

Henderson had told me a guard was bribed and helped with the escape. I wanted to get the sheriff to say it. On the record. I tried sympathetic.

"So this Dombrowsky character deliberately got himself arrested to kill Edgard Dominique? What a cold-blooded bastard."

"Looks that way."

"But how did he end up in Edgard's cell block?"

Rankin shook his head.

"Oh, come on, sheriff. Doesn't this have to be an inside job?"

Rankin worked his jaw, avoiding eye contact. It was surreal. Why did he call me over to his car if he didn't want to talk? Finally, he answered.

"I feel like I'm under siege," he said.

"First Edgard's hard drive getting erased, now this?"

"Yes."

"Somebody get bribed?" I asked, trying to make it easier for him to spit it out.

He nodded.

"A guard?" I asked. All innocent. Just trying to put the pieces together.

He nodded again.

"So who's the guard?"

The sheriff leaned back in his seat and stared at nothing for a moment. "His name was Garvin."

Was.

"About a year ago, his wife left him. He started drinking too much. Got suspended once for showing up with alcohol on his breath. Could have let him go, but the guys felt sorry for him so we took him off the street and reassigned him to the jail. He was a regular over at the dog track poker room. Henderson saw him there a few times. And he wasn't doing well. Our thinking is somebody may have gotten their hooks into him over gambling debts. Be nice if Dombrowsky were still alive. We could grill him about that. Likely we'll never know now."

"How come?"

"FHP found Garvin's car in a canal off Alligator Alley. Drowned."

"When did that happen?" I asked.

"About four hours ago. Looks like they were tying off loose ends. And you were next."

We were both quiet for a minute as I digested what he'd told me. I felt a shiver work its way up my spine, and I instinctively pulled my sport coat tighter around me. Rankin noticed.

"We'll protect you."

"You think I still need it, after this?"

He gave me a rueful smile. "It really doesn't matter what I think.

Word spreads fast. You risked your life to save Henderson. I couldn't keep our guys away if I wanted."

"Sheriff, that's not quite right. Henderson came to help me."

Rankin turned in his seat and looked at me, frowning. "That's his job. That's what he gets paid for. You, on the other hand, are a civilian. And when Henderson went down, you attacked those thugs. You used your car as a battering ram. You pulverized their vehicle. Then you ran through the field of fire to help a downed officer. You'll never get a ticket in this town again. I'll probably have to give you a medal."

He shook he head. "At least one of us showed some courage today."

I looked out the windshield. Onlookers still hugged the outside of the police tape and the news vans were broadcasting live.

"You said a moment ago you wanted to keep this tight, close it, without all the sordid details getting out," I prompted.

"I hate politics," He removed his glasses again and looked me in the eye. His were rimmed with red and glassy. "I'm not a career cop. This uniform—I didn't earn it. I won it in an election. The department's finances were a mess. I'm a numbers guy. I promised to fix things. And I did. But I know what I don't know. I delegate thoroughly to my certified staff and I trust them. When we discovered Edgard Dominique's laptop had been compromised I couldn't believe it. Not right before an election. I stopped thinking like a professional and started acting like a politician. That's what fear will do."

He took a deep breath. "I should have just come out with the truth about Dominique's laptop, his murder, the jailbreak, all of it. But I thought we might clean it up. Save the department some embarrassment. Save me some embarrassment. I compromised my integrity. And your pal, Judge Goodfellow, sniffed it out. And as you saw, he's holding it over my head. I even tried to shift the blame to Henderson. Spineless, right?"

He looked at me, his eyes pleading.

"Pretty fucking spineless," I said.

"Yeah. Well, I'm done with all that."

He sounded defeated but sincere, and I felt sorry for him, which could cost me my membership in Cynics Anonymous, but there you have it.

"So what are you going to tell them?" I asked, nodding toward the television vans.

"The truth."

I thought about that for a moment. "How much truth?"

He nodded and ventured a weak smile. "A version of the truth. We still have to protect Maria Martinez, assuming she's still alive. I won't compromise that. I will hold a press conference in a few minutes in which I will say Detective Jim Henderson was wounded while pursuing an escaped felon. That's the truth. A deputy responding to the scene shot and killed the escaped felon who both shot Henderson and his partner. That's also the truth."

"And about the jailer, this Garvin guy?"

"FHP's already put out a press release on the discovery of the car and the identity of the man inside."

"You going to say anything about his connection to the jailbreak?"

"Not yet. We suspect that. We're pretty sure. But we still have to dot our i's and cross our t's. I'm not going to hide from it. But we have to be certain."

"What about Dombrowsky? You going to ID him as Edgard Dominique's killer?"

"Yes."

We were both quiet for a moment, then he asked, "What about you?"

"What about me?"

"I can withhold your identity."

"That's your call."

"If I do, you think they'll let it go?" he asked, nodding toward the television vans.

"Not unless they're brain-dead. Any reporter worth his salt will start chatting up witnesses, start putting pieces together, and if they do, so be it. My name will be in the incident report, in any event, and that's a public record."

"We'll redact your name."

"They'll sue you. I would sue you."

"Yeah, but it will buy some time."

"Again, your call." I may have conspired to keep Maria's kidnapping away from the press, but this was a different matter. Revealing my name would not interfere with finding her. Clearly, the bad guys knew me. That said, if the Sheriff's Office did redact my name, I certainly wouldn't object.

He turned in his seat. "Thank you for helping Jim."

Jim.

"He's a good cop. He tried to talk me out of all this deception. Said he wouldn't go along with it. Said if I didn't tell the truth, he would."

"That why you created this special task force, why you hinted he might have some culpability in the hard drive going blank?"

"Yes. Shitty, huh?"

He wasn't going to get an argument from me.

"One more thing, sheriff. You have my okra in your lab."

"Okra?"

"I think it was poisoned. Henderson turned it over to the lab the day Maria's body—or whoever she is—bobbed up in Goodland. I think somebody tried to poison me. Damned near killed my dog. Henderson said Russians are into that sort of thing. Dombrowsky. Sounds Russian to me. And I think he may be the guy who did it."

"You thinking maybe this wasn't the first attempt on your life?"

I shrugged my shoulders. "Maybe you could light a fire under somebody and speed up the tests."

"OK," he said. "I can do that." His face brightened a little. Like I had handed him a lifeline. At least he now had one thing he could do resembling actual police work instead of politics.

We climbed out of the big SUV. Rankin walked over toward

Wiggins and a CSI who were engaged in conversation. The CSI pulled a yellow, coiled rope out of a paper bag and showed it to the sheriff. Wiggins pointed to the burned-out Buick, its trunk lid sprung open. It appeared they found the rope inside.

My car's trunk was crushed beyond recognition and scorched. So much for my satchel and my company camera and iPad. Edwina would be pissed. But the front half of the car looked intact. I walked over and looked on the passenger seat and found my cell phone. At least something survived the crash.

Gwenn waited for me at the entrance to the restaurant and I headed her way.

I grabbed her by the elbow. "Where'd you park?" I asked. "I gotta get out of here."

"They're done questioning you?"

"I don't care. I'm leaving."

She pointed to a far corner of the parking lot near Nordstrom Rack.

"Where to, man of the hour?" she asked as we seated ourselves in her Camry. Solid. Reliable. Dull. Once she started piling up those billable hours with Judd and Holkamp, she could upgrade. She'd look good in an Audi ragtop. Heck, she'd make anything she drove look good.

"You know where the Naples Car Rental place is?" I asked.

"Across the street from the Waterside Shops, on Seagate, I think."

"That's our destination."

"The car you crashed into," she said. "It was a rental?"

"Had a NCR sticker on it."

"You going to ask them about it?" She sounded excited, eager to be in on the adventure.

"That and get a new set of wheels until I can get my insurance straightened out."

She smiled. "I can help you with that. They give you any trouble, give me a call."

I didn't think the insurance company would be swelled up about me using my car as a battering ram.

"You think I could get the sheriff's office to say I got rear-ended in the parking lot?" I asked.

She laughed. "Honey, after today, you can get anything you want."

CHAPTER 25

As WE PULLED into car rental parking lot, I noticed the lights were out. The sign on the front door said it closed at six o'clock.

Now what?

"No problemo," Gwenn said cheerfully. Perhaps more than one glass of Jordan had accompanied her hamburger. "You can spend the night at my place."

I turned to look at Gwenn and her big green eyes were wide open, waiting for my response. I put my hand behind her head and gave her the very best kiss in the inventory. Since the invention of the kiss there has been only one better, but although Gwenn put Princess Buttercup to shame, I was no Wesley. Still, she seemed to like it.

"Oh," she said when I withdrew.

Then she grabbed me and kissed me again.

"You know," I said in my best Bogart, which I had a hard time pulling off since I hadn't breathed in about two minutes, "this could be the beginning of a beautiful friendship."

She put her hand high on my thigh, leaned in, and nibbled on my earlobe.

Captain, the nacelles, they can't take much more!

"My place, then?" she cooed.

"Uh," I said.

For the record, "uh" is exactly the wrong thing to say in a moment like that.

"What?" she asked, drawing back.

I recovered more quickly than is usual for me when I stick my flip-flops in my mouth. "I would love to go to your place. Let's do it. Let's grab your toothbrush and a change of clothes then head to Goodland. I want to show you my boat."

"Oh." She frowned. "But Goodland is so far."

"I know. And it's asking a lot. But, I have a little problem."

"Problem?"

"Yes, his name is Fred. And I need to take him for a walk."

"You live on a boat *and* you have a dog."

"Yes."

"Well, it just so happens I love dogs and I love boats. Is it a sailboat?"

"No, a trawler."

She wrinkled her brow.

"Kinda like a tugboat," I said.

"Tugboat?"

"Yeah, only a little bigger, and I have this great crew."

"You have a crew?"

"Yeah. Let's go. I'll introduce you when we get there."

Gwenn pointed the Camry south on Tamiami Trail. She rented a studio apartment above Sushi Thai Too at the entrance to Fifth Avenue. She pulled to the curb in front of a hydrant and we agreed I would watch the car while she collected her things. Alexander Strange. Man of the Hour. Nobody would give me a ticket in this town.

I pulled out my cell phone. Thank God it had survived the carnage. My poor Sebring. I loved that car. I really did. Even if insurance paid for it, though, what would I get? Maybe I could buy lunch with the proceeds.

I punched Edwina Mahoney's number and she picked up on the third ring.

"Ed, you found that investor yet?" I asked.

"What?"

"I need new wheels."

I was a little nervous about calling Ed while waiting for Gwenn. I expected her to come racing back to the car at any moment, and yakking on the phone would not send the clearest signal she had my undivided attention. Bad enough I was about to drag her to the far side of nowhere.

"I'm in a bit of a rush here, Ed, so let me give it to you shorthand."

I looked at Mickey. His hands were on nine and three. I started talking, giving her the rundown of everything that had transpired. As usual, she listened without interrupting, although I could hear her breath catch when I described the events in the parking lot.

"One more thing, Ed. My messenger bag. And the company camera and my iPad. They're toast. I've gotta replace them. Will you cover me on this?"

"Christ. You're going to bankrupt us before I can get this outfit sold. But, yeah, go ahead. Actually, do it right away. I need clean books."

"Clean books? You close?"

"Don't start on me."

"OK. OK. I'll have Pitman Photo in Miami overnight it. Thanks."

"Wait a minute," she said. "Your columns? You didn't lose them, did you?"

"They're backed up in the cloud. No worries."

"And you're alright?" Took her long enough to ask.

"Yeah, I'm fine, Ed. Thanks. I'm on my way back to Goodland right now. A friend is giving me a lift."

"Who?"

"Gwenn Giroux."

"I see." Cold.

"What?"

"Nothing."

"No nothing. What?"

"You and women." She hung up.

Like what would she prefer? Me and goats?

Women!

I checked Mickey again. The little hand was now halfway between the nine and ten. The big hand was on the eight. Gwenn had been upstairs in her apartment for twenty-five minutes. How much time does it take to pack a toothbrush?

My phone buzzed. Rivers had seen the news reports from the Mercato on TV. "They didn't mention your name, but something told me this could be your handiwork."

I gave him an abbreviated rundown and told him I would be back to Goodland soon.

"I'll meet you at the boat," he said. "There's someone who wants to talk to you." No further explanation.

I pushed the red button ending the call and checked my watch again. I love my Mickey Mouse watch, but it's a bitch to tell time on it. His big white-gloved hands were now overlapping one another between nine and ten. Gwenn had been gone for more than half an hour.

I stepped out of the car and began walking toward the stairs leading to her apartment. Could we have been followed again? Could someone have been waiting for her upstairs? Could she be another loose end to be taken care of? Why hadn't that occurred to me before? And where were the cops who were supposed to be watching out for us?

I grabbed the handrail, swung onto the steps, and started racing upward. Then Gwenn appeared at the top of the landing. She saw me below and smiled.

"Sorry it took so long. Thought I should freshen up here. Didn't know about facilities aboard the boat, you know?"

Women!

CHAPTER 26

LESTER RIVERS AND a man I didn't recognize approached us when Gwenn and I arrived at the boatyard.

"Good evening, Ms. Giroux," Lester said. He turned to the man standing beside him. "This is my colleague, Colonel Lake."

Gwenn's smile gleamed in the moonlight. "Good evening, *Major*," she replied. She hadn't missed that, either. She turned to the other man. "Colonel." We all shook hands.

"You're with The Third Eye," I said.

"Yes," Lake appeared to be in his fifties and wore a suit with an open-collared shirt. Like Rivers, he suffered from follicle impairment. Maybe the stress of peering through keyholes eats away gumshoes' hair.

"Would you care to come aboard?" I asked.

"No, thanks," Rivers said. "The hour's late, but I wanted you—both of you—to meet Colonel Lake. He's been sharing some interesting information with me that bears on our case."

"What you need to know," Lake began without preamble, "concerns the similarities in the deaths of Edgard Dominique and the body that surfaced here. A rope with an identical knotting pattern was used in both cases. In the Dominique case, the rope was discovered in his cell block, the other under this boat, right?"

I nodded.

"The knots on both of those ropes and that method of execution, are signatures of a small subset of the Russian mafia known as Stalin's Hangmen."

"Russians?" I asked.

"Yes."

"They just ID'd the man who killed Edgard Dominique. His name sounded Russian. Dombrowsky. Arseny Dombrowsky."

Lake extracted a small notepad and pen from his jacket pocket and wrote the name down.

"Police also found a length of yellow rope in the trunk of their car."

"Oh, Jesus," Gwenn said. "What is this?"

"A little background may help," Lake said. "Brighton Beach, historically, was the center of Russian mob activity in the United States, but in recent years Miami has surfaced as another epicenter of activity. The Italian Mafia considers Miami to be open territory, and the Russian mob appears to operate similarly."

A brief smile appeared then vanished. "There's something about Miami that seems to attract mobsters."

"Florida's a weirdo magnet," I said.

"The Russian mob is organized, more or less, like the Italian gangs," Lake continued. "Names are different, but they operate with similar structures, cells, and hierarchies. Russians are a bit more secretive, more compartmentalized. They're into extortion, drug trafficking, prostitution and, especially down here, real estate. A great deal of money is funneled into real estate by both the Italian and Russian mobs. We know of at least five cells centered in Miami and three in Tampa. There are doubtless more."

"And these guys, Stalin's Hangmen, did you say?"

"Ah, yes, the hangmen. During Joseph Stalin's reign, he murdered millions of his countrymen. The henchmen in charge of that carnage were known as his hangmen. They were very powerful and fearsome. We believe what we are seeing here, however, is a small *bratva* of contract torpedoes. We're not sure how many there are, and we don't know their names. They've taken the appellation Russian Hangmen, evidently as both an *homage* to Stalin's thugs and to bolster their reputation for ruthlessness. They do not seem to be attached to any one of the *pakhan*—the crime bosses—but rather are freelance enforcers. We know about them through rumor and other sources, but mostly from their handiwork. Their victims, ordinarily, are other criminals and, consequently, they have not attracted as much attention from police as, perhaps, they should. Their signature method of dispatching their victims is by hanging."

"Bit theatrical, isn't it?" I asked.

"We think that's the point. To send a message. Stay in line or the hangmen will be at your door."

"What about the cannibalism bit?" I asked.

Lake grimaced. "Yes, that is disturbing."

"It's sick," Gwenn said.

"No argument. We estimate in the past three years there have been at least fifteen murders in South Florida we have traced back to the Russian mob. Not all by hanging, but there have been six homicides like the two here. We are talking about dangerous people. And at least one of them may be seriously deranged."

"Or just hungry." I don't know why I said that. I really don't.

"Perhaps," Lake said, deadpan. "More likely some twisted sexual aberration. But the young woman who died here is not the first to be mutilated like this. There have been two other cases, both women, one in Key West, one in Miami Beach. Both initially were presumed drowned and the facial disfiguration was not mentioned in news reports. We have gone back, now, and reviewed the autopsies and there does appear to be a pattern. Unfortunately, both of those bodies were cremated, so to a certain degree any connection is speculative."

"These Russians," I said, "when they're not hanging people, they seem to favor poison."

"What's that?"

I told Lake about my okra issue, how my dog could have been killed. He'd been cool until I mentioned Fred. Then his face empurpled and he started to say something, but clenched his teeth, and turned quickly to Lester.

"I'm getting video from the deli," Lester said.

"No need," I said. "I recognized Dombrowsky. He's the guy who poisoned my okra."

A sheriff's cruiser pulled up outside the boatyard's fence. A deputy stepped out of the car and scanned us with his flashlight.

"Alexander Strange?" he asked.

"Yes."

"I'll be here until sunrise," he said, "then someone else will be taking over."

I walked over and shook his hand. His nametag said Templeton. "Thanks deputy. I can't tell you how much I appreciate this."

"Yes, sir." He walked back to his car.

When I turned, Rivers and Lake were approaching the gate.

"We'll leave now," Lester said.

Lake shook my hand. "Good meeting you. What you did today was commendable. We should talk some more."

"Well," Lester said, "you've had an eventful day. What say, we reconvene tomorrow morning and share notes. If you will forgive me, I hear a nightcap calling."

"Thanks, Lester."

The two men walked off into the shadows.

I picked up Gwenn's overnight bag. It weighed twenty thousand pounds.

"Can I help you up the ladder?" I asked.

She kissed me and said, "No, I'm good." Then she stepped on the rungs and climbed upward. She wore a tank top and very short shorts. I followed her up the ladder and wished for better light.

I unlocked the door to the lounge of the trawler and ceremoniously waved her inside. She took one step in then shrieked.

"Ohmygod!"

"Oh, sorry," I said. "Gwenn, this is Mona; Mona, Gwenn. I assume you already know Mr. Spock."

She turned on me, visibly annoyed. "Why do you have a mannequin on your boat?" Like I might be a perv or something. Like Mona was weirder than a Vulcan.

"Mona is a rescue mannequin," I said. "See that bullet hole?" I pointed to where Deputy Garcia shot her in the chest. "She's only here until she heals."

"Who shot her?" she asked. Her eyebrows were making big rainbow shapes.

"You know the deputy, the one who iced the thug in the parking lot? Him."

"But why?"

"He came aboard the trawler during the search. Mona scared him. Only thing is, unlike you, he packed heat."

Moonlight drifting in through the windows dimly illuminated the cabin, but I could see the questioning look on her face. "This is going to be different, isn't it?" She gave Mona a hard stare.

"Better is always different," I said. "Would you like a drink?"

"In the worst way."

"The worst way? Ever done it upside down?"

"Drinking or sex?"

"Yes. That's why they call it bottoms up."

She walked into my arms. "You're crazy."

CHAPTER 27

THE NEXT MORNING, I quietly slipped out of the berth in the bow of the trawler, taking care not disturb Gwenn. I climbed the short set of stairs into the galley and padded over to the Keurig and turned it on. The machine gurgled as it sucked in water to heat, and I dropped in a K-Cup. These fancy new coffee makers don't make the best coffee, but they make brewing easy. Although I do feel guilty about all the plastic they send to our landfills. Chalk it up as another victory of sloth over principle.

I fetched a Batman mug off the counter and placed it under the drip. While the coffee maker did its thing, I checked my mail. A solicitation from a Nigerian prince to help him claim twenty-five million dollars somehow slipped through my spam filter. I also received a reminder from Progressive my auto insurance premium was due. Couldn't wait to talk to them about that. The Tropic Press noted that on this day in history in 1980 a tanker rammed the towering Sunshine Skyway Bridge in Tampa Bay and 35 people plunged to their deaths. The House Judiciary Committee opened impeachment proceedings against Richard Nixon in 1974. And it was Billy Joel's birthday.

I put down my phone and spotted a sticky note attached to Spock's chest. I hadn't seen it last night, but I had been distracted by a gorgeous woman. "Alex, I fed Fred before I left. Call me sometime. Gabby." She left her number.

Instinctively, I glanced down toward the berth where Gwenn still slept, feeling vaguely guilty, which was foolish. If I had a coffee can I could have hidden Gabby's note in there. Instead, I peeled it off Spock and dropped it in the trash.

The Keurig finished dripping and I grabbed a small carton of half-and-half from the galley's little refrigerator. I poured it into the cup until the coffee turned a nice milk chocolate color. I heard Gwenn behind me. She placed her hands on my shoulders.

"Oh, somebody scratched you," she said.

"A wildcat attacked me last night." I turned, pulled her into me with my free hand, and kissed her.

"That for me?" she asked, looking at the coffee cup.

"Of course. Just about to bring it in to you." A lie, but harmless, right?

"How did you know I take cream?" she asked.

Lawyers.

"Lucky guess."

She snickered. "Sugar?"

"Great idea. My batteries are recharged and I'm ready for action."

She pinched me. "Not that kind of sugar."

"Oh."

I keep a small supply of restaurant-style packets in a drawer. As I fetched them I heard somebody outside. I looked over the gunwale to see Lester approaching the trawler.

"Ahoy!" he called.

"It's Lester," I said. "And he's carrying to what my keen reporter's eyes appears to be a bag of doughnuts."

"What kind?" she asked.

"I dare not use my X-ray vision for fear of setting the bag on fire."

"I better throw on something," she said and scampered out of the galley. She wasn't the first nude woman I'd seen scampering, but I could recall no finer.

I followed her down the stairs and climbed into a pair of cargo shorts and a Jimmy Eat World T-shirt while she slipped on her panties and bra. We were bumping into each other and giggling.

"A little crowded down here," she said. "Especially with all these books."

Uncle Leo had left a bookcase filled with detective novels in the berth. I was working my way through the ones I hadn't read before.

"All my heroes are detectives," I said.

"What about Batman?" she asked, bumping into me on purpose.

"World's greatest detective," I said.

Of course, Elvis Cole might take issue with that.

Lester reached the top of the ladder when I opened the lounge door. I walked over and offered him a hand.

"I've got it," he said, giving me a little surly.

"Hey, I would offer a hand to anyone, not just a cripple," I said.

His face cracked into a broad grin. "I know. I know. I'm a bit testy about being self-reliant."

"Well, at least hand over the doughnuts. If you fall on your ass, I don't want them squashed."

He tossed the bag to me then stepped onto the deck. He was dressed in Full Cleveland again: knee-high black socks, Bermuda shorts and his straw boater. Maybe he read some edition of *GQ* edited for dorks. Or maybe he wore what he wanted to and didn't give a damn what anybody thought.

"We just got up and I'm making coffee," I said. "Welcome aboard."

I started to turn to re-enter the cabin and he grabbed my arm.

"You all right?" he asked, concern in his voice.

I nodded. "I'm good."

"He's adequate," Gwenn said from inside the boat.

Adequate?

We decided to take our coffee and doughnuts out onto the poop deck to enjoy the cool, clear morning.

"How are Mona's injuries?" Rivers asked.

"I found a place online that will patch her up, but it costs a small fortune."

"We'll sue the county," Gwenn said. "We'll sue the sheriff. We'll sue that trigger-happy deputy."

"Well, he did save my life," I said.

"All right, we'll give the deputy a pass."

"Must have been some scene over at the Mercato," Rivers said.

I walked him through it, starting with my conversation with Henderson earlier in the day, the weird encounter with Geneva and Ricky Perez, the search of Maria's condo, and the shootout in the Mercato parking lot.

"Deputy was like Wyatt Earp," I said. "He never flinched, not even when that fuckwad Dombrowsky drew down on him. He just stood his ground, aimed, and pulled the trigger. Then he covered the car so I could get over to Henderson. I was a nervous wreck. I don't think he even broke a sweat."

"We definitely are *not* going to sue the deputy," Gwenn said.

The doughnuts were gone and the temperature was climbing. We retreated to the shade of the lounge and I plunked another K-Cup into the Keurig.

"I'm appalled you're using one of those things," Lester said. "Aren't you millennials supposed to be environmentally conscious?"

It took me a beat to realize he was talking about the plastic coffee pod I was holding.

"You know how many times you can circle the planet with used pods like that?" he asked. "It's killing our landfills."

"So you don't want another coffee?" I asked.

"Didn't say that."

"They're working on biodegradable pods, I heard," Gwenn said.

"Good, I'll switch to them as soon as they come out," I said. "But now we need to plot our moves."

"Let's see the note," Lester said to Gwenn.

"First, *major*," I said, "you gotta tell me about Colonel Lake."

"Ah." He removed his straw hat, tossed it on the counter, then slipped a handkerchief out of his back pocket and wiped his brow. I fretted for a moment that perhaps I should have waited to ask that question when we were alone. Then again, we were all in this together: The Three Mouseketeers.

"Colonel Lake and I have a little history together. From overseas when he was my commanding officer."

"Did the other members of your unit also have aquatic names?" I asked. "Perhaps a Captain Cove. A Sergeant Swamp. A Private Pond?"

Gwenn hissed, *"Alex!"*

Rivers shot me a brief smile. "You do love your alliterations."

I held up my hands in surrender.

"No," Rivers said, "it's all right. I served in the Army for many years, and mostly with INSCOM—short for the Army Intelligence and Security Command. In-country, we often employed cryptonyms for our clandestine work."

He had been staring at the floor while sharing all that. He raised his head and chuckled.

"Protocol required using code names, but it felt a bit over the top. So we started doing silly stuff. One time we named ourselves after trees. Another time, mountains. I became Captain Everest at one point. Anyway, during my last tour, we settled on bodies of water. I was Major Rivers the day I lost my leg."

"So is Lake one of the organizers of The Third Eye?"

The corner of Rivers' mouth twitched. "The Third Eye knows all and sees all. But The Third Eye does not tell all."

I said, "I shouldn't have asked. Really, it's none of my business."

"Actually, I would have been a little disappointed in you if you hadn't."

"So, just keep calling you Rivers?"

"I use it all the time now," he said. "Besides, a lot of names are strange, right?"

I ignored that. "You really don't sell toilet seats, do you?"

"Urinal screens. Not anymore. But I did sell them for a while, right after I got out of the Army. I was out of sorts, not sure what to do with myself. My life was a mess. Sound familiar?"

I ignored that, too.

"And you really don't play the trombone."

"Oh, but I do. Learned it on the streets of New Orleans as a young man playing for tips. I learned you either get good at what you do and do it fast, or you go hungry."

"So you got good fast?" I asked.

"No. I joined the army."

CHAPTER 28

DETECTIVE WIGGINS CALLED while we plotted how to spend the day, and I agreed to meet him at the Sheriff's Office after Gwenn drove me to the rental car office to get a new set of wheels.

While I did my thing, Gwenn would drive to Fifth Avenue. There's a little shop that sells Haitian arts and crafts called The Lady From Haiti. Gwenn would ask the shop's owner to translate it for us, make sure we got the idioms right. Better to have it done by a real person than stumbling around online.

Lester would contact his people at The Third Eye with the passcode information Maria hid in her notebook. While we had the codes, we did not have the user IDs she might be using. I checked my email from her. The earliest was from her business address at *The Nation*. More recent emails were from the account we assigned to her at the Tropic Press. But we did not know any of her personal addresses, which were more likely to be used on some of the sites.

"If we could talk to her aunt it would speed things up," Lester said. "Odds are she has Maria's personal email. Maybe other useful things."

"Ricky hauling her off has made this more difficult," I said.

"Yes it has. I have her husband's contact information. He, technically, is our client. I'll call him, too."

"I thought Colonel Lake was going to call."

"He did. Left a message. No answer. I'll try again."

"Think he'll talk to you?"

"We'll find out. If not, I'd like to know why not? They gave us no explanation whatsoever for firing us. Something about all this just doesn't feel right."

We had two potential trails to follow:

* See what Edgard's note might tell us. That could be point, game, match right there.

* Hack Maria's accounts and see what we could find. Among the various parenthetical abbreviations on her list were the letters IC. We hoped that might mean iCloud. If she backed up to the cloud, it could be huge. Assuming somebody else hadn't already gotten there first. Lester assured us that the hackers at The Third Eye were even better than the Chinese and they most likely would discover a pathway for us quickly.

Gwenn and I listened to the radio on the drive to Naples. The shoot-out at the Mercato dominated the news. The stories seemed to follow the script Rankin said he would use. My name was not mentioned, but someone had speculated the "Good Samaritan" who came to Henderson's rescue might be an undercover cop. No idea where that came from. Listeners were invited to call in to chat. Manny from Estero said they should give a medal to Officer Garcia. Miss Anthelia from Bonita Beach, who identified herself as a psychic, said Detective Henderson would recover and that he, too, would get a medal.

When Wiggins called earlier, he told me Henderson was in the intensive care unit and his doctors said the next twenty-four hours would be critical, I hoped Miss Anthelia got it right. If so, maybe she could land a job at The Third Eye. Can't have too many psychics in the crime busting business.

After coverage of the shootout, the news switched from local to state. Tampa vice cops were concerned the upcoming End of Days

Convocation would lead to an influx of prostitutes downtown. Police were drawing up plans for "hooker-free zones" around the Tampa Bay Times Forum.

The convocation was the brainchild of the Rev. Lee Roy Chitango, who had been demonizing the tree-hugging, baby-seal saving, Caitlyn Jenner-worshiping hedonists who would be consumed in the apocalyptic end of days. Tickets for his convention were a thousand dollars a head, which included a lottery entry to escape the end of days on the soon-to-be-completed Ark II.

I kissed Gwenn goodbye in the parking lot of the car rental place on Seagate Drive.

"Good hunting," I said.

She gave me a thumbs-up and drove off. No mushy stuff, all business. I liked that.

There were no other customers at the counter when I walked in. It's like that in Naples once the season is over. Some days, you could shoot a cannon down the Tamiami Trail and not hit a single Rolls Royce.

The young woman behind the counter wore a green shirt under a black vest. Her nametag said "Cindy."

I pulled out my driver's license and a credit card. "Hi, Cindy," I said. "Any chance you guys have a car I can rent?"

"We do," she said enthusiastically and gave me a big smile, revealing a bit of an overbite.

"Happen to have any black Buick Regals?" I asked.

She turned to her computer terminal. She hummed to herself while she scanned their inventory, then said, "Oh."

"Oh?"

She looked around to make sure she couldn't be overhead. "I shouldn't tell you this," she said, "but we did have one, leased out of our airport location, but it was destroyed yesterday, over at the Mercato. Did you see it on the news? Big shootout, burning cars. Like something in the movies."

"That was your car?" I asked, innocently.

She looked down at the screen again. "Yes, our only black Regal."

"Wow, that's something," I said, lowering my voice a bit to mesh with her conspiratorial tone. "Were the police here?"

She nodded. Up and down, up and down. "My manager talked with a sheriff's detective. He wanted to know who rented the vehicle."

I leaned in and in a hushed voice asked, "Who was it?"

"Oh, I'm sorry, I can't give out that information," she said. "In fact, my manager told the detective the same thing. Said he would have to get a warrant."

"I'll bet that made the cop's day," I said.

She shook her head. "He was definitely not a happy camper."

"This detective, was he medium height, brown hair, copper colored oval glasses? Youngish guy?"

"How did you know?" she whispered.

"His name is Wiggins. Ring a bell?"

"Yes." It came out as a squeak. "Like Wiggins Pass, I remember."

Delnor-Wiggins Pass State Park is a pristine beach in northern Collier County, named after an early homesteader named Joe Wiggins. Maybe the detective was related.

"Do you know him?" she asked. She looked around again. "I didn't get to talk to him, but he's cute."

"I'm going to see him as soon as I get my car. Want I should tell him you said that?"

She blushed. Then nodded.

The door behind the counter opened to a small office. "Your boss back there?" I whispered.

She shook her head. "No, he's out. He takes lunch early. He should be back any minute."

"You know, getting a warrant is just a formality, right?"

She nodded hesitantly.

"If you could just tell me who rented that car, it would save everyone a lot of time. And I know Detective Wiggins would be very grateful to you."

She grimaced, clearly worried about her job.

"It would just give us a head start is all," I reassured her. "And we would never tell."

We.

Cindy pursed her lips and instinctively glanced down at the computer screen. Then her brow wrinkled.

"Hmm," she said. "A company rented it."

"A company?" I asked.

Her head bobbed up and down again.

"It's a funny name," she said, crinkling her nose. "FFFA PAC."

"That *is* a funny name. But surely, there has to be an authorized driver."

She looked back to the screen, but then the office door opened and a middle-aged man in a black and green polo shirt walked in. Cindy looked up and froze.

"How's it going, Cindy?" he asked.

She forced a smile. "Just fine." She glanced down at her computer terminal, hit a few keys, and I knew I'd gotten as much as I could.

She looked back up at me. "Now, let's see about that car you need…"

CHAPTER 29

I PHONED LESTER during my drive to the Sheriff's Office. I was behind the wheel of a Hyundai Santa Fe. Cindy upgraded me to a model with navigation, a panoramic sunroof, and heated and air-conditioned seats. The inventor of the seat cooler deserves the Noble Prize.

"You ever heard of a political action committee called FFFA?" I asked.

"You know how many PACs there are in America?" he said, giving me bored.

"Nope."

"Over four thousand."

"Wow. What a racket. Maybe I should start one."

"So what's with this PAC?" he asked.

"I charmed the girl at the counter over at Naples Car Rental. That's who she said rented the Buick those two thugs were driving."

"FFFA?"

"Well, that's what she got off her computer, but tell me something, Lester, you're a bad guy, you don't want anyone to trace you back through your car, do you?"

"I wouldn't. But I'm not a bad guy."

"Then again..." I paused, thinking about the events of yesterday afternoon.

"Then again, what?"

"Then again, maybe they figured tying off a loose end like me would be a cake walk. They didn't count on getting ambushed by Henderson and Garcia."

"And you, hoss. Give yourself some credit."

"Just trying to stay alive."

"Rubbish. You wanted to stay alive, you would have hightailed out of there. You were trying to kill them."

I didn't have anything to say to that.

Then Rivers added: "I like that about you. So does Colonel Lake."

"You've reported in."

"Yes. They're hacking Maria's accounts as we speak."

"I've been thinking about that," I said. "Maybe the password's a name, you know, based on the letters on the phone buttons."

"Good thought. Twenty of the alphabet's 26 letters are represented by 8675309. Virtually pointless to explore."

"How about Tommy Tutone."

"Who?"

"He sang it." I'd finally remembered. "The song is called *Jenny*. Jenny's phone number was eight six seven five three oh nine." I think Jenny or Jennifer or something like it could be Maria's middle name.

"You are so full of helpful suggestions. I will be sure to pass along all your insights to our technology team."

Smart ass.

I was in the left-hand lane on Tamiami Trail, heading southeast, where the highway bends toward Miami away from downtown Naples. A red Mercedes SL 550, a car costing over a hundred grand, shot over from the far right-hand lane and slid into the narrow space between me and a Chevy Tahoe then hit the brakes as traffic slowed for a red light.

Did he not know I was the newest driver in the Demolition Derby?

I smashed the brakes and gave the idiot some room. James Bond would have pulled his Walther PPK and shot out the Benz's tires. Kinsey Millhone would have done the same although it would have killed her eardrums. Jack Reacher would have driven to the driver's side window, rammed his fist through the glass, and crushed the driver's neck.

"So Lester, you never did say how Colonel Lake possessed all that intel on the Russian mafia."

Lester went quiet and I waited to see if he would answer. The Third Eye sees all and knows all but does not tell all.

The red Mercedes changed lanes again, no signal, of course, swerving back into the right lane. A BMW X3 laid its horn on him. The Benz driver was either drunk or a tourist. We get a lot of both and they aren't mutually exclusive.

"Budget cuts."

"Huh?" It took me a moment to reconnect the dots. "Could you be more enigmatic, please?"

"Because of budget constraints, the federal government increasingly offloads work to private contractors. Doesn't save the taxpayers any money. Actually, costs more. But keeps the books clean."

"Like Blackwater in Iraq."

"Precisely. We do a lot of intel work for Homeland Security, principally regarding foreign criminals operating on American soil. FBI used to handle all of that, but they are, justifiably, more focused on preventing the next nine-eleven."

"That's how Lake crossed paths with these Hangmen guys?"

"The Hangmen are freaks, but there are many bad guys out there who are far more worrisome. As Colonel Lake said, the Hangmen mainly occupy themselves killing other gangsters. For the most part, who cares, right?"

"But now, not so much."

"Yes, this has triggered additional interest. Colonel Lake briefed me last night while you were otherwise occupied playing bumper cars. The agency has been asked to step up intelligence gathering on the Hangmen."

"Wouldn't you guys have done that anyway with Maria missing?"

"Sure. But it is always nice to get paid a little something extra."

"Where are you now?" I asked.

"I was on the boat. It's as good a place to work as any, but a little warm. I opened the back door to get some ventilation. I'm taking Fred for a walk right now. We're over by that seashell museum."

"Hey, thanks, Lester."

"My pleasure. Fred is a very nice person. Better than most humans I know."

I had no argument with that.

"Oh, two guys from a glass company were here a little while ago. Said they were hired by the county. They removed your damaged window and took out the frame, too, so they would make a replacement. Custom job. Afraid it's going to be breezy on board for a couple of days."

At least something was getting fixed on that tug.

"I moved Mona onto the poop deck to make room for them," he said.

"You put some sun screen on her?"

He hung up.

I turned left at Airport-Pulling Road then right into the county government complex. There's an outdoor lot north of the courthouse and on the opposite end of the campus from the garage where we parked the day before. I spotted an empty space and cut across lanes to pull in and nearly collided with pickup truck headed straight for me. I'd forgotten that the aisles in the lot are one-way. The truck driver horned me and swerved around. Sheesh! How many cars did I want to wreck in one week?

I met Wiggins in the lobby and he escorted me through security back to his desk.

"How's Henderson doing?" I asked.

"Out of ICU. He's going to make it."

"Can he have visitors yet?" I asked. I still wasn't sure I trusted him completely, but he did come to my rescue. I wanted to drop by and say thanks. Maybe, bring flowers? Or a fresh box of bullets? Although, in retrospect, he never got a shot off.

"You can call and see. I got the number right here." He tore a page off a yellow notepad and copied the information for me.

We picked up the conversation where we left off at the Mercato, although I'd already given him a full rundown of what happened in the parking lot. He said he just had a few more questions.

"You ever see those guys before?" he asked.

I recognized the big guy. He tried to poison my okra."

Wiggins gave me a what-the-fuck look, and I told him the story.

"Anything else you can tell me about them?"

"No. But the sheriff said the guy Garcia plugged was in Edgard Dominique's cell block the night he was hanged."

Wiggins set his pen down and leaned back. "Yeah, he mentioned that at the press conference, too. We were keeping that close to the vest. It surprised me."

"It would get out eventually, anyway," I said.

"Sure."

"Let me backtrack a bit," I said. I told Wiggins how I got the keys to Maria's condo from her aunt and that I searched the place looking for anything looking out of place. And when I left I spotted their car.

He listened attentively, scribbling notes, letting me talk, but when I finished he shook his head.

"That's a crime scene," he said. "You shouldn't have been there."

"Wasn't taped off and Geneva gave me permission," I said.

He tapped his pen on the notepad a few times, thinking. "Find anything?"

Lester and I anticipated this question. Would I tell the truth or would I obfuscate? As usual, when we discussed it, I ran through all the on-the-one-hands-this and on-the-other-hands that. Lucky I only have two hands. Then Lester stopped me.

"You have to tell the truth."

"You're right."

"But that doesn't mean we have to turn the notebook over immediately," he said. "Wouldn't mind a head start. How about you?"

"Agreed."

I told Wiggins about digging the plastic bag from the bottom of the coffee can and finding the small notebook in which Maria had transcribed the phone message from Gwenn, and that The Third Eye was hacking Maria's online accounts even as we spoke.

"A coffee can, you say?"

"Yes."

He stuck the end of his pen between his teeth and chewed on it for a few moments, frowning, as if what he just heard gave him indigestion.

"You should have turned it over right away," he finally said.

"My bad. Must have slipped my mind, playing Demolition Derby and all."

I could have said that if the Sheriff's Office had done its job properly, they would have found it before me.

He rubbed forehead as if he were in pain. "Where's the notebook now?" he asked.

"You getting a headache? Want I should find you some aspirin?"

"The notebook?"

"Oh, that. Gwenn has it."

"She needs to turn it over."

"Hmmm."

"What?"

"The notebook could be a problem," I said.

"Why?" He gave me a dead-eye stare.

"It's a communication between a lawyer and her client. It may be privileged. Not sure Gwenn will give it up. Not sure you can make her without a court order."

As if I were on his side. That darned Gwenn.

"We'll see," he said.

On the face of it, I didn't have a problem giving him the notebook. But I also didn't know what the message written in Creole said. I wanted to do everything possible to help find Maria, assuming she was still alive, but I liked Lester's idea that we should give ourselves a head start. Rankin, and by extension his department, had proven themselves unreliable and untrustworthy.

Wiggins said he would drive to Goodland and meet me there after he made a few phone calls. He escorted me to the front door.

I asked him if he could check the file for Geneva's contact information. He said he'd bring the number with him when he met me in Goodland. He was stalling, of course, Maybe looking for something to trade. Clever.

"Oh, Wiggins," I said, as I walked outside. "You remember a girl at the rental car place when you were there earlier today?"

"Yeah. You were there? After me?"

I nodded. "Needed new wheels. Also discovered the ID on who rented the car Beavis and Butthead were driving yesterday."

"What? How'd you do that?"

"Used my Jedi powers. It's a political action committee: FFFA PAC."

"What's FFFA stand for?"

"Beats the shit out of me."

"So much for the Force."

"Oh, I promised that girl, her name's Cindy, that I would mention to you she thinks you're cute. Bet you don't get that every day."

"More than you would think," he said.

Everybody's a comedian.

THE STRANGE FILES

Gators, Crocs, and Panthers, Oh My

By Alexander Strange

Tropic©Press

This edition of The Strange Files is dedicated to animals in the news:

Rescue workers fished an elderly woman out of a South Florida canal where she was discovered thrashing about earlier this week. Police speculated she tried to commit suicide by drawing the attention of one of several alligators that inhabit the canal.

"This was a first for me," Collier County Sheriff's Deputy Arnolfo Garcia said. "I've heard of suicide by cop, but this was my first suicide by gator."

Speaking of reptiles, the Turkey Point Nuclear Generating Station reported that the warm water in its cooling canals have spawned a record number of crocodile hatchlings. They offered no comment on how many of those newborns might be crossbreeds with the aggressive Nile crocodile.

Gators and crocs are fearsome, but they are not the only reptilian predators in the Everglades. Wildlife officials released photographs this week of a monstrous boa constrictor discovered in the swamp that burst open after swallowing a Key Deer.

And wildlife officials, intent on saving the endangered Florida panther, announced plans to capture some of the big cats and move them to new areas of the state to expand their range.

The Florida panther was nearly hunted to extinction. So few remained that heart defects from inbreeding were killing them faster than bullets. That's when somebody got creative and imported female Texas cougars to save the species. And it worked. The new crossbreeds are so tough one scientist called them "the Arnold Schwarzeneggers of cougars."

This was before Arnold got caught with the scullery maid, so no offense intended to the big cats. Nor shall we stoop to a discussion of catting around.

STRANGE FACT: Cats have more than one hundred vocal sounds; dogs have about ten.

Weirdness knows no boundaries. Keep up at *www.TheStrangeFiles.com*. Contact Alexander Strange at Alex@TheStrangeFiles.com.

CHAPTER 30

I WALKED BACK to the rental, pushed the Hyundai's start button, and waited while the AC performed its magic. I slipped out my cellphone and checked for messages. I'd received three calls but the phone hadn't rung. What the heck?

I checked the little switch on the side of the iPhone and saw it had been turned to silent mode. Jostling around in my cargo shorts, it does that sometimes.

The first message was from Gwenn. She had driven downtown to the Haitian gift shop on Fifth Avenue but the owner took the day off. Said she'd figure something out and call me later.

The second call was from Edwina. I'd missed the deadline for my column. Yes, yes, she understood things were rough, but now was not the time to slack off. We all needed to pull our weight, yadda, yadda, yadda.

I'd already written that day's submission. Two more columns were also in the pipeline, part of my emergency stock of material. I retrieved the columns from the Dropbox folder on my cell phone and pushed SEND.

The third call was from a Miami area code. I hoped it might be Geneva. I tapped the redial button.

"Yes?" a man's voice replied after the third ring.

"Hello," I said, polite, but disappointed not to hear Geneva's voice. "We received a call from this number." I didn't identify myself. It was probably a scammer. Or worse, a Jehovah's Witness.

"Is this Alexander Strange?" Solicitous. He spoke with a slight foreign accent I couldn't place. Fucking telemarketers.

"No, I'm his personal assistant." I crack myself up sometimes. "And if you're selling magazine subscriptions, Mr. Strange is not interested."

"Oh, no," he said. Cheerful. "Not magazines."

"You're not a Jehovah's Witness, are you? If you are, I can tell you right now you're wasting your time."

"No. No. Delivery service." he said.

Oh, good. My camera and iPad.

"Is Mr. Strange there now?" He read off the street address of the vacant lot where the *Miss Demeanor* was drydocked. "Someone will have to sign."

"Someone will be there," I assured him. If not me, then Mona.

There's no left turn out of the county lot at Airport-Pulling Road, so I turned right, then U-turned when I cleared the median. At the light, another left and I entered the Tamiami Trail headed toward Goodland. About a hundred yards ahead something caught my eye. Yellow. A Volkswagen Beetle, the same color Bug that Maria drove.

I dialed Rivers again.

"Now what?" he answered.

"I'm following a yellow Volkswagen," I said.

"Why?"

"Maria drove a yellow Beetle. It's missing."

"I'm aware. But do you know how many yellow Volkswagens there are in Naples?" he asked.

"Yes. Thirty-seven."

"Fuckhead."

"Mr. Fuckhead, to you." I heard what could have been a chuckle.

"I'm going to try to catch up and see if I can read the plate. Hang on."

The Volkswagen chugged along in the passing lane, driving about five miles per hour below the speed limit. I couldn't close the distance between us because of intervening vehicles. A Harley soft tail hugged the Bug's rear. Now cars behind me were snugging close to me then passing on the right. One elderly woman in a Caddy shot me the bird as she passed.

What do you say to that?

I could see the back of the VeeDub driver's head through the rear window. Couldn't tell anything about him, though. Maybe a her. Up ahead, at the approaching light, left-lane traffic would be forced to turn. The Bug driver slid over to the right-hand lane. No signal. But why should he be different? The Harley turned left.

The VeeDub's lane change allowed me to pull closer and I caught the plate.

I read the numbers and letters to Rivers.

"Got it," Rivers said.

"How long will it take to see if it's Maria's?" I asked.

"One nanosecond."

"How can you do that?"

"Downloaded a copy of the missing persons report Lawrence Marcano filed on Maria. Her tag is on it."

Dammit. Why didn't I think of that?

"And...?"

"Maria has a vanity plate."

"What is it?" I asked, deflated. Wouldn't it have been cool to have stumbled onto her car driving down the highway? Maybe I'd win the lottery, too.

"Hmmm."

"What?"

"This is very annoying."

"What?" The guy drove me crazy.

"Maria's plate is JENNY867."

"Modesty prevents me from telling you I told you so."

I made the turn south on Collier Boulevard. The yellow Volkswagen did not, continuing southeast on the Tamiami Trail. A few decades ago, before the completion of Interstate 75, a.k.a. Alligator Alley, the Trail was the only west coast route between Tampa and Miami, hence the unusual name.

"Hey, Lester," I said, "somebody's going to be delivering a package in a few. If I'm not there in time you may have to sign for it."

"Now what are you talking about?"

I told him about the phone call.

"Meet me in the parking lot across from Stan's." Then he abruptly hung up.

Like what? He couldn't do me a solid?

Traffic thinned southbound on Collier Boulevard. The road is a straight shot through swampland. I passed the entrance to Isles of Capris on the right after a few minutes and then crossed the Jolly Bridge onto Marco Island. I hooked a left on Barfield Road and another left on San Marco Road, passing block after block of houses on canals leading to the Gulf, most with boats tied up at backyard docks. I slowed at a "Bobcat Crossing" sign and again at a "Tortoise Crossing" warning. There were no "Snowbird Crossing" signs. They're not an endangered species.

In ten minutes, I turned right onto Goodland Drive and slowed down. Water covered the narrow road for about thirty yards. The bay, on the left, overflowed the road into the swamp on my right. I carefully entered the stream and kept going. At one point I thought I might stall as the water rose nearly to the door jam. But I finally cleared. I couldn't have made it in the Sebring. Goodland had become its own island until the king tide receded.

Lester stood next to a sheriff's cruiser in the grassy parking lot across from Stan's holding Fred on a leash. I walked over, squatted down, and gave Fred a pat on the head.

I looked in the window of the patrol car. The deputy was young, female, with brown hair and a stern face. She stuck her hand out.

"You Strange?" she asked.

"So I've been told."

"Name's Henderson. Linda Henderson."

"What a coincidence," I said.

"Nope. He's my granddad."

"How's he doing?" I asked.

"Talked to him earlier. He's a tough old fart. He's going to make it."

If I ever have grandchildren, please Lord, don't let them call me a fart.

"We have three units rotating around Goodland for the next several days," she said. "I'm off in a few. Deputy Templeton will take my place. He'll come by and introduce himself."

"Thanks," I said. "Actually met him last night."

"Good. We got you covered," she said, then rolled up her window to contain the AC.

Henderson's granddaughter. Small world.

I heard a truck engine off to my left and I turned to see a white panel van pulling past Stan's. It stopped in front of the chain link fence separating the boatyard from the street. Water was dripping from its underside.

We could hear, but could not see, the sliding door on the far side of the van open. There were muffled voices. A man dressed in black jeans and a black T-shirt and carrying something long and cylindrical walked over to the gate and swung it open.

Odd looking package, I thought. Not my new camera. Maybe a new crankshaft for the boat? That notion vanished when he raised the cylinder to his shoulder and sighted down the tube where a bell-shaped device protruded from the end. The man in black pulled a trigger and there was a deafening crack and a burst of flame and smoke as a projectile hurtled toward the *Miss Demeanor*.

Something hit me in the back and I landed face-first in the dirt. It was Rivers.

"RPG," he said in my ear, his voice hushed.

I looked up and the rocket propelled grenade left a smoke trail streaking right through the empty window in the bow and out the open back door. Never touched the boat at all, but Mona teetered back and forth, buffeted by the projectile's wake. The smoke trail arced across the marina and into the bay.

"Get the fuck off me, Lester," I yelled, rolling over, trying to stand.

He grabbed the waistline of my cargo shorts and pulled me down. He was stronger than I imagined. "Stay low," he said. Calm. Like this wasn't his first time to deal with a lunatic holding a bazooka. Guess it wasn't.

The man in black was swearing. Something Slavic, maybe Russian. He ran back to the van. Maybe going for more ammo.

He never got the chance.

The rear wheels on Deputy Linda Henderson's cruiser begin spinning, throwing up a shit storm of dirt and grass as she dropped the hammer and accelerated toward the van on a collision course. But a split second before she would have smashed it, the van lurched forward, burning rubber and heading east on Harbor Place, the little road in front of the boatyard. Henderson hit her brakes but still slammed into the fence, and the cruiser's cow-catcher became entangled in the chain link when she tried to reverse out of it.

I knew Harbor Place ended in a few yards at Papaya Street. If the van turned left, it would become ensnared in a labyrinth of one-lane streets that would lead back to where we were. It didn't. It turned right toward Pear Tree Avenue. That, in turn, would dead end where the van driver would face another choice. Left would lead to yet another series of cul-de-sacs. If the driver turned right, he would hit Goodland

Drive and have a clear path off the island. I knew this route well. I ran it almost every day.

I tore free from Lester and sprinted over to Henderson's stalled cruiser. She was wrestling a tangle of chain link trying to open her door. I pulled on the door and grabbed her hand and helped her out. "This way," I yelled.

She unholstered her sidearm as I led her toward the intersection of Harbor Place and Goodland Drive, right in front of Stan's. "They gotta come by here," I shouted.

"You don't have to yell," she said. Calm.

Everybody was calm but me.

We saw the van skidding around the corner to our left and then it turned onto Goodland Drive heading away from us.

"Dammit!" Henderson said.

"Come on," I shouted, and began running after the van.

"Are you nuts?" she said, but followed.

"High water," I shouted back at her. Tide's rising fast. They may stall out."

Twenty yards ahead, the van plowed into the swamp water covering the road sending up huge wakes on both sides. And then it rolled to a stop, wobbling a bit from side to side, momentarily floating.

I love it when I'm right.

Henderson sprinted ahead toward the left-rear of the van, assumed a two-handed shooting stance, legs spread.

"Police. Come out of there. Hands in the air," she yelled. Just like on TV.

We heard the sliding door open on the other side of the van. She sloshed over and turned the corner to face the rocketeer. Only this time he brought up a rifle.

Henderson didn't hesitate. She fired four shots in rapid succession and the man flew backwards and splashed into the water.

We heard the driver's door open, but couldn't see it at our angle.

Henderson began to wade over to the other side of the van, but I caught her arm.

"What?" she hissed at me, never taking her eye off the vehicle.

"Look down," I said, softly. "But don't move."

She glanced at her feet and saw the snake. It was an enormous python, more than fifteen feet long, swimming from one side of the street to the other.

"I fucking hate snakes," she growled, never taking her eyes off the van. "Tell me when it's gone."

It took only seconds for the python to slither across the submerged asphalt. "We're clear," I said, and we continued wading our way around to the other side of the van. Henderson closed on the rear bumper, took a breath, then threw herself around, following her gun.

Nothing.

She turned to me and put a finger to her lips.

Off to our left, we could hear splashing.

"He's trying to escape through the mangroves," I said.

Henderson keyed her radio and called it in, asking for air support to find the fleeing man.

Then she turned to me. "I'm going after him."

"No," I said and grabbed her shoulder to hold her back.

"Don't tell me no!" she hissed and shook off my grip. Who did I think I was, anyway, interfering with a cop?

I seized her right bicep and pulled her to me. Maybe a little more forcefully than I had intended. I leaned into her. "You are not going in there. You have no backup. And there are snakes and gators and maybe even crocs. I've already got one Henderson on my conscience. I won't have another."

There was more splashing, not far from our line of sight. Henderson pulled away from me and turned. She aimed toward the sound, and shouted, "This is the police. Come out of there right now with your hands in the air."

A pistol cracked and the driver's side window of the van shattered.

Henderson rose to her full height and opened fire, emptying her magazine, aiming down toward the waterline, making sure her rounds didn't go flying off into God-knows-where in Goodland. The splashing in the swamp stopped.

"You think you got him?" I asked.

"We'll see."

Then she looked at me and cocked her head. "Do you know what happened to the last man who grabbed me?"

I imagined my life as a eunuch, then decided to change the subject. "Let's check out your first victim."

We waded back to the passenger side of the van. The rocketeer lay submerged.

"Should we drag him to high ground?" I asked.

"I guess."

We each grabbed a foot and tugged. He left a bloody trail in the water from four small entry wounds in his chest, four gaping exit wounds in his back.

Deputy Linda Henderson had stood in the middle of a flooded road facing killers armed with rifles and rockets, two against one, and she shot one of them to death and chased the other into a swamp filled with man-eating monsters and, in all likelihood, shot him to death, too.

Note to self: Do not fuck with the Hendersons.

We could hear sirens approaching. And in the distance, I could see a chopper.

"Freaking Annie Oakley." I patted Henderson on the back. "Where'd you learn to shoot?"

"Spent half my childhood on the range," she said.

By the time a wrecker arrived to remove the stalled van, the tide was receding. In addition to a platoon of cruisers, Wiggins pulled up in his unmarked Crown Vic. So did Garcia in his own car—he'd been suspended pending the pro-forma investigation that's always held after a shooting, but somehow he got the word.

I introduced them to Lester. And to Fred, whom Lester protected through all of this.

Mrs. Overstreet wandered over from the Little Bar where she had been waiting tables. Half the residents of the island were already there, gawking.

"Alex, what is going on here. This looks like a war zone," she said.

"I'm afraid I may have made a few enemies."

"I never thought of you as a troublemaker," she said. "You've always seemed like such a nice boy. Now look at this. All the police. My goodness." She gave me the once-over. Her look was less scornful than concerned. But more for Fred than me, I gathered.

"Give me that," she said to Lester. He handed over Fred's leash.

"Freddie will be staying with me until you get this straightened out," she said. She turned on her heels and walked back to the Drop Anchor trailer park.

I felt a stab of guilt. I liked Mrs. Overstreet, but now I felt like I had disappointed her. I had brought all this violence to Goodland. I looked around at the faces of the rubberneckers. I saw worry and concern. They had welcomed me to this little patch of civilization in the Everglades. I felt like I had betrayed their kindness.

Lester stepped over. He'd read my mind. "Shake it off, Alexander. By tomorrow, they'll be hounding you for details, buying you drinks. This is the most excitement Goodland's seen since the time that cross-dresser ran for queen of the Mullet Festival."

The next several hours was a law enforcement and media circus. Sheriff's cruisers set up a checkpoint on Goodland Drive and turned back non-residents. That included three TV vans and several carloads of reporters and photographers. They were unable to stop two TV choppers from shooting aerials from overhead.

A van loaded with crime scene investigators showed up to

photograph and secure evidence. One of the women—at that time, all the CSIs in Collier were female—approached Linda Henderson and took her gun, unloaded it, and bagged it.

Ponytail spotted me and walked over.

"You know, we could use a day off now and then. Could you hold off killing anybody else for a while." She turned and returned toward the rocketeers' van, but looked back over her shoulder. "I still need your prints."

A UPS delivery truck was allowed through and it pulled up to the boatyard.

"What happened here?" the driver asked as I signed for my new camera and iPad.

"Couple guys were impersonating a delivery service," I said. "Cops shot one of them and ran the other off."

The driver gulped and the color drained from his face. Good thing he wore brown.

Gwenn got caught at the checkpoint, and called me on my cell. I asked Detective Wiggins to escort her in. I should have known better. Wiggins told the deputies at the checkpoint to clear her, but he insisted on getting in the car with her to direct her to a parking spot.

I walked over to her car and she jumped out and gave me a neck-breaking hug.

"What the fuck?" she whispered in my ear. "How many did you kill this time? And what's with this?" She backed away, brushing grass and dirt from her blouse.

"Not me. Annie Oakley over there," I said, nodding to Linda Henderson.

She glanced in Henderson's direction and frowned.

Uh, oh.

"You two know each other?" I asked innocently.

"Oh, yeah."

She turned around to face me and I felt her hand slide down into my undershorts.

"We could try to slip off somewhere," I said.

"Don't I wish," she said. "That detective, Wiggins, insisted I turn the notebook over to him." Wiggins exited the car and walked toward us, talking on his cell phone. "Honestly, I really don't care," Gwenn said, "but I wanted to talk to you first."

"This the notebook?" I asked, patting the front of my shorts. Didn't feel that big.

"No. I learned my lesson. It's just a copy of the note. The entire notebook's in a safe at my office."

"So tell Wiggins the truth," I said.

The detective stepped up to us.

"The notebook?" he asked Gwenn.

"I don't have it on me," she said. "It's locked in a safe at my office."

She turned her back on him. "Sorry I took so long. After I locked up the notebook, my new bosses wanted to talk. They're concerned about what I've gotten myself into."

Wiggins interrupted. "I need the notebook, Ms. Giroux." Before he could continue, his cell phone rang again and he walked a few steps away to take the call.

"Let's go," she whispered.

"What did the note say?" I asked as we walked in the direction of the boatyard.

"I'm afraid it still doesn't make a lot of sense, but I'll tell you what I found out when we're alone."

Alone was exactly what we were not.

The medical examiner arrived. Then the sheriff and more deputies. Agents from ATF and the FBI finally showed up and immediately began bickering over which federal agency would take over. There were so many cops fighting for jurisdiction they practically needed a peace negotiator.

Finally, Sheriff Rankin suggested they take their moveable feast over to Stan's, which with the blockade of Goodland, was nearly deserted. Garcia scared up some water for everyone. Gwenn, Lester and I were told to stick around, they would have questions for us.

I intercepted an ATF guy carrying the rocket launcher in a large, clear plastic bag. "What is it?"

"It's a Russian-made RPG-27 *Tavolga*. One shot. Anti-personnel explosives. Using a RShG-1 thermobaric rocket," he said.

"Ah, just what I thought."

The ATF guy laughed and continued walking.

After the cops huddled among themselves for what seemed like an hour, they finally asked me to come talk to them. I passed Linda Henderson on her way out.

"How'd it go?"

"I told them you were a big help," she said.

"Aw, shucks."

"Hey, I'm sticking around a bit. Before I go, I've got something to give you," she said.

I wondered what that was about.

The cops were gathered around a circular white plastic patio table. Before they could start grilling me, I asked if they'd identified the dead rocketeer.

The FBI guys were surprisingly forthcoming. Said they'd printed him, photographed him, and emailed it all to Washington." If he's in the system, we'll have an ID shortly," one of them said.

Just like in the movies. Some things actually do happen fast.

I opened the recording app on my iPhone and set it in front of me on the table. The FBI and ATF agents were recording, too, and they raised no objections, which I found a little surprising. Feebs I'd encountered elsewhere were pretty stiff. These guys seemed more chill. Maybe it's a South Florida thing. I wanted the recording for my own notetaking, and I would also transmit it to Edwina Mahoney just in case.

I started my story with the day I met Maria at the Lee Roy Chitango press conference and included everything except the details of my evening at Maria's condo and my time with Gwenn. Otherwise, I left nothing out.

After I told my story, they began asking questions: Who would kidnap Maria? Any ideas on the contents of Edgard's computer? Why did I think they were hunting me? Why were they being so aggressive?

"And what's the big deal with you?" asked Rankin. "You know something you haven't told us?"

That was for show, playing tough cop. I'd felt a little sorry for him earlier. Now I felt foolish for doing so. Once a shit weasel, always a shit weasel.

"I've given it to you straight," I said.

"Then we're missing something," an FBI agent named Cao said.

"Like maybe they think I have something and they're wrong?" I asked.

"Or maybe they think you have something and you don't know you have it."

I shook my head.

"It has to be about the list. I don't have the list. You have the computer. I gather you have not recovered the list."

Cao hesitated before answering, but then said, "That's right."

We all thought about it for a moment.

"So, maybe, they think Maria Martinez got the list and somehow shared it with you," Cao said.

"And why would they think that?" I asked.

"Maybe because she told them that," Wiggins said.

We all stared at him.

"Maybe it's keeping her alive."

"That could explain the attacks," Cao said. "But it wouldn't be very smart."

"How so?" I asked.

Cao leaned back, stretched his arms behind his head, and stared into the starlit sky for a moment gathering his thoughts. "The problem with just killing you is the list could still be out there. Maybe that's why they confronted you in the parking lot yesterday—they didn't want to kill you, they wanted to grab you."

"And today?" asked Wiggins.

"Maybe a two-for-one?" Rankin said. "Take you out and if the list was on the boat, it goes up in flames with you." He might be a shit weasel, but he wasn't entirely stupid.

"Or maybe you guys are overthinking it," I said. "Today wasn't the first time they tried to ice me, remember." I had told them about the poisoned okra, how that fuckwad Dombrowski almost killed my dog.

"Fair point," Cao said. "Maybe they're just stupid."

Some heads nodded.

Wiggins asked about the notebook again. I told him Gwenn would get it for him tomorrow.

When they were done, they asked me to send Gwenn in.

"They're going to ask you about it," I told her on my way out. "I said you'd get it for them tomorrow."

"And when they ask me what it said?"

"Again, tell the truth. It doesn't make any sense."

"And tomorrow?"

"Tomorrow's another day."

CHAPTER 31

THE SUN HAD set and the party began to break up. Gwenn took me by the hand. "I don't want you to spend the night out here," she said.

I pulled her into me and held her. "Go home," I whispered into her ear. "I'll be all right, and you'll be safer away from me."

"I'm afraid. I don't want to be alone right now," she said.

Linda Henderson lingered nearby and caught some of that. "You guys have nothing to worry about," she said. "They found the other body, ten yards from where the truck stalled, in about two feet of water."

"Jesus," I said. "You killed both of them."

She shook her head. "He was crushed by a python and drowned."

"The python you didn't shoot. So you got him either way."

She waved her hand dismissively. "Like I said. Things should be calm tonight. There will be a deputy out front of your place and Garcia and I are spending the night here, too."

"But you're off duty, right? Pending a shooting review?"

"Yeah, so's Garcia. We got nothin' better to do."

I was touched; Gwenn not so much. In fact, I sensed a very real possibility she might throttle Henderson.

"All right," Gwenn relented. "We'll be safe enough here."

"So you're staying?" I asked, stupidly.

"Why, yes, I think I will," she said then turned to Henderson and gave her the stink eye.

I couldn't wait to hear the story behind all of that.

Lester walked over and suggested the remaining stragglers head over to the Little Bar.

"Drinks are on The Third Eye," he said.

Wiggins and Garcia joined him, but Gwenn and I said we were calling it a night.

"We'll regroup in the morning," I told Lester.

Linda Henderson motioned toward us as we walked back to the trawler. Gwenn and I were holding hands and she tightened her grip but said nothing.

"Heading back to the boat?" Henderson asked.

"I've got to check on Mona and Spock," I said. I gave her a smile. She gave me confused. And I remembered she had never met my shipmates.

"Come over here for a second," she said. "I've got something for you."

Gwenn and I walked over to her cruiser. The car had been freed from the chain link fence and was scratched up. Henderson reached into the back seat and pulled out a shoulder holster rig with a semi-automatic pistol inside.

"You know how to use one of these?" she asked.

"Yeah," I said, "although it's been years since my uncle took me to target practice."

Henderson popped the clip, showed it to me, and slid it back in the handle. "You pull the slider to load a round into the chamber," she said, then did it. She popped the clip out again and then ejected the round. She loaded the bullet back into the clip and then reinserted it.

"You have to use this," Henderson said, "aim for the center of body mass and don't stop pulling the trigger until the target is down."

Target.

"Try not to kill anybody else. Even most experienced cops can't hit shit much beyond ten yards."

Most, but not her.

"I didn't think police officers were allowed to loan out their service weapons," I said.

"That's right. We're not. And this isn't. It's grandpa's, but not his department piece. When I talked to him this morning, he asked me to go by his house and get it out of his gun safe and give it to you."

"Don't I need a permit or something?" I asked.

"You kill somebody," she said, "make sure it's a bad guy."

CHAPTER 32

WE WERE BACK aboard the *Miss Demeanor*. I'd brought Mona inside and duct-taped a black plastic garbage bag over the missing window in the bow. A hint of rocket propellant lingered in the cabin's air. Acrid. A marked sheriff's cruiser sat outside the damaged boatyard fence.

"Gwenn, you gotta tell me, what's the deal with you and Henderson."

"Whatever do you mean, sugah?" she replied in a faux Southern belle accent.

Her back was to me, mixing cocktails for us at the galley, so I couldn't see her face when she said it.

"Oh, please."

Gwenn finished topping off the Cuba Libres with a final dash of Coke and set them on the little table in the lounge. She raised her drink and we tinked glasses.

"I've had two run-ins with her," she said. "On both occasions, Henderson was the arresting officer of young men I represented. One for burglary, the other for domestic assault. They both told similar stories of being treated roughly by her. My burglar had a gash on his forehead where he claimed she slammed him into the doorframe of her cruiser when she placed him in the back seat. The other guy, the one arrested for assault, said she threatened to, quote-unquote, shoot his balls off if he ever hit a woman again."

"She *is* quite a shot," I said, realizing it was exactly the wrong thing to say as soon as the words left my lips. But Gwenn surprised me.

"From what we saw today, I couldn't argue with you. However, when I brought both of those complaints to the court on behalf of my clients, she not only denied them—which I expected—she filed formal complaints against me with the Bar."

"How could she do that?" I asked.

"Anyone can for any reason. But she accused me of manufacturing the accusations to win leniency for my clients. In other words, she accused me of lying to the court."

"Oh."

"Yeah."

She took another drink. "But fuck her. I've got something to show you."

Gwenn leaned over and pushed me back in my chair. For a brief and exciting moment, I thought we were about to initiate festivities. Instead, she slipped her hand into the front of my shorts and extracted the note she'd hidden there.

"Unfortunately, none of this makes sense," she said. "Maria's question to Edgard Dominique was straightforward and easily translatable. It reads: 'Was that your computer?'"

"Good question."

"Yes, but Maria didn't know Edgard already admitted he stole it. But his answer is stupid: *Kaka epi ale.*"

Which means what?" I asked.

"Roughly, go poop."

"Poop?"

"Yes."

I examined the hand writing for a moment and then asked, "But there are three words here not two."

She nodded. "There is a Haitian woman who works at Judd and

Holkamp. One of the secretaries. She said, literally, it reads poop and go."

"Kaka is poop? I thought a kaka is a bird in New Zealand."

"It may be, but in Haitian Creole it means to take a bowel movement."

"Poop."

"Yes."

"That's what she said, 'poop'?"

"Yes, and she seemed a little embarrassed about it. She wore a cross and I got the sense she might be religious. She actually crossed herself after translating it for me."

"Poop and go. Dump and go. Crap and go. Shit and go."

I caught my breath.

"SHIT AND GO!" I shouted, startling Gwenn. She jumped back, bumping into Spock and spilling some of her drink. Spock said nothing. Typical.

"What?" Her voice sounded nervous.

"Shit and go? You've never heard that?"

She shook her head.

"How about Chitango?"

"Ohhhh."

Let's Hear It for the Gulf of America

By Alexander Strange

Tropic©Press

State Rep. Hayworth Stephens has proposed a bill in the Texas State Legislature to rename the Gulf of Mexico the Gulf of America.

Stephens, a Democrat, said he proposed the bill to make fun of his more conservative colleagues "who want to slam all minorities, but especially Hispanics, and especially all those Mexican rapists and murderers storming across our borders."

But not everyone gets the joke.

Florida state Sen. Lamar Hillcrest of Panama City, heard about it and now has proposed an identical bill in the Florida Legislature.

"It's time to stand up for America," he said in a press release announcing the proposal. "And that starts right here on our shoreline. It's not Mexico's Gulf, it's America's."

I called Stephens at his office in Austin and asked him what he thought of that.

"Well, I suppose imitation is the sincerest form of flattery," he said, "but, like, is he for real? Even the dumbasses here in Austin knew it was a joke."

When Stephens isn't legislating, he makes his living as a funeral director, an occupation not well known for humor. And he's an amateur magician.

"I just like saying abra-cadaver."

STRANGE FACT: Mondays are the busiest days for funeral homes. More heart attacks happen on the first day of the work week than any other.

Weirdness knows no boundaries. Keep up at *www.TheStrangeFiles.com*. Contact Alexander Strange at Alex@TheStrangeFiles.com.

CHAPTER 33

LEE MEMORIAL HOSPITAL is an hour north of Goodland in downtown Fort Myers. It is the regional trauma center for southwest Florida, where the victims of major accidents and gunshot wounds are transported. And it is where Detective Jim Henderson had been transferred from Intensive Care to a private room. I was doing 75 on I-75 heading there. I wanted to thank Henderson for saving my bacon, and to tell him how sorry I was that he got shot. I also wanted to ask him if he wanted his gun back.

Gwenn and I had spent a restless night, both of us feeling exposed and vulnerable on the boat. Me feeling guilty and stupid for dragging her into all of this. She torn between being loyal and having the *kaka* scared out of her. That's what happens when the adrenalin finally leeches out of your system: Reality sets in.

I slipped out of the berth at sunrise and tip-toed to the galley. I thought for a moment about going for a morning run, but I couldn't leave her alone on the trawler. Imagine her reaction if she awoke and I was AWOL. I did that to another woman once, and things didn't turn out so swell. Not that I'm superstitious or anything. Not that I felt any anxiety about jogging through Goodland with crazed Russian killers lurking in the mangroves or anything.

I needn't have worried.

"Hey," she called up from the berth.

"Yo."

"I need coffee."

When the Keurig finished its magic, I took two mugs below.

"You know Lester's right about all those K-cups," she said.

"You, too?"

She had a pillow propped behind her, basking in the pink light of dawn seeping through the portholes. She pulled the sheet up to her neck and pinned it in place under her arms. Either she was being modest or her body language was suggesting she needed a security blanket. I handed her the Wonder Woman mug and sat down on the berth beside her.

"How come you got Bruce Wayne and I get Diana Prince?" she asked. Cute. She knew their secret identities.

"Wanna trade?"

Gwenn blew on the coffee and took a sip. "Nah. I like Wonder Woman."

As we sipped our coffee we plotted our day.

"First things first," I said, "we're off this tug."

She gave me big eyes and nodded eagerly. The sheet slipped a bit down her chest exposing more of her alabaster skin and freckles to the early morning light. A hint of cleavage revealed itself.

"I'm sorry, Gwenn, we shouldn't have spent the night here. At the very least, I should have insisted you go home."

She shook her head no, and her eyes turned moist. She pulled the sheet back up.

I didn't say anything for a beat, letting her compose herself.

"Don't do that," she said, her voice tight.

"Do what?" I asked, stupidly.

"We're in this together."

Oh.

I took the mug out of her hands and set it on the narrow shelf by the bed. I held her in my arms for a full minute, then I gently kissed her on the lips and lowered her back onto her pillow.

"You've been amazing. I don't know what I would have done without you. Thank you."

She nodded.

"But I may not be back tonight."

"Why not?" She gave me curious instead of hurt.

"You ever see that movie with Ben Stiller, *Night at the Museum*?"

She nodded.

"I'm thinking I'm going to drive over to Fort Myers, visit Henderson, then head over to Chitango's place, look around, see what I can find."

"And spend the night?"

"Edgard's note indicated the laptop belonged to the Sermonator, but from his note it sounded as if he didn't like him so much, calling him Shit-and-Go. Be nice to know exactly what his relationship was with His Holiness."

"How are you going to do that?"

"Not sure, exactly. But, for starters, I thought I'd spend the afternoon there, maybe chat up the help, see if anyone remembers Edgard. I'll need to get a photo of him to show around. Could you email that to me?"

"Sure," she said, "but what's that got to do with spending the night?"

"*Welllll*, I'm flying by the seat of my pants, but the thought occurred to me if I could manage to hide away somewhere in the museum until after it closes, maybe I could prowl around, see if there's anything to be discovered."

"Like in the movies." Giving me sarcastic.

"Yeah, I know. And probably it won't work out that way. Might not be able to figure out how to pull it off or might not think it's worth it to try. Just saying, I might be out of pocket this evening."

"But you will be in touch."

"Absolutely. In fact, if you don't hear from me, call out the cavalry."

In a little while, Rivers dropped by and we reviewed our moves. I thought he would give me some static about my *Night at the Museum* stunt, but he didn't.

"You know how to pick locks?" he asked.

"I'm a writer not a shamus," I said.

"Well, then, if you plan on snooping around behind locked doors, you're going to have to figure out how to get in. I suppose you could try to Watergate it."

In 1972, five men broke into the Democratic National Committee headquarters at the Watergate office complex in Washington, D.C. It began a chain of events that led to President Richard Nixon's resignation and Bob Woodward and Carl Bernstein becoming the most famous investigative reporters in the nation's history. The break-in was a low-tech op. Earlier in the day, one of Nixon's burglars placed tape over a door latch so it wouldn't lock properly. That's what Lester had in mind.

"Got to worry about alarm systems, too," he said. "And cameras. But you might get lucky. Most security systems are built to catch break-ins and internal doors are frequently unarmed. There will likely be a night watchman. So you need to understand this carries some risks."

"You think it's stupid?" I asked.

"Just weigh the risks and rewards."

"You know how to pick locks?" I asked.

"Sure. All us gumshoes do."

"Wanna come along?"

"Thought you'd never ask."

We agreed we'd meet at the museum at noon.

Lester said the FBI had asked The Third Eye to keep in touch. The feds also contacted Ricky Perez and told him they were prepared to take over the case as a kidnapping.

"Guy from the Bureau said Perez sounded weird about it. Thought Perez would be pleased, but instead he argued there's no evidence it's a kidnapping, same line he used during our meeting with Judge Goodfellow."

"He's an asshole, but he does have a point. There's no ransom note or anything like that," I said.

"You think he's right?"

"No. Either Maria is dead—and I'm still not convinced the body in the morgue isn't her—or somebody has to be holding her captive."

"Geneva thinks so, too," he said.

"Speaking of which, did the feds talk to her?"

"No. Just Perez."

"How about you guys, you reach her?"

"Colonel Lake finally contacted her husband, and he said Geneva's frantic and he wants us to redouble our efforts to find Maria. He said *he* never fired us. He gave us a cell phone number for Geneva, but I can't reach her. Apparently, she's on her way back to Connecticut. Tried last night after we broke up our confab. I'll try again today."

"I don't like the smell of this," I said.

"Me, either."

"What do you need me to do?" Gwenn asked.

"Can you start digging into Chitango?" Lester asked. "Anything you can find. His history. Contributions to his church. Tax filings. I think he has some kind of foundation. Pull his 990s from the IRS. Who's donated to his foundation? Where does its money go? We need to follow the money and see what we find."

"I'm on it right now." She pulled her iPad out of her purse and began tapping away.

I added, "and see what you can find out about this FFFA PAC, if it even exists."

"Oh, I've got something there," Rivers said. "The rental car, somebody from the FFFA PAC filed a stolen car report with the Sheriff's

Office about an hour after the shootout. Wiggins told me about it last night."

"Huh. Wiggins have anything else on the PAC, who's behind it?"

"No, but he said his task force is all over it."

"His task force?" I hadn't put that together. So Rankin had tapped a junior detective to upstage Henderson. What a prick.

"Alright, move that to the top of your list."

"Doing it right now," Gwenn said while typing on her iPad.

"There's something else for us to consider," Rivers said. "Lee Roy Chitango isn't just a big-time televangelist with a crazy end-of-days Ark scam, he's deeply entrenched in right-wing politics. Hell, he's one of the president's so-called spiritual advisors. He speaks at political gatherings, he's a mouthpiece for some of the most extremely conservative ideologues. And some of the wealthiest. The *Tampa Bay Times* published an article the other day saying the President may actually speak at his big religious convocation in Tampa."

"That's where Chitango's going to draw the lottery tickets, right? See who gets saved come the second great flood?"

"Not too late to buy a ticket."

"Maybe we can steal some when we're at the museum."

Gwenn asked, "When's the Ark II going to be ready?"

"The *Miami Herald* quoted Chitango saying it's nearly ready," I said. "There's going to be a special cruise out of St. Petersburg before his End of Days confab for a select few, presumably high rollers, to visit it at its secret location."

Gwenn turned her iPad to us. "Take a look. Chitango is more than a little connected to the evangelical right. He's a major bankroller."

Her iPad screen showed a website called OpenSecrets.org, which keeps track of political action committees and campaign contributions. Lee Roy Chitango was listed as the founder of For a Free and Faithful America—FFFA.

"Oh, boy."

"I think we're on to something here," Gwenn said.

"Yeah," I agreed. "But we're dumping a lot on you while Lester and I go gallivanting about."

She brushed that off with a wave of her hand. "I love researching. It's the best part of being a lawyer."

I pulled Edwina Mahoney's business card out of my wallet and handed it to her. "I'll update Ed on what we're up to in case you need some reinforcements. We got a couple reporters who live and breathe database research."

"Good," Gwenn said. "If I start pulling up some big files, I'll give her a call."

"Back to Chitango," Rivers said. "With his political connections, how comfortable should we be sharing information with the sheriff, who, as we know, is running for re-election and will be scratching around for donors? And isn't Chitango lining up behind Ricky Perez's run for the Senate primary nomination?"

We thought about that for a moment.

"This is getting weird," Gwenn said.

"Weirdness is my business," I said.

She rolled her eyes, then said, "Help me understand this. I don't get putting the rental car in the PAC's name. Seems awfully careless."

"If criminals weren't boneheads, our jails wouldn't be so over-crowded," Rivers said.

"Gwenn, I'm curious about that, too," I said. "But look at what's happened. A face-eaten corpse, an amateurish attempt to frame me, maybe poison me, rocket-fucking-launchers, for chrissake. These people are nuts."

"Or Russians," Rivers said. "But that may be redundant."

"Back to your, point, Lester," I said. "I don't trust Rankin. There's something off about him. And Perez is a creeper. We need to keep things close to the vest until we get some answers."

"I'm down with that," Gwenn agreed. "And that fucker Henderson didn't level with me about Edgard Dominique and what happened. I don't like him."

Or his granddaughter.

After a beat, Gwenn asked: "What about the note? Wiggins will be all over that today."

"Here's a thought," I said. "Don't give it to Wiggins. Call that FBI agent, Cao, and ask him if he wants it. Then if Wiggins pesters you about it, tell him to go talk to the feebs. Stall him."

"Gotcha. But this Wiggins guy is on the ball. He'll be heading down the same path soon enough. He'll tumble to Chitango's involvement."

"So we better saddle up," I said.

We clambered off the boat and walked Gwenn to her car. On the way, we told the sheriff's deputy parked outside the boatyard we'd be out of pocket for a while, not to worry.

"I'm supposed to stay with you," the deputy protested.

They had a shift change during the night, and a new guy, named Sebaly, had replaced Templeton. Sebaly said he would call it in and get instructions. I was grateful, but we didn't need nannying right now.

"It'll be all right," I told Sebaly as we walked away. "You seen deputies Henderson and Garcia around?" I asked.

He nodded.

"Check in with them. They'll understand."

We kept walking.

CHAPTER 34

JIM HENDERSON SAT upright in bed watching a program on the wall-mounted television called *The Best of The Young and the Restless*.

"I am *so* going to rat you out," I said.

"Jill and Genevieve are about to have a mud wrestling match in the park," he said. "It's a rerun, but I thought it might cheer me up."

"Well, for a guy who's been gut shot, you're not looking so bad."

"Got lucky," he said. "Bullet nicked a corner of my liver and just missed an artery, but they were able to patch me up. Missed the ribs, so no bone frags. In an out. Should be out of here in a few days."

"Good."

He looked at the TV for a few seconds, then turned the volume down. "Thanks," he said.

I nodded. "Jim, I might be dead if you hadn't shown up when you did. Thank *you*. And I'm so very sorry this happened."

"I'm withdrawing my retirement papers," he said.

"Having too much fun?"

"Nah. Now, I can get disability. It's an even better deal."

I sat down in the chair by his bed, making sure I didn't trip over the tubes leading to his wrist from a drip bag suspended beside him.

"Your granddaughter's heck of a shot," I said.

He beamed. "I've had her out on the range since she was a little girl. She's something, isn't she?"

"Sure is," I said. "Probably make sheriff someday."

"FBI director."

"Even better."

The TV caught his attention and he turned up the sound. Jill and Genevieve were slinging mud and rolling around.

"I assume Wiggins is keeping you posted," I said.

He nodded. "Said he's tracking down this political action committee that rented the car."

"You buy that the car was stolen?" I asked.

He shrugged, then winced from the motion. I'm no doctor, but I couldn't imagine he'd be out of the hospital any time soon.

"Wiggins, he's a bulldog. He'll get to the bottom of it," he said. He sounded dismissive. Maybe just weak. Or maybe time to let somebody else grab the baton.

I reached out my hand. He took it. "Get well," I said.

"Where you off to?" he asked.

"I plan to get to the bottom of it, too."

I started toward the door, then remembered a question.

"You ever get anything back from searching my boat?"

"No DNA. Not yet. And no matching prints or hair samples."

"Hmmm."

"What?"

"I don't know, just thought, if they were clever, they might have planted hairs or something onboard, make a better case against me."

"That's what you would do. That's because you're smart. You got imagination. Don't overthink this stuff. It almost never plays out like that. It's not like TV. It's rare we build a case on that kind of thing. Usually it's witnesses, idiots who talk too much, stupid stuff."

"What about the smart, imaginative criminals?" I asked.

"We don't bat a thousand."

"Huh. Anything else turn up?" I asked.

"Yeah, got a call a little while ago. This is odd. Jane Doe, the floater in Buzzards Bay. The ME found tiny bits of chicken feathers in her hair."

"Chicken feathers."

He waited for me to put the pieces together.

"Chicken feathers, like from the feather flicks on Edgard's computer?"

"Either that, or she was a farmer."

"Sonofabitch." I was certain the word "feathers" hadn't crossed the ME's lips when we met with Judge Goodfellow.

I turned to leave.

"Hey, Strange, Linda give you the piece?"

"Oh, yeah, and thanks. I've got it in the car. You want it back?"

"No. You keep it. You take care of yourself. These fuckers. They think this is the Wild West or something. Never seen anything like this. They're crazy."

"I'll be careful."

"Listen," he said. "That gun, it's unregistered. It's untraceable."

I looked at him, wondering for a moment what he was trying to tell me.

"Just saying."

CHAPTER 35

LESTER AND I were standing beside a replica of Noah's Ark, watching worshipful visitors, most with children in tow, ascend the gangplank to explore the innards of the giant wooden ship. Well, a cross-section of it. The building wouldn't hold all 300 cubits by 50 cubits by 30 cubits.

"Know how big a cubit is?" Lester asked.

"Foot and a half," I said.

"Right."

"No, seriously."

"Prove it."

I pointed to a sign by the entrance to the ramp.

"Oh."

A drawing beside the entrance displayed a tiny figure of Noah leading the animals into the ark. There was Noah, then two giraffes, two dogs, two bears, two Tyrannosaurs Rex, two bunnies, two Velociraptors, and two horses marching aboard the miniaturized replica.

A boy, maybe ten years old, holding his father's hand, examined the drawing, too.

"Dad, how come T-Rex didn't eat all the other animals?" he asked.

"Well, son," his dad replied, "it says right here." He pointed to a sign next to the exhibit. "Back then, all the dinosaurs were vegetarians."

Nearby, cordoned by red velvet ropes, rested a thirty-foot scale model of the Ark II with a poster advertising how worshipers could buy lottery tickets for their chance at salvation come the Next Flood. Conveniently, tickets were being sold at an adjacent kiosk where no fewer than fifty people were queued up.

"I don't know whether to be offended or jealous I didn't think of it," Rivers said.

"Maybe we could start selling lottery tickets to the Ark II's lifeboats," I suggested.

"That's my partner."

Earlier, we examined a mural explaining how scientists had gotten the carbon dating of dinos all wrong. They really did not become extinct 65 million years ago:

"Since we know the earth is only 6,665 years old, how can carbon dating show dinosaurs were alive millions of years ago? The answer is simple: Carbon dating measures the radioactive decay of the carbon element in former living things. So, clearly, the rate of radioactive decay was much faster 6,000 years ago than it is today. Radioactive decay is slowing down. That's how scientists have been fooled."

"This place makes my skin crawl," I said.

"You believe they expose children to this?" he asked.

"They'd be better off watching porn."

Dad overheard me and scowled. "Come along, Jimmy, let's go see the Ark."

"Mommy, who's that man?" a little girl asked. She pointed to a giant mural beside the exhibit.

"That's Noah, honey."

Rivers and I took a look.

"Fuck me," I said. He just groaned.

The face in the image was unmistakable. Under the robes was none other than Ronald Reagan.

"Look around," I said. "Maybe Moses will be played by Newt Gingrich, Cain and Able by the Koch brothers."

We decided earlier to prowl around the museum for a bit, get a thorough sense of the place before trying to buttonhole employees about Edgard Dominique. Now, it was two in the afternoon and we were both getting tired of walking. "Let's get a bite to eat," I said.

As we weaved through crowds of visitors toward the lobby restaurant, we spotted an arched entryway to a large room with a sign overhead that said:

The Chitango Legacy

Lester grabbed my elbow. "We need to see this."

A scale model of the theme park under Plexiglas filled the center of the room. It displayed a series of walking trails around a pretty, kidney-shaped lake in the center of which was a large fountain. On a small island in the pond, the Virgin Mary held the baby Jesus in her arms. At the entrance to the museum, a towering eternal flame erupted from the ground encircled by marble tablets translating the Ten Commandments in various languages. The towering cathedral where Chitango lived and held services stretched skyward directly behind the museum. The structure looked like a pointy Catholic bishop's mitre. A cobblestone courtyard separated the museum from the church. A walking trail from the courtyard led to a complex of what appeared to be guest cottages. Toward the back of the theme park, at the far end of the campus, stood an unlabeled outbuilding.

"What do you make of that?" I asked.

"Maybe we should find out."

On the walls of the room were dozens of enlarged photographs of the Rev. Lee Roy Chitango, all double life-size. Chitango as a boy growing up in Oklahoma. Chitango in what appeared to be divinity school. Chitango at the altar of his church here on the museum grounds, all robed up, silver hair flowing, eyes ablaze as if in direct contact with the Almighty.

"You know Chitango got his divinity degree online, don't you?" I asked Rivers, nodding to the classroom photo of His Holiness.

"That so?"

"Yeah, from a site called the Universal Life Monastery. Sells ordination certificates online. For thirty-five bucks, you, too, can be a minister."

"Nice."

At an adjacent gift shop the faithful could buy an assortment of plastic dinosaurs, Bibles, cups, pencil holders, purses, backpacks, hats, postcards, and copies of the Sermonator's autobiography for $25.99. For $45.99 you could get an autographed first edition.

The fast-food restaurant off the lobby was jammed with chattering children and moms and dads. We queued up to order. After five minutes we finally made our way to the cashier. I ordered a Creation Cheeseburger, hold the fries.

"Would you like it with chili?" the helpful girl behind the counter asked.

"What kind of chili?"

"Noah's Chili, of course."

"Yes, please," I said. "Good enough for Noah, it's good enough for me."

Rivers selected an Eden Salad.

We carried our lunches over to the drinks stand. I got a Diet Coke, Rivers an iced tea. Then we made our way to an empty table.

"Never order iced tea at a fast food restaurant," I told Rivers when we sat down.

"Why not?"

"Nine times out of ten it's terrible."

He took a sip and screwed up his eyes. "Tastes like Velociraptor piss."

I took a bite of the Creation Cheeseburger and it was to die for. Of course, the worst cheeseburger I ever ate was wonderful.

Thank you, Noah, for saving the cows.

"You know what gets me?" I said to Rivers after a couple more bites. "This is actually a beautiful museum. The curating is some of the best I've seen anywhere. The planetarium movie on the Big Bang rocked. I'm no scientist, but it strikes me about ninety percent of everything in here is right on the money, scientifically. Then they twist it all at the end."

"That's the nature of a successful swindle," Rivers said, his mouth full of salad, his head bobbing up and down in agreement. "You gotta have enough truth woven in to make the marks believe the con."

I just shook my head.

"The truth is scary," Rivers said. "People take comfort in myths."

"Yeah, I get it, and I'm not bashing religion. I just don't see what's the big deal. The planet is billions of years old, so what?"

"Because they take the Bible literally."

"OK," I said, "but what's with all the dinosaurs?"

"Look around you," Rivers said. "Kids love dinosaurs. You think you could get this kind of crowd if all you showed was that horrible Old Testament violence? Abraham cutting his son's throat? Cain killing his brother? Plagues? Stonings? Animal sacrifices? Slavery? All that begatting? Parents would leave here and rush their crying kids straight into therapy."

"It's all about marketing," I said.

"It's all about money. Money, sex, and power. It's always about at least one of those three."

"You're even more cynical than me," I said.

"I've lived longer."

All around us, people seemed to be having the time of their lives. Everyone except us.

"We may go to hell for this," I said.

"Cheer up. When you're done with your burger, I'll buy you a Christian Cone for dessert."

CHAPTER 36

THREE HOURS LATER, Rivers and I met outside by the fountain of Mary and Jesus. The museum was closing.

"Any luck?" I asked.

Rivers shook his head. "I showed Edgard's picture to, maybe, two dozen employees. Nobody recognized him."

"Same here," I said.

"How did people react to you when you asked about Edgard?" Rivers asked.

"Uniformly, they were nice, respectful, tried to be helpful."

"Anybody act suspicious, wonder what you were up to?"

"No. And that's weird. Like they were all on meds or something."

"Like a scene out of *Stepford Wives*?"

"Exactly," I said. "After a while, it got to be annoying. Mostly I talked to tour guides and gift stand clerks. Finally got around to buttonholing a couple of security guards. Figured I'd get a rise out of them, for sure. But no. They were just as polite and helpful and unsuspecting as they could be."

We had agreed we would divide up the museum and tell the same story: We were looking for a friend who worked there, but we weren't sure where. Could they help? Did they remember seeing him?

"Maybe they spike the drinking water," he said.

"Or maybe they only hire nice, naïve people."

"Even security guards?"

We talked about simply walking into the Human Resources office and asking the staff if they recognized Edgard, but finally decided to be more indirect, at least at first. HR departments are notoriously rule-bound and legalistic. Back when dinosaurs roamed the earth, they were called Personnel Departments. That's when they actually cared about the persons who worked there. Might get us thrown out, now, and we didn't want that.

"May have to go back to Plan B," I said.

"Tomorrow," Rivers said, glancing at his watch. "It's after six now and the offices will be closed. We can try tomorrow and if we strike out we can always try your original idea. I wandered up to HR and have a better sense of the security system and the locks. I think we can break in, but I need a few tools I don't have with me right now."

"Notice any good places to hide?" I asked.

"Maybe inside the Ark?"

"You know those displays of Adam and Eve, where they're lounging in the Garden of Eden with the sabre tooth tigers and wolves?" I asked. "Bunch of foliage in there might give us some cover."

He nodded.

"By the way, Eve was hot, didn't you think?"

Rivers shook his head. "Looked like Bristol Palin."

"I take it back."

"With any luck, you won't have to hang out with her. Why don't we walk over to that outbuilding we saw on the scale model? Maybe we'll get our answers there."

I agreed.

We couldn't see the building from where we sat by the pond, but we knew it was on the far end of the campus and sheltered from our view by a patch of bald cypress and low-lying shrubs left as a kind of nature preserve to separate it from the rest of the park.

Rivers pulled out the tri-fold map to the theme park. He used a pen to mark where we were by the fountain, but noticed that the outbuilding, which we'd seen on the scale model inside the museum, was missing.

"Guess they don't want tourists straying back there," I said.

"It's right about here," Rivers said, pointing to a spot beyond the small stand of trees.

We took the sidewalk alongside the pond and headed in that direction until the sidewalk began circling back. We were about to cut across the grassy lawn toward the tree line when a sudden rippling erupted on the surface of the pond.

"Did you see that?" I asked.

Then we felt a trembling beneath our feet, like a small earthquake, a vibration that lasted only a moment, but unlike anything I'd experienced in Florida before.

"Fracking," Lester, said.

He pointed to a tower about a half mile to our east, past the museum's grounds.

"I saw that operation on my way over here," he said.

"Isn't fracking illegal in Florida," I asked.

Lester rubbed his thumb and forefinger together. "Money talks."

"That was strong," I said.

"Probably right under us. These days, drillers can bore horizontally for miles."

Another ripple spread across the pond and we felt another vibration underfoot. Then it stopped.

"Let's get going," I said.

The further we walked from the manicured area of the park, the wilder the terrain became with tall weeds, palmettos, and the occasional pine tree among the bald cypresses.

"Watch out for pythons," I cautioned.

"And gators."

After a hundred yards we encountered a sand-covered service road heading in the right direction and we stayed on it as it cut through the preserve. Lizards skittered across the trail at our feet and a trio of turkey buzzards circled overhead. Ominous. Rivers, who'd taken point, suddenly pulled up short.

"What is it?" I asked.

He pointed to a red and black snake lounging in the sunshine on the trail ahead.

"I hate snakes," he said.

"You and Linda Henderson. Don't worry. It's a corn snake. Harmless." Rivers remained motionless, so I moved into the lead. As I approached the snake, it looked up, stuck its tongue out at me, then slithered into the bushes.

The dirt road ended at a two-story, windowless structure. It looked like an ordinary utility building, steel framed with corrugated metal siding, painted pea green, probably to blend into the landscape. Sliding double-wide doors guarded the entrance, and as we approached I could see a padlock holding the doors in place.

"Now what?" I asked.

I needn't have.

We heard a rustle in the shrubs behind us and as we turned, two security guards emerged, pistols drawn.

CHAPTER 37

THE WIDE DOUBLE doors to the metal barn clanked shut. We heard a metallic, scraping sound as the guards reattached the padlock outside. Inside, it was dark except for a dim light penetrating the gloom through the open door of a small office in the far corner of the structure.

Lester and I were lying on the floor, our wrists and ankles tightly wrapped in duct tape. I would have said something clever, but that's tough to do when your mouth is also wrapped with tape. There were a handful of lawn mowers, two tractors, and a table piled with leaf blowers and weed trimmers. Bags of fertilizer and weed killer were piled against one wall. The air smelled of gasoline, chemicals, and cut grass.

The lawn mowers gave me an idea. If I could crawl over to one of them, tip it over, and if the blades were sharp, maybe I could cut the duct tape off my wrists. Of course, I'd just as likely cut my wrists and bleed to death, but at least it was an idea.

I glanced at Rivers. He stared at his hands, as if in prayer. Slowly, and painfully, Rivers sat up, then began raising his bound hands over his head as if he were beseeching the gods above. I followed suit. Not sure what he had in mind. Maybe we were going to do some meditation. Or yoga.

Instead, he swiftly flung his arms downward while pulling sideways as hard as he could. I heard a muffled scream behind his taped mouth. Rivers toppled over and struck his head on the concrete floor and lay still.

I copied his maneuver. It hurt like hell. Thought my shoulders would pop out of their sockets. But I noticed the tape around my wrists had loosened, stretched by the violent motion.

Lester appeared to be dazed, so I raised my hands again and thrust downward. This time a seam popped loose. I began wriggling my wrists under the tape. And in a few moments, I was free.

I then ripped off the tape covering my mouth. Big mistake. I damn near tore my lips off.

I saw Rivers stirring. "My hands are free, Lester. I'll help you as soon as I can unravel my ankles." He barked out a muffled acknowledgement.

Within a few minutes I freed myself and I pulled Rivers upright. He had a knot on his forehead. I gently pulled the tape off his mouth.

"You still with us?" I asked.

"Just get me out of this."

It took a couple of minutes, but I finally unwound his wrists. We both worked on his ankles until the last of the tape peeled off.

Rivers started to stand up, but I put my hand on his shoulder and held him down. "Look at me," I said.

"What?"

"I want to check your pupils; you could have a concussion."

He pushed me aside and scrambled to his feet. "Leave me alone. I'm fine."

"You sure?"

"Yes. Look around and see if there's anything we can use for weapons."

We settled on shovels. We'd bash their brains out the minute they stuck their Neanderthal heads through the door. We flanked both sides of the entrance, and as we waited we calmed down enough to think.

"Lester, I'll stand guard by the door. Why don't you go back to that office and poke around, see if you can find anything on Edgard

Dominique. And check out what's under the big tarp in the back of the barn." He hesitated a moment then headed for the office, still carrying his shovel. A good soldier never abandons his weapon.

I could hear him shuffling papers, opening file drawers, then I heard the click-clack of computer keys.

I put one ear to the door straining to hear anyone approaching. Nothing. I looked at the shovel. What happens to the guy who brings a shovel to a gunfight? This plan looked dumber and dumber with every passing minute.

When they came back, it wouldn't be just the two of them. They'd be bringing someone at a higher pay grade, someone to question us. Three against two. Minimum. Guns against garden tools. I'd be better off using the shovel to bust a hole in the wall of the building so we could get the hell out of there. I began inspecting the walls of the building. Could I jam the shovel blade between the sheet metal seams and pry a panel open?

I didn't want to do that on the front wall where it would immediately be seen by the returning guards. But to experiment elsewhere would mean deserting my post by the door.

"Lester, how's it going?" I called out in a voice he could hear but I hoped would not penetrate the building.

He emerged from the office, shaking his head.

"It's all groundskeeping stuff. There was a shift schedule on a bulletin board, but Edgard's name wasn't on it.

"I heard you on a computer."

"Yeah, I hoped it would be connected to the Internet so I could reach somebody, but it's password protected."

"What's under the tarp?" I asked.

Rivers stepped over and lifted a corner of large blue sheet of plastic. He looked up at me and in the muted light from the door I could see him shaking his head.

"You won't believe this," he said, then tugged on the tarp and it fell away. Underneath sat a yellow Volkswagen Beetle.

"Sonofabitch."

Rivers opened the driver's door and a light came on inside. He looked around for a minute then stuck his head back out.

"Empty. And no keys."

"Can you hotwire it?" I asked. I had a fleeting vision of ramming the Bug into the doors to bust them open. But those were heavy doors with a solid padlock. It probably wouldn't have worked.

"I missed that class in Shamus school," Rivers said. He pulled the tarp back over the Beetle and joined me back at the door. "Any activity out there?"

"No. But I thought I could pry open a seam in the wall with my shovel."

"Give it a try. I'll watch the door."

I ran to the back of the building and began jamming the shovel into one of the metal panels, but I couldn't get purchase.

After a few minutes, Rivers called out. "I hear voices."

I ran back to the front. "I don't like our odds," I said.

"Neither do I," he said. "Follow me."

Rivers led us back to where the guards had left us on the floor. "Set your shovel down where you can reach it, and let's put the tape back on, enough so they won't notice we're still not tied up. Maybe we can catch them by surprise."

It didn't take long to place the sticky tape over our mouths and across our wrists and ankles, but it wouldn't fool anybody once they got close.

We heard a rattling outside the barn and the double doors slid open. Three men stood in the entrance, silhouetted in the late afternoon sunlight.

"Let's have a chat," one said, and they began walking toward us. As they stepped out of the sunlight that had backlit them, I recognized the two uniformed guards who waylaid us and a man in a suit whom I'd never seen before. The guards' pistols were holstered.

I don't know who jumped first, Rivers or me, but as the nearest guard approached I could see his eyes go wide. He reached for his sidearm. I leapt off the floor, pulling the shovel with me, and smashed it into his face. It made a sickening thunk and the guard went limp and toppled backwards. Another smack sounded to my right. I turned and saw Rivers, pointing his shovel at the man in the suit. The guard nearest him lay unconscious on the floor.

"If you're carrying," Rivers said, calmly, "I will bash your head in before you can reach it." The man took a step backward toward me.

"Hands in the air," I said, my voice surprisingly steady, not betraying the anxiety I felt. Mostly that manifested itself in a strong desire to pee. But real men do not pee in a crisis. Real men are resolute. Of course, it could simply have been that second Diet Coke I had at lunch.

I shoved the wooden handle of the shovel into the suit's back. He froze. Rivers jumped on him in a flash. Who knew he could move so rapidly? Rivers' forefinger plunged into the man's neck and he bent over, gagging. I popped him on the head with the shovel, just enough to stun him. He hit the ground, curled into a ball and retched.

Rivers reached inside the man's jacket and extracted a semi-automatic handgun. As the man thrashed, trying to regain his breath, Rivers patted him down. No other weapons, but he came up with our cell phones, wallets, and car keys.

"Get their guns," Rivers said, nodding to the unconscious guards.

I pulled their handguns out of their holsters and checked their necks for pulses. They were out, but they were alive. "What should I do with these?" I asked Rivers, waving the pistols.

"Set them over there," he said and gestured toward the table covered with leaf blowers. "Then grab some rope. I saw some in the office."

I ran to the office. "Bring a chair, too," Rivers shouted.

While Rivers trained the pistol on the suit, I tied him to the desk chair I found in the office, then tied up both guards, wrists and ankles, and left them lying on the floor.

Lester dragged a box over by the suit and sat down. "Shut the door so nobody can hear the screams," he said, never taking his eye off our prisoner. I walked over and slid it shut leaving a small gap so we could hear if anyone approached.

When I returned, Rivers held his prosthetic leg in his hand.

"Now, we can do this the easy way or the hard way but either way you are going to tell us what we want to know," he said.

"Lester, what are you doing?" I asked.

"I'm going to torture him," he said. "And I'm going to beat his sorry ass to death with my leg if he doesn't tell us what we want to know."

With that he smacked the suit in the face. It knocked him and his chair over sideways.

"Put him back up," Rivers ordered, his voice cold.

"Where'd you learn that trick?" I asked, heaving the suit back into an upright position.

"Abu Ghraib."

The guy's eyes widened. Blood dripped down his face from a cut on his forehead.

Rivers leaned toward me. "You know, I haven't tortured anyone in years, let alone beat somebody to death. This brings back fond memories. You wanna give it a try?" he asked, gesturing his prosthesis toward me. "It's loads of fun."

"No. No. You got this."

Rivers returned his attention to the suit. He gave him a wide, evil grin: Heath Ledger's Joker. "Ready for some more?"

"What do you want?" the man sputtered. "You're fucking crazy."

CHAPTER 38

WE LEFT THE suit and the two guards tied-up in the barn and rolled the double doors closed. I tossed the padlock into the weeds, then followed it in a few steps to relieve myself. While I did that, Lester talked on his cell phone.

"You get ahold of Cao?" I asked when I returned.

He had his phone up to his ear and shook his head no. "Left a message. Trying to reach Colonel Lake right now." He pushed the speaker button on the phone so I could hear the conversation, but it rolled over to a recorded message.

At the beep, Lester said, "We have a situation here and are leaving the area. We were attacked, bound, and gagged, but managed to escape. There are three bad guys hogtied in a barn at this location." He read the geo-coordinates using an app on his mobile phone. "All three have suffered injuries and will need medical attention. We have reason to believe the Russian Hangmen are heading this way. Could be an opportunity for Cao to capture them. I called him and left a message. Call back when you get this."

While Lester talked, I kept an eye on the trail we had followed to the barn. It was dark, clouds obscuring the moon, but the white sand was visible against the dense foliage surrounding it. If the Hangmen were coming, this would be their route.

When Lester hung up, I motioned him to follow me along the trail. I figured if we hurried, we could beat any incoming traffic. But a few steps along the path, the clouds parted and a crescent moon illuminated a narrow trail to our left, one we hadn't noticed earlier. I had point, and Lester grabbed my shoulder from behind, pulling me to a halt.

"Look." His voice was hushed, worried.

I turned toward the newly discovered trail.

"Did you see that?" Lester whispered.

"Yeah. It looks like it leads to the parking lot. Could be a shortcut."

"No, look closer." His voice sounded strained, urgent.

I peered up the trail and thought I saw a flash of movement. Could it be the Hangmen heading this way?

Lester and I crouched at the edge of the path and stayed still, waiting. We didn't have to wait long. In a few seconds a figure stepped out onto the trail just as it meandered to the right, maybe forty yards ahead.

The moon had moved behind the clouds again and it was too dark to make out details, but it appeared to be a woman—a tall woman—in a long dress. She stood in the center of the path for only a moment, then turned and vanished around the bend.

Lester gripped my shoulder again. "What do you make of that?"

Before I could answer, a pair of headlights appeared up the main trail heading in our direction.

I glanced back at Lester. "We gotta chance it, Lester. Those lights. That's gotta be the Russians." He nodded and we set out along the little pathway toward where the mysterious female figure had disappeared. When we got there, she was nowhere to be seen. Behind us, the lights and sounds of a vehicle whipped past where we had been walking on the main trail.

"Dude. We dodged a bullet."

"It was her," Lester said.

I knew what he was thinkin—that it was his guardian angel. And who knows? Maybe it was. Or maybe it was another museum visitor who got lost wandering around like we were. No matter, our bacon would have been cooked without her. We would have been caught dead—you will excuse the term—on the maintenance trail if we hadn't followed in her footsteps.

The suit Lester tormented was a thug named Harvey Turnbull, Chitango's head of security. He'd heard we were pestering employees about Edgard Dominique and he ordered a pair of his guards to find us and to hold us for questioning. That, of course, confirmed our suspicion that Chitango must be implicated. It ultimately took Lester a bit more persuasion to get Turnbull to spill his guts.

"I want a lawyer," Turnbull pleaded at one point.

"You're not going to need a lawyer," Rivers told him, casually. "You're going to need a surgeon."

"You make me talk under duress, it's inadmissible." A *Law & Order* fan, no doubt.

"Let me show you duress.' Rivers said, then threatened to pop him again with his prosthesis.

"No, stop," Turnbull shouted. "Enough already. Jesus."

"You recognize this guy?" I showed him a picture of Edgard Dominique on my iPhone.

"Yeah. I warned the reverend not to trust him."

"Why's that?"

"He look white to you?"

"Give me that," I told Lester, gesturing to his artificial leg. He ignored me.

"And what did Edgard Dominique do?" Lester asked.

"He ran errands. Brought the animals."

"Animals?" We said it simultaneously.

"Chickens, mostly."

"You fry 'em or what?" I asked.

Turnbull started hyperventilating and Rivers gave him a moment to gather himself.

"You know the apartments, over on the north side of the campus? We have, uh, special events, parties for certain guests. Most of them, they're normal, just want pussy. But some are queer and trying to recover. Some need other things. One guy, he likes chickens. The reverend, he gives them a chance to release their demons. It's therapy, part of his ministry."

"And how are chickens therapeutic?" I asked.

"This one guy, he strangles them while getting off."

"Who would do a thing like that?"

"You wouldn't believe me if I told you."

"Try us."

"I don't remember his name, but I recognized him from TV. On the news. He's a congressman. From Miami."

Lester and I looked at each other. His eyes were wide. Mine probably were, too.

"It just keeps getting weirder and weirder," I said.

"How do you know all this?" Lester asked Turnbull.

"Seen the videos."

"Movies, like on Edgard's laptop?"

"We have tons of videos. All of the guest suites are videotaped."

"And why is that?"

"Why do you fuckin' think?"

"Blackmail, right?"

He just rolled his eyes.

"And is the Russian mafia involved?" I asked.

"I'm not talking about that."

Rivers picked up a shovel.

"All right, all right. They supply the 'tang. Mostly, they bring them up from Miami. But Edgard kept lobbying the reverend, said he could get hookers closer to home, cut out the Russkies. He was obsessed about it. He wanted a bigger role in the ministry. I warned the reverend we had to do something about him."

"He break into the reverend's car?" Rivers asked.

"No, he broke into my car. Stole my laptop. Fucked up my door when he did it. I was sitting right outside his apartment when the cops raided his place. I wanted to get it back before that asshole could cause any trouble."

"You say Edgard damaged your car?"

"Yeah, it's in the body shop."

I played a hunch. "So, you driving a rental?"

"Huh? No. Not now anyway."

"That was your rental the Russians were driving when they came after me."

He shook his head and Lester leaned down to him. "Too late for games."

He relented. "Yeah. The dumbfuck Russkies boosted it. But I got those assholes. I reported it stolen."

"Speaking of dumbfuck Russkies, what can you tell us about the Hangmen?"

Turnbull started breathing heavy again. "They're really scary, man. We had this one hooker, a spick, she thought she would get smart, blackmail the reverend. The Hangmen, they fixed that problem."

"Fixed? How?"

He took a deep breath. "One of these guys, we call him Hannibal, he likes to, he likes to…"

Turnbull turned his head, which was awfully considerate given the circumstances, and spit on the floor. "He's a cannibal, man. He hanged that girl, here in the barn, then ate her face right off. It was horrible."

I showed him a picture of Maria Martinez on my cell phone. "Was it her?"

He shook his head. "That's her car back there." He nodded toward the tarp in the back of the barn. "She showed up the day before

Hannibal ate that Mexican chick's face. He did it right here, he nodded to a space behind us in the barn. The girl in the car, they'd already taken her off, kept her in one of the guest lodges. We had to guard it, make sure she didn't escape."

"Is she here now?" I asked.

"No. She's on her way to the boat."

"What boat?"

"The fucking Jell-O Boat."

The boat to which Turnbull referred was the *Monkey Business Too*. It was docked in St. Petersburg and the property of a strip-club magnate who had operated "gentlemen's establishments" in a dozen Florida cities. He recently retired and claimed to have discovered Jesus thanks to the Rev. Chitango. He donated the use of the yacht to Chitango for his cruise out to the Ark II construction site.

"Why do you call it the Jell-O boat," I asked.

"You ever seen its swimming pool?"

Lester slipped his prosthetic leg back on. "Our people will be here very soon," he said. "The FBI, too. Tell them just what you told us."

Turnbull laughed.

"Your people." He spit on the floor again. He didn't bother to turn his head this time. "We'll be gone by the time they get here. You think I spilled my guts 'cause I'm afraid?" He sneered. "Been buying time. *My* people will be here any second and you assholes will be Hannibal food."

Lester and I were at our cars, ready to head out. "You sure you don't want us to handle this?" he asked.

"Time is running out on us, Lester. I can't wait."

Lester and I had agreed it would make getting a search warrant easier if we spotted Maria aboard the *Monkey Business Too*. That would be preferable to telling the cops we beat a confession out of one of Chitango's people. We'd be the ones who landed in jail. Which meant we needed to stake out the harbor.

"But what about her car? Isn't that enough, us finding it here?" I'd asked.

"That should be enough to get a warrant to search the museum and grounds, but we've only got Turnbull's say-so that she's aboard that boat. We get lucky, and he spills his guts to the FBI, they'll be all over it. If not…"

"If not," I said, "we need to tell the cops about what Turnbull told us. Even if it means we end up in jail."

"Come on," he said. "We gotta get out of here."

"Right."

"You got everything you need?" he asked me.

"Yeah, in the back of my SUV."

"I checked my watch, barely visible under the light of a street lamp. Mickey's little hand rested on eleven, his big hand on two. How time flies when you're torturing people.

'I'll call you when I get to St. Pete, soon as I check in with Gwenn."

"She's not going to like this."

"I know."

Lester opened the door to his car and prepared to ease himself in. "Hey, Lester," I said, "level with me. Were you really at Abu Ghraib?"

"Nah. But it got his attention."

Something in my face caused him to pause. He looked at me for a moment, cocked his head, then said: "That bothered you, didn't it?"

"It's not my usual interviewing technique."

"Have you thought about what they would have done to us if we hadn't turned the tables on them?"

"I get that. And I also understand the urgency. But, I don't know, I don't feel good about myself right now."

"Or me, either, I imagine."

I didn't argue the point.

"You ever feel good about hurting people," he said, "get help."

CHAPTER 39

THE *MONKEY BUSINESS Too* more closely resembled a small ocean liner at 225 feet. Tied up at the City of St. Petersburg's Cruise Port Terminal One, it was a gleaming white, four-tiered vessel with a swimming pool on the stern of the main deck. I was observing it from the bushes at the entrance to the Knight Oceanographic Research Center about fifty yards away. I couldn't tell if the pool was filled with Jell-O, but it had an unusual shade of pink, so maybe so.

The eastern sky turned golden across Tampa Bay, and a heavy sea mist clung to the water, thickening, then thinning, massaged by an uneven onshore breeze that for moments allowed the yacht to fade into the fog, like a seaborne Brigadoon, only to re-emerge as wisps of vapor rose off the water's surface. In the breeze, the harbor water wrinkled, then settled back into a glassy calm.

It was after two in the morning by the time I'd arrived in St. Petersburg. Turnbull said the guests on the *Monkey Business Too* would be arriving early. He didn't say how early, so I reckoned I should stake out the yacht as soon as I arrived. I parked on a side street across from the nearby Salvador Dali Museum and walked to the port. It was a lonely vigil, not another soul stirring in this corner of the city in the pre-dawn hours.

I focused on the yacht and pushed the shutter release on my new

Canon 80D. I was using a 70-200 millimeter telephoto lens attached to the camera. If faces appeared on deck or dockside, I'd get tack-sharp images we'd be able to enlarge.

I set my camera's controls to wirelessly transmit my pictures to Canon Image Gateway, a service the camera maker provided. Back in Goodland, Lester would be monitoring that, getting transmissions from my camera as I uploaded them.

For all this technological wizardry to work, I had to have a wi-fi connection. The good news was that I got a strong signal outside the circular entrance to the Knight center. The bad news was that I couldn't get as close to the *Monkey Business Too* as I would have liked without losing my wi-fi link.

About five minutes after I snapped the picture of the *Monkey Business Too*, my iPhone vibrated in my pocket. Lester sent me a text confirming receipt of the picture.

Now all I had to do was wait for Maria to show up.

I'd called Gwenn while en route to St. Petersburg. As Lester predicted, she was not ecstatic about my plan.

It was a simple plan, really. I would do what I was doing now, stake out the yacht, see if I could identify the people Turnbull assured us (with some inducement) would be boarding first thing in the morning. Among them, I hoped, would be Maria. The moment I saw Maria, I would call Lester and he would alert the Coast Guard to keep the yacht in port, and he would notify the FBI that there were reasonable grounds to search the vessel. A photo of Maria, if I could get it, would give the Feds irrefutable evidence.

Turnbull told us the yacht, if not interdicted, would make its way into Tampa Bay then out into the Gulf of Mexico, under the Sunshine Skyway Bridge, for a leisurely cruise south along the Ten Thousand Islands to Key West, then on to the secret location of the Ark II.

There would be drinking and there would be a special performance by the Boogie Barbies in the Jell-O pool. But he knew nothing about anything kinkier, certainly no beastiality, Chitango's regular chicken procurer having been hanged in the Collier County Jail.

I'd asked Gwenn to check out the boat's registry. Calling the *Monkey Business Too* a boat was akin to calling the nearby Dali collection a nice bunch of paintings. Gwenn got the information online while we talked. The registry showed the yacht boasted twelve staterooms and accommodations for a crew of 24. Records showed it weighed 2,280 tons, and had a draft of only 12 feet, which would give it maneuverability near shore. It had a closing speed of 16 knots, not that much faster than Uncle Leo's trawler.

Maybe they'd like to trade.

Gwenn told me she'd spent a frustrating day investigating For a Free and Faithful America and where its money came from. It was registered for tax purposes as a 501(c)(4) "social welfare" organization. Outfits as diverse as the National Rifle Association and the Sierra Club were 501(c)(4) nonprofits. But since the U.S. Supreme Court ruled in its 2010 *Citizens United* decision that "corporations are people," political campaigns had been using these so-called charities as their personal ATMs. IRS regulations did not require them to disclose their donors, so they provided perfect smokescreens for funneling money to political campaigns. These so-called Super PACs were raking in millions and millions of untraceable money.

"I've hit a wall trying to figure out where the money's coming from," Gwenn said. "And it's nearly as hard figuring out where it's going. It's so vague. Tens of thousands of dollars for consultants, media, outreach. It's gibberish."

"Wonder how much Chitango is pulling down," I said.

"We're working on that." Gwenn had eventually called Edwina and asked for help plowing through all the data.

We talked some more about the paper trail. And next steps. But finally she cornered me on my plan to surveil the yacht.

"Why you?"

"Have camera, will travel."

"No, seriously, why not let one of Lester's people do it?"

"There's no time. And, besides, I need to know if Maria's on board," I said.

Ricky Perez was right about one thing: I got Maria into this, and if she were still alive I couldn't sit on the sidelines.

"Be careful," she finally said. "I hate breaking in new boyfriends." Then she hung up.

Lester called about six in the morning. His voice sounded grave. "It appears we got out of there just in time," he said.

"How's that?"

"It took our team a while to get out there—they arrived at the same time as the FBI—and they found all three dead, double taps to their heads, execution style. Could have been us, too, if we hadn't skedaddled when we did."

"Jesus Christ."

"I called Detective Wiggins and I'm heading over to the Sheriff's Office to give him a statement. So you know, I intend to tell him what Turnbull said about Maria and the *Monkey Business Too*. Should be enough to get a search warrant pretty quickly."

Unsaid was the fact there no longer was anyone left alive to complain about how Lester extracted that information.

"Wiggins said he wants a statement from you, too."

"Lester, if Turnbull told us the truth, this yacht will be leaving pretty soon. I need to stay here and see what I can find out."

"Understood," he said. "Colonel Lake is contacting the Coast Guard. These murders should give them plenty of reason to hold the ship in port while Wiggins gets the search warrant."

"Uh, there may be a problem there, Lester."

"What?"

"I'm looking over at the Coast Guard station right now. It's empty. There are no ships there."

"Hold on," Lester said.

In a few minutes he returned on the phone.

"Apparently, there is a big storm out in the Gulf and it's heading your way. Fast. There have been several distress calls and the Coast Guard is out there right now."

"Terrific."

"Colonel Lake will call the Pinellas County Sheriff's Office."

"They got boats?" I asked.

"Don't know."

"Lester, this yacht could be gone pretty quickly."

The line was quiet for a few seconds then he said, "You're going to try to sneak onboard, aren't you?"

"Any words of wisdom?" I asked.

"Don't get killed."

The fog had lifted, but heavy clouds stretched from horizon to horizon obscuring the sun. I checked my phone and the Weather Service said a tropical disturbance in the Gulf was moving ashore rapidly and would bring rain and heavy wind. I could hear thunder. It wasn't far off.

Lights were blinking on aboard the yacht. The radar antenna array began rotating. The soft rumble of the diesel engines echoed across the water and bubbles appeared at the stern. Uniformed crewmembers were toweling off chairs and tables on the decks, a pointless exercise with a storm approaching. A gangplank lowered to the dock.

In a few minutes, a white stretch limo pulled up and a group women piled out, each carrying a small overnight bag. The Dozen Dancing Virgins had arrived. I snapped away with my Canon.

No sooner had the limo left than another pulled up. Two white guys in chinos, golf shirts and deck shoes emerged. They got out and stretched, working out the kinks, most likely not used to the early hour, but they were clearly anticipating a great time at sea based on their laughter. Again, I kept the Canon busy.

This procession of vehicles continued during the next few minutes, all either black or white limos. All the men were white. While the women carried their own bags onboard, porters descended from the yacht to grab the luggage for these guys. Maria Martinez was not among those boarding and I did not see her on deck.

I was checking my camera's controls, uploading pictures, when I heard footsteps approaching. I peered out of the bushes to see Congressman Ricky Perez flanked by two men wearing *Monkey Business Too* crew uniforms heading my way. The crewmember on the right, a small, wiry, middle-aged man, held a handgun down his right thigh. The uniform on the left stood at least six-six and three hundred pounds. He flashed his teeth, showing a sizeable gap between his two front incisors.

Hello, Hannibal.

I stepped out onto the sidewalk.

"Why don't you join us, Mr. Strange?" Perez said.

I raised the Canon and snapped a picture of Perez. I had just enough time to push the "upload" control before Hannibal rushed forward and seized the camera in one of his bear-sized paws.

"Careful with that," I yelped. "It's company property. I could get in trouble if anything happens to it."

"I wouldn't worry too much about it," Perez said. He held out his hands and Hannibal passed him the camera. Perez examined it for a moment.

"Heavy. This looks like a very sophisticated piece of equipment," he said. "This lens. It's huge. You must be able to take great pictures with it."

"That's right, the camera does all the work."

"I see," he said. Then he opened his hands and dropped it on the sidewalk. It hit lens first, shattering the glass, then the body of the camera thunked onto the cement.

"Ooops," Perez said.

But I knew something he didn't know. He might have damaged the lens, but the rubber-coated magnesium-alloy body of a Canon is rugged. You could use it as body armor.

"You're a jackass, Perez," I said. "You realize that's going to come out of my paycheck?" I looked down at the camera body. It was intact.

He raised his hands, palms up, as if it were an accident.

The transmission of photos over the wi-fi network isn't instantaneous and there were a half-dozen pictures queued up ahead of the image of Perez. I needed to stay in range of the building's wi-fi connection long enough for the pictures to be sent. So I stalled for time.

"How'd you spot me?" I asked.

Perez looked over his shoulder to the dock. "Light reflecting off your lens." While overcast, the harbor was brilliantly illuminated with floodlights.

The other thug raised his pistol and gestured toward the boat. A sane person would have been scared, but I was too annoyed to be sensible.

"Hey, Ricky," I said, not budging, keeping my voice level, giving my camera time to do its job. "You much of a high tech guy?"

He didn't answer, just sneered. Once again, I noticed his overly long canine teeth.

"The picture I took of you? It's already in the hands of The Third Eye and the cops. Complete with geo-coordinates and a time stamp putting you with me, right at this spot, right at this moment. Got pictures of all your pals and the Barbies when they came aboard, too. Every one of those photos has been transmitted to the police. Game's up, Ricky. You can kiss the Senate goodbye."

Rickey's face darkened, his shoulders tensed.

"Tell me about Maria, Ricky. You kill her? This asshole"—I nodded to Hannibal—"he eat her face off? You could do that to your own cousin?"

Perez pointed his finger at me, wagging it up and down like a schoolmarm. "Not that I care what you think, but I had nothing to do with that. These geniuses," he turned to sneer at Hannibal, "that was their brilliant idea."

The geniuses didn't like Perez dissing them so much. The shorter, wiry guy with the gun turned to Perez, and, I swear, for a moment I thought he might shoot him. It dawned on me that Ricky might not be in charge. The chicken strangler might be in hock up to his ass to these hoods.

Perez noticed me reevaluating the situation. He snorted. "Maria's not dead. We're going to take her to see her uncle."

Turnbull had told the truth. Maria was still alive. I straightened to my full height. I felt as if a huge weight had been removed from my shoulders.

"The cops will be here any minute, bonehead. Why don't you tell me where Maria is and she and I can go home and you and your disturbing friends can go to jail."

Perez lurched toward me. My inner lizard sprang to life. For a brief, blissful moment I felt exhilarated, utterly free and unbound. I was one with the dinosaurs. I was one with Neanderthal man. I was going to hit this motherfucker so hard it would alter his DNA. Generations of future Perezes would wonder why their jaws always ached.

He drew back his right hand to swing, telegraphing the punch slower than Morse code. But before he could finish, and before I could step into it, a blinding flash of red erupted in my skull. The world grayed into oblivion.

CHAPTER 40

"Gwenn, tha' you?"

The woman peering down at me dissolved, reassembled, then swayed back and forth. I blinked several times and shook my head, which sent a wave of nausea through me. I leaned back, blinked a few more times and she came into focus.

"Maria," I groaned, "you *are* alive."

"Took you long enough to find me," she said.

"I thought you were dead."

"Dead?"

"Your ring, your birthstone."

She looked down at her hand. "*Si*, they took it from me."

"They took it from you and put it on another girl, then killed her, then destroyed her face. We thought you were murdered."

She sputtered something in *Espanol.*

"Your aunt, Geneva, when she came to identify the body, she said it couldn't be you. She, uh, she…she knows you really well."

Maria uncrossed her arms and reached out to a wall in the little room to steady herself as the floor underfoot suddenly tilted. When she regained her balance, she sat on the bed beside me. We were below decks in a small cabin with no porthole. Crew quarters. The boat rocked wildly. I tried to sit up but my right wrist was shackled to a rail on the bed. The yacht rolled in a giant swell from the storm that had been approaching before I got slugged. Right on cue, a thunderclap reverberated through the hull.

"How long have we been under way?"

"Maybe twenty minutes."

"Got any Dramamine?" I asked.

"No, but I have some Advil. You got a really ugly cut on the side of your head." She poured two capsules out of a small container and handed them to me along with a bottle of water. I swallowed the pills and leaned back in the bed.

"Well," she said, smiling ruefully, "I finally got you where I want you."

"Didn't know you were into bondage," I said, clanking the handcuff against the bed rail.

"So who's Gwenn?" she asked.

Oh.

"You know her," I said. "Edgard Dominique's public defender. She was, anyway."

She nodded then narrowed her eyes. "Was?"

"Yeah. He's dead. Hung in his cell. Same kind of rope they used to kill the girl they gave your ring to. Your cousin Ricky has some nasty friends."

Maria lowered her face into her hands and mumbled something again in *Espanol.*

"So, Ricky says he's taking you to see your uncle. What's that about?"

She shook her head. "You talked to Geneva. She didn't tell you?"

"Ricky whisked her away before I could ask her much of anything," I replied. "Your uncle in Key West? That's where we're going, right?"

She shook her head. "I am going further south."

"The only thing directly south of Key West is... Cuba? You said your mother got pregnant in Havana, right?"

"Yes. Mama had to go. It was politically impossible for her to stay."

"Politically…?"

"Yes. That's why, when they caught me poking around Chitango's place, they didn't kill me. It's why they've kept me locked up. Ricky's campaign, he's getting money funneled to him through Chitango and his political action committee. You figured it out, right?"

"I know about the Super PAC, but not where the money's coming from."

"Some of it's coming through Cuba."

"Cuba?"

"*Si.* From my father, before he died, and his brother. I think they're getting it from some Russian oligarch. Or something. Somebody over there wants their very own senator."

"Who the fuck was your father, anyway?"

"Fidel Castro."

CHAPTER 41

"Fidel?"

"Si."

"Castro?"

"The one and only."

"Wow. Does that make you some kind of royalty?"

"Communists don't believe in royalty," she said. 'Neither do Americans, for that matter."

"Still, you're special."

"Hardly, Papa had dozens of illegitimate children. No telling how many step-sisters and step-brothers I have."

"So then why the trip to Cuba?"

"Raul, Papa's brother, wants to meet me. Or so Ricky says."

I shook my head, which sent another wave of nausea through me. Some people never learn.

"He wants to meet you? Or Ricky is afraid of the repercussions if he kills you?"

"Either way, I'm here."

"We're here. You should have called me, told me you were going to snoop around Chitango's operation."

"I know. I'm sorry. Believe me, I've thought about this a lot. I was upset with you, but, really, I was more upset with myself, for throwing myself at you. Edgard Dominique's PD, Gwenn Giroux, right? She left me a phone message. I knew right away he was referring to Chitango. I wanted the story all to myself, to prove myself. To prove myself to you. Now look what it's gotten me."

"Us."

"Sí. Us."

"Maria, they interrogated you, right?"

She nodded. "They were careful not to harm me physically. But that first night, they taped me to a chair and gave me a shot. Truth serum, I guess."

"So, you told them about the note from Edgard Dominique?"

"Yes, I told them everything. I was powerless."

"Everything

Maria hung her head. "They asked who else knew about all this." She started crying. "I'm sorry. I gave you up."

At least that explained why they were so interested in me.

"Shake it off, Maria. Ricky won't get away with this. My guess, the Coast Guard will be here any minute."

I brought her up to speed on what had happened while she was imprisoned, including my confrontation with Ricky dockside. Her eyes grew wide when I told her about the shootout in the parking lot and the RPG attack in Goodland. But she freaked out when I told her about the face-off with Ricky.

"You told him you took his picture and sent it to the police?"

"Yes."

"And you think the Coast Guard will intercept this yacht?"

"I'm certain of it."

Maria's eyes bulged. "Oh, no!" She began crying again.

"What?"

"Don't you see? They can't possibly let us be discovered on this boat. Ricky will have to eliminate us."

"Oh."

I hadn't thought of that, but it made perfect sense. Perez taunted Maria about taking her back to see her uncle, and, stupidly, told her about the funny money being funneled into his campaign. He was a braggart and she couldn't hurt him once she was in Havana. The money from Russian through Cuba was untraceable, laundered through Chitango's political action committee. Sure, Ricky might take some flak for being on the Jell-O boat if it were boarded by the Coast Guard, but that would be the worst of it.

Which raised a question.

"Have you seen Ricky onboard since we got under way?" I asked.

She shook her head no.

If he were smart, Perez would have hightailed it out of St. Petersburg and never set foot on the yacht. He could explain away the photo as a meeting with me I'd arranged. Where's that pesky Strange now? How should he know?

"You haven't seen Chitango on board have you?"

Again, she shook her head no.

At any moment, I expected the cabin door to fly open and we would be dragged on deck, probably shot, then dumped overboard wrapped in chains.

"I've got a sinking feeling about all this," I said.

"Is that supposed to be funny?"

I shrugged.

"Whatever happened to your computer?" I asked. "We have people hacking your accounts, trying to find something useful."

"I left it in my car. I have no idea what they did with it. And, no, nothing like Edgard's list or anything like that was on it."

"I searched your place," Maria. "It appeared a suitcase and some clothes were missing."

She nodded. "I packed some things when I decided to spend more time in Immokalee, to talk to more people there and at the museum. I got a motel room. When they caught me at the museum, they found my hotel key card and cleaned out my room." She nodded to a small closet in the stateroom. "It's all in there."

"The Third Eye traced your credit cards, trying to locate you, but didn't see anything," I said.

"I paid cash at the motel," she said. "My credit card is maxed. I was only going to spend a couple of nights there. Then they grabbed me."

We were quiet for a moment. The ship continued to rock, but more violently than before. The thunder was becoming a continuous drumbeat.

It occurred to me that with all this rocking and rolling the Jell-O would slosh out of the pool.

I was about to find out how right I was.

CHAPTER 42

THE CABIN DOOR swung open and Hannibal and his buddy, the gunslinger who had pistol whipped me, walked in.

Mr. Pistol aimed his semi-automatic at my head. "Arseny Dombrowsky, you know this name?" he asked in a heavy Russian accent.

Dombrowsky was the thug Deputy Garcia shot in the Mercato parking lot. I nodded. "Yeah, lousy shot. He killed his own partner."

"Shot by police," he said.

"Yep. Took three while running away."

"This your fault," he said. "You will pay for this. Arseny was my brother." He wagged his handgun at me, like a school teacher scolding a child.

"Blow me."

His face empurpled. "Take the girl," he ordered Hannibal. "Meet me topside. Do not eat her yet."

Maria screamed. Hannibal reached for her wrist, but she dodged him and tried to bolt out the door. Instinctively, I tried to leap out of bed, but the handcuff snapped tight. Hannibal slapped one enormous hand around Maria's mouth, his other arm encircled her waist, then he lifted her off her feet as if she were a rag doll and carted her out of the room, Maria's screams muffled by his gigantic paw.

Mr. Pistol gave them a minute to clear the passageway, then tossed the keys to the cuffs on the bed. "This is very nice room. I would hate to get blood on it. Don't tempt me." He thumbed back the hammer on the handgun.

It took a few moments to free my wrist from the cuff, and while I was doing that the Russian backed out into the passageway, putting a little space between us, his gun still trained on me.

"It was stupid to leave bite marks on the girl," I said while fumbling with the lock.

He nodded. "*Da*. Dmitri, he's out of control."

"And why use the same kind of rope to hang Edgard Dominique if you were trying to frame me?"

"We always use that rope. Now shut up."

"Your brother, he tried to kill my dog."

The gunslinger snarled. "*Nyet*. Poison meant for you." He shook his head. "Should have shot you. You make too much trouble for us."

I rolled off the bed and walked through the door, rubbing my wrists. He shoved the gun into the middle of my back and nudged me in the same direction Maria and Hannibal had taken.

Hawk would have made a lightning move, disarmed him, and shoved the pistol up his ass before you could say "professional thug." Joe Pike would have used either tae kwon do, wing chun or ubawazi on him, breaking at least half a dozen bones. Kate O'Hare would never have let him get the drop on her in the first place. What I would do is get myself shot if I didn't march straight ahead, which is what I did.

A stairway led upward to the stern deck. Hannibal held Maria around her neck with one of his enormous hands. She'd stopped yelling. No point. Nobody hears you scream in a tropical storm.

As we stepped onto the deck, I slipped on some pink slime and fell to my knees. Yep, the Jell-O was definitely sloshing out of the pool. The Russian popped me on the back of my head with his gun barrel.

"Stop that," I yelled.

"Up," he ordered.

I "upped" and staggered to the stern rail toward Maria. Hannibal wasn't armed, but with his size he didn't need to be. Was he always so big, or does eating faces build muscle?

"Dmitri!" the gunslinger shouted to Hannibal, "Hold him while I get ropes."

Hannibal reached out and grabbed me by the back of the neck, too, just like Maria. No doubt that if he wanted to snap my vertebrae he could do so effortlessly. Mr. Pistol switched the weapon to his left hand, still training it in our direction, and reached toward a large rectangular container secured to the rail with bungee cords. He slipped as the deck rolled over to starboard and stumbled. But his gun stayed pointed in our direction.

"In here, *da?*" he yelled to Dmitri.

Before Hannibal could answer, the ship rocked violently and Hannibal let go of our necks momentarily to grab the rail behind him. A split second later, before either Maria or I could react, a blinding flash of light and a deafening blast stunned us.

A painful tingly heat instantly shot from my feet to my groin as the current from the lightning strike spread across the sodden deck. Mr. Pistol screamed, his gun flying free as he fell. The lid of the container flew open and a dozen chickens burst from their cage, cackling and flapping only to be swept over the stern in the tornadic winds raking the yacht. I turned to Hannibal. His face was blackened, his shirt burning, his hands welded to the rail. He looked like a gigantic deep-fried Frankenstein.

Maybe there is a God, the God of the Old Testament, smiting my enemies. I marveled at that thought for a moment, but then, suddenly, Hannibal's eyes snapped open.

Someone should have screamed, "It's alive!"

But it wouldn't be Maria, on her hands and knees, crawling back toward the stairwell through the pink ooze awash on the deck.

Nor Mr. Pistol, also on his hands and knees, groping for his missing gun as if he were blind.

It wouldn't be Hannibal, who was bellowing *"arrgh, arrgh"* in a lousy Johnny Depp imitation of a drunken pirate.

And it wouldn't be me because in that moment I lurched over to Maria and scooped her into my arms. Then I turned and sprinted across the heaving deck to the starboard rail. My foot hit a patch of pink Jell-O slime and I fell headfirst, sliding toward the edge of the yacht. I pushed Maria's head down and the two of us slid under the rail and over the side into the roiling Gulf of Mexico below.

CHAPTER 43

WE SPLASHED INTO the water head first. Thank God the lightning short circuited the yacht's engine or we might have been chopped to bits by its propellers.

I lost my grip on Maria as we fell, and after I kicked furiously back to the surface I looked around for her. A wave smacked me in the face knocking me under. I clawed my way back to the surface, gasping for air.

"Maria," I shouted. No reply. I looked to my left, then to my right. Still no Maria. I yelled her name again. Still no answer, but I thought I could hear her coughing.

I rose on another wave, and when I did I could see her, twenty feet away, arms splashing in the water, trying to stay afloat. I swam over to her and she grabbed me around the neck, pulling us both under.

I let myself sink, and she let go. Learned that trick during lifeguard training in high school. I powered back to the surface, swam around her, and held her from behind.

"I've got you," I said. "Just relax or you'll pull us both under again."

Another wave smashed into us, but we rode it upward. I clung tightly to her lest we become separated. It was a miracle I found her; I wouldn't lose her now.

"Maria, I want you to take my hand."

She did.

"We have to get our shoes and clothes off or they'll drag us down."

We rose upward on another huge wave and I saw the yacht drifting away, carried by its momentum. That was a relief. I ducked under water and wrenched one of my Nike's off and brought it to the surface then let it go. "See? Now you do it."

We bobbed up and down in the swells for a few seconds while she screwed up her courage, then she reached down and ripped off one of her shoes. Then without waiting, dove again and got the other one.

"Good girl," I said. "Now, keep an eye on me and grab me if we start to drift apart," I shouted. I reached into the water and slipped out of my cargo shorts. Then I tore off my shirt. As my shirt came off, she grabbed my arm and nodded at me. She got the drill, and repeated the same motions, stripping down to her bra and panties.

"All right," I said. "Let's see if we can't figure out where we are."

We floated up on another swell and I saw the yacht had drifted further away. Good. Now that we were free of gunslingers and cannibals, all we had to worry about were sharks.

"Your head is bleeding again," Maria gasped.

Great. Blood in the water.

Still, we were a hell of a lot safer in the Gulf than aboard the Jell-O boat. I didn't worry about drowning—I could teach fish to swim. After mom drowned in that cave, I vowed I would never end that way. Joined the swim team in high school. Swam second-string for Texas in college.

I spotted the Sunshine Skyway Bridge east of us, so we were just outside Tampa Bay. And that meant we would be in or near the ship channel. To the south, I found what I hoped I would find: A buoy, its lights blinking, marking the channel boundary.

It took half an hour of hard swimming in rough water to make it to the buoy, taking our bearings as we crested the waves, then pushing on. Maria was a champ, she kept pace with me, helping to navigate.

Every once in a while, I would glance back over the top of the white-caps toward the yacht, afraid it might come after us.

Shortly before we made it to the buoy, a lifeboat dropped from the side of the *Monkey Business Too*. I couldn't see who was in it, but no sooner had it splashed into the Gulf than it turned back toward Tampa Bay.

"The Russians are leaving, the Russians are leaving," I huffed.

"What?" Maria swallowed a mouthful of seawater and gagged.

"Come on," I shouted. "We're almost there."

In a few minutes we were clinging to the edge of the buoy.

"How long will we be here?" Maria asked once she regained her breath.

"Shouldn't be too long," I said. "When the storm clears, there will be ships passing through. We'll signal one of them, get help."

After resting for a few more minutes, I heaved myself out of the water and onto the base of the buoy. I'd seen seals do that in Santa Barbara. Figured I could, too. I pulled Maria up after me, and when I did she raised up on her toes and kissed me on the cheek. "You sure know how to show a girl a good time."

I had my arms around her, steadying her, intensely aware she was nearly naked.

"Why don't we try to sit down on the edge of this thing," I said. I let go of her and lowered myself. But as I did—I couldn't help myself, I really couldn't—my eyes passed her wet underwear: Maria Martinez had not shaved her pubic hair.

She sat down beside me and gripped my arm, steadying herself.

"Uh, Maria," I said. "I've got a really sensitive question to ask you."

She looked up at me. "Go ahead."

"Please don't think I'm a perv or anything, but I couldn't help noticing your pubic hair."

"WHAT!"

She wrenched away from me, slapped me on the shoulder, then

toppled back into the water. Gasping and crying, she shouted at me in *Espanol*, and, using my Jedi skills, I deduced she was not praising my powers of observation.

"Maria, give me your hand," I yelled down to her.

She flailed around for a few moments, still fussing, but finally allowed me to haul her back aboard the buoy.

"Let me explain," I said, and after another minute of angry yammering in *Espanol*, she relented. I told her how Geneva argued the body in the morgue could not be her because the corpse's public area had not been shaved.

"Geneva!" Maria blurted. Then she started laughing hysterically. At first I worried maybe the heat and dehydration were getting to her. We'd been out in the water for nearly an hour. The storm had passed and the blazing sun was baking us.

"I called Geneva before I met you for dinner," she said. "She was so excited I had a date. I explained it was business, but she wouldn't listen. She gave me all this advice. Finally, she told me to be sure to shave."

I guess I looked at her funny at that point and she laughed again.

"I shave my legs every day, but Geneva was talking about something else. She said all the porno stars shave their privates. Those were her words. Men like it, she said. I asked her how she knew this and she said Uncle Larry said so."

"So you told her that's what you were going to do?" I asked.

"No. She told me to do it. She insisted. And to get her off my back I said OK."

And if that conversation had never taken place, Maria and I might not be sitting on a buoy in the Gulf of Mexico waiting to be rescued. She'd be on a slow boat to Cuba, never to be seen again.

Weird.

The sun continued to beat down and I could tell she was fading. Me, too.

"MJM." I said, trying to distract her. "Your middle name is…"

"Jennifer. It's my mother's first name."

"Ah."

"You ask, why?"

"Like I told you, we were trying to crack your password."

She looked puzzled.

"Eight six seven five three oh nine," I sang. I was trying to keep her spirits up, but for some reason she frowned.

"We were playing with things like Tutone, Jenny, trying to figure out what MJM8675309 might be about."

"It's my password. For everything."

A wave rolled the buoy and I nearly slipped off. "That's not safe, you know, having the same password for everything."

"Can't you tell. I like living dangerously. How many girls you know hang out like this in their underwear."

A half-mile away, a cutter, painted white with a broad red diagonal stripe, steamed in our direction.

"Looks like the cavalry's on the way," I said.

Maria grabbed my arm and squeezed.

We heard a whooshing sound behind us. Startled, we turned to see a silvery pod of dolphins curling in and out of the water. The closest dolphin surfaced again, blew water out of its blowhole, then disappeared.

"Flipper!" Maria cried, her voice cracking.

She smiled like a little girl on her first trip to Sea World.

The dolphins surfaced and dove around us for a few minutes. Likely, the buoy attracted smaller fish, food for Flipper and friends.

One of the dolphins popped up at Maria's feet and began chirping at her, his beak breaking into the smiley shape that humans translate as friendly but, really, is just the natural curvature of their jawline. Alligators have the same upturn at the corners of their mouths, too.

"Look!" Maria cried. "He wants to help us."

The dolphin began flailing its tail and climbing its way out of the water. As it did, it nudged Maria's leg with its beak. She didn't like that so much.

"What's he doing?" she asked, her voice wavering.

"I think he's hot for you," I said.

Dolphins are notoriously horny and have been known to try to have their way with scuba divers from time to time.

"Give him a hand job and he'll go away." I was just trying to be helpful.

Maria hugged the buoy, putting as much distance as she could between herself and Lothario. "It's not fair, it's just not fair…"

The Coast Guard cutter pulled alongside the *Monkey Business Too*. A boarding party clambered onto the yacht.

"Will they see us?" Maria asked. She sounded weepy.

"They'll find us."

I reached out to her, keeping one hand on the buoy.

"Let me cheer you up," I said, giving her shoulder a squeeze. "I've composed a song in honor of our experience."

"A song?" she asked, shielding her eyes from the sun, a faint smile crossing her chapped lips, trying to be brave.

"Yes. I don't do music very much. Gives me earworms. But my mother used to sing this Barbara Streisand number. I've changed the lyrics. Ready?"

"Sure."

I have a godlike singing voice. I know this because the only time I ever went to a karaoke bar, my date spent the entire evening muttering, "Jesus Christ, Jesus Christ."

"Sing along if you like," I told Maria, then began:

"People
People who eat people
Are the hungriest people in the world…"

Before I could continue, there was a loud splash as the dolphins simultaneously dove and began swimming furiously away. What got them so riled up?

A few minutes later, we heard a whop, whop, whopping sound approaching rapidly.

We looked up to see a massive helicopter, painted in the Coast Guard's signature white with a broad red stripe. As it neared, I noticed a thin blue line in the design, too. Patriotic. The chopper lowered and hovered over the water a few dozen yards away. Two rescue swimmers jumped out and splashed into the water.

The cavalry, indeed, had arrived.

CHAPTER 44

THE CHOPPER SOARED over the Sunshine Skyway Bridge en route to Albert Whited Airport, a short walk from the Port of St. Petersburg. The crew gave us water during the brief flight and supplied us with blue fatigues and flip-flops, which they kept aboard for waterlogged people pulled from the drink. Maria's outfit drooped off her small frame. I had to leave most of my buttons undone. But we weren't complaining.

The pilot advised us there would be a reception committee waiting for us. As the tarmac rose to greet us, I spotted two patrol cars—St. Petersburg PD and Collier County sheriff's. They flanked an ambulance and a black Camry. A redhead stood next to the Camry, her hair and skirt windblown by the chopper's downdraft.

Crew members helped Maria and me down from the chopper. No sooner did my flip-flops touch the ground than Gwenn dashed over, ignoring the still-swirling blades overhead, and flung herself into my arms. She kissed me hard and hugged me so tight I thought my ribs would crack.

She pulled back and looked me in the eyes. "You scared me to death. I thought I'd never see you again." A tear rolled down her right cheek.

"I will always come back for you, princess," I said.

She rolled her eyes.

Lester ambled over and took Maria's hand. "So good to finally meet you, Ms. Martinez," he said. "My name is Lester Rivers, and I am with The Third Eye. Your aunt, Geneva asked us to find you. She will be so relieved you are alive and well."

Maria smiled. "I'm relieved, too. Thanks to him." Maria turned to me. "I never did thank you for saving my life."

"All in a day's work." I turned back to Gwenn. "I believe the two of you know each other." Trying to be polite, sensing a little tension.

Maria offered Gwenn her hand and they shook, Maria giving Gwenn a full body scan. "Thanks for leaving that message. It's what broke this open."

Gwenn nodded and offered a tentative smile.

Maria nodded in my direction. "You get tired of him, let me know." She turned and began walking toward the waiting cars.

I took Gwenn by the hand.

"You getting tired of me?" I asked.

"I don't know. Things have been kinda dull around you lately."

The medics wanted to know if we needed anything, but we assured them that with the water we'd gotten aboard the chopper we were fine. They bandaged the cut on my head and gave us some more bottles of water. I poured some into my hands and washed my face, getting the crusted salt off. Maria followed suit.

"You've been through hell," I said to her. "You sure you don't want to get checked out at the hospital?"

"No," she insisted. "I want to get on with this." Not unfriendly, just all business. A pro.

Detective Wiggins walked over and pulled me aside. He would need an affidavit regarding the incident at Chitango's outbuilding.

"I already took Rivers' statement," he said. "You're lucky to be alive."

"Lester told me the three security guys, they were executed?"

He nodded. "The FBI has taken over the investigation. But we're helping out."

I nodded.

"Remember that feeb, Cao? He's got the point. We're going to see him and some local detectives now."

The drive to the St. Petersburg Police Department's crumbling headquarters on First Avenue North took just a few minutes. I rode with Wiggins and Maria. Gwenn and Lester followed in her car. We were led to a conference room brimming with cops. It must have been eighty degrees in there.

"What's with the AC?" I asked nobody in particular.

"They're working on it," a voice to my left replied. The FBI agent, Cao.

"You guys at the federal building got air conditioning, right?"

"Yes. Always better to work for the people who print the money."

He pointed to a group of empty chairs on the other side of the conference table.

I knew several other people in the room: the ATF agent from the other night, a man I recognized from television as the Pinellas County sheriff, and at the far end of the table, Wiggins. Others included a uniformed Coast Guard officer and several guys in short sleeves and ties that I took to be local police detectives. A suit sat next to Cao. An assistant U.S. attorney named McCarthy.

"Let's begin," Cao said. Then he faced Maria and me. "We will be recording this conversation. And, to be clear, you are here voluntarily, but anything you say will become part of the permanent record of this case. If you wish legal representation, you are entitled to that."

"Our attorney is here," I said, nodding to Gwenn.

Maria led off, describing her kidnapping while prowling around Chitango's headquarters. She'd been held captive in a guest house on the grounds of the museum. She was drugged after her capture but otherwise unharmed, but she was under constant surveillance by a handful of men who spoke what sounded like Russian. She fingered Ricky Perez as her kidnapper, and revealed how he confessed to receiving campaign funds that were being funneled from Russia through Cuba and then through Chitango's political action committee. She said Perez planned to smuggle her to Cuba where the government agreed to hold her. She said she was the illegitimate daughter of Fidel Castro, and that's why she wasn't killed.

Everyone at the table listened without interruption as she reeled out her story, although eyes bulged and heads shook at various intervals. When she revealed her relationship with Castro there were a couple of audible gasps. When she finished, the questions began pouring out.

"Why were you investigating Chitango?" McCarthy asked.

Maria turned to me and I filled them in on Dominique's arrest, how a source told me about the missing data on Dominique's computer, and how I turned the story over to Maria to investigate for the Tropic Press.

McCarthy looked up from his note-taking. "Your source?"

"You know better," I said.

He gave me a few seconds of prosecutorial intimidation, then said, "We'll get back to that."

Gwenn recounted her conversation with Maria, who wanted to interview Edgard Dominique at the jail, and how Gwenn forwarded a note from Dominique to Maria.

"Our assumption," I said, "was that the missing data on the computer held a list of people implicated in some sort of sex scandal. The question is: How could the hard drive on the computer be wiped? As agent Cao knows, the FBI has been working with the sheriff's office on that."

"We still don't know the answer for sure," Cao said.

Wiggins jumped in and shared how a jailer had been bribed, how Dominique was hanged, and he gave a recap of the shootout in the Mercato parking lot, the rocket attack in Goodland, and the bribed jailer's mysterious death along Alligator Alley.

I recounted the attempt to frame me for what appeared to be Maria's murder and how my search of her condo led to the discovery of the missing note from Edgard Dominique.

"So you hid the note in a coffee can?" McCarthy asked Maria.

"I used it as a kind of safe deposit box."

Wiggins spoke up: "A coffee can, you say?"

"I don't drink coffee, myself, it's my aunt's. She likes Folgers." Maria said.

Wiggins shook his head. "Here's the thing. I helped search Maria's condo. It was me, Henderson, and a CSI. I didn't see a coffee can in your pantry. If I had, I would have done exactly what Strange did. So I'm confident it wasn't there. It also wasn't there yesterday when I searched your condo again. I was specifically looking for it and it was gone."

"It *was* there when I searched the place," I said. "If it wasn't there before and it isn't there now, something very odd is going on."

That got the room buzzing.

McCarthy finally rapped the table with his knuckles. "We need to wrap this up. I want to get warrants and get going. He turned to me. Can you finish?"

I recounted how Lester and I were ambushed. That we managed to free ourselves. I did not disclose how Lester beat the information out of Harvey Turnbull. I continued with my confrontation with Ricky Perez dockside, how his goon slugged me, and how Maria and I escaped.

When I got to the lightning strike, Wiggins whistled out loud. "Holy cow. And he lived?"

"The guy's the size of a great ape," I said. "You'll need an RPG to take him out."

The Coast Guard officer had taken a phone call during my part of show-and-tell and came back in the room just as I finished up.

For his benefit I ended with, "and that's how the Coast Guard saved the day."

"Not quite," he said. "We searched the *Monkey Business Too* from bow to stern. Congressman Perez was not on board. Nor were the men and women Mr. Strange said he photographed while boarding."

"Maria and I saw a small boat leaving before you guys arrived," I said. "I guessed it was the two Russian hitters. They on board?"

"No. Your guess could be right."

"So, Ricky scuttled his plans for the Jell-O Boat cruise, probably blamed it on the weather, and set the boat sailing for Cuba?" Lester asked.

"Or just into international waters," the Coast Guard officer said. "Captain of the yacht said he was ordered to take the vessel twelve miles out and wait for further instructions."

"Would that have stopped you guys?" I asked.

The officer smiled. "No."

"They just needed to get into deep water and dump you two overboard" Lester said. "If they'd succeeded, we wouldn't be here now."

McCarthy and Cao conferred quietly between themselves for a few minutes, then turned their attention back to the rest of us.

"Ms. Martinez, Mr. Strange, I appreciate your cooperation," McCarthy said. "I am going to ask you to fill out and sign affidavits attesting to the events you described here. We will then execute search warrants at the homes and offices of both the Reverend Chitango and Congressman Perez."

McCarthy wanted us to drive over to the federal building in Tampa to complete the paperwork, but I balked.

"Why can't we do that right here, right now?" I asked. "Time is not our friend."

The two St. Pete detectives chimed in. "We can go upstairs and type all this up."

Maria and I were shown to two adjoining desks with computer terminals. We plopped down and began writing. Midway through the narrative, I noticed the two cops peering over my shoulder.

"What?"

"You sure type fast."

"It's my super power."

Gwenn and Lester left the building to find us some chow. They returned with burgers and Cokes for Maria and me and doughnuts for the cops. We ate while we wrote. When we were finished, McCarthy's assistant copied and pasted our stories onto affidavit forms and printed them out. We signed the forms and Gwenn witnessed them.

Wiggins asked for copies.

"You still need a statement from me about what happened at Chitango's?" I asked.

"This will do for now," he said.

Cao said four agents from the FBI's Miami Field Office were already en route to the Museum of Holy Creation, and other agents in Miami were standing by and would raid Ricky Perez's office and home as soon as the warrants arrived.

It was already past three in the afternoon. It would be after five before we got back to Naples. My camera gear, my cell phone, and my rental car keys would be at the bottom of the Gulf by now. Bad enough they tried to kill me. Now I'd have to stand in line at DMV and get a new driver's license. And the credit card companies, God, what a nightmare that would be. And the people at the rental car company. They would be pissed.

And what would I tell Edwina about *this* camera?

Maria grabbed me by the arm. This got a look from Gwenn.

"We need to write," Maria said. "It's time."

Congressman and Televangelist Implicated in Sex Ring and Political Scandal

By Maria J. Martinez and Alexander Strange

Tropic©Press

ST. PETERSBURG—U.S. Rep. Ricky Perez has admitted receiving illegal foreign campaign contributions, funneled to him through a political action committee run by conservative televangelist the Rev. Lee Roy Chitango.

Perez has also been involved with a sex ring based out of Immokalee, Fla., home of Chitango's Museum of Holy Creation.

It was at this religious theme park that Perez, running for Florida's GOP U.S. Senate nomination, confessed his illegal activities to Tropic©Press correspondent Maria Martinez while he held her captive in a guest house on the theme park's campus. Martinez is Perez's cousin.

Martinez was presumed dead for several days after a body matching her description was discovered floating dockside at Stan's Idle Hour in Goodland, a small fishing village southeast of Naples. The dead woman's face was eaten off, but she wore a birthstone ring identified by Tropic©Press columnist Alexander Strange as belonging to Martinez. The corpse had ligature marks indicating she had either been strangled or hanged.

Not until a relative of Martinez asserted the corpse was misidentified did authorities realize the reporter might have been kidnapped.

Agents of The Third Eye, the Boise, Idaho-based detective agency, identified the ligature marks on the corpse as being consistent with the work of a group of Russian mob enforcers known as Stalin's Hangmen. It is believed the illegal contributions flowing into Perez's campaign originated in Russia and were laundered through Cuba.

In the past several days, four of those Russian mob enforcers have been killed in a pair of spectacular shootouts with Collier County sheriff's deputies. Also, a Collier County jail guard was found murdered. He is believed to have arranged the jail-cell hanging of a Haitian native who claimed to have incriminating evidence involving Chitango and others in a bizarre sex cult involving, among other things, the ritual killing of animals—often chickens—during orgies.

Two Russian hit-men kidnapped Martinez as she explored the grounds of Chitango's museum. The mobsters made two unsuccessful attempts on Strange's life—once in the parking lot of the upscale Mercato shopping center in north Naples, the other at his residence in Goodland. In both cases, the gunmen were felled either by their own bullets or by sheriff's deputies.

Earlier today, three employees of Chitango's operation were found murdered, execution style, in a barn on the Museum of Holy Creation campus. Police suspect Russian hit men in those assassinations, too.

Another pair of suspects, accompanied by Perez, ambushed Strange while he was photographing the boarding of a massive luxury yacht in St. Petersburg earlier today that featured a swimming pool filled with pink Jell-O.

Ten men were seen boarding the yacht in the early morning hours today, along with a half-dozen women.

However, the yacht set sail without those passengers when Perez learned that Strange transmitted photographs of his guests to The Third Eye and police. Strange was assaulted, held, and handcuffed in a crew cabin below decks when the yacht, the *Monkey Business Too*, set sail out of the port during a sudden tropical storm.

Strange and Martinez managed to escape their captors and were rescued by the Coast Guard.

The FBI has issued warrants for the arrest of Perez and Chitango and agents were en route to their residences and businesses as this report was being filed...

CHAPTER 45

MARIA AND I gave the story one last look and then I pressed the send button, transmitting it to Edwina Mahoney.

"You know," Edwina said when I called earlier to let her know we had a story coming, "your job was to write about weird news, not make it."

"Was?"

"Congratulations, you now work for Simplex Digital Media Holdings."

"Sounds like a sexually transmitted disease."

"It's a holding company. We're the third independent online news service they've acquired. The idea is to put all of us on a common advertising platform, combine our news resources, have a common brand."

What brand?"

"Tropic Press. They like the name."

"Will I still work for you?"

"Yes, our team stays intact. In fact, I've been named publisher of the whole shebang. That was part of the negotiation."

Of course. Edwina wasn't just a great editor, she knew her way around a spreadsheet, too, and I couldn't imagine her selling the service and stepping aside.

"And your check is in the mail," she said.

"How much?"

"Enough to buy that scow you live on."

Which reminded me of Uncle Leo. It was his scow, after all. "Uh, Ed, could you do me another favor?"

"Name it."

"I'm about to write the best story you've ever read, but I need to let Uncle Leo know I'm OK. You guys are still on speaking terms, right? Could you call him? I'm really pressed for time."

Edwina Mahoney and Judge Leonard D. Strano were a number for a while. I didn't know that when she hired me at the *Phoenix Daily Sun*. It's all about connections, right? But it still was a sketchy point between Edwina and me.

"No problem," she said. "I'll let him know."

Maria and I finally were done writing and we got out of our chairs. I turned to her and gave her a hug. "We'll need to stay in touch," I said. "This isn't finished."

She nodded.

Rivers stepped over. "I'm hitching a ride back to Naples with Wiggins," he said. "Ms. Martinez, would you care to join us?"

"I guess." She looked at me for a moment, then turned back to Rivers. "Where will I stay?"

Wiggins chimed in. "I have a set of keys to your condo. Will you be comfortable returning there?"

"I suppose so."

I walked over to Gwenn and took her hand. "Take me home."

"Home," as it turned out, was a suite at the Hilton Hotel just down the street from the marina. She'd booked a room while Maria and I were hammering away at our keyboards.

A cart of delicious food and drink greeted us as we stepped into the room. A bottle of Dom. BLTs. Fries. Strawberries. There are benefits to dating a high-powered lawyer.

"This is fabulous," I said. I pulled her into my arms and gave her the very best kiss in the inventory. Eat your heart out, Dread Pirate Roberts.

"First things first," she said and pointed to the bathroom. It felt good to get the salt and grit off. The hotel even provided a toothbrush and a razor, of which I took full advantage.

I pulled a white terrycloth robe from the closet after showering, wrapped it around myself, and walked back into the bedroom. I needn't have bothered.

Gwenn was draped on the bed, naked, a glass of champagne in hand.

"Come and get it," she said.

I dropped my robe.

"As you wish."

CHAPTER 46

LESTER CALLED THE next day. "We've located Perez." We meaning The Third Eye.

"That was fast," I said. "Let me guess. He's in Cuba."

"Was. For maybe an hour or two. Our sources say he never got out of Jose Marti airport. They packed him off on the first flight to Venezuela."

I thought about that for a moment. "How do you know all this?"

"If I told you I'd have to kill you."

"So, can Perez be extradited from Venezuela?"

"On paper. In reality, the government there rarely cooperates with the U.S. Caracas is filled with ex-pats dodging the law from all over the world."

"So now what?"

"Well, our government can sit on its hands, or it can request the assistance of an off-the-books organization such as ours to extract him."

"How hard would that be?"

"Not especially. We'd use a honey trap."

"How's that work?"

"A team flies in. Commercial. It's only a three-hour flight out of Miami. We track him down, watch him, see where he hangs out, how he spends his time. We have several capable female agents who are experienced at this. The basic setup is they meet him, they flirt with him, then they lure him to a spot where we bag him. After that, we take a charter flight out of the country. Get back, turn him over to the feds. Tell them we found him on the side of the road. Government's hands are clean."

"Maybe instead of a female operative, you could just find a very attractive chicken."

"*Buck, buck, buck, buckahhhhhh!*" Lester was in rare form.

"Seriously, though, Lester, I got a very weird vibe from that guy. I mean, did you see his teeth, those canines? Who knows what he's into."

"You're still obsessing about the Army of the Strange, aren't you? Those vampire names they use."

"They called it on the cannibal."

Lester nodded. "Yes, they did. Be good to know who they are."

We were quiet for a moment. "This Venezuela gig, it going to happen?" I asked.

"Maybe. Just because we can do it doesn't mean it won't take the bureaucrats a while to build up the nerve. We'll see. If it does, you want in?"

"I thought you'd never ask."

"Well, I'm asking. Or more accurately, Colonel Lake is asking. I've been authorized to offer you a position with The Third Eye."

"A position?"

"Yes. You've impressed people."

"Mostly I ran around trying not to get killed."

"Consider it. I can tell you the pay is generous. There is always adventure. And every now and then we're able to do some good."

"Sounds like my current job, except for the pay part. And doing any good."

"You wouldn't have to give up your position with the news service," he said. "In fact, its good cover."

"Not sure about the ethics of that," I said.

"Something to work out."

"Would I get a neuralizer or a shoe phone or something?" I asked.

"Just think about it."

The Rev. Lee Roy Chitango Discovered Mutilated Deep in the Everglades

By Maria J. Martinez and Alexander Strange

Tropic⊚Press

The ravaged remains of the Rev. Lee Roy Chitango have been discovered deep in the Everglades a day after he is believed to have hijacked a van transporting exotic snakes that was en route to the Naples Zoo.

Video captured by an airborne Florida Highway Patrol drone shows Chitango ditching his sedan at a Marathon gas station at the intersection of the Tamiami Trail and State Road 29 on the edge of the Big Cypress National Preserve. Video then shows Chitango assaulting the driver of the van and driving south toward Everglades City.

This occurred shortly after arrest warrants were issued for the televangelist. Chitango was pursued by police after his role in funneling illegal contributions to a U.S. Senate campaign was revealed by the Tropic⊚Press. He was also tied to a sordid sex and bestiality ring based out of his Museum of Holy Creation.

Police said Chitango appears to have driven into a little-used swamp-buggy trail east of Everglades City, where the van collided with a cypress knee and became mired in mud several miles into the swamp.

Hunters, attracted to the site by a swarm of buzzards overhead, found a crocodile dragging Chitango's corpse away from the van. A police spokesman said the hunters fired several rounds into the crocodile, described as "at least" eighteen feet in length, before the reptile ripped off Chitango's left arm at the elbow and submerged.

"That weren't no regular croc, I'll tell you that," one of the hunters,

Bobby Keith Jennings, told police. "I shot that bad boy three times and it didn't even flinch. When it tore that poor fella's arm off, it turned and glared at me hateful like. I've hunted gators all over the 'Glades and I ain't never seen nothin' like that. Crocs, they're different. I swear, his eyes were the eyes of the devil. They glowed."

Chitango, police said, appears to already have been dead at that point, crushed by one of the Burmese pythons the van was transporting. All of the snakes, which can grow to nearly twenty feet in length, were missing from the van. The cage housing the reptiles appears to have been jarred open by the force of the van's collision with the tree.

"It was horrible," said Sgt. John Reetz of the Collier County Sheriff's Office. "His chest, it was pulped. His arm, it was gone. It's the most awful thing I've ever seen. Even worse than that time my wife made me watch the Kardashians."

Chitango's body also appears to have been mauled by other animals in the swamp, police said. His face was devoured, they said, with both eyes chewed out.

Deputies said panther tracks were visible in the mud near the body.

"We don't know for sure, of course," Reetz said, "but the Fish and Wildlife guys think maybe a panther got to him after the pythons and then the panther was run off by the crocodile. If those hunters hadn't shown up, there wouldn't have been anything left but his shoes."

However, a man calling himself the "Skinkster" said Chitango was the victim of the Skunk Ape. "He was huge. I saw him foraging around this part of the swamp earlier. At one point, he turned to me and snarled. He had a huge gap between his front teeth, but his face, oh man, his face, it was burned to a crisp. I'll admit it. I ran away. And I don't run from anything."

The van containing the exotic snakes was en route to the Naples Zoo where the pythons were to be included in a new exhibit highlighting the destruction the invasive species is wreaking on Everglades wildlife.

Now, of course, they are on the loose.

Chitango's brief flight from justice followed the disclosure that he appears to have been working with a Russian criminal gang known as Stalin's Hangmen, and was using his political action committee, For a Free and Faithful America, as a conduit to funnel illegal financial contributions to the U.S. Senate campaign of congressman Ricky Perez.

Warrants were issued for the arrest of both Chitango and Perez. Perez's whereabouts is unknown.

The Hangmen have been implicated in at least two recent murders: An unidentified woman whose body surfaced at the docks in Goodland, and an inmate at the Collier County jail, Edgard Dominique, who was preparing to offer testimony against Chitango. The Hangmen have also been implicated in the abduction and attempted murders of these reporters.

A spokesman for the *Oh God, Oh God* radio and television franchise and the Museum of Holy Creation, said, "The ministry will live on. We are blessed that the Reverend Chitango had the foresight to name his successor. His son and associate pastor, Elroy Chitango, will assume his dearly departed father's duties and continue the work of the church as we approach the end of days.

"Elroy Chitango is the Chosen One."

CHAPTER 47

I PUNCHED THE send button and the story made its way to the news service.

We were in Maria's condo working on her new laptop, a gift from Aunt Geneva. Ricky had put Geneva on a flight back home to Connecticut shortly after driving back to Miami from Naples. Geneva told Maria she was so furious "with that miserable, self-indulgent prick I almost kicked him."

I called Geneva to thank her for having the courage to give me the keys to the condo. That allowed us to unravel the mystery of Maria's disappearance. Doing so, right under Ricky's nose, involved more risk than either of us knew at the time.

"I'm very sorry, Mr. Strange, that I was rude to you," she said. "I wasn't thinking clearly. I was upset. I hope you understand."

"Of course."

"I've always known there was something wrong with that boy," she said. "To think I was in the same car with him. And all the while he was keeping my Maria a prisoner. The bastard!"

We were working at Maria's place because the *Miss Demeanor* was in dry dock on Marco Island finally getting repaired. The check from the sale of the Tropic Press had arrived. It was bigger than I expected, and I asked Uncle Leo to sell the boat to me.

He refused. But he said if I paid for the repairs he'd sign the title over so long as I would allow Judge Goodfellow and him to borrow it from time to time for their traditional maritime festivities.

"Only if you don't run it aground," I told him.

"All right, then you come with us and you can drive."

We had a deal.

Gwenn wasn't wild about the idea of me spending more time with Maria, especially at her condo, but we needed to work somewhere. I called my contacts at the *Naples Daily News* and asked if we could borrow a couple of desks, but they gave us the cold shoulder. I got that. We'd just cherry-picked a fantastic story in their own back yard and they didn't like it. I wouldn't either.

Finally, I put it to Gwenn like this:

"If this relationship is going to have a future, it will have to be built on trust."

She agreed. "You can trust I will cut your balls off if you touch that bitch."

You see? This is what I'm talking about. Trust.

I was staying at Gwenn's apartment while repairs to the trawler were under way. We were both furiously busy, she at her new job, me with follow-ups on the story. We ate dinner every evening at different restaurants on Fifth Avenue. Our goal: to dine at every single one and then rank order them against a list of criteria we developed:

- Best cocktails.
- Best wine selection.
- A subjective 1-10 rating of the food.
- Service.
- Price.
- Quality of sex afterwards.

So far, Vergina and Citrus were neck and neck in first place with Alberto's and Bha Bha Persian Bistro close seconds.

I'm not big on collaborative writing, but Maria turned out to be surprisingly pleasant to work with. It helped that I insisted she have top billing on our double-bylines. Seemed only fair since it was her story and she got kidnapped pursuing it.

Gwenn was not so generous.

"None of this would have happened if she had talked to you first," she insisted one night over dinner. "She might not have been kidnapped and that poor girl who ended up in the bay might not have been killed."

That's what you get when you date a lawyer.

All the major news services and television networks would be running the story about Lee Roy Chitango's death we just transmitted. Edwina called after she got it to tell us our new investors at the venereal disease corporation were ecstatic about the coverage.

We were hard at work at Maria's when the he doorbell rang. Miss Ellie, the elderly lady who had ambushed me when I came to toss Maria's place, was standing at the door. She held a bright red can of Folgers's coffee.

"I am sorry, my dear," Ellie said to Maria, "I forgot to return this."

"Return it?" Maria gasped. "You've had it?"

"I do apologize. I ran out so I came over and borrowed yours. I have a key. Well, that was the first time. I only took a few scoops—I usually only drink a cup a day, first thing in the morning to get the old heart started. I was going to bring the can right back, but it slipped my mind. Next thing you know there were coppers all over the place and I waited for them to clear out before I returned it."

"You returned it?" I asked.

"Yes. I intended to go to Wynn's Market and get some more, but I got lazy and figured I could do without for a while. Then a few days later I wanted some more—I was having one of those mornings, no get-up-and-go—so I came back over and I'm afraid I borrowed yours again. So, here it is. You ever run out, you can borrow some of mine. I went to the store today."

Maria turned to me, her eyes wide. I burst out laughing.

"What's so funny, you?" Ellie grumped.

She took a step inside to get a bead on me. "Oh, I remember you. You were snooping around here before. Said your name was Alice. Give me a break."

She walked out the door and shuffled back down the walkway.

"Alex. Not Alice," I shouted after her. It landed on deaf ears.

CHAPTER 48

WE HAD SOLVED the mystery of the disappearing coffee can. Wiggins didn't see it during the initial search because Ellie had borrowed it. And when he came back after I found the note in the can, it was gone once again thanks to Ellie.

I told Gwenn about our surprise visitor that evening over dinner at Yabba Island Grill. We were sipping sauvignon blanc and waiting for our entrees. I'd selected the sweet and spicy steak and she'd ordered the rasta pasta.

The food finally arrived, delivered by a familiar face, but her hair was now blond instead of green.

"Hey, Alex."

"Hey, Gabby. New do?"

"Wig."

Gabby studied Gwenn for a moment then refocused her attention on me. "Your date is beautiful. I see now why you never called." She turned and sauntered back to the kitchen.

Gwenn was frowny. "Care to explain?"

I felt myself blushing, like I had done something wrong and gotten caught. Hell of a thing to be perfectly innocent and still feel guilty. Hey, I threw her note away, didn't I?

"She worked at Stan's," I said. "You know Mrs. Overstreet, the lady who keeps Fred for me? She's her niece."

"No. When did she ask you to call her?"

"Oh. That. Uh, well, she left me a note onboard the boat. Invited me to call her. I never did."

"She's been on the boat?"

"Yeah, she returned Fred from Mrs. Overstreet's..."

"Just how many women *have* been on your boat?" Her voice sounded strained and she was giving me heat vision.

"Where you going with this?" I asked, giving her a little attitude back.

"I'm not interested in being part of anyone's harem," she said.

What the fuck?

"And that mannequin of yours. Every time I see it, I mean, a girl-friend gave it to you. It's a reminder. And what's with her tits?"

"It was a friend, not a girlfriend. You want me to get rid of Fred, too?" Now I was being pissy.

"Of course, not. I love Fred. I just don't want to be part of your catch and release program."

Catch and release?

I took a deep breath, collected myself. "You know perfectly well I have not been seeing anyone else since you and I got together. When would I have had time?"

Or energy?

"Never mind."

"No 'never mind.' Spit it out."

We were sitting at an outdoor table and she glanced a clutch of tour-ists strolling by on the sidewalk.

"Gwenn," I said, drawing her attention back. "If this is about Maria, me working at her condo, I can fix that."

She shrugged.

"Tell you what," I said. "We've just about got this thing wrapped. Maybe I'll write from your place for the rest of it."

"It's not just that," she said.

Just?

She took a deep breath. "This isn't fair." She paused. "To you, I mean."

I nodded, but had no idea where she was going with this.

"Tomorrow, I turn thirty."

"Oh? Gosh, I'm sorry. I guess I should have known."

She shook her head. "Don't be silly. I don't know your birthday, either. I mean, think about it. There's a lot we don't know about each other. We haven't had time."

"We can make time."

She smiled and reach across the table and patted my cheek. "You're a sweet guy."

"So what is it, then?"

She took another sip of wine. "You hear that ticking sound?" she asked.

I had no idea what she was talking about.

"It's my biological clock."

Uh, oh.

Gwenn took another sip of her wine. I decided to match her. Only mine was more of a gulp.

"Gwenn, like you said, we've only known one another for a couple of weeks. They've been insane, but still. What do you want from me?"

"If you don't think this is going to last, tell me sooner than later, alright?"

I didn't know what to say, because I wasn't sure how I felt. I'd lived alone for most of my life. Even as a kid, I spent most of my time by myself. My best friends were Tom Swift and the Hardy Boys. I liked the solitude. And, if I were honest with myself, I found living with Gwenn these past few days a little claustrophobic. Not that I would rather live with someone else, it's just that I didn't know if I wanted to live with anyone at all.

When we returned to her apartment that evening, I just held her until she fell asleep.

CHAPTER 49

GWENN LEFT EARLY the next morning, hitting Pilates class before work. I admired her discipline. And the results of her hard work showed. Ordinarily, I'd be off for a run myself, but our conversation the night before haunted me, so, instead, I wandered down to Starbucks and ordered a Venti Pikes Place, room for cream. Thought I'd sit for a bit and think about things. The cup came filled to the brim and I poured some out in a trashcan to make room for the half-and-half. I wondered how many millions of gallons of Starbucks were similarly discarded each year. What is it about "room for cream" that doesn't register with the baristas?

I sat at a wrought iron table on the patio and sipped my coffee. Was I ready for the kind of commitment Gwenn wanted? If I had to ask myself that question, the answer seemed self-evident. But might I be after a while? And how would I know?

What I did know was that I wasn't interested in anyone else. That would have to do for now.

I pulled out my iPhone and clicked on the *Naples Daily News* app. A small item listing the promotion of Sheriff's Deputy Naomi Jackson to lieutenant surprised me. I should drop by and high-five her.

I finished my coffee then walked back toward Gwenn's place and my new rental parked outside at the curb, a gray Honda Civic. I planned to go car shopping in a few days to spend some of my newfound money.

Jim Henderson had been released from the hospital and was at his home in Golden Gate Estates, east of downtown, recuperating. I wondered if he might be up for visitors and punched in his number.

"Thought I'd drop by and give you your gun back," I said. I had taken it off the boat and shoved it in my satchel. I was nervous walking around with a concealed weapon, but I didn't want to leave it on the boat.

"Keep it for a while longer," he said. "Those Russians are crazy and there are still some of them running around."

"You up for some company?"

"Maybe in a couple of days. Call me next week and we'll get together."

"Will do."

"Oh, I almost forgot," he said. "Should have told you sooner. Got the lab results back on your okra."

"And?"

"And you were right. It was cyanide."

I cranked up the rental and drove toward Pelican Bay, to Maria's, to talk about what was left for us to do. En route, I thought about Miss Ellie and her crazy coffee can adventure. What would have happened if she hadn't a key to the place?

Well, Henderson and Wiggins would have found Maria's notebook, that's what.

Right?

Of course.

Hmmm.

Something felt off. I couldn't put my finger on it. I tried to clear my thoughts, think through what nagged at my subconscious.

I drove more than a mile on autopilot, letting my mind run free, at one with the Force, then it registered. It was what Maria said about being injected with truth serum and how she told her captors about the notebook. They'd snatched her car and condo keys. Wouldn't they have tried to steal the notebook from Maria's place?

I wondered if Miss Ellie, little busybody that she was, might have seen something—or someone.

I pulled into the condo complex, took the stairs to the second floor, and rang Miss Ellie's doorbell. I could hear her yelling from inside. "I'm coming, I'm coming, hold your horses."

She had a big smile on her face when she swung the door open, but as soon as she saw me, her eyes screwed up and a few more wrinkles grew around her mouth.

"You!"

"Yes, me." I said, pleasantly. "Thought I'd take you up on that rain check and come in and have a sit. Is now good?"

She cocked her head. "You know it's not nice to tease little old ladies."

"Miss Ellie, I promise you I would never tease you."

"Then why'd you say your name was Alice?"

"Alex."

"Yeah, Alice. What's with that?"

I smiled, unleashing all 400 watts. It might blind her, but sometimes collateral damage is unavoidable. "Why don't we sit a spell and we can talk about it?"

She looked at me, leery, but finally said, "All right. Come on in."

Her condo's floor plan matched Maria's. Her drapes were wide open and light poured in from her balcony. I scanned the room. "Good grief, Miss Ellie, that's the biggest television ever." It must have been seventy inches, covering half the wall across from a pair of upholstered arm chairs separated by a circular, mahogany end table where a cigarette smoldered in the ashtray. I could feel my sinuses closing.

"I watch a lot of TV. And my eyes aren't the best anymore."

Nor her ears.

I nodded and tried breathing through my mouth, but somehow that only made it worse. My eyes were watering.

"This smoke getting to you?" she asked. "Here let me open the sliding door. It's still nice and cool out. This place could use a little fresh air."

I thanked her.

"So what's your story?" she asked.

I sat down in one of her chairs, and as I did an eruption of stale cigarette odor burst forth from the fabric. I'd have to burn my clothes.

"Well, I guess that begins with a Grateful Dead concert…"

"Grateful Dead! Last time I saw them was at Woodstock."

"Miss Ellie, you were at Woodstock? No offense, but you…ah…"

"I'm too old, that what you're saying?"

"It's just…"

"Hah. You kids today. Well, I was there. Slept in a tent, too. But I was working. I was a roadie!"

"You were a roadie?"

"That's right! With Country Joe McDonald."

"With Country Joe?"

"Yep."

"You were there when he yelled out, 'Give me an F…'"

"Sure was."

"Wow, that's something. Historic, even."

Miss Ellie grinned and bobbed her head.

"Well, my mother wasn't a roadie, and she wasn't at Woodstock," I said, "but she was a Deadhead. I was conceived at one of their concerts."

I was six-years old when my Mom shared that story with me. Imagine being so young and hearing your mother tell you, "It's where I popped my cherry."

Mom and I never stayed anywhere for very long. Making friends was impossible. Near the end, though, mom landed a real job in a flower shop. We had an actual apartment. I had an allowance, which I spent on comic books. The only Christmas there, mom bought me a set of coffee cups with the emblems of all my favorite super heroes. "Someday, you can drink real coffee out of these," she said. And, knowing I'd become a fan of old Star Trek reruns, she gave me a life-sized cardboard cutout of Mr. Spock.

Then she died.

"My mom joined this radical environmental group in Austin and she and some others staged a sit-in to stop a developer from bulldozing a cave in Barton Hills. They believed an endangered species of spider lived there, although nobody ever saw one. A gully washer hit during her shift and she drowned, although her body was never found."

"Oh, you poor boy."

"My uncle adopted me, got me through school. I live on his boat now."

Miss Ellie tut-tutted about that then decided to make us some coffee, which she delivered with a plate of Girl Scout cookies—Thin Mints, my faves. Finally, I got down to why I came to visit.

"Miss Ellie, you mentioned yesterday you waited until the police finished searching Maria's condo before returning the coffee can."

"That's right. I'm not in trouble, am I?"

"Oh, no. But I have a question. I know you're a really good neighbor and keep an eye on things, right?"

"You saying I'm a busybody?"

I smiled at her. "Yes."

"Ha!" She slapped her thigh. "I knew I liked you. Yeah, I'm a regular Mrs. Kravitz."

I had no idea, and my face showed it.

"Gladys Kravitz. The nosey neighbor on *Bewitched?*"

"Oh, sure."

"Hey, you know what? The actress who played her. She was an Alice, too. Alice Pearce."

"Alex."

"Right."

"Well then, Mrs. Kravitz, you know by now Maria was abducted."

She nodded.

"We're tying up loose ends. You and I met after the police were here, right?"

"That's right. There was this big search party. Couple of men, detectives, I guess, and a lady, the CSI person. They dusted for prints and looked everywhere inside. They left the door open and I could see them. It was very exciting."

I nodded. My way of encouraging her to continue

"Then, like you said, you showed up. *Alice!*"

I gave up trying to correct her. "And that was it? Nobody else showed up to look around? How about before then?"

She thought for a moment, screwed her face up in concentration, as if trying to capture an elusive memory. "Well there was that private eye. He knocked on my door. Wait a second." She walked back into the kitchen and returned holding a business card. It was Lester's. He said he'd talked to a neighbor.

Getting Miss Ellie to reach back into her memory was like an archeological dig. As we excavated each layer, another appeared. I had a hunch there was at least one more.

"Was there anyone else you can recall? Anyone earlier before Maria's place was searched by all those detectives and the CSI person?"

"Let me think. Let me think." She was quiet for a few moments, squinting in concentration, then her eyes sprang wide open. "Oh. How could I forget? A sheriff's deputy came by. This was earlier, before the big search party. I saw her walk past my front window. She was a colored woman."

"Did you talk to her?"

"I opened the door to say howdy, but she told me to go back inside. She wasn't very friendly."

"Can you describe her to me?"

She did.

CHAPTER 50

JUDGE HENRY GOODFELLOW lived in Aqualane Shores, an upscale neighborhood south of downtown Naples. Houses there overlook the Gordon River, which feeds into the Gulf of Mexico, or onto canals leading to the river. While not the billionaire palaces of Port Royal, we're still talking real estate prices in the seven and eight figures.

It was six in the afternoon on a Tuesday and I hadn't called ahead. But I hoped the judge would be home from the courthouse by now. I pulled my rental to the curb in front of his house and stepped out of the car, slipping my new backpack over my shoulder, a gift from Gwenn. A Tumi. She even had it monogramed for me.

The front door opened as I walked up the driveway.

"Mr. Strange," Goodfellow said. He seemed tired. "I wondered if I would be seeing you."

He waved me inside and directed us to a comfortable sitting area at the front of the house, filled with cream-colored leather sofas and chairs, arranged in a semi-circular pattern to encourage conversation. A large wet bar occupied the back half of the room. A three-dimensional chess board sat in the center of a round, copper-topped coffee table, three layers of glass boards with pieces on all levels. A game in progress.

"Something to drink?" he asked.

"No, thanks. That a game with Uncle Leo?"

He smiled. "No, actually, I'm playing my most cunning adversary."
He let it hang so I gave him a raised eyebrow, an invitation to finish.
"Myself."

I smiled. "Who's winning?"

He laughed. But it sounded hollow.

"Tell me why you're here," he said.

"I think you know why." I settled into an armchair, gave him relaxed, confident, and waited, hoping he'd volunteer what I needed to confirm.

He leaned back into his chair, too. He reached for a drink on a side table and took a sip. My move.

"Are you black or white?" I asked.

"I'm actually playing myself," he said as if he had no recollection of our exchange only moments ago.

I leaned over and examined the game.

"My black bishop is in danger on level two," he said.

"I see that. But if you move him you'll expose your knight on level three."

He stared at me, cold. "Sometimes sacrifices must be made, wouldn't you agree?"

"But why sacrifice Naomi?" I asked.

He crossed his legs and squinted at me. Game on.

"Does she know the extent of your involvement?" I asked.

"Do you?"

I gave him a brief smile. Let him think the worst. "You know the problem with chess as a metaphor for life, don't you?" I asked, all philosophical.

"Enlighten me."

"In chess, the rules are known to both players, all the pieces and their positions are visible. All the players can do is manipulate that which is known. Even in three-dimensional chess, everything is transparent, including the boards."

"Is there a point here?"

"In life, there are unseen variables, events you can't anticipate, players showing up on the board out of nowhere."

He took another sip and nodded. "It's why no plan of battle ever survives contact with the enemy."

"Exactly. And in our case, we're talking about a little old lady named Miss Ellie."

"Ellie?"

"Yes. The reason the police didn't find Maria's notebook in the coffee can when they searched her place is because the coffee can was missing. Miss Ellie, a neighbor, ran out of coffee and borrowed the can from Maria's pantry. She didn't return it until after Henderson and Wiggins searched the condo. It was also missing earlier when Naomi showed up right after Maria's disappearance."

Goodfellow ran his hands through his hair, and sighed. "And the only reason Naomi would be there would be on my behalf. This is what you've deduced?"

"Yes," I said. "But why?"

"Why did I send Naomi?" His fingers rattled a drumbeat on his lips as he contemplated how to answer. Or, perhaps, whether to answer. Then he did. "I couldn't very well let myself into Maria Martinez's apartment. I'm too recognizable and I would have no plausible reason for being there. Naomi, on the other hand, is a uniformed law enforcement officer. She could easily explain her presence if need be."

"I hope you gave Naomi a reason sufficiently plausible that she can deny criminal intent."

Goodfellow finished his drink and walked over to the bar. He grabbed a crystal decanter and refilled his glass, neat.

He settled back into his chair, took a tug on the drink, and set the glass down on the table by the chessboards. It landed with a clank, ungracefully. He reached across the table to the chessboards and moved the black bishop, leaving his knight vulnerable.

"When this comes out," I said, "it won't just ruin you. Is it really necessary to drag Naomi down with you?"

"Sacrifices…"

I bolted out of my chair, grabbed the chess boards, and hurled them across the room leaving a trail of black and white pieces and broken glass scattered on the tile floor.

"Goddammit," I bellowed, "this isn't some fucking parlor game. People have died. People have been abducted and their lives threatened. How dare you sit there and smugly talk about sacrifices. She's not a fucking pawn."

Goodfellow didn't flinch. He sat stone faced. Finally, he said, "Sit down, Mr. Strange."

I thought, momentarily, about throwing him through the window. But there was more I wanted to hear from him, so I sat.

"You're right about life," Goodfellow said. "It is often not what it seems. I have certain needs that cannot be satisfied in traditional ways. I used to accommodate those desires during my occasional trips to Las Vegas. Where I met your uncle."

He saw the alarmed expression on my face and held up a hand. "Never fear, Leonard is not involved, nor is he aware of my peccadillos."

I leaned back. "So, you're into chicken crushing? That your need?"

He offered a brief, rueful smile. "No. I'm into pain, if you must know. Not animals." He took another sip of his liquor, his hand trembled slightly. "Immokalee is much closer than Las Vegas, and for the past two years I have indulged myself at Rev. Chitango's facilities. I won't bother you with how I made the connection. It's immaterial to the matter at hand."

I nodded, saying nothing. He was on a roll. Better to let him talk.

"A few days after Edgard Dominique was arrested, I received a frantic call from Chitango. He was panic-stricken. It was only then I learned Dominique worked for him. And that the list, the one on the computer hard drive, was of Chitango's clients."

"Including you."

"Indeed. Chitango made sure I understood that."

"So when Naomi tipped me off about the hard drive being erased, all so you could embarrass the sheriff, you didn't know the true nature of its contents?"

He nodded. "A terrible blunder. But I got lucky. Instead of running with it, you assigned the story to that Maria person. A rookie. And she couldn't put two-and-two together." He paused for a moment. "Why was that so hard?"

"I handed the story off to Maria based on the information I got from Naomi. But Maria couldn't confirm it."

"Confirm?"

"You think we would run a story based on hearsay from an unnamed source? Would you admit that in court? You think your standards are more rigorous than ours? It wouldn't be ethical."

Goodfellow rolled his eyes. "Ethics? Blood suckers have ethics?"

"Blood suckers?"

"You're all blood suckers."

Throwing him through a window became more appealing.

Goodfellow took another pull on his drink and examined the glass for a moment. Then said, "Where was I?"

"Edward Dominique."

"Indeed. Dominique was becoming restless. He needed to be silenced. I had nothing to do with that and I told Chitango I wouldn't. But I was in too deep by then. They owned me."

"Sacrifices," I said, rubbing it in.

Goodfellow was gazing out the window and he ignored my remark.

"Chitango called me when they caught Maria," he said, his voice softer, weak. "They had administered some sort of truth serum and, under the influence of the drug, she told them about Edgard Dominique's note, the one identifying Chitango as the owner of the computer."

Goodfellow took another sip of his drink and shook his head. "Chitango was crazy with fear. Let's face it, the guy was never very stable to begin with. Those ridiculous rants of his. And this Ark. As if it's really being built. What a con man…"

He was drifting. "Back to Maria," I coaxed him.

"Yes. Chitango, he was losing it, said he was going to send his Russians to search her apartment. Well, I had to put a stop to that. Can you imagine a bunch of foreign hoodlums tearing through a condominium in Pelican Bay? My God. I told him I would handle it for him. Naomi doesn't know the real reason I asked her to retrieve the coffee can. I told her it would help us figure out who was behind the hard drive's erasure, that it was time for us to take matters into our own hands. We couldn't trust the sheriff."

"You exploited her."

Goodfellow shook his head and his voice cracked. "She said I'm the most honorable man she's ever met, that she would do anything for me, no questions asked."

"Judge, you knew this would eventually blow up on you."

He took a deep breath. "Of course. I just needed some time."

"Time for what?"

"I had a few moves left. I needed time to settle my affairs, make arrangements to leave."

"You're leaving?"

"Yes. I'm flying out within the hour. My driver will be here momentarily. He doesn't like you very much. He blames you for the death of his brother."

The gunslinger!

"You really should leave now, before he gets here."

"Let me guess," I said. "You're headed for Venezuela."

The color drained from his face.

"How…"

"It won't work, your honor. Perez has already been spotted there.

Plans for his extraction are already under way. You'll just be dragged back along with him."

He reached for his glass and drained it, his hands shaking visibly now.

"And this Russian?" I said. "You think he's going to give you a lift to the airport? Are you crazy? You know too much. You need to call the cops. You're the one who needs to get out of here before he arrives."

He looked up. His eyes were wide, as if he were the recipient of this great epiphany.

"Checkmate," he said, softly, to himself.

"Come on," I said. "My car's outside."

"Too late," he said, staring at the window.

A black Chrysler 300 pulled up behind my rental. "Oh, Christ," I hissed. "Call 911."

He just sat there, catatonic.

I picked my backpack off the floor and reached in to grab my cell phone, but my hand landed on the sidearm Henderson had loaned me. I pulled it out, chambered a round, and clicked off the safety.

"Get down," I said. But Goodfellow sat immobile.

With my left hand, I pulled out my iPhone, fumbled it, and it fell with a clank on the brass tabletop, cracking the screen.

"Oh, fuck."

The doorbell rang.

My heart hammered in my chest. I pointed the pistol toward the door and yelled, "The cops are coming. Get the hell out of here if you know what's good for you."

I pushed Goodfellow to the floor and hopped behind the chair to put something, anything, between me and the Russian.

I looked up and saw him peering through the window. He held his pistol at his side.

I jumped up, aimed my gun at him, and pulled the trigger.

But nothing happened. The trigger wouldn't budge.

What the fuck?

I looked at the weapon and realized I had flicked the safety on not off.

Terrified, I glanced out the window again, certain to see the gunslinger ready to shoot me, but he had fled. I heard a screech of tires and saw Chrysler tearing down the street.

I leapt over the chair and charged toward the door, but as I reached for the handle the gun slipped from my grasp. It clattered to the stone floor. I hesitated for a moment then bolted outside, hoping to catch the Chrysler's plates.

By the time I reached the end of the driveway, the car had rounded a bend and was gone. I ran after it for a dozen yards, but it was pointless. And what would I do if he slowed down and let me catch him?

I shook my head in frustration and turned back to the house. I needed to call 911.

I almost reached the door when the sound of a gunshot exploded from inside.

CHAPTER 51

GWENN AND I were asleep in the berth of the trawler when the Storm Warning app on my iPhone blared. It was 6 a.m.

"What is it?" Gwenn asked, sitting up in bed, groggy and rubbing her eyes.

"Weather Service. Big thunderstorm heading our way. They're predicting quote-unquote excessive lightning, winds up to fifty-five miles an hour, and golf-ball-sized hail."

"Of all the days," she groaned.

It was a Wednesday, but her law firm was taking the day off to attend the funeral of His Honor Judge Henry Goodfellow. Every lawyer in town would be there. Even in death, the Chief Judge, irrespective of his misjudgments or sexual aberrations, could still command an audience. Graveside ceremonies were scheduled for noon.

"Maybe it will pass over by then," she said, then slumped back into the berth.

The cremated remains of the Rev. Lee Roy Chitango were also to be interred later in the day. All the media would be there. As the details of the sex scandal continued to unfold, it was a national sensation.

And it was the career boost Maria J. Martinez always dreamed of. She was on every network and regularly quoted in *The New York*

Times, the *Washington Post* and other newspapers. She was slated for the *Tonight Show* in two days.

Gwenn asked me if I was jealous. But that's not me. This was always Maria's story and I was happy for her. Job offers were pouring in and soon she would be heading to bigger and better things. Good for her.

Honestly, I was weary of it all.

It had been the now all-too-familiar cops-and-media circus outside Goodfellow's home after I called 911, and I was stuck there talking to a phalanx of detectives until nearly midnight. Had I scored the yellow tape franchise for Naples, I could have made a killing.

Why was I at Judge Goodfellow's house? What were we talking about? Whose gun was that? What's this crazy story about a Russian mobster?

But I caught a break: The Russian gunslinger made a wrong turn and headed south on Gordon Drive, toward the dead end at the tip of Port Royal, instead of north to freedom. Naples cops bagged him after he banged into the gate of a mansion while trying to turn around. The gate probably cost more than my boat. He was the first and only of the Hangmen to be caught alive. Maybe they'd ship him to Guantanamo for a little friendly conversation.

Meanwhile, I had to convince the cops that I didn't do it, the judge shot himself. This was a Naples PD operation, not sheriff's, but Wiggins showed up and he spent some time filling in the city cops. Eventually, they let me go.

Wiggins walked me to my car. "What aren't you telling them?" he asked.

"Goodfellow was being blackmailed. He was one of Chitango's clients. Not a chicken fucker, though. Just your ordinary S&M. But he was going to run away. Then realized he didn't have a chance."

(I didn't tell Wiggins where the gun came from. This is the first time that has been publicly disclosed. I have wrestled with that. I eventually talked to Henderson, asked his advice. He would be dragged into it were I to reveal where I got the weapon. "I don't care what you do," Henderson said. "I'm retired now."

(I also did not mention Naomi's involvement. And I wouldn't except she decided to reveal her role to the prosecutor. It was the right thing to do. Better than have it hang over her head. But it would never have come from me. In the end, after weeks of internal hearings, an endless colonoscopy of questioning, she was cleared of any wrongdoing and returned to her duties.)

The judge's suicide was big local news, but the cops withheld the more sordid details. In the grand scheme of things, he was a bit player in the larger drama. When I shared my conflicting emotions about all this with Edwina, she was her usual cynical self:

"Alex, you bagged a crooked U.S. congressman, disrobed a phony televangelist, exposed a bunch of Russian hit men. Who gives a fuck about a corrupt Florida judge? Leave that to the local paper."

Maria felt the same way. She was working on a piece for *The New York Times Sunday Magazine* and said she might include it there. She said it would be an interesting nugget.

What a tombstone: *R.I.P. Judge Henry Goodfellow. A nugget.*

Maria was more amped about what she learned from the FBI guy, Cao. He said the FBI's technical staff finally figured out how the computer stolen by Edgard Dominique was erased.

"Like they guessed, it was some kind of program that killed the computer," she said. "But it was a lot more sophisticated than the stuff you can buy online. They think maybe Russians were involved with that, too."

Naomi Jackson was devastated by Goodfellow's death. I'd called and asked if I could visit her at home on the pretext of offering my condolences.

Her wife, Suzette, was with her when I broke the news of the judge's confession to me. I'm glad she was. Naomi fell apart. She had been betrayed by a man for whom she would do anything, a man she trusted and believed in. And when the news of his involvement in the sex scandal finally came out, she would look like a fool.

Later that day, Lester checked in. "You five-by-five?"

"Yeah. Long story. Buy me a beer and I'll fill you in."

"How's Gwenn handling all this?" he asked.

"What do you mean?"

"You know, for a smart guy, you're really dumb."

"Meaning?" I asked, stupidly.

"You let that girl slip away, you'll hate yourself for the rest of your life."

Uncle Leo surprised me when I called him with the news.

"It's about Henry, isn't it?"

"You already know he committed suicide?"

There was a long pause.

"No, but I'm not surprised."

"Oh?"

I could hear him breathing in an out. "Henry called me the other night. He was rambling. Drunk. Kept begging my forgiveness. Started crying at one point."

"What for?"

"For deceiving me."

"About what a weird sexual pervert he was?" I asked.

Again a pause.

"No, but since you mention it, nephew, I guess, in retrospect, I shouldn't be surprised about that, either. All those years we met in Vegas, then in Florida, Henry constantly yakked about women and his conquests. But I never saw him with one. You know how it goes, right? A man who talks about his sex life all the time, usually doesn't have one."

"At least not a normal one."

I heard ice tinkling in a glass. It was after five in Arizona, so Leo would be having the first of several cocktails to end the day. Then he asked, "How weird was this sex ring?"

"Chickens."

Leo began hacking and coughing and making horrible sounds. Then, disturbingly, he began laughing.

"Of course. What else?"

This was not what I wanted to hear. "You knew?" I asked.

"No, no, nephew. It's just, if you're going to be weird, be really weird, right?"

Weird, as it turns out, also involved cheating at long-distance chess. Leo and Goodfellow had been playing online for the past two years, and Goodfellow always won.

Leo is not the most tech-savvy person in the world, but his wife, Sarah, is more attuned. This may be because she's twenty-five years younger.

Sarah talked him into downloading a popular chess program, and Leo began comparing Goodfellow's moves to the computer's.

After a while, it became clear.

"Henry cheated," Leo said.

"Why?" I asked.

"My guess? Henry was losing it. I think he was in the early stages of Alzheimer's. Too proud to admit it. Not to be cruel, but I really looked forward to our next match on the boat where he couldn't pull that shit."

I could hear his glass tinkling. Sarah was saying something in the background I couldn't make out.

"Leo, before we hang up, can I ask you question?"

"Shoot."

"Do you think I'm a blood sucker?"

"A blood sucker?"

"Yeah, that's what Goodfellow called me."

"And you care what a corrupt sexual pervert thought, why?"

"Dunno. It just got under my skin a little bit. He said all of us in the news media were blood suckers."

"Of course he did. He didn't bring all this on himself, he was a victim. If I had a million dollars for every time some crook told me that in court, I'd be rich."

"Funny."

"Nephew, you're too fly for an identity crisis. Just because you get all those tips from vampires does not make you a blood sucker.

"Fly?"

"Yeah, fly. I can speak millennial."

Leo said he wouldn't make the funeral, but would come visit later in the summer. I promised him we'd take the boat out. "We can play chess, if you like," I said. "Would be good for your ego."

Speaking of the boat, Gwenn and I had settled on an arrangement we hoped would work for us. For the short term, anyway. I would live aboard the *Miss Demeanor*, now tied up a few blocks away from her apartment at the Naples City Docks. We would see each other as often as we wished—which, so far, meant nearly every day—and we would spend our nights together as we wished—which also meant nearly every night, so far. But we would respect each other's space.

Her space at that moment was under the sheets in my berth, spooning against me.

A while later, as we lay entwined, the wake from a deep-sea fishing boat leaving port rocked the trawler.

One of Leo's paperbacks fell from the bookshelf with a thunk, just missing Fred in his little bed.

"What was that?" she murmured.

I looked at the floor. My favorite Raymond Chandler novel.

"The Big Sleep," I said.

"Sleep."

Afterword

The FBI arrested U.S. Rep. Ricky Perez six weeks after his disappearance when an anonymous caller spotted the disgraced congressman outside the Blue Marlin Motel in Key West. A baffled Perez told police he had no idea how he ended up back in the United States. He also complained about an aching jaw. Before Perez was jailed, doctors at Lower Keys Medical Center diagnosed he suffered from a fractured mandible.

The Tropic Press was nominated for the Pulitzer Prize for Public Service for its stories exposing the Rev. Lee Roy Chitango's connections to the Russian and Cuban governments.

The Associated Press was similarly nominated for its stories exposing Chitango's Ark II lottery as a fraud. Using satellite imagery, the AP proved there was no ship under construction in the Caribbean matching Chitango's claims of a vessel more than five hundred feet in length. Funds from lottery tickets were traced by the AP to a Swiss bank, which was under investigation by Interpol.

Chitango's sudden rise to fame was no accident, according to those news reports. His sponsors in Moscow and Havana hoped to use him to blackmail elected officials and, consequently, influence American foreign policy. A thumb drive found on Chitango's ravaged remains in the Everglades contained several lists of clients who had accepted the good reverend's hospitality.

The FBI and the Justice Department refused to release the list, citing exemptions in the federal Freedom of Information Act. However, the names of clients from Collier County were shared with investigators at the Sheriff's Office. Alexander Strange obtained a copy through an anonymous source, and published the names. He also quoted unnamed sources who said federal agents were interviewing several high-ranking members of Congress who were on the other lists.

Federal prosecutors demanded that Strange reveal his source in the Sheriff's Office. He refused and was cited for contempt of court and sentenced to federal lockup. Before he could be incarcerated, his attorney, Gwenn Giroux of the Judd and Holkamp law firm, filed a successful appeal, staying the sentencing. As this was written, *Strange v. United States of America* was unresolved.

Chitango's Tampa convocation was delayed a day when Hurricane Icarus bore down on Florida, eventually scraping the state's west coast and slamming into Louisiana. Several maritime excursions aboard luxury yachts, including the *Monkey Business Too*, were canceled as a result.

Chitango's grizzly end in the Everglades, far from scuttling convocation plans, led to an overflow crowd, his followers believing that his demise was a validation of the coming end of days. Replacing Lee Roy Chitango at the altar was a young man, heretofore unknown to the public, who claimed to be the Serminator's godchild and designated by the Almighty to be his successor. His name: Elroy Chitango.

A vice squad sting resulted in 16 arrests on the eve of the gathering in Tampa, but that did not deter local strip clubs, which reported record business during the event. One club featured a recording of thunder when pole dancers were tipped, matching the stormy weather outside. Others lured faithful with ads such as "come party like a heathen" and "the poles are open all night."

At high noon on May 19, the skies grew suddenly dark over Immokalee, Florida. It wasn't the Apocalypse (obviously), an eclipse of the sun (verifiably), nor an alien invasion. Rather, it was the smoke from a monstrous fire that erupted on the campus of the Museum of Holy Creation when a horizontal drilling bit from a nearby oil-exploration rig accidently chewed into the natural gas pipeline feeding the towering "eternal flame" sculpture at the museum's entrance.

The resulting explosion hurtled a tremendous fireball hundreds of feet into the air, and the spreading conflagration consumed the museum and the adjacent cathedral where Chitango once preached and his Barbies once boogied. The fire was so intense, the hungry flames fed by natural gas for so long, that not even a single cubit of Noah's Ark could be found in the ashes.

The Twitternet erupted with speculation this was the Almighty's revenge on a religious fraud. Chitango's lingering followers saw it as confirmation the End of Days had begun. Rather than rebuild, the Sermonator's heir, Elroy Chitango, sold the site to a local real estate developer who quickly excavated a sprawling retention lake in the center of the property and surrounded it with stucco-tiled town-houses, carriage homes, and an eighteen-hole golf course.

Elroy Chitango promised his followers to use the funds from the sale to launch a revitalized ministry after a "proper period of mourning and reflection." He was last spotted in Monte Carlo by a correspondent for *People* magazine arm-in-arm with a pair of former Boogie Barbies.

Who said mourning and reflection need be lonely work?

Author's Acknowledgements

I owe a deep debt of gratitude to many people in the creation of this book. Foremost to my friend Alex Strange for allowing me to tell this story and for his detailed audio notes that made it possible.

I have chosen to write this in first person, with Alex as the protagonist, as this is his tale to tell. I am merely his scribe. Why didn't Alex write it himself? As he told me, "I'd rather have a colonoscopy than write a book."

While most of the details of this story flow from the detailed recordings Alex provided, I did fill in gaps here and there, including his internal dialogues extrapolated from our conversations. If in the course of creating this narrative I have introduced any errors, I'm blaming the internet.

The names of some characters in the book have been changed to honor confidentiality agreements and to avoid tedious legal entanglements. The names of some places, businesses, and locations have been similarly altered. There are a lot of people in the world, so it is inevitable that some of the characters in this book will have the names of actual people. How many Dombrowskys are there? How should I know? But if that's your last name, and you are alive, and you're not a Russian mob enforcer, well, dude, this isn't about you.

Special thanks to Edwina Mahoney, editor of the Tropic ⊚ Press LLC for her assistance and guidance and for her permission to use articles published by the news service. Similarly, a shout out to Gwenn Giroux, Maria Jennifer Martinez, retired Detective Jim Henderson of the Collier County Sheriff's Office, and Major Lester Rivers (United States Army, Retired) for their contributions.

Also, thanks to all who assisted me in preparing this for publication, especially my trusted readers, editors, and web designers: Sandy Bruce, Logan Bruce, Kacey Bruce, Kristina McBride, Mickey Gargan, John Fenstermaker, Jess Montgomery, and Ron Rollins. I am indebted to John and Cindy Hawkins for their help with nautical terminology. And a big shout-out to my International Thriller Writers coaches Meg Gardiner, Gayle Lynds, and F. Paul Wilson for their inspiration and guidance. And endless thanks to the many friends in several writers' groups for their input, criticism, and encouragement over the years.

CPSIA information can be obtained
at www.ICGtesting.com
Printed in the USA
LVHW042233280420
654695LV00001B/139